CW01456077

Louise Candlish is the internationally bestselling author of 17 novels, including *The Only Suspect*, winner in 2024 of a Ned Kelly Award and a Capital Crime Fingerprint Award, and *Our House*, winner of a British Book Award for Crime & Thriller Book of the Year and now a major ITV drama. Louise lives in a South London neighbourhood not unlike the ones in her books, with her husband, daughter and a fox-red Labrador called Bertie.

For up-to-date news catch her on
X @louise_candlish, Instagram @louisecandlish,
or facebook.com/LouiseCandlishAuthor.
www.louisecandlish.com

Also by Louise Candlish

Our Holiday
The Only Suspect
The Heights
The Other Passenger
Those People
Our House
The Swimming Pool
The Sudden Departure of the Frasers
The Disappearance of Emily Marr
The Island Hideaway
The Day You Saved My Life
Other People's Secrets
Before We Say Goodbye
I'll Be There For You
The Second Husband
Since I Don't Have You
The Double Life of Anna Day

Novellas
The Skylight

A Neighbour's Guide to Murder

LOUISE CANDLISH

ONE PLACE. MANY STORIES

HQ
An imprint of HarperCollins*Publishers* Ltd
1 London Bridge Street
London SE1 9GF

www.harpercollins.co.uk

HarperCollins*Publishers*
Macken House, 39/40 Mayor Street Upper,
Dublin 1, D01 C9W8, Ireland

This edition 2025

1
First published in Great Britain by
HQ, an imprint of HarperCollins*Publishers* Ltd 2025

HB ISBN: 9780008640934
TPB ISBN: 9780008641016

This book is set in 10/15 pt. Sabon by Type-it AS, Norway

Printed and bound in the UK using 100% Renewable
Electricity by CPI Group (UK) Ltd

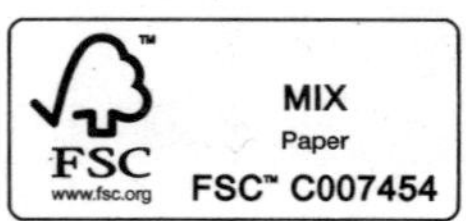

For more information visit: www.harpercollins.co.uk/green

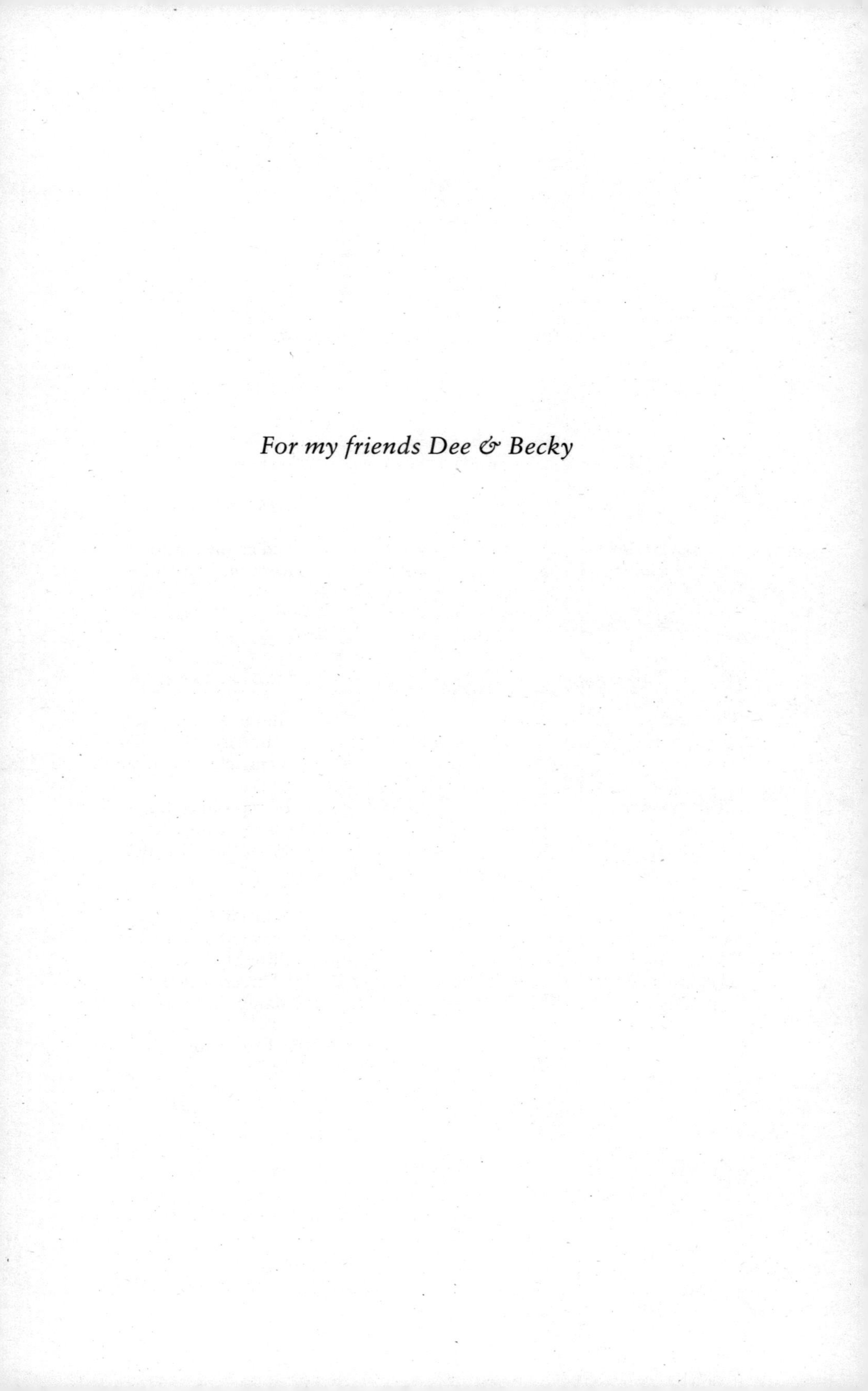

For my friends Dee & Becky

Prologue

Her hands are pleasingly steady as she makes the call. Not that she is completely without nerves – in all her decades she's never had to dial 999 and she hopes she never will again – but it's important to remain level-headed in an emergency. The last thing the authorities need is a hysterical female, especially one of a certain age.

She's damned if she'll give them cause to make a stereotype of her.

The line rings. She's sure she read somewhere of their commitment to answer within ten seconds but already they're at ten, eleven, twelve ... Honestly, someone could be bleeding out here!

'Hello, emergency service operator ...' *Finally.* Fifteen seconds and yet the call handler is completely unrepentant. 'Which service do you require?'

'Police, please.' She glances at the still, silent figure by the window and it strikes her that she'll be interrogated about their interaction, not only by the police, but also by the media. After everything that's gone on in the building this last year, they'll all want to know how it came to this ... this *awfulness*.

A new voice comes on the line and asks her where she's calling from.

'Columbia Mansions. The big mansion block on Clayton Street,

Queens Oak.' As she recites the postcode and explains which door to use, there's a moan from the window and she meets her friend's gaze. She's expecting to see remorse, or at the very least shock, but the other woman's eyes are utterly devoid of emotion, their colour lovely in the young summer light, an almost romantic shade of—

Lovely? Romantic? Has she lost her mind? There's a dead body in the room!

She gets a grip of herself, returns her attention to the call, to the question she realizes is being repeated in her ear with some insistence: 'What is the nature of the emergency?'

'It's my neighbour,' she says, a catch in her voice. 'He's been murdered by his tenant.'

A Neighbour's Guide to Murder

by Gwen Healy

1

Alec's message to Pixie is as good a place to begin as any. You can see for yourself why it might have given the poor girl hope – she was, after all, emotionally bruised as well as in urgent need of a place to live.

> Hey. Got your SOS. Room might still be free, depends. Could come to an arrangement regarding the rent?

The funny thing is she almost didn't see it because it was in hidden requests and she usually deleted those without reading them. Every so often, though, she scrolled through them 'for the lolz'. Of course, being the ancient crone that I was – I only used Facebook and even that stupefied me with its ever-changing wizardry – I had to ask her to explain what 'hidden requests' were.

('Lolz' even I knew and frankly had thought old hat by now.)

Anyway, for those who don't know, they are unsolicited and potentially offensive messages on Instagram. Brazen strangers professing curiosity as to one's 'sexy baby side'; religious blessings from self-anointed priestesses; gobbledegook from malfunctioning bots. You know the kind of thing.

But in this case, the name caught her eye – @queensoaklandlord – and it didn't take long to deduce that this was the man whose spare room she had recently viewed in Columbia Mansions.

Alec Pedley was his name. You'll be seeing it a lot in these pages because he is the protagonist of my story. Or should I say *an*tagonist? Hero or villain, you decide.

But back to that hidden request. You'd have thought that his not having had a more direct way of communicating with her – her phone number, for instance – would have been warning enough not to involve herself with him, but when I made that point to her she disagreed. *There's a bit of a story there, Gwen* (there often was). He only had her friend's number because she'd lost her phone in a club, and her ex-boyfriend, with whom the device was still linked, reported its location as twenty-five miles away in the Watford area, so she knew for a fact it had been stolen and she was never going to get it back, which meant ordering a new one. What with missed deliveries and other miscommunications, it took three days for her to be connected again.

'Oh my God, Gwen, it was like I was on witness protection or something. Like I wasn't even *me* any more.'

'It all sounds unnecessarily complicated,' I told her, but complicated arrangements were a hallmark of Pixie's lifestyle and, in any case, by the time I made the comment we had significantly bigger things to worry about.

But, look at me, I'm plunging into this at totally the wrong point. That shows you how disordered my thoughts are, how tormented I still am by everything that's happened. I need to compose myself, tell this tale chronologically.

Let's go back to the first time she met Alec, a damp, sun-streaked afternoon in late September – though neither damp enough nor sun-streaked enough to produce a rainbow.

You might as well know at the outset that rainbows don't feature a whole lot in this story.

2

Alec was one of two leaseholders in Columbia Mansions who'd taken advantage of the company's recent vote to allow the government's Rent a Room Scheme. I remember him citing 'cozzie livs' in one discussion, a term I found distasteful, but struggling with bills was not an experience our co-directors Dee or Noel had ever had, and Dee in particular had been amused by his roguish slang.

Pixie was the last of thirty or so people to troop in and out of his flat that Saturday in the hope of being picked as his new roommate, the inaugural one, a nurse called Yasmin, having moved out the previous weekend. He'd scheduled candidates in groups of four so they could enjoy the 'frisson of competition', as he put it.

'Sounds a bit like speed dating,' I told him.

He scoffed. 'Why, you want to throw your hat in the ring?'

'Hardly.' I narrowed my eyes at him through my glasses. 'I'm quite happy with the accommodation I've got, thank you very much.'

'I'm sure you are.' He winked at me then, though it's possible I imagined that. He had an unreconstructed sense of humour, Alec, a pouncing, ribald wit that is no doubt considered outmoded now, if not downright offensive. His look was as bold as his character: strong nose, craggy eyebrows, tar-black eyes with that depthless quality many find so unnerving – a sense of some inner void, perhaps. His style of dress was unfussy, even unkempt, and he'd let himself go physically (corpulent is the word I'd use), but we all have our battles with willpower, don't we? In years, he was pushing fifty.

'Anyway, it'll be more like a bidding war if I'm lucky,' he said.

'Is that fair, Alec? Fifteen hundred is a lot to begin with.'

He chuckled as if fairness were an absurd notion. When he'd told me what he charged, my jaw had dropped; £1,500 was a shocking sum to charge for a spare room, even with its own en suite shower and in a landmark building like ours. (Now I'm thinking it all through, I wonder if that en suite was the detail that stopped me from being concerned for Yasmin, also young and pretty. Then again, she did have a boyfriend built like a pro wrestler.)

'I'll tell you what's not fair,' Alec said. 'The way this government has screwed landlords. Can't do this, can't do that, law after law. No sense of the bigger picture.'

'I agree with you on that,' I said, though we both knew he was not a traditional landlord and could earn £7,500 before having to pay any tax. That wasn't a sum to be sniffed at from where I was standing.

Anyway, back to Pixie. It was four o'clock when I returned from Tesco Metro and came upon a slight young woman on our landing. Assuming she'd arrived early for her viewing, I was about to move past her with a polite nod when something gave me pause. It might have been her natural grace, the way she ran her hand over the polished banister, the rest of her quite still, like a well-born deb about to be presented to court. Or perhaps it was her fashion sense, her get-up of orange jumpsuit startling against the olde-worlde dark-wood wainscotting. Think Christine Keeler prowling Cliveden in an astronaut's costume.

'Waiting for Alec? I understand there's stiff competition for the room.'

'Sorry?' She turned quickly, strands of a shining dark bob catching on her lipsticked mouth. Brushing them free, she smiled, her naturally downturned eyes almost closing. 'Oh. Well, that's okay.' Then, playful, 'Can I tell you a secret?'

'Of course.' I gave a little giggle. Though not generally a giggler, I seemed to be responding to her childlike, offbeat charm in a completely involuntary way.

'I'm just a time waster. I've literally just paid the deposit on another place.' Her eyes flared in mock horror and I saw now the irises were an uncommon indigo colour. 'Plus the first six months' rent.'

'*Six* months? Is that how it works now?' Perhaps Alec wasn't such a shark after all.

She shrugged. 'I mean, yeah, if you want to beat the rich foreign students. Nearly seven grand I had to find.'

'That's quite a down payment,' I said.

'I know. I had to get it from my dad.'

'Where's the flat? In Queens Oak?'

'No, up in New Cross. One of those new blocks by the station? I move in on Saturday. It's just a studio, but I'll have it all to myself.' She sighed. I would soon learn she was much given to sighing; it was her preferred form of expression, and this first one was long and sensuous, as if solitude were the most erotic thing in the world (I knew the feeling). 'They had, like, forty other applicants but luckily I had everything right there, ready to go. References, all of it. First time in my life I've been organized and, boom, turns out it pays off.'

'Yes, it does,' I said, thinking of my own meticulous bookkeeping. She was holding my gaze with unusual candour, even trust, and I again couldn't help responding in kind. 'If I've learned anything in this life it's to keep on top of your own affairs, because no one else is going to.'

From behind Alec's door there came a bellow of his laughter and a reciprocal burst of titters from the group in there with him. Poor things, I thought, having to laugh at a middle-aged man's jokes to be in with a chance of having a roof over their heads.

'Is he your landlord as well?' Jumpsuit Girl asked.

'Oh. No. He only lets one room. They're all two-bedroomed flats.' I gestured to my door, directly opposite Alec's. 'I live here.'

'Of course. You must own.'

Because I was old, she meant. She probably thought I was ninety. They all do, these youngsters. The women, anyway. The men don't think anything at all, just shoulder past without so much as a by-your-leave, not even actively ill-mannered.

'Lucky you,' she said. 'I love this area so much. The square by the station, the pedestrianized bit? It's like Europe.'

'It *is* Europe,' I corrected her, but gently because I'd learned never to presume that any young person was cognizant of the continent in which they resided. 'Well, I'm sorry we won't be neighbours. If you'd looked at this one first, it might have worked out differently.'

'Oh, there's no way I could afford this building,' she said. 'Not long term. This is only one of my porn viewings.'

'I beg your pardon?'

'Property porn? Last week I went to see a place in town. That was three thousand a month. Oh my God, it was so amazing, there were these—'

I never did discover what 'these' were because at that moment Alec's door swung open and he emerged with three women, all in their twenties or early thirties. One was noticeably more attractive than the others, blonde and statuesque, and if I'd been having a flutter, she was the one I'd go for. Gentlemen still preferred blondes, if you could classify Alec as a gentleman (I certainly could not, even then).

As the women departed, he turned to my new acquaintance. 'Pixie, is it?'

What a perfect name for her, I thought. Whimsical and bewitching. Had it suited her from birth, her parents claiming it for her at first sight, or had she grown into it, adapted her personality to do it justice?

Alec was evidently less charmed. 'How did you get in?' he growled. 'I didn't hear the buzzer.'

'Oh, someone was coming out so I snuck in.'

'Careful, Gwen here will want to message the WhatsApp group about a security lapse like that,' he said, and I threw him an unimpressed look.

'Was that bad?' Pixie said. 'I thought I could just piggyback on the next one?'

'There is no next one.' As he made to turn, she stepped towards him, almost theatrically contrite.

'I'm *so* sorry. I missed my train and the next one was cancelled and I didn't know whether to bother you so I decided to—'

'Fine.' He silenced her with a raised palm. 'Since you're here, come on in.'

'Thank you *so* much.' She shot a look behind his back as if to say, *Let's have some fun*, and I hovered for a moment after they'd gone inside, just basking in the mischief of it. Mischief was an ingredient so long missing from my life that I'd quite forgotten its gorgeous, intoxicating effect.

As far as I'm aware, her inspection of his spare room passed without controversy and so it was that, following the New Cross flat debacle, which I will come to shortly, and having mislaid her mobile, she used a friend's phone to call the other landlords she'd met during her search. She confessed to being in tears on some of the calls, she felt so desperate.

When Alec didn't pick up, she left a voicemail, but his returned call was ignored by her friend (as I said, unnecessarily complicated) and it was only when her new phone arrived and she was back on social media that she discovered the Instagram message that would upend her life – and mine.

The way she saw it, she had nothing to lose when she replied:

What sort of arrangement?

3

I assumed I'd never see her again, that she'd installed herself in her New Cross studio while the corporate blonde prepared to take possession of Alec's spare room, but the very next Saturday, as I was returning from Gail's with my weekly cinnamon buns, a solid old Skoda double-parked at our entrance and I spotted her in the passenger seat. She and the driver, a big-boned young man with tattooed forearms, peeled out and began unloading boxes from the boot, ferrying them into the building. The boxes hadn't been taped shut and various items poked out: wooden salad tongs, a sheepskin cushion, a mirror decorated with butterflies; a book called *The Digital Nomad Handbook*.

In the lobby, I waved a hand as she approached and was gratified that she recognized me. 'Hello again! This looks like a change of plan. What happened to the place in New Cross?'

'Oh.' She drew up next to me and lowered her box to the floor. Clearly there was no short answer. 'The flat didn't exist.'

I frowned. 'I don't understand. You imagined it?'

'No, I mean it *existed*, it just wasn't his to rent out. The guy I met? Turned out he'd just rented it himself for a week and was pretending it was his. The whole thing was a scam.'

'What about your deposit? And the six months' rent?'

Tears rose in her eyes. 'Took it and disappeared, didn't he?'

'Oh!' Talk of such wickedness was very upsetting to me for reasons we'll discuss later, but I controlled my emotions and looked at her with normal levels of sympathy. 'I've read about that kind of thing in the papers. They set up fake agencies, don't they, so it all looks completely above board. You mustn't blame yourself.'

'I know. Though I did have this weird feeling it was too good to be true.' She turned to address her friend, who was advancing towards us with a large cheese plant in a mouldering woven pot. 'I said that to you, Ash, didn't I?'

'Yeah.' The young man peered from behind face-sized leaves. He was a foot taller than Pixie, with smooth skin and longish hair, its shine dulled by a powdery purple rinse. The tattoos on his arms featured a variety of insects, including an oversized beetle on his right wrist. 'Could have happened to anyone,' he added.

'How did you find out?' I asked.

'When I went to pick up the keys. I'd arranged to meet the owner in the flat – the *fake* owner – but when I got there, there was this Italian couple having breakfast. They'd never heard of him. I thought there must have been some mix-up, but we got in touch with the holiday let company they used and it was all exactly like they said.'

'The police couldn't trace the fraudster through his bank details?'

'He'd already withdrawn the money, they said.' Even though it was only the second time we'd met, I could see she'd been altered by the crime. Aside from the rumpled clothing and disarrayed hair of moving day, she had a raw quality to her now, as if a layer of skin had been scrubbed away. 'Reckoned he used a stolen ID to open the account in the first place.'

'He's probably doing the same thing right now with some other flat,' Ash said, transferring the plant pot from one hip to the other like a mother with a toddler. The angle was precarious, a clump of soil in danger of spilling onto the carpet.

'What about your bank? Can they not cover it through their insurance?' I asked.

'I haven't phoned them yet,' Pixie said. 'I wanted to speak to my dad first. I got hold of him last night and he says I'll never get the money back. Those fraud helplines, it's all AI, he reckons. Either that or people sitting in bed in their pyjamas.'

I chuckled. Her dad sounded like our resident misanthrope, Elliot in flat 7, who had many sharp things to say about Broken Britain on the residents' WhatsApp group. Her friend moved on, breathing heavily as he took the stairs, but even though I'd been looking forward to my Gail's bun all week I felt strangely reluctant to follow.

'I'm really sorry you've had to go through that, but thank God you've been able to secure this place instead. Did Alec come down on the rent?'

She looked puzzled. 'How d'you mean?'

'I thought you said it was out of your budget?' And that was before this unfortunate defrauding. Perhaps her father had stumped up again. I already had the sense that men orbited her in that way you sometimes found with girls who had a quality of fragility, of disorganization. Looks too, of course. I've mentioned her striking eyes, but I ought to emphasize too the almost Slavic loveliness of her face, the fine brow and high cheekbones. Had she chosen to style herself more conventionally she'd have been quite the classic beauty.

'Yeah, well. I mean, no, the rent's the same.' She looked unsettled, distracted by horns in the street: their car was causing congestion.

Ash came jogging back down, his tummy jiggling under his T-shirt. 'C'mon, Pix, let's bring the rest in before I get a ticket.'

'Can I help?' I offered.

'It's okay,' she said. 'We've got it. But thanks.'

She probably thought I was too frail to heft boxes, even though I knew I had upper body strength to match hers, thanks to the Older Bodies Pilates I'd been doing weekly for several years. I wondered if Alec was in to welcome her to her new home. If so, then plainly *he* wasn't lifting a finger to help. No doubt sitting at his keyboard with his headphones on, creating some mediocre melody no one would ever want to listen to.

But no, that's naive of me. He's probably never been more successful, his melodies the soundtrack to a million breathless true-crime fantasies.

After what I've seen of folk this last year, I wouldn't be at all surprised.

4

Can I just say before I go on that I am not what you think. The lonely neighbour twitching the lace curtains. The childless spinster searching for waifs to mother. As you'll discover, I have two children of my own, both grown up and still making regular demands on my time and patience.

Nor, since we're on the subject, am I a former good-time girl, ageing and embittered and only able to get my thrills vicariously. I've never been one of those women men wanted to chase. Since my marriage ended fifteen years ago, I've not had a single opportunity to enter into a long-term relationship (I rather wish I hadn't entered into the one with my husband, to be honest, said offspring notwithstanding).

No, what I am is a decent person. A feminist who will intervene without a qualm if she thinks a man is abusing a woman. Scrap that: if she thinks a person is abusing another person. A humanist then. A defender of victims and underdogs.

By the way, who 'you' are is at present unclear to me. It's even possible that *you* may turn out simply to be *me*. We'll see. You're certainly not my daughter, Maya, whose idea it was for me to get all of this down in writing on the grounds that it's therapeutic. 'Journaling' they call it now, she tells me, though that feels too informal a term for an account of destroyed lives.

'Unburdening' is better perhaps.

Or maybe plain old testimony.

5

A little bit about Columbia Mansions. It was – still is, I think you'll find – a masterwork of Queen Anne architectural symmetry, constructed of identical quarters, each with four floors containing two mirror-image flats that extend from the front of the building to the rear, and distinctive for its extravagance of exterior flourishes. Crested gables, turrets and chimneys, ornamental brick panels and the like. Each 'house' has its own entrance, the recessed double doors painted the same immaculate ivy green, though those at the southern end are known as the 'main doors' by virtue of their having the building's name painted above them, along with the date of its construction, 1896. This is invariably the one to feature in estate agents' photographs.

And media coverage, of course.

My flat was one of the end units that benefited from a desirable extra aspect of windows, though I was on the first rather than the coveted top floor, and at the less prestigious northern end that overlooks the car park. But I genuinely believe that after what happened with Brian and the loss of our family home in Surrey, I would have been happy in a single windowless room in that building. All that mattered was that the apartment was mine and mine alone.

Well, technically.

‘Daniel,’ I called to my 36-year-old first-born, letting myself in and turning right into the spacious living room at the rear of the flat. ‘I’ve got the buns!’

‘Great,’ he called back from his bathroom, where he liked to take epic hot showers.

I wondered if he would be dressed when he surfaced.

In the kitchen (unchanged in the years I’d been here, but there was plenty of life left in its solid pine fittings), I made a pot of coffee, put the buns on plates and sat at the table I’d salvaged from the Surrey house. It, too, was made of pine and bore a lifetime’s worth of marks and scorings.

A few minutes later, Daniel joined me. He was tall and spare, with dark hair curling over his ears and down his neck and a more handsome face than you’d detect at first glance on account of its rarely being lifted by a smile. He took after my side of the family, a genetic accident for which I felt daily gratitude: the thought of clapping eyes on Brian several times a day via the face across the table was not appealing.

‘Did you get me one or two?’ he asked. Still depressed but at least dressed, that was my assessment this morning. And not so depressed that he couldn’t wolf pastries. In spite of his new reclusive lifestyle, he never seemed to gain weight.

‘One. They’re £3.60 each, Dan.’ Six months he’d been here and not once had he thought to get off his backside on a Saturday morning and treat *me*. ‘Alec’s new lodger’s moving in,’ I said, between divinely buttery mouthfuls. ‘She’s called Pixie.’

‘What a stupid name,’ he said, chewing.

‘I really like it. It suits her.’

‘Why, got green skin, has she? What happened to the other one?’

‘Yasmin? She and Casper have moved into their own place. Ilford, I think it was.’

'Really? Why would they want to go there? Terrible place.'

Dee, and lots of other women I knew, spoke of their grown-up children still being their babies. *He'll always be my little boy*, they cooed. This was not an experience I related to. Perhaps because Daniel had never been particularly babyish in the first place, not beyond the first year anyway; he'd been too sharp and an early talker. In place of tantrums, he'd had opinions. Now, in negative mode since being ditched by his wife, he voiced those opinions in disdainful abbreviated form.

'What are you up to today?' I asked, and he looked bamboozled, as if I'd challenged him with a quadratic equation. 'Got any work on?'

'Nope.'

He'd left his permanent job as a data analyst a few months before he'd been ousted by Nella and I'd long since ceased viewing the two as coincidental. He did not suit unemployment – sorry, freelancing – and she'd identified that early.

'We could do a big walk?' I suggested.

'Not sure I wanna do a small one.'

'Then perhaps you could hoover while I'm out? Maybe give your bathroom a clean?'

'And there it is,' he said, raising an index finger in pointless, childish triumph.

My patience snapped. 'Daniel, it's not outrageous to ask you to pull your weight a bit. And could we talk about a contribution to the utilities? My bills have gone through the roof since you've been here.' You might assume that a boomer like me would have been mortgage-free by now, but my ex-husband's destruction of our finances had put paid to that and I remained at the mercy of mortgage lenders and interest rates.

Daniel tilted his head from side to side, as if to say you could be right, you could be wrong. 'I'm still paying towards the Stoke Newington flat.'

'Then you need to sort that out with Nella. You need to decide who will buy who out. You need your money for yourself.'

He scowled. *Need, need, need.* He'd always disliked repetition. I wondered for the umpteenth time how my relationship with my children had come to be so troublesome, so lacking in basic affinity – especially when with a newcomer like Pixie the sense of kinship could be natural, immediate – and came to the usual conclusion: you don't choose your family. They are God's gift to you, as the saying goes; at least they *think* they are.

'Alec's getting £1,500 a month from his lodger,' I told him.

'The pixie?'

'Just Pixie. There's no "the". And he'll expect her to do her share of chores on top of that, I'm sure.'

'Bully for him.'

Bun finished, I got to my feet to take my coffee to the sofa overlooking the communal garden. On the way, I tripped on Daniel's laptop cable and there was a horrible pulling sensation inside my right knee, which had been acting up of late. I'd need to monitor it on today's walk, perhaps even strap it.

He came after me, toeing the cable aside. 'I'll tape it down later.'

Always later, never now. *You can't let him encroach, Mum*, Maya had warned when he'd moved in, but encroach he had and I often found myself retreating to my bedroom as if he were the owner and I the 'temporary' guest.

Below, Alec had evidently roused himself to give his new roommate a tour of the garden. It was unusually elaborate for a block of this size, with a generous lawn and two picnic areas. English willows and yews were interspersed with more exotic palms and fruit trees, spectacular in all seasons but especially so at this time of year when summer passed the baton to autumn.

His manner was engaged, I saw, even attentive, and my mind wrested a line from years ago: *Tell me what you're hiding.* Tucked it away again.

'Mum? All right if I finish this?'

I broke from my reverie to see Daniel brandishing the coffee jug, a look of sufferance on his face. 'Go ahead. But turn the machine off, will you?' He had a habit of returning the empty jug to the hotplate, causing it to scorch.

He tutted; even the smallest request prickled him.

Pixie's body language was quite different from Alec's – and from when she and I had chatted in the lobby – her arms wrapped tightly around her chest and her expression guarded. As he advanced towards the side of the building (only the ground-floor flats had direct access to the garden, the rest of us had to walk around from our front entrance), she did not immediately follow. Instead, she turned her back to him, making a visor with her right hand as she scanned the plot of land before her. It was almost as if she were assessing its dimensions, searching for an alternative exit.

I've lost count of the times I've thought that had it not been for Daniel's occupancy we might have avoided the catastrophe ahead. The bloodshed (okay, there's no blood in a suffocation, but metaphorical bloodshed). I could have rescued Pixie from Alec's clutches earlier and provided safe harbour. It wouldn't have been ideal, with her enemy still living across the landing, but it could have been a life-prolonging manoeuvre.

A handbrake turn, if you like – before the car careered off the cliff.

6

If *I'm* not what you're thinking, then nor was Alec. An outlier in the building, he was someone you'd be more likely to find in a loft apartment in Bermondsey or Shoreditch, not low-key suburban Queens Oak. We were quiet-life people here, not spotlight seekers.

Hard to believe now, I know.

Anyway, back in the Nineties he'd been a keyboard player in a rock band called Empty Cloud, whose number one song – 'Take Me If You Want Me' – promised a glorious future but turned out to be a one-hit wonder. They were too minor for there to be much to see now on YouTube, just a couple of videos, an appearance on the German equivalent of *Top of the Pops*, an interview in which a baby-faced Alec and his bandmates spoke of conquering America and being bigger than the Beatles and other rock clichés.

A short entry on Wikipedia added only that he had continued to work as a songwriter, so what I knew of him beyond this I'd had to gather from our own conversations and general building chatter. He'd inherited the flat from his aunt, my old neighbour Jeanette, who'd not long been widowed when I moved in and who had no children of her own. Then based out of town, he'd initially used the place as a city bolthole before splitting with his second wife and notifying the board that he intended moving in himself.

Strange now to think that I'd viewed him as a potential offender even before we met, though my fear back then had been to do with noise. Ageing rockers, whether still commercially active or not, tended to have professional quality kit, electric guitars that they blasted in home studios that weren't properly soundproofed. And given that one big hit, he likely lived off royalties and didn't need to do anything inconvenient like get up in the morning for the office. We had guidelines about noise issues and I confess to poring over them before he arrived.

As it transpired, Alec was no more or less noisy than any other neighbour. Yes, he liked a drink, but you could hardly complain of Bacchanalia across the landing and any songwriting was done on computers and using headphones – not that he talked much about his music. He was just a middle-aged bloke, mostly jocular, often entertaining, occasionally grumpy.

Among other unstarry activities, he joined the boules team based in Winifred Gardens and became a regular support to Steve, our part-time gardener. When one of our board directors moved out, he was elected in their place, quipping in his first meeting that the financial settlement he'd just reached with his second ex-wife was an incentive to keep service charges down.

'You don't have to be divorced to serve on the board, but it helps,' Dee joked back.

She texted me afterwards:

I can see we're going to have a lot of fun with Alec!!

By then I had mixed feelings about him, but I was damned if I was going to confide in her about that. I spent some time considering the appropriate response before settling on a single thumbs-up emoji.

I'm thinking this might be a useful point at which to note that all of the text messages I've included in this account are in their exact original form. In the unlikely event that anyone should want to check, I imagine the police could verify that. Most of us have had our devices examined by them at one time or another, as I understand it.

7

The first time I heard them arguing, I put it down to teething problems. In a publicly advertised rental like this, neither party knew much of the other and had everything to discover. As a victim of fraud, Pixie had been desperate enough to take a room she couldn't afford, while Alec's vetting methods had been superficial to say the least – had he even asked for references? I suspected he'd allowed pity to play a part in choosing her over candidates whose affairs might have been less fraught.

Whatever their differences, they flared quickly because it was only a matter of days before that first contretemps. It wasn't a blazing row, don't get me wrong, but hostile enough for me to be aware of it through the thick wall that separated our living rooms. Initially I couldn't make out more than the odd word, only their fractious tones, until Alec raised his voice in a sudden escalation:

'Come on, you know the deal.'

There was an answering grumble from Pixie and then silence.

I wondered if this had something to do with her working from home. She did something freelance with websites, I'd learned from a brief chat with Alec, and it was possible she was already getting under his feet in the way Daniel did mine. It seemed to me he had got used to having his cake and eating it with Yasmin, who'd taken extra shifts at the hospital while saving for her flat deposit.

In any case, the incident unsettled me sufficiently for me to make a point of checking in with Pixie when I saw her sitting alone in the garden a few days later.

'I thought it was you,' I said, as though the grounds teemed with young women dressed in tie-dye print leggings and fluffy pink hoodies. On her feet were scuffed grey UGGs, leaves stuck to the soles. 'Are you settling in okay?'

'Oh. Hi.' She looked disorientated, struggling to focus on me. 'I was meditating.'

'I'm sorry. You had your eyes open.'

'I know, I'm rubbish at it.' She giggled, shifted along the seat. 'Come and sit under this gorgeous tree. What even are those fruit?'

'They're pomegranates,' I said, sitting.

'Really?' She reached to finger one of the fruits, pressing gingerly as if expecting it to drench her with liquid, though it was unripe and rock hard. 'I'd love to know this stuff.'

'Where did you live before? Did you not have a garden?'

'No, I was staying with friends in their top-floor flat. Before that, I was with Dylan in Tooting. We had a bit of outside space but it was where the bins were kept and smelled really grim.'

'Dylan's the ex-boyfriend?'

'One of many.' She gave a fatalistic sigh, as if resigned to being forever unlucky in love, and though obviously intended to amuse me, it concealed, I thought, a very real sorrow. I longed to be able to help.

'Are you working at the moment? Alec said you design websites?'

'Content, yeah. I just finished a project. I'm getting a bit worried actually. Everyone's cutting budgets. It's like a total hellscape.'

'If you just want something to tide you over, I noticed they're looking for people at Bageri Møller. The new Danish bakery on Station Square?'

'Bakery' was a little prosaic for the emporium that had just opened in Queens Oak, the kind of place that referred to its customers as a community and where you could sit the whole day at your laptop – presumably on the understanding that you'd break at some point to order a pastry or a plate of herrings. I'd yet to be lured from Gail's.

'I was about to head that way now. We could walk down together if you like?'

She agreed, though more in the spirit of failing to find an excuse than of actively wanting to. But once on our way, she brightened, as most would, for the route took us through Winifred Gardens, the charming Victorian square that separated Columbia Mansions from the tangle of streets near the station that constituted Queens Oak proper. With its bandstand and folly and raked-gravel boules pits, it was at its most winning on a fluorescent-skied day like today.

'Getting on okay with Alec?'

'Fine,' she said.

'I hear him grumbling sometimes.' I kept my tone light. 'That's middle-aged men for you.'

'He's free to grumble. It's *his* place.'

'Yours too now. I hope you'll enjoy living in Columbia Mansions. It really is a lovely group of people. Very sociable. I don't know what I'd do without Scrabble Club and Older Bodies Pilates.' Pixie looked quizzical and I explained. 'It's slower and gentler than a younger person's class.'

'So is everyone …' She tailed off, suddenly awkward.

'Old?' I guessed, laughing. 'Not at all. We have three families in the building, including Sadie and her twins just below you, and a few younger couples as well. Plus my son Daniel is staying with me at the moment. He's in his thirties. You'll meet everyone at the bonfire party.'

'Oh, when's that?' she asked.

'November the fifth?' I chuckled. 'You've heard of Guy Fawkes, haven't you?'

'I thought that was to do with fireworks.'

'Yes, but bonfires too. Traditionally his effigy was burned.' Lord knew what they'd been teaching in schools these last decades for her not to know this. 'When I was young, we used to take him around in a wheelbarrow. And before you ask, yes, there were cars on the road and we did have electricity.'

We'd reached the far end of the gardens, the Beehive gastro pub right ahead and Crown Road leading to Station Square on the left, a scruffy but charming assemblage of outdoor café tables, bicycle racks and planters. On arrival at Bageri Møller, Pixie duly asked for details about the vacancy – general assistant, £12 an hour – and was given the link to fill out an online application, while I ordered our coffees.

We sat at the bar in the window, all the regular tables already taken by young people with laptops and AirPods. They looked very important as they scrolled through feeds and inspected spreadsheets, apparently undisturbed by the nattering of fifty-plus other people within earshot. Some sort of folk music played, with fiddles and the accordion, not unpleasant.

Below my elbow, a woman dipped her head to kiss the miniature dachshund suspended in some sort of sling around her chest and, catching us looking, smiled up at Pixie.

'What a total cutie,' Pixie said.

'I know, he's my angel. He needs his nap soon. Wait, I had some thoughts on optimization,' she added sharply, evidently segueing into a conference call, and I marvelled at what passed for professionalism these days.

'I love dogs,' Pixie told me. 'I want a whole pack of them. I'm going to be like that wrinkly old French actress and live by the sea with my own little fur babies.'

'Brigitte Bardot? Well, I hope you won't share some of her political views. They're a little unforgiving.'

'Oh, I don't follow politics. It's too depressing. I've got friends out on marches every weekend and I'm, like, why? Nothing's going to change.'

'Just being part of some rent-a-mob is pointless,' I agreed, 'but having a cause close to your heart can be very rewarding. I speak from personal experience.'

'Why, what's your cause, then?'

'Girls' education in developing countries. My ex-husband and I used to run a charity that raised funds for projects in India and rural Bangladesh, but we had to close, sadly. I still donate, but it's not the same.'

She looked mournfully at me. Her emotions were quick to see-saw, I was learning. 'Why did you have to close?'

'It was about the same time Brian and I split up. Let's just say the two things were linked.' I paused, ignoring the ache in my centre, the wound her sympathetic gaze was reopening. 'Anyway, that was before Malala came along. She's quite the force. What we did was a drop in the ocean compared to what she's achieved.'

As I was outlining Malala's accomplishments, our coffees arrived. They were served in rustic stone beakers, presumably fired in a Copenhagen kiln, and came with a little cake that I believe is a *financier* and not Danish but French.

Pixie nibbled hers, speaking as she chewed. 'Thanks so much for treating me, Gwyn.'

'Gwen,' I corrected her. Though a little hurt by the mistake, I laughed it off. 'Alec obviously hasn't mentioned me then, even though we're next-door neighbours and directors of the residents' management board. We're the worker elves who keep the building going.'

'Elves?' she repeated, puzzled, but I decided not to get into the Brothers Grimm.

'Yes, so any complaints about your neighbours, you know who to come to. Unless it's about me, of course!' Generally, the last thing I wanted was to encourage petty complaints – yes, I used the word 'petty' in relation to this poor girl – because there was already more than enough to keep us busy in our roles. But this was different and not only because of my instinctive liking for her. Knowing she'd been the victim of such a horrible scam, I wanted her to know my door was always open, my experience hers from which to benefit.

'How is your friend?' I asked. 'The boy who helped you move in?'

'Ash? He's good. He's moved back in with his parents down in Kent, so I won't see him much for a while.'

'It's not that far away. You could invite him up for the bonfire party?'

She pouted. 'Nowhere to park. And the trains from his place don't come in anywhere near here. It's not worth it.'

'Couldn't he stay over, make a night of it? Alec usually has people over afterwards, actually, so you'd be right where the action is.'

Pixie shook her head. 'I'm not allowed overnight guests.'

That knocked me out of my groove. 'Really?'

She looked curiously at me. 'Actually, you said about this board ... Is it a rule of the building then? No guests?'

'Of course not. People have them all the time. Is that really one of Alec's conditions? Sounds a bit restrictive.' Not to mention newly introduced for I knew for a fact that Casper had stayed over regularly with Yasmin. You'd see them going out for a run in the morning, returning with take-out cups of some lurid-coloured juice. 'Can I ask, do you and Alec have a written contract?'

She gave a slightly shameful shake of the head. So, he could turf her out without notice.

'Well, I don't see how he can prevent you from having guests. What if you have a boyfriend?'

'I told you, we split.'

'I mean someone new. Or you might have family who need to stay a few nights. Your dad, maybe?'

'Oh, he won't want to stay.'

'Would you like me to have a word?'

She looked a little alarmed. 'With my dad?'

'No, with Alec.'

'Oh. It's fine. I've probably not understood properly.'

'Let's do your application, shall we?' I said, sensing her mood plunging. 'Might as well send it off while you're here. Get it out of the way.' There were shades of my dynamic with Daniel in this rallying, but unlike him she obliged quite cheerfully, opening the form on her phone while I ordered more coffees. We then spent a lovely hour with her reading out the questions and me proposing answers (Which element of the Bageri Møller brand most resonates with you? *The caffeine, but only if it's a double shot ;-)*), but even before she'd submitted her answers, the member of staff she'd spoken to on arrival came over and scheduled a trial shift.

'Needn't have bothered with the questions,' she said, sliding her phone into the pocket of her hoodie.

'Amazing,' I said, though it was becoming clearer by the moment that in spite of her averred bad luck, she had a charisma that drew strangers to her, encouraged them to please her. 'I did that once at the charity. Hired someone on the spot as my assistant. She had no experience or much in the way of qualifications.' I paused, gulped air. I so rarely spoke of Cyndi, I'd taken myself by surprise. 'But sometimes you just know someone is going to be brilliant.'

'Well, I hope you paid her more than these Danish guys are paying me,' Pixie said, already disgruntled with her rate and she hadn't even started yet.

Incidentally, four coffees, plus service, came to almost £20. As I entered the amount on my spreadsheet that evening, I despaired of the government's money-printing madness that had led to this inflation.

8

As it happened, the next meeting of the management board took place just a week later.

For the record, directors are volunteers elected by the members of the Company to manage the development in the best interests of the residents collectively and must own properties in the building. In our case, all four of us used them as our principal residences – Dee, our chair, occupied flat 32; Alec, flat 4; Noel, flat 18, and me, flat 3 – and bar Noel, a married gay man in his early 50s, were divorced and single. The families and young couples in the building were understandably far too busy to want to spend a precious free evening debating whether we should switch our insurance provider or sanction a neighbour for crimes against recycling. Organize a vote for the umpteenth time on whether the no-pets restriction should be reversed.

Of course, the topic that caused the most discussion at this time of year was the service charge, specifically whether it would need to be increased for the subsequent period. The answer was yes – insurances had soared, and roof repairs could be delayed no longer – and we'd need to devise a payment scheme before sending out demands.

But none of this matters (actually, the service charge *is* relevant): the reason I include the meeting here is because it was the first time I'd seen Alec since I'd overheard his sniping with Pixie and been made aware of his no-guests stipulation.

He and I arrived at Dee's together. Hers was the best flat in the block, situated on the light-drenched top floor and featuring two of the building's distinctive corner turret rooms. The one in the living room had a window seat upholstered in blue velvet and it was here, at a gleaming walnut table, that we convened for our meetings.

'Come in, guys, grab a pew.' Dee spoke in a kind of purr, possessing a charm quite different from Pixie's, the honeyed kind you'd be forgiven for mistaking for ingratiation (and that I'm now inclined to believe was).

'New lamp?' I asked, noticing a mushroom-shaped copper addition under her framed black-and-white photograph of Helen Mirren, her hero.

'Yes, it's Tom Dixon. I saw it in the *Telegraph* and just knew it would look perfect there. Glass of Madeira, either of you? Noel's having one.'

'Never touch the stuff,' Alec said.

She tried to press a glass on me – 'It used to be your favourite, Gwen' – but my stomach rolled at the sight of it. 'I'm happy with water,' I insisted.

'You're looking good, Dee,' Alec said. He tended to be on best behaviour at these meetings, his bonhomie so polished you could see your reflection in it. 'Lost weight, have you?'

'No, I think it's just this dress. It's surprisingly slimming.'

In fact, the dress – a denim number with raglan sleeves – was only slimming because she *was* slim. Tall, too, with still-good legs, a costly haircut of silver and blonde highlights, the ends softly layered on her shoulders. Fashionable reading frames drew attention to her hazel eyes. Almost ten years retired from a career in hospitality, she was categorically, unassailably, the dowager queen of the building (though divorced rather than widowed) and I had long admitted defeat in any attempted rivalry.

Not only was she younger, richer and, as we've just established, thinner than me, her children were also more accomplished (we'll come to that) and even her relationship with her ex-husband was of a superior calibre. Richard, a retired TV chief of independent wealth, was often seen dropping by with a stack of fold-up chairs or the extra Le Creuset casserole she needed for an extended family gathering, at which he and his second wife would be present. When complimented on this open-spiritedness towards her successor, Dee would say, *Oh, you know, too few to mention*, which was her catchphrase (as in regrets, I explained to Pixie. 'From the song "My Way"?' But like the Guy Fawkes effigies and so much else, she couldn't be quite sure she'd heard of it).

All of which is quite a lot of detail, I realize, but I think it's important you have a clear picture of Dee, since she is an important player in this story.

And believe me, 'player' is the word.

Refreshments taken care of, we motored steadily through our business: an insurance claim; a lost key fob for the car park; a change of tenant in flat 19 – the vast majority of the flats were owner-occupied and the board had to approve all prospective rental tenants.

'Last but not least,' Dee said, 'Bonfire Night. As we know it's a Tuesday night, so we're not expecting to be mobbed.' The team was united in its suspicion of newfangled safety guidelines and it was a point of principle that our annual party should defy the nanny state by featuring an actual bonfire on the actual date, regardless of school nights and other objections. 'About eighty, so a nice easy number. Obviously, you and Steve are building the bonfire, Alec. Noel, you're doing the hot dogs, Hester's in charge of the mulled wine and the toffee apples order is confirmed. You're picking those up on the day, Gwen, aren't you?'

'I am,' I said.

'Daniel's still able to help out?'

'He's with Steve and me,' Alec said, which was news to me.

'Are Stella and Rafferty coming?' I asked Dee.

'Stella, yes, but Rafferty's working, unfortunately. How about Maya?'

'Busy, I think.' There was a sense of 'probably just as well', which I had to admit I shared. 'There'll be a few overnight guests in the building,' I said, with a glance at Alec. 'Hopefully residents will remember to issue their guests with parking permits if they're staying on the next day.'

'Otherwise, they'll be heading off with a nice fat ticket,' Noel said.

'Will you or Pixie have anyone staying over for it, Alec?' I asked, and thought I saw a flicker of wariness in his eyes.

'Not that I know of. Why the sudden fixation on visitors?'

'Security,' Dee said, answering for me. 'Non-residents don't always close the main doors properly and the Queens Oak forum has just warned again about opportunistic break-ins. Thanks for raising it, Gwen. I'll put up a notice about not sharing entry codes. Everything working out with Pixie?' she asked Alec helpfully. 'She seems like a lovely girl. So pretty too.'

He nodded. 'Early days, but so far so good.'

'It's awful how she was deceived over that other flat,' I said. 'You were very kind to step in and rescue her.' I shared details of the scam with Dee and Noel, who weren't aware of it. 'Alec was quite the knight in shining armour.'

'Gwen's exaggerating,' Alec said, leaving it to me to field all the questions I'd previously asked Pixie about police enquiries and bank insurance.

'Good on you, Alec,' Dee said, reaching to squeeze his shoulder in approval. 'We haven't had this sort of charitable spirit in the building since Irina moved out.'

Irina was a Homes for Ukraine refugee, taken in by Dee's neighbour Karishma but widely known as Our Ukrainian. Though not normally permitted, flags had been in evidence in the building for a good year, an exception having been made for such an important cause.

'I'm not sure I'd call Pixie a charity case,' Alec said. 'She's paying rent.'

'Yes, she'd hate to be treated as vulnerable,' I said, perhaps a little proprietorial given the infancy of our friendship. 'Maybe I shouldn't have mentioned it. It's not my story to tell.'

But Dee said I'd been right to, that it made us all more vigilant. 'These fraudsters are operating with impunity right under our noses,' she said, shaking her head.

'Or from scam factories in China,' Noel said. 'Did you read that awful story in *The Times* about the one in Myanmar?'

'They're in a right old mess out there,' Alec said. 'Wouldn't go near the place if you paid me.'

As he digressed, it struck me that he was uncommonly eager to discuss Southeast Asian politics, not a natural subject for the group, and I cut in at the earliest opportunity. 'You don't have to be in a country ravaged by civil war to find yourself taken advantage of. Look at poor Pixie.'

He gave a bark of laughter. 'Don't say you're gonna go all vigilante on us, Gwen. Even a gargoyle like you couldn't scare off these grifters. I mean that with affection, of course,' he added, as Noel and Dee looked a little shocked by the insult.

I sought his eye with the aim of transmitting general disapproval, but when our gazes locked, I was in for a surprise. Malevolence burned behind that façade of merriment, almost as if *he* were warning *me*.

My brow twitched, but otherwise I succeeded in holding my nerve. 'Of course, Alec,' I said, patting his hand, Dee-style. 'Goes without saying.'

9

If Dee had too few regrets to mention regarding her ex-husband, then I had plenty to spare about mine. Truly, the remainder of my life wasn't long enough for me to plot and execute the appropriately maximized levels of pain and suffering Brian deserved. I have neither the space nor the energy to outline the whole saga here, so you'll have to make do with the basics of his crime and judge for yourself its impact on our family – and beyond.

I trust it will also inform your response to any opinions he might have chosen to contribute to my current predicament.

He was found guilty of fraud by abuse of position at the charity, fiddling his expenses to you and me, and while it may not have been on an industrial scale like the scam factory Noel mentioned (and that I read about avidly on my return from the board meeting), it was serious enough for our accountant and me to be investigated alongside him and subsequently removed from our roles. Our beautiful family home had to be sold to repay the embezzled funds.

I wanted to throttle him then and I still want to throttle him now, but worry not: he is safe from me. He lives with his second wife and three step-children eleven and a half thousand miles away in New Zealand.

'You had the hubris to believe you would get away with your theft indefinitely,' the judge told him in court before handing him a two-year suspended sentence. 'I remain unconvinced that any regret you claim to feel is for your having deprived those you were trusted to help, but rather for your having discovered that your peers consider your conduct beyond the pale.'

In other words, he was an arrogant self-serving pig.

I suppose it's easy in retrospect to think that I conflated Alec and him in some warped psychosis, some unstoppable transference of lust for revenge. But let me assure you that I was able to keep their faces – and their crimes – quite distinct.

As for the meting out of punishment on a private basis, well, what can I say? That was dictated entirely by opportunity.

10

Motivated more by instinct than strategy, I dropped into Bageri Møller the next day and quickly located Pixie behind a gargantuan coffee machine, working her way through a row of tickets. She was dressed in the café uniform of white shirt, black leggings and grey apron, her hair tied in a tight ponytail that exposed a flush across her neck and collarbone. She moved quickly, if a little haphazardly, slopping milk over the top of the jug, scattering coffee grains, knocking into objects at hip and elbow level. As she called their names, young people in yoga or cycling gear stepped forward to collect their drinks, much too preoccupied with their phones to proffer even a muttered thank you.

The music today was frothy and sung in accented English. I'd preferred the fiddles.

When there was no longer anyone waiting, I signalled hello. 'You're getting good at this.'

'It's not hard.' She was bashful about compliments, I'd noticed. But she smiled with her eyes, exuding warmth. 'How are you, Gwen?'

'Good. I won't distract you, I just wanted to say I'm having a few of the girls over tomorrow night for dinner and I wondered if you'd like to join us?'

Without wishing to sound as if I had her under surveillance,

I had noticed how rarely she left the building in the evenings and it had struck me as odd that someone so likeable and attractive socialized so little – until I remembered the small fortune she'd lost in the rent scam. She must be strapped for cash.

'Girls?' She looked at me, quizzical, guileless.

'Women. Some of the other residents.'

'Not, like, the Scrabble group Dee told me about? Because I haven't got time to learn how to play. I'm on shift here all day tomorrow.'

I felt a clench of protest at the thought of Dee approaching her, which I suppose speaks to my early intuition that she and I had – or were destined to have – a special bond. 'No skills required, just a basic dinner party. And no need to bring anything. You probably haven't been paid yet.'

I asked if there was any news from her bank and she grimaced. 'Yeah, they came back to me this morning. Said it's my fault.'

'Why?'

'They said there were all these warnings before I made the payment and I clicked yes to them and that means I was satisfied this guy was a trusted payee or something.'

I frowned. 'Well, I'd appeal that. The point is they should be more aware of fraudsters operating in the rental market and even if *you* thought it was safe to send the payment, *they* could have blocked it.'

She looked a bit taken aback and I wondered if I'd sounded sterner than I'd intended. 'So how would I even do that?' she asked, mopping a spillage with a fistful of paper napkins. 'Appeal, I mean?'

'You usually need to make a written complaint, asking them to reconsider. If that doesn't work, then you can take it to the Financial Ombudsman Service.'

'Right.' But her tone was vague. I couldn't understand her reluctance; the sum stolen was significant by most people's standards.

A colleague appeared at her shoulder with a new ticket. 'Two cortados and a ginger tea, Pix.'

'On it.' She turned to me. 'I'd love to come tomorrow, thank you. What time?'

'Let me take your number and I'll text you the details.'

After she'd plugged her number into my phone, she said, 'Wait, Alec isn't invited, is he?'

'No, no, just the girls.'

'Great. See you then, Gwen.' She placed an emphasis on my name, presumably to reassure me that it was fixed in her mind now and that she would never again forget it.

Which I think it's fair to say she never did.

*

I had scheduled the meal for Daniel's monthly outing with the only friends he'd kept up with since the breakdown of his marriage – or who, I suspected, had insisted on keeping up with him. It involved a football match in North London and he'd be staying out late so I had a clear run of it.

Besides Dee, Pixie and me, there were three other residents, Columbia Mansions stalwarts all. Hester was a recent empty nester in her fifties who shared my love of rambling, as well as being that rare creature who understood that conversation involved listening as well as speaking. Liz, who lived on the ground floor at Dee's, had, since becoming a smidgen confused with age (she was well into her eighties), taken on the status of resident 'character'. She also had some issues with her gums ('I can't watch her eat,' Daniel observed, unhelpfully). Finally,

Sadie, who lived with her husband and twin boys in the flat below Alec's, and was in her late thirties but looked younger, having the lustrous hair of a teenager and one of those girlish upturned noses. Besides Pixie, she was the only representative of child-bearing age at the dinner.

Proudly fecund or post-menopausal, we had one thing in common besides our postcode, and that was an appetite for Tesco's Chenin blanc, served with the own-brand crisps and nuts I'd supplied, as well as a bowl of Dee's overpriced but admittedly delicious olives that were reportedly all the rage in her daughter's chi-chi East London neighbourhood.

'Daniel's still in the spare room, I take it?' Hester said, even though I'd tidied his work station and removed the various socks and zip-up fleeces he'd left in his wake. Clearly his presence was still discernible; perhaps he'd contributed to a change in the scent of the place, the way a pet does.

'You don't think there's any hope for him and his wife?' Sadie asked.

'No, Nella's getting the flat valued, wants to buy him out. She's instructed her solicitor. He's dragging his heels, but he doesn't have much choice.'

'Have you had any contact with her?'

'Not since before the split,' I said.

'One of them must have someone else, do you think?' Hester suggested.

'Well, it's not him. He hardly ever sets foot outside.'

'He might have one of those women who aren't really there,' Liz said. 'I was reading about them in the *Daily Mail*. Pretend girlfriends. What's it called again, A1?

'AI, Liz,' Dee said. 'The A1 is a motorway.'

Pixie giggled and tipped her near-empty wineglass to her

lips. She was a little shy with the others and drinking at a rate of knots. I fetched the bottle and refilled her glass.

'He's certainly online a lot,' I said. 'It's as if he's completely dropped out of normal society.'

'They call that lying flat in China,' Sadie said.

'Really? I call it being bone idle.'

'At least there aren't any children caught in the crosshairs,' Dee said, with characteristic positivity. 'And, as you say, it's lovely to have so much time with him.'

I had said no such thing, but everyone acted as if I had. Times had changed and where once a friend might have demanded to know why I didn't just give him his marching orders, now it was common for grown-up children to boomerang – if they'd even flung themselves off in the first place.

'My two are so booked up, I practically have to formally request to see them,' Dee continued. 'Imagine having to wrangle with your own children like it's a dentist's appointment. "I've got a cancellation on Tuesday at five? Would that work?" Honestly.'

'What do they do, Dee?' Pixie asked.

'Rafferty is a pilot, he works for a private jet charter company based at Stansted, and Stella's a journalist with the *Sunday Times*. Though she's pregnant with her first baby so we'll see how much writing she gets done with a newborn in the house.'

'She'll write about being a new mum, I imagine,' Hester said, explaining to Pixie, 'she has her own column. I'm surprised you don't know her, she's quite a well-known young feminist.'

Pixie sparked. 'What, like ... Who was it again, Gwen? Malala?'

'Goodness, not in that league,' Dee said, laughing. 'Malala won the Nobel Peace Prize!'

'Is she on Instagram?' Pixie took out her phone and found Stella's feed. 'Wow, she's like model good-looking, Dee.'

'Well, *I* think so, but *she* would say that's the last thing she wants to be recognized for.'

Servicing wine refills, I kept my head down. I would not be directing Pixie to my own daughter's social media – and Maya had considerably more followers than Stella.

'I can't imagine my boys being actual grown-ups,' said Sadie. 'It sounds as if they still need quite a lot of support. Do you have to help them find a job? Homework is stressful enough.'

'Mine were very lucky that they identified their passions early,' Dee said modestly. She didn't mention the fact that Richard was a retired but still well-connected big cheese in the media, though, to be fair, there were no airline pilots in the family.

'How old are they?' Pixie asked, and on hearing that Stella was twenty-eight, close to her own age, looked thoroughly dismayed. Learning of a contemporary's superior status and accomplishments was not easy at any age – look at my own permanent state of eclipse at Dee's hands – but particularly harrowing in hormone-drenched youth.

'Not everyone can be a star,' I said good-humouredly.

'Oh, no one's saying they're stars,' Dee said, sweetly. 'They're still helpless babies to me.'

I somehow knew to catch Pixie's eye at this. While I was in Dee's direct line of sight, she was not and when she pulled a face it felt like the most thrilling act of rebellion.

'Where do your parents live, Pixie?' Hester asked.

Pixie took another healthy swallow of wine. She was flushed and tipsy by now. 'I grew up in Kent. On the coast, near Herne Bay? My mum died when I was fifteen and my dad is still down there.'

'Has he seen your new digs yet?'

'Not yet.'

'Well, good on you for being so independent.'

She gave Hester an uncertain smile. 'I don't *feel* very independent.'

'You don't live in your parents' spare room and expect your laundry to be done for you,' I said. 'You pay rent. You're independent.'

'How did your mother die?' Liz asked. Cause of death was a regular topic of small talk in the older reaches of the community.

'Heart disease.' Pixie pulled a face. 'Everyone says my dad drove her to an early grave.'

'Why?'

'Oh, just that he's a character. He used to be always out on work stuff. She wouldn't know if he was even coming back.' His business had been recently sold, she added, and I supposed this had been the source of the funds spirited away by the criminal non-landlord. 'So how often do you do your Pilates class?' she asked, changing the subject.

'Once a week, Friday morning at my place,' Dee said. 'Would you like me to add you to the residents' chat? That's where we share updates on our get-togethers.'

'No, I'm all right,' Pixie said politely.

Dee took the demurral with a good grace. 'I'm sure Alec will keep you up to date on anything that affects you directly,' she said and it seemed to me Pixie's expression darkened at the mention of her landlord's name.

'How old do you have to be to join?' she asked, rallying. 'Pilates, I mean?'

'It's at our discretion, but I'd say fifty-five plus.'

'It's really helped my frozen shoulder,' Liz told her.

'I meant to ask, Gwen,' Hester said. 'How's your knee?'

'Getting worse.' I adjusted it slightly and, feeling fresh pain, imagined the cartilage worn away to nothing, the old bones grinding together. 'Oh, Pixie,' I cried, as her earnest gaze turned my way, 'promise you'll enjoy your healthy young body while you can!'

There was a moment's surprise at this heartfelt plea and then, as the double entendre echoed, everyone laughed and said how funny I was and Pixie replied, with a game smile, 'I'll try, I suppose.'

I feel awful about the faux pas now, but at the time the oven pinged and I got up to tend to my Rick Stein fish pie without giving it another thought.

11

I hadn't been entirely truthful with my dinner guests – or Daniel, for that matter – about not having seen his estranged wife. In fact, I'd paid Nella a call about a month into their separation, when he'd entered a malaise even deeper than the one that gripped him now, unable to give a reason why they'd parted or estimate how long for. Had it been a more promising exchange – or even a more ambiguous one – I would certainly have told him, but sadly that was not the case.

I arrived unannounced at the flat in Stoke Newington, early enough on a weekend to have a good chance of finding her at home. She came to the door wearing exercise kit, ropes of dark hair swinging in a high ponytail, skin glistening. A pitying smile reinforced what I already suspected: there was no hope.

'There's nothing you can say, Gwen.'

'I'm not trying to plead on his behalf,' I said, 'just to understand.'

Her catlike gaze softened and she invited me in for coffee. The flat, a top-floor one bed that leaked heat in winter and retained it in summer, was unchanged beyond the few new plants in an already thickly forested collection, an extra velvet cushion or two on the oversized white sofa. Daniel, who'd left with only his clothes and laptop, had yet to remove his decorative effects.

'If I'd known you were coming, I'd have got your cinnamon

buns,' Nella said, delivering my coffee in the Emma Bridgewater mug she knew I liked best, and I felt a string pluck inside me. In her thoughtfulness, her attention to my needs, she'd always been far more daughterly to me than my own daughter. I would miss her.

But this wasn't about me, this was about Daniel. 'Oh, Nella, I can't make head nor tail of how this has happened and I'm not sure he can either.'

She groaned. 'The fact that he doesn't know is sort of the point.'

'Is that fair? I know my generation put up with too much in our marriages, but even so. If he doesn't know what he's done wrong, could you not just tell him?'

'He won't be told,' she said, and I sensed a loosening then, a willingness to divulge a little more. 'I just think maybe he's the way he is because of his dad going to jail? That whole scandal with you guys?'

I'd never grown used to her knowing about our family disgrace and it didn't help that time erased the nuance, leaving only 'that scandal' and 'you guys'. Though I'd been exonerated, I seemed only to grow guiltier. As for Brian, I didn't protest that his sentence had been suspended and he hadn't actually been jailed. To my mind, he should have.

'The way he is?' I queried.

'You know.' She tore the scrunchie from her hair and fanned her silky locks over her shoulders. 'Negative. Distrustful. He wills things to go wrong, then when they do, he acts all I told you so. He's not sad because things have gone wrong, he's happy because he was right. It's childish.'

I couldn't have described my son better if I'd tried. 'He was quite mature as a young child. He's developing in reverse. Regressing.'

'Well, I can't have a family with a man-child. I'm sorry.'

I eyed her abdomen. 'You're not ... ?'

She shuddered. 'No, but at some point, yes. With the right person. We should *never* have got married. We did it to keep things going.'

Marriage as a last-ditch rescue remedy. I'd come across this before among my generation's offspring and it seemed to me to be an expensive way to mark the end of a relationship. Even without that shudder, that emphasized 'never', this was definitive stuff.

'Did you come on the bus?' she asked. 'Do you think you could take his things?'

I was about to protest, but it was only one small box, the tiniest of lots. The flat was not unchanged because he hadn't yet removed his effects, I realized, but because he'd contributed so few in the first place. I felt profoundly sad for him then.

But having a little rootle through the box on the bus home I found old Valentine's cards she was returning to him, one containing a limerick he'd penned – *There was a young lady called Nella/Who always had toast with Nutella/He once gave her jam/She cried out Oh damn/And threatened to find a new fella* – and I felt my sympathies slide back towards her.

Back home, I popped the box among the clutter in his room, knowing he wouldn't notice its arrival, and decided it was a good thing that he cared so little for possessions. We kid ourselves that they are key to our identity, but the instinct to acquire fades with age and is surprisingly freeing.

You can't take it with you – as greedy Alec discovered.

*

Speaking of material wealth, I had close to £40,000 in savings when all of this began, a decent rainy-day fund, I'm sure you'll agree. And yet, within a few short months, an unprecedented downpour had washed much of it away.

The health expenses were the first to make a dent and those I don't regret. *He who has health has hope* and all that. It was our Pilates instructor, Saoirse, who, at the next session after that dinner party, suggested I get the mole on my left forearm looked at. According to her, it had a suspiciously ridged texture. She had a cousin in Cork who had died of a melanoma and she knew her onions.

As soon as the class was over and I was back in my flat, I rang the GP and entered into the usual catch-22 exchange with the receptionist about whether or not the need was urgent. If you said no, it wasn't urgent, you went to the bottom of the list and if you said yes, they sent you to A & E, where you entered a race between seeing a medical professional and catching MRSA. No wonder all calls were now preceded by a recorded message about zero tolerance of abusive language.

'I'll book you in for the next non-urgent,' she said, finally, but starting to imagine I could feel the mole metastasizing, I also consulted a private GP, who duly arranged a biopsy.

'I noticed you're experiencing discomfort when you walk,' he said, and we discussed the nature and severity of my knee pain. 'Let's get a scan scheduled, shall we?'

And so began a programme of medical appointments that basically turned me into exactly the ailment-fixated oldie that I'd mocked in my youth and vowed never to allow myself to become.

'Sounds rough,' Daniel said when I updated him, both his empty expression and lack of active questioning signalling an absence of interest that only proved my point.

To be honest, I'm wondering if this medical stuff might be as dull for you as it was for him? It's so hard to tell when you're the writer – we are all the hero of our own story, as the saying goes. Just know that it had a measurable effect on my psychological state and in that sense must surely be significant. I felt impaired, limited, at exactly the time I intuited a need for full fitness.

No one wants to go into battle with a limp.

12

To recap, my disapproval of Alec at this stage had to do with little more than his attempts to curtail Pixie's domestic rights. I trace the moment I grew suspicious of something darker to a chance encounter in Station Square.

I was approaching the café that wasn't Bageri Møller or Gail's, but a small independent that had a long trestle table with bench seating on the pavement, a popular pit stop for cyclists and runners. On this occasion, one end was crowded with a group of young women, including one with a spaniel on her lap, its water bowl on the table next to her coffee (this struck me as unhygienic, but who cared what *I* thought?) and another who wore a fuchsia woollen beanie over smooth blonde hair and whose face was naggingly familiar. It was only when she burst into laughter that I remembered: she'd been the attractive forerunner among those viewing Alec's spare room.

I drew to a halt at her shoulder. The other women looked up and, seeing I was older and therefore of no relevance, resumed their chat. 'I'm sorry to stare,' I said, 'but I think you came to see my neighbour's spare room last month. In Columbia Mansions?'

'That's right. He really messed me around on that, actually.' She was crisply spoken, eager to vent. 'He told me I'd got it, right after the viewing it was. Oh my God, I was so happy. Then a few days later he changed his mind, literally just blew me off in a text. I'd already given notice on my other place by then; it was completely out of line. I found somewhere else in the end, but it's not as nice. I love Columbia Mansions. I was so gassed when I thought I'd be moving in. It's so iconic.'

While this was perhaps the most overused adjective of her generation, I never tired of young people admiring the building. Not because I wanted them to envy those of us in possession of these covetable apartments, but because it meant that they had taste; they valued heritage, artistic quality. The decline of Western civilization might be underway but it was not quite complete. 'Did he not give any reason?' I asked.

She sent me a narrow, betrayed look. 'Said he'd decided not to rent the room after all. Needed to let his niece use it. It's not fair how she just rang up her uncle and took someone else's room just like that. Lucky for some.'

As I've mentioned, I have an instinct for impropriety, and that instinct was not so much buzzing as clanging. *He'd decided not to rent it ... Needed to let his niece use it ...* Why couldn't Alec have just told her the truth? It wouldn't have made up for the inconvenience, but to know she had lost out to someone in greater need, a victim of crime, might have lessened the sting.

As I turned to depart, a strong feeling of unease flooding my stomach, the girl called after me, sharply enough to set the spaniel barking: 'If you see him, tell him Cara's not very happy, yeah?'

*

Should you by now be picturing me as some second-rate Jane Marple or Jessica Fletcher – Vera would be my preference, if we must have a fictional point of reference – then you'll be pleased to know that we've reached a breakthrough in the case.

Soon after that interaction in Station Square, I was returning mid-morning from the chemist, where I'd been treated like a street junkie for trying to obtain something stronger than paracetamol for my knee pain, when I came upon Alec at the main door, signing for a delivery. He was barefoot, wearing only a thin towelling robe in spite of the October drizzle, and, as he was apt to do with blue-collar workers, engaging in a bit of banter. His robe gaped open during an eruption of laughter and I averted my eyes from the flash of belly.

Upstairs, the door to his flat had been left wide open and, a little concerned about security, I peeked in to check that everything was as it should be. Thanks to a freak combination of half-open doors and a hallway mirror, I caught a glimpse of Pixie standing in her bedroom doorway in her underwear, stretching her arms high above her head. To see her there so scantily dressed with her door open took me aback. Wouldn't she want to keep it closed if Alec was about to return at any second? Especially when he himself was semi-naked?

It was only when I was back in my own flat, boiling the kettle for tea, that it occurred to me that since Alec's flat was a mirror image of mine, Pixie's room – the equivalent of Daniel's – must be the smaller one in the centre, its door just across the hall from the flat's entrance. And yet the bedroom I'd seen her in was at the front, the larger of the two, the master. I suddenly understood. She and Alec must have struck up a physical relationship. They were both in a state of undress because they'd got out of bed at the same time – *together.*

I don't mind admitting that my blood ran cold at the thought. Whether it was a premonition of disaster or simply an Older Body responding in disgust to what might once have been perfectly acceptable, I couldn't say, but I knew it was pointless to overreact. I needed to apply a bit of rational thinking.

As I drank my tea by the window, soothed by the sight of our mighty willows beginning their seasonal shedding (trees are decidedly more reliable in their behaviour than any human I've met), I reminded myself that it happened all the time, this 'roommates with benefits' thing. It was a staple of romantic plots and sitcoms, the ultimate sexual convenience.

I considered the women I'd seen Alec with over the last few years. In their forties usually, and extrovert, with a tendency to cackle on the balcony with a cigarette late at night. Since none had been brought to Columbia Mansions social events, I'd assumed he was a dyed-in-the-wool commitment-phobe, in which case dating a flatmate might be a complicated business.

As for that charitable instinct he'd been credited with for housing Pixie, well that was obviously nonsense: he'd changed his mind because he'd fancied her more than Cara the blonde. Both were young enough to be his daughter, but again such relationships were common enough and not only in the high-end parts of London where billionaires kept their lairs. The UK was a country in which over forty per cent of marriages ended in divorce and ... Well, have *you* ever met a second wife who was older than the first?

Fine, Queen Camilla, but besides her?

I thought not.

Overcoming an urge to text Pixie and share my opinions on her change of status, I persuaded myself it was better to wait for the right moment. I'd have a discreet word with her at the bonfire party when Alec would be in charge of the fire, which I knew from previous years would occupy him all evening.

In charge of the fire: now there's a line begging for reinvention as a metaphor.

13

Unlike last year, when we'd been gifted sublimely crisp conditions, the weather was not ideal for our bonfire party. Swollen cloud hung so low that it merged with smoke from the blazing fire as if one and the same, an illusion I found unsettling.

Others' spirits were not so adversely affected. Alec, Steve and Daniel tended the fire with enthusiasm (I'd watched from the living room window as Alec and Steve constructed it, as tenderly industrious as expectant swans). Noel and his husband Ethan were full of cheer as they dispensed hotdogs with all the trimmings, Hester and Dee equally perky in their ladling of mulled wine. Karishma circulated with a tray of Indian sweets, smiling indulgently at the building's children, all of whom had invited friends and were dashing about in duffel coats and bobble hats.

My role as toffee apple seller proved a lucky option, the teeth-endangering product selling out in under an hour and leaving me free to focus on Pixie. At first, I didn't think she'd come, but then I spotted her, standing on her own about as close to the fire as you could get without being singed, dressed in a vinyl trench coat, Doc Marten-style bovver boots and what looked like a genuine Stetson.

'Pixie?' My voice was lost in the crackle and swoosh but, in any case, she was too bewitched by the flames to hear me – it was as if she believed that if she just stared long enough the truth would be revealed.

'Don't get too close.' I took her arm and gently steered her back a pace or two. 'You don't want your lovely coat to melt.'

'Oh, Gwen.' She turned gratefully to me. 'I went into a bit of a trance there.'

'I know you did. You were like a toddler mesmerized by the candles on their birthday cake. Which reminds me, I saved you one of these.' I handed her a toffee apple, its cellophane wrapper reflecting the orange of the flames, and she held it to her sternum like a posy. Her gloveless fingers were bony and white, with several chunky rings featuring hearts and bows.

Knowing we would not be alone for long, I decided to plunge straight in with my concerns, careful to keep my emotions on an even keel. 'So, I gather you and Alec are seeing each other?'

'What?' I couldn't tell if the flush was from my question or the heat of the fire, but her shock was unmistakable as she met my gaze. 'Who told you that?'

'No one. Like I say, I gathered. From my long decades of observing human behaviour.'

She glanced away. 'Oh. Okay. Wow.'

'Tell me to mind my own business ...' – she was far too sweet to do that – 'but I worry that he's a lot older than you. And as the person you pay rent to, he's also in a position of power and I'm not sure that's an advisable dynamic for a romance.'

'Don't worry about it, Gwen,' she said, politely enough, but I could tell she was dismissing my misgivings as those of someone who didn't understand on account of her advanced age, because dating was done differently now and people no longer had dance cards and chaperones.

'Pixie, I just—'

'I said, don't worry about it. Honestly. It's fine. It's not forever.'

I stared at her. It would have been easier not to worry had she not looked so deeply un-fine. It was awful to see this lovely girl so downcast. Over her shoulder I could see Dee advancing with the pregnant super-daughter Stella and her partner, and again I felt – and crushed – a pang of rivalry. Given this confirmation of an entanglement with Alec, Pixie needed more than little old me in her corner: let Stella and her man model a same-age relationship of equity and mutual respect.

'Don't say anything, will you?' she said, anxiously. 'About ... him and me. I don't want anyone to know.'

'Understood,' I said. 'But beware, this is the famous journalist daughter. She has a nose for gossip. I'm kidding,' I added, seeing her alarm.

'Greetings, ladies!' Dee, resplendent in a fake fur animal print coat and a trendy brand of wellington boot, placed herself between us. 'Pixie, I wanted you to meet my daughter Stella and her partner Cam.'

'Stam', as Daniel had dubbed them after a single encounter, were exactly the smug metropolitan duo you're probably picturing: tall, well-dressed, bright-eyed, the beneficiaries of unimpeachable orthodontics. He had a trimmed beard and she an abundance of inky hair that snaked in attractive twists down her back, but otherwise they were interchangeably delightful.

'I love your coat,' she told Pixie in smoky tones inherited from her mother. 'I can't wait to get back to belted waists. Or any kind of waist to be honest with you.'

I enquired after the baby's due date and birth plan and she said how thrilled and relieved she was to have snared her first choice of male doula.

'I'm not sure I know what that is,' I said.

'A doula who's a man,' she said.

'No, the doula bit.'

'I'm messing with you, Gwen.' As she outlined exactly what the doula was to do (get under the feet of the midwife, from what I could tell), I tuned into Dee's account to Cam and Pixie of the Bonfire Nights of her youth.

'Did you burn an effigy of Guy Fawkes back then?' Pixie asked and I thought, *well remembered*, with the pride of a teacher. She was soon giggling – truly, her capacity to change mood on a sixpence was breathtaking – and launching into a story of her ex-boyfriend's failed attempts to light a fire in a cottage they'd once stayed in, which had led to the fire brigade being called out to help. I'd read that false alarms of this nature cost the tax payer a billion pounds a year, but I kept that statistic to myself, not wishing to hurt her feelings. In any case, there was nodding and smiling to be done as to Stella's thoughts on whether she should order a £300 sock that monitored the baby's oxygen levels or some such though it was obvious she was going to buy it no matter what my view (which was, for the record, that you'd have to be mentally impaired to want such an item).

'You can't put a price on peace of mind,' she said.

'It sounds as if you can.' Maybe it was the effects of the spiced wine, but I was starting to enjoy myself.

It was then that I noticed that Alec had paused in his fire-stoking duties, a beer pressed to his forehead, presumably to try to cool down, and was looking our way. Pixie was at our centre, four faces turned to hers, but he didn't look the slightest bit interested in joining us, utterly incurious as to our gasps and giggles. For all he knew we could have been discussing *him*.

'Anyone want another mulled wine?' Cam asked, adding that he was drinking for two. 'Pixie?'

‘I’ll come with you,’ she said, and watching them stroll over to the stand, where Hester had been left by Dee to toil alone, I wondered if Alec had clocked the attention this attractive young man was paying Pixie. But when I checked he’d returned to his work, soon lost to the Dickensian fog.

Later, when the boozing and male bonding continued in flat 4, I imagined Pixie tucked up in bed, earbuds in, struggling to sleep. Was she in Alec’s room or her own? Given they had a flat full of guests, it must be the latter if she hoped to keep their attachment private. I thought it a good sign that she didn’t want to go public with their coupling. She obviously wasn’t confident it would last – or had any intention of letting it. Best-case scenario they would go back to how they were, landlord and tenant, no harm done.

Incidentally, *doula* is from the Greek for ‘slave’, which surely meant its days among the millennial metropolitan elite were numbered.

14

Inevitably, I was even more attuned to the dynamic next door after that, keener to pick up snatches of conversation through the living room walls, even to rue the efficacy of the soundproofing that I'd previously valued very highly indeed.

But what can I say? I'm of the generation that airs rooms occasionally and the morning after the party, getting wind of activity on Alec's balcony, I eased open my own French doors and cocked an ear.

'No, I'm telling you,' Pixie was saying, voice gravelly, hungover. 'She totally does. She asked me straight out.'

I caught Alec's answering mumble, along with the scent of tobacco, but not the actual words.

'No,' Pixie said, 'just that we're together.'

Another mumble. Short of sticking my head out, I was going to have to piece together the conversation from her half of the exchange.

'I don't know ... Yeah ... I just feel bad ... I don't think she's *jealous*. That's mad. She's not gay, is she? We're friends, that's all. Good friends.'

It was fair to assume they were talking about me. There was a splutter of laughter from Alec and his next reply was just about audible: 'Not you, babe. Me.'

I almost cried out in protest: the conceit of the man to assume *he* was the prize! Typical of males of a certain generation, of course. Next thing, a cigarette end went flying onto the terrace below, an act that was strictly forbidden in the conditions of the lease, though I supposed that since the ashes of a large bonfire sat a short distance away, I could let it go.

As the two of them retreated inside, I told myself to ignore their remarks about jealousy and focus instead on Pixie's statement: *We're friends. Good friends.* We were indeed, and it gave me a warm feeling both to hear her say it and to repeat the words silently to myself. Too early, perhaps, to talk of kindred spirits, but when you know you know, as they say.

Anyway, it was important not to obsess and distraction arrived in the form of my biopsy and scan results, processed with laughable efficiency – this must be how it felt to live in Switzerland or Japan! The mole was benign but the knee officially screwed and a replacement recommended. The timing coincided with the non-urgent appointment I'd secured with my GP, so I took the results along in the hope of booking the procedure on the NHS.

'I'll make the referral now,' the doctor said, a promising dynamism soon snuffed out by the news that the waiting list was not the best-practice eighteen weeks promised on their website but unknowably longer. 'The problem is the cancellations,' she explained. 'You can feel like you keep going back to the beginning.'

Eighteen weeks – four months – was bad enough, but this might conceivably be a year, and as soon as I got home, I googled the cost of having the surgery done privately: £14,000. Sweet Jesus.

It was depressing being the only one in Pilates the next morning to have to declare an injury. Even Liz's shoulder had eased. Saoirse checked regularly that I wasn't causing myself undue strain and reminded the others more than once of the importance of improving bone density before it was too late.

'At least it's not *both* knees like Stella's boss at the *ST*,' Dee said, and everyone agreed, relieved that she'd teased out the positive where they had been at a loss. No one pointed out the illogicality of her statement – one hospitalization for two procedures would have been more efficient in several ways, including cost – but I'd found that if you challenged Dee's thinking you only made yourself look an idiot.

*

Indulge me, if you will, in a short appraisal of Stellar Stella's *Sunday Times* column. When she'd first got the gig, I'd read it every week and flattered Dee with regular discussion of it, but over time it had become a chore, if not outright torturous, and I'd let the habit go. However, having seen Stella at the bonfire party, I made a point of catching up online on her latest offering.

Her style was what I believe the young call wholesome and I would describe as cute, applied on this occasion to the subject of priorities, because no woman can have it all even if she really, really wants it.

(Cute *and* unoriginal.)

Why Three Into Two Won't Go

A wise woman once said to me that at any life stage you can only do two big things well. Toss a third into the mix and you tip into mediocrity.*

Work and Frolics with Friends™ have always been my big two, but now motherhood looms (did I mention I'm pregnant with my first baby?) I find I have a bit of a three-into-two problem.

**My mum*

On it went, as if she were the first woman ever to have considered the compromises and sacrifices of breeding.

> *It's not forever – even if it will occasionally feel like that – but while my child needs a car seat, friendships will have to take a backseat. Don't give up on me though, party people, will you? Because I'll be back. I'll be back if it's the last thing I do.*

That phrase again: *it's not forever.* It was all too easy at the time to link Stella and Pixie by its usage, to file it as the motto of the never truly committed, for I did not yet understand the profound difference between these two young women.

I do now, of course. For Stella, sacrifice was self-actuated, a conscious choice, not an act of desperation, and if something wasn't forever it was because *she* set the timeframes. I'd go so far as to say now that of all of the women in this story, she was the only one with a true crusading intelligence.

And an instinct for self-preservation that never once wavered.

15

The next altercation between the lovers was noisy enough for us to get wind of it over the combined clamour of the TV and a squall of lashing rain. It was a Friday night and Daniel and I were watching an old episode of *Criminal Minds*, when I lowered the volume. 'Can you hear that shouting?'

'Leave it, Mum.'

Ignoring his advice, I struggled to my feet and headed for the door. Out on the landing, the exchange was clearly audible, taking place, from what I could gather, in Alec's hallway.

'Get it out of here or I will!'

'Don't be so mean!'

'Give it here, you stupid—'

'No, get off! I hate you!'

I hate you? I crossed the landing and rapped on their door. 'Pixie? Is everything all right in there?'

The door was flung open and Alec bore down on me, hot with anger. 'Oh good. *Here's* someone qualified to resolve this. Tell her, Gwen.'

'Tell her what?'

But before he could reply, I saw for myself: Pixie emerged from the shadows like Orphan Annie, with a small brown dog in her arms, a terrier of some sort. She wore torn grey jeans and some sort of mesh top, her feet bare.

'I've told her she can't have a pet in the building and she's refusing to remove it,' Alec said.

I downgraded my assessment of the incident from critical to manageable. 'I'm sorry, Pixie, but Alec's right. It's in the building's lease restrictions. We tried it on a trial basis and we had problems with allergies and barking and—'

'And the rest of it,' Alec interrupted. 'We almost lost Steve over it. He got fed up of treading in dogshit.'

Pixie stepped towards me, the animal rigid, its eyes afraid and ears pricked. 'It's only for the weekend, Gwen! Ash is away and he couldn't find anyone else. You know Ash,' she appealed, as if the fact that he was not a figment of her imagination might swing the situation in her favour.

'Could he not have left it with his family?' I asked.

'That's who he's away with!' Her injured gaze drifted beyond me and fell on a fresh target, Daniel, hovering in our doorway. 'You think it's okay, don't you?'

But he remained slack-mouthed, about as useful as a goldfish.

'Gwen?' Alec prompted. 'Are you going to back me up here?'

'One night,' I decreed. 'We can't put an animal out overnight in this weather. But you need to make alternative arrangements first thing in the morning, Pixie.'

'Oh no,' Alec said, 'I'm not having this. If you're so happy to break the rules, Gwen, *you* take the mutt.' With this, he tore it from Pixie's arms and thrust it into mine. 'There. That's what you get for being an interfering busybody.'

'Please do not speak to me like that,' I protested, but he was already closing the door in my face.

'I'll bring his things over,' Pixie yelled from behind the door. 'Just give me two minutes!'

The dog began to wriggle and I tightened my grip, scared I would drop him. His coat was wiry and slightly greasy. Once inside, I set him down and let him explore while I messaged the residents' WhatsApp to brief everyone on the emergency animal rescue.

More shouting could be heard before Pixie finally arrived with a lead, a carrier bag of food, and a stained dog bed, which she dumped on the floor in the kitchen. She'd added an oversized yolk-yellow cardigan and fluffy green socks to her outfit, as if having feared a plummeting in temperature on the other side of the landing. 'Oh,' she said, 'I forgot his bowl! Can I borrow one for his water?'

'In the cupboard next to the oven. Help yourself.' Though the burn of having been outmanoeuvred – and insulted – was still strong, my animosity was directed purely at Alec and I had no beef with her. Her colour was very high, I saw, her breathing shallow. 'What's his name?'

'Draco. From Harry Potter?' She filled one of my best china bowls with water and encouraged the dog to drink from it. 'So many rules in this building,' she grumbled, then looked up at me, stricken. 'Wait, you won't get sacked for this, will you? From the board or whatever it is.'

'No, no. I've explained on the group chat that it's a one-off situation.'

'It really is! Thank you, I'm so grateful. I was wondering, Gwen ...'

She was eyeing the sofa and I guessed what was on her mind. 'Do you want to sleep here tonight? Let Alec cool off. He seemed disproportionately enraged.'

'Disproportionate,' she repeated. One of the things she did that I liked very much was make me feel as if I'd used the exact right word, one she couldn't hope to improve on. 'Can I? That would be so great.'

'You've met Daniel, haven't you?' He was on his haunches,

petting the dog. He'd begged for one as a child but Brian had claimed to be allergic.

'Of course,' Pixie said. 'We talked on Bonfire Night. At the after-party.' I'd assumed it had just been the men boozing into the night at Alec's but she'd been involved too, clearly. 'Were you really fucked up the next day?' she asked him.

'I was,' Daniel said, unfolding himself to his full height. 'Were you?'

'Yeah, little bit.'

'I'm glad I came straight home,' I said, though I had not been invited. Remembering this was not only a dispute about building rules but also a spat between partners, I thought Pixie might be in need of a drink and so I put off fetching bed linen in favour of opening a bottle of wine.

'Do you want me to make myself scarce?' Daniel said, seeing the two glasses I delivered to the coffee table.

'That might be—' I began, for I'd been true to my word and said nothing to him about Pixie's entanglement with Alec, which meant we wouldn't be able to speak freely in his presence.

But she interrupted me: 'No, it's okay. Stay.'

She shuffled up to create space on the sofa and I went to fetch a third glass. By the time I returned, Draco had hopped into the space between them and there was no longer a spot for me, so I took the armchair I'd been avoiding since my knee had been playing up, it being of an awkward pitch and harder to get out of. My groans as I lowered myself into it attracted her attention.

'How's your knee, Gwen? I heard you're getting a transplant?'

'It's not a transplant. It's a replacement.'

'Isn't that the same thing?'

Daniel wheezed with laughter at this, but I found I'd temporarily lost my sense of humour.

'When're you getting it done?' she asked.

'I haven't decided if I'm doing it privately or not. I can't really afford to pay, but there's a crazy NHS waitlist and at my age you don't want to waste months and months stuck indoors. I've got limited time.'

'Don't say that,' she protested, either distressed by the thought of my dying or too young to be able to comprehend mortality.

'No, seriously,' Daniel said, still chuckling at my expense. 'She's got this life expectancy calculator. She knows exactly how old she'll be when she dies.'

He was beginning to seriously piss me off. 'It's not *my* calculator, it's a freely available health tool on the government website.'

'I think it's better not to know how long you've got,' Pixie said, taking a moment to stretch her exemplary joints. 'So what's your score then, Gwen?'

'Currently, I'll last till I'm eighty-eight.'

'What d'you mean, currently?'

'Every year you live, the number goes up.'

'I don't get it,' she said. 'Doesn't that mean it just goes on forever?'

'Well, it does run out eventually. None of us is immortal.'

'You wish you were, though, don't you, Mum?' Daniel said, affecting a joking tone that didn't fool me for a second. 'You'd love to watch over us forever. Carry on disapproving till the end of time.'

'What a horrible thing to say,' I told him, though it was obvious he was just showing off in front of Pixie, who I was pleased to see took no notice of the nitwit. I returned the subject to her recent drama. 'Do you *really* hate Alec?'

'At this point, totally. I don't see why he needed to be so extra. What's his problem? It's not like I had, I don't know, a snake in there or something.'

'Did you see that guy who took his python surfing?' Daniel said.

Nasty digs at me aside, I was heartened to see him so animated. 'Apparently, it's animal cruelty. They don't like the water.'

As he brought up the video and shared more facts about the preferences of reptiles, there was a knock at the flat door, followed by Alec's voice from the landing: 'Is she coming back over?'

'She is not!' Pixie screamed, startling both Daniel and Draco. She scooped Draco onto her lap. 'Sorry, baby.'

'You've left your key,' Alec called. 'I'm not waiting up.'

'I don't want you to!' she called back.

'Go away,' I yelled for good measure, though he'd likely gone back into his flat by then. 'No one wants to speak to you, Alec!'

Just so you know, I certainly do *not* seek to extend my life with the express aim of disapproving of my children. I can think of better ways to spend borrowed time.

Oh, and I categorically reject the term busybody.

16

It strikes me that the background I'm about to share might answer some of the questions you're probably asking yourself by now. Like, *why on earth is this woman so obsessed with her young neighbour? She claims Pixie isn't a substitute for the daughter she never seems to see – in any case she's already told us Nella filled that role, keep up! – but there must be* something *pushing her buttons.*

Indeed there is. Guilt. Shame. Regret. A powerful latent desire to do right where once I did wrong.

I said earlier that I define myself as a proud defender of victims and underdogs, that I will intervene without a qualm if I suspect mistreatment, but we all know actions speak louder than words. So, as I strive to be truthful with myself about the events of this last year, I don't think only about Pixie and my staunch defence of her that got me into so much trouble. I think as well about the victim I did not defend – in order to keep myself *out* of trouble.

That young colleague I mentioned, Cyndi (she'd been named after Ms Lauper, though from what she inferred about her birth parents, precious little had been done to facilitate girls having fun). She arrived in our office at the age of twenty as part of a scheme for those who'd been brought up in disadvantaged circumstances; a social worker had noticed her obliging nature and work ethic and was helping her secure entry-level work to pay for a room in a private shared house. Did I need an assistant?

Well, what an excellent assistant she turned out to be! Not only meticulous at admin but also fast on her feet at events and in meetings, to the extent that after little more than a year I was able to send her to support Brian at a conference in Edinburgh when a crisis with teenage Maya kept me at home. I imagined us working together for years to come, helping thousands of young women access education and have a stake in their own futures.

None of that happened, of course. Brian put paid to that – as he put paid to everything.

*

She'd been with us for about eighteen months when the discrepancies involving expenses began to come to light. In short order, investigators had invaded the office and begun sequestering documents and devices, Brian had withdrawn to the family home to start to piece together his defence, and the rest of our staff put on leave.

I'd clawed a private space from which to field calls from clients and donors and it was there, one particularly trying day, that Cyndi came by to see me. I'd missed a few calls from her and, assuming she'd come to ask about pay, felt fresh trepidation at the thought of our frozen business account.

'Is Brian coming in?' she asked, her expression wary. If you need to picture her, then think of the sales assistant whose hair colour you struggle to recall the moment you've left the shop, or the friend in the background perpetually outshone by the skinny, doe-eyed one. She was pretty only when smiling, which she was very much *not* doing as she sat facing me.

'Over my dead body,' I said, answering her question with real bitterness. 'Don't worry, you're completely protected. I've told the police, if *I* didn't know anything, then you couldn't possibly have.'

'It's not that. It's something else.' As she gestured with her hands, I saw they were shaking. Her face was stained with high colour. Whatever it was she had to say, she was terrified I would not receive it well.

'I'm hardly my husband's greatest fan, Cyndi. Complain to your heart's content.'

'Okay.' She reclasped her hands. 'What it is is, he's been ... he's been bothering me.'

'Ignore him. If he thinks you have anything that can incriminate him, that's pure paranoia.'

'No. It's not that kind of ... It's, well, sexual. It happened on the trip to Edinburgh.'

The breath was sucked from my lungs. 'Are you saying he ... ?'

'I don't know what to call it really.'

Two minutes later, I knew exactly what to call it. A coerced sexual act in my husband's hotel room that could be construed as assault, even rape. Succeeded, she confessed, by the threat of my sacking her if she said anything (*my* sacking her, note, not him. As if we preyed on young women as a team!)

'This is dreadful, Cyndi. I can't believe it.'

'It's true!' she cried, crushed.

'I mean I believe you, of course I do. I'm just dumbfounded. He's never done anything like that before.'

He'd never embezzled hundreds of thousands of pounds from his workplace before, either, but apparently there was a first time for everything.

'I was wondering, should I say something to the police? Since they're already investigating him?'

I gaped, my mind a kaleidoscope of faces – Brian, Maya, Daniel, the flinty-eyed officer who'd already questioned me twice at length – with Cyndi at its centre. 'Can I ask you to give me a chance to think about it?'

'Of course. I also wanted to ask, will we be paid? This month. You can't get behind on the rent where I am. It's weekly and if you're late they readvertise the room.'

'I'll do my damnedest to make sure of it.' I hugged her goodbye and watched at the window as she emerged from the building and trailed down the street, automatically giving way when a man came bowling down the centre of the pavement.

I remember so clearly the sky that day for it was a squeaky-clean French ultramarine, taut as the skin of a drum. Selling the lie that all was well with the world – not only well but glorious.

It made me want to take a blade and slice right through it.

17

Both Pixie and Draco enjoyed their overnight stay enormously. She reported being perfectly comfortable on the sofa and chatted happily over coffee and toast, giving every impression of having forgotten the previous evening's sourness.

'Isn't he just the best?' she said, as the dog whined and pawed at her shins. 'We've totally bonded.'

'Do you think he might need a pee?' I suggested.

'Oh, yeah. I forgot about that. Can I borrow a coat?'

She took Daniel's moss-green peacoat from the stand by the door and departed, Draco clutched to her like an infant. Moments later, she came into view in the communal garden and lowered him onto the lawn. As he circled, she chatted on her phone.

'Bag it up!' came Alec's bellow from next door's balcony, when the dog finally squatted and she showed no signs of having noticed.

She swung towards the building, face burning with defiance, and yelled back, 'I was going to!'

Not quite forgotten, then.

She came back up with the news that a mutual friend of Ash's and hers, the ridiculously named Bear, would be arriving within the hour to take custody of Draco. 'He was like, how come you're not allowed pets in a posh block like that? And I'm like, I don't know. It makes no sense. Rich people normally do whatever they want.'

'Not everyone here is rich,' I said firmly. Clearly, her shouting match with Alec had disrupted her previously good mood. 'And as we said, it's been put to the vote more than once. It's democracy.'

'Bear' arrived, texting Pixie from his car, and she hurried out, trailing Draco and his various bits of kit. I relocated to my bedroom window to get a look at the cavalry: a tomato-red Fiat 500 blocked access to our car park, its hazards blinking, while the friend waited on the pavement. He was Pixie's sort of age, his sandy hair styled like a squirt of cream, and more of a buffed type than Ash; indeed, I wondered if he'd been interrupted during a workout, given the gym shorts and flimsy vest he wore on this chilly November morning.

As they talked, Draco's things scattered at her feet, I opened the window to call down to ask them to move the car, but catching a fragment of their conversation I decided to hold fire (yes, I realize I'm characterizing myself as an inveterate eavesdropper, but if you think that all of this took place over several months, there was actually relatively little I gleaned by this method. I wish I'd done it more often, to be frank).

'You *know* I don't want anyone to know,' Pixie said with an air of remonstration.

'We already do, Pix.'

'I mean new people. I don't want anyone new to know. They'll treat me differently.'

'You haven't done anything wrong.'

'I know, but still. It's ... shaming.'

Shaming, like a word from a Bright Young Thing of the Twenties. This couldn't be about Alec, could it? A relationship with her landlord, an older man, a Nineties has-been. Ill-advised, yes, but shaming?

'It's so awful for you,' the friend said, and I could tell even without seeing his face that he wore an adoring expression. And she couldn't cope with that – I can't stress enough my certainty that she never wilfully exploited her beauty – changing the subject at once, changing her tone.

'How's it going with the new job?'

'Oh. Dunno really. Don't think I'll stay.'

Next thing, someone was indicating to enter the car park and the two of them piled themselves and the dog into the car and reparked further down the block.

I turned my attention to the WhatsApp residents' group, where messages were amassing following the exchange in the garden.

Elliot
Everything OK with the girl in Alec's flat. Pixie, is it? Is she on here?

Hester
Don't think so. Alec is tho.

Elliot
Heard some shouting earlier.

Sadie
Me too. Last night as well. What's going on?

Karishma
Was that a dog in the garden?

It was no surprise that Alec had not contributed any explanation. I jumped in to remind everyone of the message I'd sent the previous night and to confirm that the dog had now been removed from the premises. No further comments appeared. Pixie returned, sans Draco, and regained access to her own flat without returning to mine. She'd left her yellow cardigan, which I folded and set aside for her, noticing as I did the scent of jasmine from the fragrance she used.

An hour or so later, just as I was about to leave for my afternoon walk, Alec knocked at the door with Daniel's coat and a bottle of Pinot Noir.

'Sorry,' he said, with a sheepish, twisting smile.

'Thank you.' There was nothing to be gained from refusing either the apology or the wine.

'It's a nice one,' he said, as if I'd suggested otherwise, and lingered, shifting his weight from foot to foot. 'I still can't believe she smuggled the stupid thing in.'

'It was just a dog, Alec. A small one at that.'

'You know I don't like them. I always vote against. But I shouldn't have lost my rag.'

'No, you shouldn't. And if you ever heard someone shouting at me, I hope you'd knock on my door and check that *I* was all right.'

'Sure, though I'd say it was fifty-fifty in the shouting stakes. She's got a mouth on her, that one.' He gave no indication that he knew I knew about their having begun a relationship, let alone whether or not it had survived the bust-up. 'Anyway, I shouldn't have said what I said.'

'Hmm. You of all people know how hard I work for the smooth running of this building. It doesn't look good for us to fall out and if we do then I don't see how we can continue to work together. We'll lose the confidence of our leaseholders.'

I could hear how pompous I sounded and normally he wouldn't think twice about mocking me, but on this occasion, he let it go. 'No, you're right. Absolutely.'

'I wonder if this is working out,' I said. 'I mean Pixie renting your spare room. Might there be more compatible lodgers out there?'

'You know what? I think there might be,' he said with a smirk.

Finding his levity inappropriate, I said, slyly, 'Actually, I bumped into someone in the village who said you'd offered her the room first.'

'Oh yeah? Wasn't anything binding.' But he sighed heavily, no doubt reflecting that he would never have got himself into a messy relationship with the jettisoned blonde. Nor would she have smuggled in a hound.

'I don't remember these sorts of dramas with Yasmin,' I pressed.

'Yeah, I know. The problem with Pixie is she's got no ...' He struggled to find the word, settling at last on 'sense'. 'She's too impetuous. Disorganized. She needs to get used to living with rules.'

Living with rules. He said it in such an agreeable, matter-of-fact way, but when you consider the sentiment now, after the fact, it really is quite chilling.

*

Thanks to increasing pain in my knee, I restricted my walk to an unambitious single circuit around Nunhead Cemetery. It was, however, long enough for me to return in possession of a brainwave – thanks perhaps to the influence of those poor Victorian souls resting in peace, their lives undoubtedly far more challenging and unsatisfactory than my own.

'I've had a brilliant idea!' I announced to Daniel, as he emerged from the shower, wet hair dripping onto the shoulders of a stained and crumpled T-shirt (I've never understood why people clean themselves only to dress in dirty clothes). 'Why don't you and Pixie swap?'

'Swap what?'

'Rooms.'

His eyebrows shot up, brow crinkling. 'You're joking, right?'

'I'm not joking at all.'

He looked at me as if I were completely demented and I itched to tell him about the relationship that had sprung up next door, that shouting matches like those we'd witnessed were more dangerous in the context of a couple, but I remembered my promise to Pixie and held my tongue.

'Is this because of the barney about the dog?' he said, finally.

'Yes, but not just that.' My tone grew beseeching. 'There's real tension there. You know that as well as I do.'

He ran his fingers through his damp hair, smoothing it from his ears.

'Didn't you say she pays £1,500 in rent? Where am I going to find that?'

'The idea would be that she continues to pay it and he continues to take it. That part of the arrangement wouldn't change. They get some space from each other, that's all. Cool off a bit.'

'Sounds like something out of *Friends*.' He opened the fridge, extracted the orange juice, and poured the last of it into a glass before returning the empty carton to the shelf. There was not a snowball's chance in hell that he'd buy a new one to replace it. 'I suppose she could have my room when I'm at Dad's?'

'You mean at Christmas?' Since settling in Wellington fifteen years ago, Brian had paid for Daniel and Maya to visit him every Christmas and New Year's, often booking them on flights that arrived on Christmas Day itself to keep costs down (to be fair, they were both in their thirties and really ought to be funding their own fares by now). Apart from anything else, Daniel's offer meant he expected to still be in my spare room in late December and beyond, but now was not the time to address that. 'I'm talking about right now. Today, if possible.'

'Today?' He drained the juice, leaving a trace of orange on his upper lip. 'Why don't *you* move in over there and she can move in here?'

'That's ridiculous,' I said.

'Yes, it is. Don't suggest it to them, Mum. They'll think you're a complete nutter. I didn't mean it, by the way,' he added gruffly. 'What I said last night.'

He meant his remark about my everlasting lust for disapproval, I supposed. Two apologies in one day, how about that?

'Don't worry about it. I know things have been hard for you these last few months. We all lash out.'

He was right about the nutter part, though. It was madness to reach for a sitcom solution to a real-life problem, a problem I wasn't yet able to define, though I soon would.

And on that note, I think it's time to cut to the chase. I've kept you waiting long enough.

18

You'll be pleased to know that this wasn't one of my overheard exchanges puzzled together from snippets. The truth arrived in direct confession – and I'm confident I remember it word for word.

I was in Winifred Gardens experimenting with a compression sleeve and stick combo for my knee when I saw Pixie crossing from the far end, presumably following a shift at Bageri Møller. It was several days after the brouhaha involving the dog and as far as I could tell there had been a period of calm at flat 4, with not a whisper from behind their door or via our adjoining balconies. Had she and Alec stopped speaking altogether, I wondered? Or made up their quarrel, lapsing into loved-up bliss?

Both scenarios were disquieting in their own way.

As we were about to meet, I raised my free hand in greeting and drew to a halt. The sun was low, the air vibrating with light, and when she passed me, I assumed she hadn't seen me for the dazzle. I turned and hurried after her, my stick out of rhythm with my stride, knee grinding painfully. 'Pixie, wait!'

She slowed but did not stop and I limped on at her pace. 'I haven't seen you since dog-gate. He was returned to Ash without further incident, I hope?'

She gave a curt nod. 'Draco's fine.'

'You left your cardigan. Do you want to pop over and grab it? Have a cup of tea?'

'Maybe.' But she continued to look ahead, unwilling to engage.

'Is something wrong? You don't seem yourself.'

'No. I mean, yes.' At last, she stopped, putting me out of my physical misery. Her lower lip was trembling. 'Alec says you think he should throw me out.'

'What? That's not what I said at all,' I protested. 'I just asked if he thought it was working out. And I didn't say anything about knowing about the two of you, by the way. I gave you my word on that.' At this, her expression clouded, impossible to read, and so I made an educated guess that they'd split and she was – inexplicably – upset by this. 'Unless you're not an item any more?'

'An item,' she repeated darkly. 'We've never been *that*.'

We were forced apart then by a young child wobbling on a bike and I suggested we take advantage of a nearby free bench. As she sat, her chest rose and fell, her agitation growing.

'Pixie, what is it? You're really worrying me.'

'Don't, Gwen.'

'Don't what?'

'Be nice to me.' To my great concern, tears began rolling down her cheeks. Evidently her feelings for Alec were far deeper than I'd imagined.

'I had an idea,' I said. 'Daniel thinks it's completely mad, but what if you and he swapped rooms? Just for a few weeks while you decide if living with Alec is working out.'

She blotted her eyes with her sleeve, flashed me a quick, grateful smile. 'I'd actually love that, Gwen, but there's no way he would agree.'

'There's no harm in asking. He might see it's good for him too. Get your relationship back on a platonic footing?' Remembering

Daniel's misunderstanding, I added, 'It would just be his lodger who changed. He'd still get his rent, of course.'

'That's the thing,' she said, and this was the moment when I sensed it rise to the surface, the explanation to all this ambiguity. 'I'm not paying what you think.'

'You mean you negotiated him down? I did wonder how you were affording it after what happened with the first flat.'

'No.' She stared miserably in front of her. 'We agreed on a different deal.'

'What deal?'

'I don't pay anything.' She paused, still not meeting my gaze. 'I have sex with him instead.'

My mouth fell open. 'Did you just say … ?'

'Yes.' Now she looked directly at me, desolation in her eyes. 'Instead of rent.'

My mind spun, processing this extraordinary information. Pixie – sweet, giggly, guileless Pixie – was some sort of live-in escort? 'Whose idea was that?'

'His.' She took no offence at the implication that it might have been hers. 'The joke is I wouldn't have known it was even an option. You remember I'd lost my phone? He sent me a message on Insta and it went into hidden requests. I hardly ever look at those. But I was doing a clear-out of all the junk when I got my new phone and I saw it.'

'What did it say?'

'That we could come to an arrangement. You know, about the rent.'

'And you replied?'

She rolled her eyes in ironic mockery, causing more tears to leak. 'Uh, I wouldn't be here if I hadn't, would I? Where was *I* going to get £1,500 a month? I told him that at the viewing when he offered it to me on the spot. Then everything happened with the New Cross flat and, yeah, I wasn't in a position to choose. It sounds so grim,' she added with a little moan. 'Not something *you* would ever do, Gwen. In your younger day,' she clarified, my being so visibly past my sell-by date. 'I mean, it's not something I ever thought I'd do myself. I feel like such a—' The thought was lost to another moan, this one more forcible.

'Oh, Pixie.' I grasped her hands in mine. 'You clearly felt you had no choice. It's not you who's committed the crime here, it's him.'

A flicker of protest crossed her face. 'I'm not sure we can call it a *crime*. More a transaction.'

This must be Alec's term for it, I thought. It was important not to alienate her by being corrective or judgmental. For all the 'calling out' of unacceptable behaviours by a feisty minority, most young women were, I'd learned, just as likely as their forebears to overstate their own guilt in ambiguous situations involving consent.

'Fine,' I said, 'a transaction. A borderline *criminal* transaction.'

She then permitted some gentle questioning as to how the 'arrangement' had unfolded once she was installed.

'It wasn't the first night or even the second, but after that. The fact that he didn't say anything those first few days made me think ...' She gazed forlornly into the distance as if that version of herself had been tragically credulous. 'Well, I hoped he'd changed his mind. But that was dumb. Why would he let me live there for free without getting something in return?'

'So, what, he just came into your room one night and got into bed with you?'

She screwed her eyes shut as if the image was too unbearable to behold. 'The way it works is he invites me into his.'

'And you can't say no?'

Again, she hesitated. A cavapoo scurried up to sniff the legs of our bench, but she didn't reach to pet it as she usually did an approaching dog. Ahead, stringy cloud obscured the sun, clinging like curdled egg. 'I can, but I haven't. At least, once, maybe, at the beginning, but then I said yes.'

I thought of that first argument: *You know the deal.* 'But you wouldn't have chosen to sleep with him if you'd been able to pay the rent?'

'No, but I wasn't and it's what I agreed.' She shook her head as if to dispel further ideological objections. 'This is a thing, Gwen. I've looked it up and it turns out loads of girls have to do this. Half the people in this city, they don't have any back-up. They're not like Daniel, or Dee's kids, all the people *you* know. They don't have parents with spare rooms. They don't have options.' There was no anger in her voice, only an awful heartbreaking acceptance.

'And it's been every night since then?'

'Not every night, no.'

'But regularly?'

'Whenever he likes.'

I waited for two dads to pass, both pushing compact prams with one hand and gripping trendy oversized water bottles with the other. One glanced at Pixie, his expression altering as he registered her distress, and I caught his eye – *I've got this* – urging him to move on. 'Pixie, this isn't right. Even if it is a "thing" and lots of girls are doing it, you should only ever have sex with someone you want to have sex with. Whenever *you* like.'

She exhaled gently. 'That's the dream.'

'It's not a dream, it's a right. And for clear reasons: look how upset it's making you.'

'It has affected my mental health,' she agreed. 'But I was already pretty low anyway after the split with Dylan and the fraud and … everything else that's happened. I don't know.' She straightened, wiped her wet face, collected herself. 'Like I said, everyone has problems, don't they?' In front of my eyes, she was downgrading her emotions from despair to acceptance, as if we were talking about some lesser renter's hazard, mould in the bathroom or mice. 'I'm not special.'

'You *are* special,' I said fiercely. 'And you're the one we're focusing on here, so let's not worry about anyone else's problems for now. This sounds very much to me like a young woman in a vulnerable period of her life being exploited by a man who should know better.'

'Yeah, well. I'm not in a position to do anything about it, not right now. As soon as I can get that money back or save up again, I can move on.'

'Could your father help you out again?' I suggested.

'I can't ask him for more after what happened.'

'Then maybe you should move back in with him for a little while?'

'That's not possible.'

'What about grandparents or other relatives? Even if they're not in London, they—'

She cut me off, losing her patience: 'I want to be here, Gwen! London is my home. No one's telling *you* you can't live where you want, are they?'

I didn't say that this was exactly what had caused me to come to Queens Oak, a neighbourhood I'd known only from Maya having rented here briefly after university, that I'd lost my previous home in a crisis of my own, and nor did I point out that seniority usually conferred the advantage of greater choice, that it was foolish to imagine that the mere fact of wanting something entitled you to it, even though all of this was true.

Instead, I just listened as in another of her customary gear changes she persuaded herself she'd made a positive lifestyle choice. 'I just have to do whatever it takes until I can set myself up. It's a journey and this is just a bump in the road.'

'A bump in the road? It's more than that, Pixie.'

But the subject was closed – for now, at least. 'You won't tell anyone, will you?'

'Of course not.'

'Promise.'

'Promise,' I agreed. It occurred to me that this was what she must have meant when talking to her friend Bear about her 'shaming' secret. Not that she was dating Alec but that she was being used – or, more accurately, abused – by him. If so, then she'd already confided in others besides me; he'd said 'we' already knew, hadn't he, not 'I'?

I worried she might not possess the natural discretion needed for keeping secrets of this magnitude, even if I did.

19

It didn't take much googling to discover that she was right about one thing: there *was* a lot of it going on and it had an established name – sex for rent.

While not a front-page issue (at least not yet), the stories existed, and there was an escalating seriousness to the headlines in recent years:

Cost of Living Crisis Sparks Sordid New Trend

Landlords Seeking Sex for Rent 'Normalized'

Home Secretary Considers Sex for Rent Law

It does what it says on the tin, said one 'explainer', rather tastelessly.

> *The tenant pays her rent in the form of sexual favours. This might involve an agreed number of liaisons a month or work on a more ad hoc basis.*

Ad hoc? They were talking about women's bodies here!

Accounts from the victims themselves were hard to read:

Caught in the Sex for Rent Trap

Shania was working in a care home, gradually getting her feet back on the ground following a period of mental health crisis, when her employer offered her extra hours. She gladly took them, only to find that her bolstered earnings had rendered her ineligible for the top-up benefits she counted on to pay her bills.

With rent benefits also withdrawn, she went to her landlord to ask for time to build up her earnings.

'He said no,' Shania remembers. 'If I couldn't find the rent, he would have to evict me. But then he said there was another way we could resolve the problem. He didn't say exactly what he expected, he just called it "being nice" to him. He would let me know he was visiting and that was when I would "be nice".

I was sick with dread when I knew he was coming over. I had to get drunk on vodka to get through it. It wasn't in my bedroom, it was on the sofa. That felt like something, like my bedroom was still my private space. But then it grew into him expecting to stay the night.

I had no choice. I was so ashamed. I didn't tell anyone.'

Upsetting though this was, it was the second half of the account that made me catch my breath in horror.

Matters went from bad to worse when Shania made a horrifying discovery. Her landlord had filmed her performing a sex act and shared it on a porn website. 'I'd never have known if he hadn't bragged about it,' she says. 'It was like he was saying there was nothing he couldn't do to me because I was his hired plaything. On his payroll.'

With the help of pro bono legal services provided by an advocacy service for victims of revenge porn, Shania was able to get the footage taken down from the original site. However, it remains online. 'Once content of this kind is out there, it's almost impossible to chase it down,' says lawyer Esther Lupton.

'And all because I couldn't find a way to pay my rent,' says Shania.

What kind of a world was this?

Stupid question, I already knew it was a bad one. A mad one. The better question perhaps was how such dysfunction, such sickness, could have infiltrated Columbia Mansions. The only difference between Alec and these sex pests I was reading about was the relative grandeur of the accommodation.

There was also the small matter of his being a director and representative of the very community in which he was conducting these squalid practices and it was for this reason that I decided I would give him the chance to desist of his own accord before I took steps to involve the board.

*

I cornered him in the garden, where he was bagging up leaves with Steve, a considerable task that took the pair of them hours, if not days, at this time of year and at least a dozen bags were already stuffed and tied. Dressed in black jeans, donkey jacket and a beanie, he looked like an ageing roadie doing community service following a cannabis conviction.

If only that were the extent of his misdemeanours.

He did not look overjoyed by my approach, perhaps having expected the bottle of wine to have kept me at bay for longer than this. 'Someone looks like she's on the warpath,' he drawled, his breath visible in the frigid air. 'What's wrong now, huh?'

I drew to a halt. The cold ground crunched underfoot. 'Do you mind if we talk privately?'

'She means me,' he told Steve, who stood docilely by. 'You're missing out, mate.' The pair of them tittered.

'I need to get something from the van anyway,' Steve said obligingly.

'Spit it out, Gwen,' Alec said, his tone markedly less convivial once his friend had moved out of earshot. 'It's freezing out here. I'm not in the mood for guessing games.'

I gripped my stick, irritated that he'd resumed his raking, not deeming me worthy of his full attention. 'Pixie told me about your unorthodox arrangement.'

'Oh yeah.' He barely glanced up. 'What unorthodox arrangement is that?'

'You know full well, Alec. Her rent. How she pays it.' I sharpened my tone, speaking to his half-turned shoulder. 'With sex.'

Now he stopped, turning back with an almost sinister deliberation. 'I think you need to be very careful what you're accusing me of here.'

'Why? It's completely wrong and I know you must know that.'

He did not respond at once and, for a second, I feared he was about to club me with the rake. I imagined defending myself with my stick in some sort of fencing parry.

'How can you—'

'I don't want to hear it,' he cut in. 'Seriously, Gwen, you need to butt out and stop encouraging her.'

'Encouraging her?' I couldn't believe my ears. 'To do what? Refuse to prostitute herself?'

'*Prostitute* herself? Bandy that word about again and you'll be hearing from my lawyer.' He followed this threat with an unpleasant little chuckle, but I held my nerve.

'You're right, it's probably more unethical than illegal because it's unregulated.'

'Unethical?' He seized on the word, his tone crowing. 'Isn't this the pot calling the kettle black?'

I eyed him with distaste. 'What do you mean?'

'Come on, I know what happened with your charity. Your murky little part in it all. What was it again? You weren't "categorically" in the clear on suspicious payments but they gave you the benefit of the doubt?'

I felt myself flush. Though I'd thought it best to disclose my history to Dee and Noel when standing for election myself, it had not been shared later with Alec on the grounds that I'd proved myself to be both competent and dependable. How long had he been sitting on this? Not long, I guessed, remembering that I'd mentioned the charity's closure to Pixie and confidences might well have flowed both ways. And he's paid them sufficient attention to be able to quote from the official findings.

Praise God those findings did not include Cyndi.

My heart thudded painfully. 'The payments you're referring to were my ex-husband's. *I* was not prosecuted and there was no "murky little part". It was also years before I moved here, whereas *this* is happening right now, in this building. It involves you, not me.'

'You're right – whatever you think "it" is, it doesn't involve you.' He kicked the rake with his boot to dislodge a clump of leaves, before glaring at me through narrowed eyes. 'She's been manipulating you, simple as that. And she's obviously doing a brilliant job of it because you haven't got a clue.'

'You're saying she's lying?' My voice vibrated with outrage.

'I'm saying she's cottoned on to your bleeding heart and has decided to present our relationship in a way that bears no resemblance to reality.'

'Why on earth would she want to do that?'

He shrugged. 'Attention? Sympathy? Whatever she says is going on, I can promise you she'll have heard about it on TikTok or YouTube or whatever and decided to stir a bit of drama. Reimagine herself as the victim. They're all at it now. Look at Daniel.'

'He's depressed,' I said. 'And I'd ask that you keep him out of your little posse from now on. You're not a good influence.'

He barked with laughter. 'Can you hear yourself? He's a grown man! I was going to message him today, actually, see if he's about. We could do with an extra pair of hands down here.' He adopted a simpering tone: 'But if Mummy says he's not allowed to come out to play ...'

I adjusted my grip on my stick, longing to swing it at him. He thought he was so clever, distracting me again, but I wasn't having it. 'So as far as you're concerned, you're in a normal relationship?'

'As far as I'm concerned, my relationships are my own business.'

'Rental contracts are the company's business,' I retorted.

'Then put it on the agenda for our next meeting, why don't you? You can bring along whatever evidence you've got. Bring *her*. Let's have ourselves a bit of a tribunal, huh?'

Something caught his eye then as he glanced towards the building and, following his gaze, I saw Pixie at the window. She was watching us, obviously aware that we were arguing though too far away to be able to hear what we were saying. A horrible thought struck: didn't they say that if you confronted an abuser, you only exposed the victim to reprisals? I couldn't live with myself if Pixie had to bear the brunt of my interference.

'Please, don't take this out on her,' I begged. 'She didn't want to tell me. I guessed.'

'Take it out on her?' Alec grimaced. 'If that's how your mind works you're weirder than I thought.'

Now I worried I'd gone and given him the idea. Pixie had withdrawn from the window, I saw. *Run away*, I thought wildly. 'If I hear any kind of conflict between you, I'm calling the police.'

There was a silence, during which his insolent gaze scraped me up and down, coming to rest on my stick. 'Why don't you go back in for a rest, Gwen. Looks like you're on your last legs there. Go back up and pour yourself a nice glass of Madeira, yeah?'

I stepped back, the awkward angle turning my ankle. He was right, the conversation was over. Even as I hauled myself back up the stairs, regrets about this confrontation – or partly, if I'm honest, about it having been observed by Pixie – were already gathering. Judging that Alec would continue in the garden for a while longer, I knocked at the door to number 4, hoping to explain myself to her before he could. But either she wasn't answering or she'd just left for work.

I rang the café's landline and, discovering she was indeed expected in, left a message. But she didn't call back and nor did she answer my subsequent texts, even though she must have been entitled to a break at some point.

Later, when I heard her return and get into an almost immediate argument with Alec, I felt sick knowing my actions had sparked the altercation. I texted her again, asking to meet the next day – off site – and at last she responded:

Meet me tomorrow at the Arches after my shift? 6.30

'What the hell, Mum,' Daniel said, finding me in the kitchen in the dark. He snapped on the lights and his tone changed. 'What's wrong? You look like you're having a stroke.'

'I'm fine. I just stood up too quickly.'

He took me at my word, glancing at the oven. 'Are we not having dinner?'

'I'm not hungry.' I moved past him, not in the mood for domestic duties. 'You'll have to fend for yourself tonight.'

He watched as I swiped Pixie's abandoned cardigan from the side table where I'd left it, drawing it to me, a comforter while feelings were uncertain between us.

The incident delivered greater clarity on one thing, at least: my knee dilemma. Alec and I were enemies now and I couldn't allow myself to be any more physically enfeebled than I already was. I would stop dithering and ring the private clinic first thing in the morning to book myself in for surgery.

20

The Arches was a bog-standard wine bar with the usual pretensions. Ordinarily, I would have preferred the Beehive, which had more comfortable seating, but it was not my choice and, in any case, that was Alec's drinking hole and the last thing we wanted was to bump into *him*.

I arrived first and the young hostess was in the process of directing me to the table next to the toilets when Pixie walked in and we were immediately diverted to a nicer one in the window. Incidents like this were, I knew from when Maya had been keen on such things, microaggressions, in this case of the ageist stripe, though she had explained in the same breath that I had no right to claim any grievance on account of being a wealth hoarder (wealth hoarder? Well, no one can accuse me of that now). I told her I understood my rights perfectly well and would respond to ageist slights however I saw fit.

On this occasion, I merely treated the hostess to a twitch of the eyebrow and ordered a bottle of the house white before she could disappear and set about the imperative business of avoiding the customer's eye.

'Do you want anything to eat?' I asked Pixie, who was busy folding her trench over the spare chair and zipping mittens into her handbag.

'No, I'm stuffed.' She puffed out her cheeks. 'I literally just had a cheese toastie and a chocolate and pistachio slice.'

'You're allowed anything you like?'

'Pretty much. Means I don't need to buy dinner.'

Or to eat it with Alec in some grisly approximation of coupledom, I thought, though I had no evidence that dining together was part of their 'transaction'. She looked weary, I thought, with mascara smudges under her eyes and a slackness around the mouth. I hadn't swallowed Alec's line about her having fabricated her story for sympathy, not for a moment. In my opinion, if she differed from her peers in any way, it was in her *lack* of self-indulgence. *I'm not special*, she'd said and she'd meant it.

There was a jug of water on the table and she drained a glass at speed. 'Thank you,' she breathed, with fellow feeling, when the waitress delivered and inexpertly poured our wine.

It was hardly the occasion to clink glasses and we both took healthy swallows before I got to the point. 'I think you know I broached the subject of your rent situation with Alec yesterday.'

She looked at me with more determination than I was used to from her. 'I really wish you hadn't. I told you that in confidence.'

'You did and I'm sorry. But it's not as if it's news to him and he needs to be told it's not right.'

'It's not actually unlawful.' This did not sound like her phrasing and I guessed must be his.

'Perhaps, but it should be. I've done some reading since we spoke and it looks like there's a campaign to introduce legislation to stop it.'

She gulped her wine, hiccupping softly. 'But how could it be enforced?'

Enforced: again, not her wording.

'I don't know, I suppose in the same way any sexual misconduct is. By making a complaint to the police and expecting it to be investigated.' I paused to wash down the lump in my throat with wine. 'But right now, as you say, it's a grey area. What I can say with certainty is that it's not permissible in Columbia Mansions. If we put it to a vote, the members would reject it unanimously.'

'And I'd be humiliated,' she said glumly. 'Homeless, as well.'

It was hard to refute the humiliation, if not the homelessness. 'There must be somewhere you could stay instead. With one of your friends? Even if it's just on the sofa?'

'All my friends are back home or they've already got someone on their sofa.' Her eyes were glazed with weary defeat. 'I should never have told you.'

'I'm very glad you did. You need support and I'm here to give it.' I poured us more wine, returning the bottle to the ice bucket with a crack, and looked at her with a new determination of my own. 'Especially if it turns out to be more than you think.'

Fear crossed her face. 'How do you mean?'

'Like I say, I've been doing some reading.' I leaned in a fraction, suddenly absolutely certain of my instinct. 'Can I ask you a very private question?'

She gulped more wine, nodded.

'Does he film you? I mean, when you're having sex.'

'Of course not.' She squirmed, pulled away from me to sink as deep in her seat as the rigid design allowed.

'I know it's not nice to think about, but you're absolutely sure?'

'Yeah. I mean, he'd be too busy, wouldn't he, to get his phone out?'

'I don't mean he's personally holding up the phone while ... in the act. And it wouldn't be his phone anyway. I've come across some awful stories, Pixie, and I honestly think it's worth checking the flat for spy cameras. You can get these ones with motion sensors that broadcast straight to your phone.'

Her eyes were wide with alarm as she processed the implications of this. 'He wouldn't do that, would he?'

'I think he would. He clearly has no problem with degenerate behaviour. If he pays for sex, he might see nothing wrong with voyeurism.'

'He doesn't pay for sex,' she objected, loudly enough for a nearby couple to overhear and exchange looks. 'You're making it sound worse than it is. It's way more casual. It's more like, I don't know, my food at work? It's free. It's a perk.'

I bit my tongue at this preposterous conflation of a cheese toastie and her most intimate anatomy; she didn't need a lecture from me about self-respect. 'Do you know when he might be out for a few hours, so we can do a sweep of his room?'

'This is crazy, Gwen,' she said, by now a familiar refrain, and began twisting a strand of hair.

'I hope it is. But will you indulge me? Just in case? If I'm wrong, great, and if I'm right, well, it stops right there. We get you out.'

'Get me out? You make it sound like I'm a hostage, chained to a radiator or something.'

'Oh, Pixie,' I said. 'Chains like this, they're not real in the physical sense, but they're chains all the same.'

She gazed at me for a long moment, still battling denial, before capitulating. 'Fine. Just in case.'

21

On the few occasions I'd visited flat 4 since Alec had taken possession, I had only ever been into the sitting room. The mirror image of my own, with the same French doors and high arched window overlooking the gardens, it had not altered much since he'd inherited the place from Jeanette, with the exception of a home studio in one corner where he'd set up his computers and keyboards. He'd even kept most of her furniture, presumably having relinquished his own in his divorces: the pale leather chesterfield sofa and pair of lamps with pineapple-shaped bases I certainly remembered as hers. I knew there'd been renovations to the bathrooms because these had to be approved by the board and, in any case, I'd lived through the drilling and tile cutting, but the kitchen looked much the same bar a row of framed vintage French drinks ads in place of Jeanette's Constable prints.

The stale aroma of last night's takeaway curry, the congealed remains of which clung to an unwashed plate in the sink, made me want to open a window, but I resisted.

'Not much of yours in here,' I said to Pixie, nudging a tangle of earphones from a stack of history books on the coffee table before running my fingers under the table's edge. I noticed a fresh ring in the wood and thought how Jeanette had probably used coasters all her life and here he was paying no heed. Treating everything – everyone – as expendable.

'I keep my stuff in my room,' she said, no less shifty than she'd been when she'd ushered me in minutes ago, as if *we* were the ones up to no good. It hadn't helped her nerves that we'd had to wait several days for this opportunity. Alec was at an away fixture with his Sunday league boules team and based on previous absences she judged we were safe for at least three hours. 'I only hang in here when he's out or if there's other people here,' she added.

With every one of these casual details a new piece slotted into the puzzle of her compromised situation. It was horrendous that she should desire his company so little that she avoided time alone with him – only to be summoned to copulate with him at his whim.

'Should we be wearing those gloves?' she said. 'Like on TV.'

'I think it's probably okay to use our bare hands.' I hadn't thought beyond the discovery of any surveillance devices, but wondered now if she might have a point. Would we want to involve the police and, if so, shouldn't we take pains to preserve his fingerprints? 'If we find anything, we'll be careful not to touch. We'll take photos and discuss what to do next.'

It took some time to check all the fittings for the telltale glint of a camera lens – from my online research I knew they could be hidden in air fresheners and smoke alarms and the like – before we headed into his bedroom, which was logically the more likely location. Here, there were two more armchairs of a vintage that spoke of his aunt's reign, though an orange lamp in the form of a chimp with a shade on his head was likely his own addition. The walls were covered in framed tour posters of bands from his era and I wondered at the psychology of surrounding yourself with evidence of your own also-ran status. Was that sublimated in his relationships with his lodgers, feeding his need to dominate and control?

I imagined poor Pixie advancing to his bed under the gaze of those petulant Oasis brothers.

As she poked about ineffectually at a small bookcase, I reached for the bedside cabinet and, noticing, she intervened in some misplayed loyalty: 'There's not going to be a camera *inside* a drawer, is there?'

'Could be in a clock radio or something that he only brings out when he needs to,' I said, but settled for a peek. Phone charger. Painkillers. Condoms. At least he wasn't exposing her to unwanted pregnancy or STDs.

I checked my watch; we still had plenty of time. 'There's nothing in here. We should check your room as well.'

Pixie looked puzzled. 'Why? I told you we've never done anything in there.'

'I know, but he might want to watch you, you know, undressing, that kind of thing.'

'Gwen! You're really freaking me out!' But clearly there was a chink of doubt because she left his room and trooped down the hallway towards her own. I followed only after pausing to examine the nostrils of the chimp.

Her room was as chaotic as a teenage girl's, both bed and floor obscured by a thick covering of discarded clothing and footwear. More clothes hung from picture rails and over wardrobe doors. If Alec had fitted a camera in here, it was in danger of being draped with a jumper or knocked aside by a rogue boot.

Some of those boxes I'd watched arrive in late September had never been unpacked, I noticed, but remained stacked in one corner, and I wondered if there was a subconscious resistance there. An unwillingness to commit fully to this particular phase of her life. (On the other hand, Daniel's room also featured unopened boxes, for the more prosaic reason of sloth.)

I pushed open the door to her shower room. As in other apartments in the building, this en suite was a relatively modern modification and styles varied from flat to flat. Mine – currently Daniel's – had been installed before my time and had a dated but serviceable bath/shower combo; Dee's was a glorious marble and brass walk-in affair fitted a few years ago with one of her pension lump sums. Pixie's dated from Alec's recent refurb: simple white sanitary ware, slate-grey floor tiles, oversized white wall tiles with extra-wide lines of dark grouting.

I pulled the light cord, which activated a noisy extractor fan.

'There's not going to be anything in here,' Pixie protested, embarrassed perhaps by the jumble of towels and underwear on the floor, the weeks' worth of used wipes and tissues and make-up pads that kept the lid of the pedal bin from closing, the toothpaste crusted on the basin. She set about a perfunctory clean as I scrutinized the mirrored wall cabinet and other fittings, running my fingers over the wall tiles, even the sections of smooth plaster.

Nothing. Evidently her privacy had not been invaded in the heinous additional way I'd feared.

It was just as we were about to end our search that something snagged my peripheral vision, making me investigate more closely: a raised blob in the grouting on the tiled wall opposite the shower. Touching it, I found it was soft, a lump of Blu Tack-like putty, and I peeled it off to reveal a black unit about two and a half centimetres by one centimetre embedded in the grouting.

'Look at this.' I prodded the unit with a cotton bud but it was set flush to the tiles, glued fast in the grouting.

Pixie was by my side, damp towels bundled in her arms. 'That's not a camera, is it?'

'I think it is. I saw one like this online. He must cover it with this Blu Tack stuff when he's not using it. I'm really sorry, Pix.'

Dropping the towels, her hands flew to her mouth. It was ghastly to see the look in her eyes as she calculated how many showers she'd taken in the months she'd been living here. How many had he spied on? I could only pray he hadn't recorded any images or video to share online with other perverts, as had the landlord in the article I'd read.

'Don't touch it,' I reminded her, and took out my phone to take photos for evidence. But as I was fiddling with the camera app, I was startled by the sound of a voice behind us, almost letting go of the phone in fright:

'What's going on in here then?'

We spun in unison. Alec had crossed Pixie's bedroom – without invitation, I should point out, though I think we've established by now that he was not a respecter of boundaries – and come to a halt in the bathroom doorway. He was dressed in the unflattering sports gear I'd seen him wear in the boules pit on the square, but the early return told me the fixture must have been cancelled.

'Well?' he said grimly, black eyes blazing. He was blocking our exit from the tiny space and I felt a rush of fear that he might suddenly kick shut the door and imprison us. Melodramatic as it may sound, coming so soon after the confrontation in the garden it confirmed my instinct that he had a capacity for violence. There was no trace of those sneers from that earlier episode, only flat burning rage.

Whatever our discovery meant legally, it was no longer safe for Pixie to remain in this flat.

I stood my ground, meeting that intense animal gaze. 'This is Pixie's room, Alec, so if you could back off, please.'

'You've obviously been poking around the whole flat,' he growled. Was this a guess? How long had he been here? Clearly only since we'd been in the en suite, the growl of the fan having smothered the sound of his key in the door. He couldn't fail to notice the blob of black putty where I'd stuck it to the tile and so I continued on the offensive.

'Yes, we have, and as you can see, we've found what we were looking for.' I gestured to the camera. I would have liked to have taken a second shot of it but feared his dashing my phone from my hand and cracking it. Keenly aware that Pixie was in his direct line of fire, I manoeuvred around her to put myself between the two of them. 'I think it's best if Pixie comes and stays with me for the time being.'

Expecting him to be rattled out of his customary denialist mode, I was surprised to see him frown in confusion, seeking Pixie's eye. 'What's she on about?'

She refused to look at him, speaking in a mumble. 'Will you hang on, Gwen, while I grab my stuff?'

'Of course,' I said, which provoked a note of impertinence in our jailer.

'Haven't we been here before not so long ago?' he said to Pixie. 'You just need your muzzle and a bowl of dog food and you're all set.'

'What a repulsive way to speak to a young woman!' I cried, my anger erupting. 'What is *wrong* with you?'

'I could ask you the same question,' he snarled.

'I'm not the one taking sex for rent and installing spy cameras in people's bathrooms!'

Pixie, now sweeping toiletries into a sponge bag, was doing her level best to remain dignified during this, but fear made her clumsy and a couple of items fell to the floor and rolled from her reach. She squatted to pick them up, overbalancing as she did, and I shot out a hand to steady her. Only now did Alec take a step back and the claustrophobia lifted a fraction.

'You'll regret this,' he said.

I thought he was talking to Pixie, but when I looked up his gaze locked straight onto mine, ugly and unyielding. I glared back, refusing to give any hint of how menacing I found him. 'Is that supposed to be a threat?'

'It's actually …' He paused, as if he had all the time in the world to stand there and toy with me. 'A hunch,' he said, at last.

22

In my flat, while Pixie folded herself onto the sofa, sobbing softly into a tissue and sporadically breaking into a more spirited wail, I weighed up the options for police support. Since 999 was for immediate physical danger and Alec wasn't raging at our door, or even cussing from behind his own, I decided 101 was more appropriate.

'Please don't say anything about the other thing,' she begged me. 'Just the camera.'

'Understood.' I made the call and requested that someone come to investigate as a matter of urgency.

Meanwhile, Daniel had been drawn from his quarters by this latest, more explosive drama. 'What's going on?'

'Can we tell him?' I asked Pixie and she nodded before burying her face in her hands, loath to witness his reaction.

'I can't believe this,' Daniel said, when I'd outlined what had been going on under our noses all this time. He traced a hand over the back of his skull with the air of reassuring himself that the physical world still existed. 'He's an okay bloke, I thought.'

'That's how he seems at first,' I conceded, as Pixie wept afresh, 'but would an "okay bloke" do something so sleazy?' I moved past him to comfort her. 'Pixie is going to stay with us for the next few nights, so we'll need you on side, Daniel.' With my knee surgery coming up in the next few days and involving a stay in hospital, I wanted to be sure of his commitment to us, not Alec.

'Of course,' he said, expression still incredulous.

I asked both of them to use headphones if watching TV or playing video games. 'I need to be able to hear if he leaves the flat.'

'Why?' Pixie asked.

'Because he'll want to get rid of the evidence. He won't use the bins here in case the police search them. He's not an idiot. He knows exactly what he's doing.'

*

Sure enough, less than an hour or so after our confrontation, Alec could be heard leaving his flat. The police had still not materialized, so I briefed Daniel while pulling on my boots and coat and locating my stick. Outside, I saw Alec had turned right and I struggled down Clayton Street after him, praying he wouldn't strike out too far. To my relief, he made for our nearest shops, a short parade along the northern side of Winifred Gardens, halting abruptly just before the bus stop and causing a woman with a pushchair to brake and divert around him. I held my breath as he peered into a kerbside drain, wondering how on earth I'd be able to retrieve the camera from down there, but he straightened without dumping anything and headed past the chicken shop into Tesco Metro.

I waited in a nearby doorway, warming my hands with my breath. I'd left in such a hurry I hadn't brought my gloves and my fingers were already stiffening with cold. Passers-by turned their faces downward as a bitter drizzle started up, some sheltering at the bus stop.

A few minutes later, Alec came out of Tesco with a bag of groceries, munching on a sandwich and apparently heading back to Columbia Mansions – until he stopped at the bin outside the chicken takeaway and took suspicious care in dropping the sandwich packaging into it. Still chewing, he continued, passing me in my doorway without a glance. I waited thirty seconds or so before going to check the bin, arriving just as someone tossed the dregs of a takeout hot chocolate into it, dousing the sandwich wrapper (roast beef and horseradish, with a yellow discount sticker) in the process. I delved deeper and my fingers touched something cold and sticky, soon identified as ketchup from someone's bus stop snack, along with other mulchy and unidentifiable foodstuffs, soiled handwipes, an abandoned trainer, and God knew what else. The smell was revolting.

I quickly decided this was futile. No doubt helped by my rootling, the camera had probably fallen through the gaps right to the bottom and unless I could empty the entire bin, I wasn't going to be able to find it. As I withdrew my hands, I looked up to see Alec among a cluster of observers at the bus stop, his the only face with a smirk pasted across it. Everyone else looked thoroughly disgusted, including a small child, speaking to her mother in a loud, high voice.

'Lady in the bin!'

'I know,' the mother said, horrified. 'We don't do that. It's dirty.'

'Dirty,' the girl repeated.

'She might be hungry,' someone else chipped in in my defence, which was almost worse.

Luckily, there was a nearly clean paper napkin on the ground nearby and I had a small bottle of sanitizer in my coat pocket, so was able to get the worst of the muck off my hands. I dropped the napkin into the bin, by which time a bus had pulled up, drawing most of those waiting to its doors. To my great dismay I recognized one of those remaining as Karishma, who lived across the landing from Dee. She was studying her phone with conspicuous intensity, no doubt to spare my blushes – or hers.

Returning home and washing my hands properly, I felt utterly sullied by the episode, almost in tears as I reported to the waiting Pixie and Daniel that I'd failed to collect the evidence. Such was my despair that Daniel broke the habit of a lifetime and made me a cup of tea.

The police still hadn't turned up and when evening came, we had to concede that the working day for non-emergencies was likely over.

'I suppose it is Sunday,' Daniel said. 'They'll probably come tomorrow.'

'I've got a shift in the morning,' Pixie said from in front of the TV. There no longer being any need for silence, it blared at full volume, showing one of the dating reality programmes I would soon be all too familiar with. She was calmer now, her cheeks no longer blotchy with tears. Time with Daniel had done her good.

'You might need to go in a bit late,' I told her, and started at the sensation of my phone vibrating in my pocket. Expecting to see Alec's name and a torrent of abusive messages, I found instead a single message from Dee:

Just checking you're OK?

Karishma must have reported what she'd seen – or even Alec himself. I had no doubt he was brazen enough.

Fine. Whatever you've been told, it's not a big deal

OK, glad all good

'Glad all good' was another of Dee's platitudes. One she liked to deploy to avoid having to acknowledge the damage that someone's – including her own – actions might inflict on their fellow men.

23

When, finally, a police officer came knocking late on Monday morning, Pixie had been holed up for almost twenty-four hours. Dressed for work, trainers laced, she was champing to be released.

'Gwen Healy? I understand there's been some sort of dispute with your neighbour?' the officer said. He was in his early thirties, with cropped hair, clear grey eyes and a placid manner.

'Not a "dispute", no.' I didn't care for the implication that this was a trivial barney. 'The discovery of a crime. In the flat next door, number four.' I dictated Alec's full name, making sure he got the spelling right, for it had occurred to me overnight that he might already be on the police database. Offenders did not suddenly emerge in their late forties, did they? Who knew what misdemeanours lurked in his past. He'd been a rock star for a spell, after all, not a tribe known for its adherence to the letter of the law.

'What kind of crime?'

'We found a camera in his roommate's shower. Pixie here. You're happy to give a statement, aren't you, Pix?'

'Um, I think.' But she looked uneasy when her details were taken, grateful when the officer said a statement would not be necessary at this stage.

'At what stage *will* it be necessary?' I demanded. 'I'm pretty sure he got rid of it yesterday, by the way, but I took a photo when it was still in situ. It's not great quality …' This was an understatement: I hadn't realized till afterwards that the phone had jerked in my hand when Alec had startled me and the resulting image was blurred. 'If you go and have a look, you'll see the spot where he's removed it. Either there'll be a deep hole in the grouting or there'll be a section where he's redone it. Or it might have sticky putty stuff in the hole.'

The officer asked us to sit tight while he went across to call on Alec. Listening at the door, I heard Alec invite him in, all mild-mannered courtesy.

Behind me, Pixie groaned. 'This is awful. I feel so guilty.'

'Why? He's the one who should feel guilty.'

'I know, but …'

'You're confused,' I told her gently. 'That's natural. But we're here to help you see how things look from the outside. Aren't we, Dan?'

Daniel agreed, sending her a pleasingly protective look.

As we killed time with another cup of tea, she began fretting again about being late for work. 'What am I going to say? I can't tell them the real reason.'

'Say you had to help a neighbour with an emergency. Give it another half an hour.'

Before she could object – and certainly not long enough for any thorough investigation to have taken place – the officer returned.

'Mrs Healy,' he began.

'Ms,' I corrected him. 'How did you get on?'

'He allowed me to look around the property and I didn't find any device of the kind you suggested.'

'I told you he got rid of it,' I cried, exasperated. 'I saw him throw it away with my own eyes.'

'I don't think you said that.'

'I'm saying it now. Go and look in the bin by the bus stop. The one next to the chicken shop.'

'Street bins are emptied first thing on a Monday,' said Pixie, who knew about these things now she worked in the commercial zone. 'So it'll be too late.'

'Did you find the right spot in the shower?' I insisted the officer at least look at the photo again, but he was infuriatingly noncommittal. 'Was the grouting freshly applied like I told you?'

'Evidence of DIY isn't something to concern me, to be honest,' he said, his tone flat.

'Have you at least taken his laptop and phone so you can get your tech people to check for images?'

'Images?'

'Of Pixie here in the shower! He might have distributed them to other perverts for all we know.'

She gave a whimper then, and in a rare demonstrative act Daniel placed a hand on her shoulder and squeezed.

'We would need a warrant for that,' the officer said.

'Then get one! This is basic detective work, what's wrong with you? Have you taken a blow to the head or something?'

'Mum,' Daniel said.

'Ms Healy, we do not tolerate abuse of our officers.'

'Abuse? You're a grown man. I'm a senior citizen. Honestly, when you think of all the rapists and paedophiles and God knows what else you have to deal with, and you call *me* abusive.'

'It's fine,' Pixie said.

'It's not fine, Pixie. The law should be protecting *you*, not him.' But I was beaten and I knew it. Alec was no fool and he'd had all of yesterday to cover his tracks. Likely he'd been out again under the cover of darkness and disposed of the very devices I was urging the police officer to seize. I thought about suggesting the images might be on the cloud, but it was a concept I'd never really understood and Lord knew if you could police such a thing.

The officer left with an air of having done his best to take us seriously but of having decided to cut his losses.

'Thanks for nothing,' I called after him.

'What's going to happen now?' Pixie said. 'Do you think we've made things worse?'

'I think it's unfortunate Alec came home when he did. We could have got better pictures, maybe even accessed his laptop.' I exhaled, wearied by the morning's frustrations. 'The main thing is you're here now. He can't watch you here. He can't make you do anything you don't want to.'

'You think it's safe for her to go to work?' Daniel asked me, as Pixie hauled her bag over her arm.

'Yes. She'll be surrounded by people. If he comes in and tries to make a scene,' I instructed her, 'which I doubt he will, ask your manager to call the police and get yourself somewhere safe.'

'I'll walk you down,' Daniel told her. 'I was actually thinking I might apply for a job there myself.'

Though taken aback by this, I could hardly express dismay when I'd not only championed such work to Pixie, but marched her in there to get it.

She, by contrast, was genuinely thrilled. 'That would be amazing. We could do the same shifts?' She linked her arm through his as if it were already decided.

'That's what I was thinking,' Daniel said, colouring very slightly.

24

When thwarted, I redouble my commitment, even become combative. Ask Brian.

No, don't do that. Don't ask that weasel anything.

At first, following that pathetic non-intervention by the officer, I resolved to abstain from any further contact with Alec, at least while I plotted my next move, but I'm afraid to say this lasted only a matter of hours before we had our next clash.

Thanks to the weekend's furore, I'd failed to notice we'd arrived at the date of our regular board meeting, and when Dee sent a reminder in the late afternoon, I could only hope he planned to duck out to avoid seeing me.

No such luck: when I left the flat, I found him on the landing, phone and notebook in hand, about to head over.

'Evening, Gwen.' He treated me to the same contemptuous smirk he had in the street the previous day, when he'd watched me rummage in the bin. 'Any interesting scavenging opportunities over the weekend?'

'Any interesting spying on naked young women opportunities?' I shot back. As I say, I come out fighting. 'You might have got away with it this time, but they'll catch up with you eventually.'

'Who might "they" be?'

'The police, of course.'

He openly scoffed at me, close enough for me to feel the heat of his breath. 'There's nothing to catch up with, as our neighbourhood bobby confirmed this morning. This is all in your head. How's my erstwhile roomie, by the way? Having second thoughts yet, is she? Tell her the bed's still warm if she wants to come back.'

I ignored this repugnant remark. 'I'd like to politely request you don't come to this meeting, Alec.'

'I'd like to politely request *you* don't.' He glanced at my stick with disdain, then motioned to the stairs, mock gallant. 'Race you?'

To get to Dee's, we had to walk the length of the building and enter through the main doors, no great distance, but with the advantage of fully functioning joints he'd pulled ahead even before we reached our own door, letting it slam shut rather than holding it for me. By the time I'd chased him four flights to Dee's, I was so badly out of breath as to be almost doubled over.

'Gwen, are you all right?' Dee said, meeting me at the door with a freshly opened beer in her hand. I could hear Alec inside chatting to Noel as she fussed over me. 'We were worried the stairs might be a bit much. You probably shouldn't inflame your knee right before surgery. Can I get you one of these? Or a nice glass of wine?'

'I'm fine.' I limped after her to the turret, doing my best to compose myself, and acknowledged Noel's greeting. Then, ignoring Alec's warning gaze, I summoned my courage and said, 'I have a very serious issue to raise.'

'Can we add it to the agenda?' Dee handed Alec the beer and took her seat. 'I really think we need to start with the service charge. Noel and I have crunched the numbers and we're looking at a surcharge of about £3,000 per flat, I'm afraid—'

'I'd prefer to discuss this first,' I cut in, still breathing heavily. 'It's very important.'

'Okay, fine. Do you want to sit down and get your breath back? Let me pour you some water.'

I did as she suggested and she poured me a glass from the carafe. I would have liked a few sips before I spoke, but I knew my hand would shake when I picked up the tumbler and make me look overly emotional. 'Yesterday, Pixie accused Alec of a crime and I would like to suggest that he step down as a director while we conduct an internal investigation.'

'Internal investigation?' Alec jeered. 'What do you think this is, *Line of Duty*?'

'What crime?' Noel asked.

I opened my mouth but Alec beat me to it, addressing the other two exclusively, just as I had done. 'In the spirit of transparency, I'd like to disclose that a police officer visited my flat this morning at Gwen's behest. Gwen's, not Pixie's, I should stress, after she misconstrued a matter between Pixie and me. He left quite satisfied no crime had taken place. My position is, we all make mistakes and I'm sure we can settle the matter privately later. Shall we get on with company business?'

He turned to me then and actually held out his hand. I refused to shake it, outraged.

'Just because the police believed you and not us doesn't mean the crime didn't happen! Why else would Pixie be staying with me?'

Dee and Noel looked from Alec to me, both bewildered.

'What are we talking about exactly?' Dee said.

'It relates to sexual imagery,' I said. 'Captured on a hidden camera.'

'That's complete fantasy and you know it,' Alec said.

'It's the truth,' I insisted. 'And *you* know it.'

'Look, I'm sure we're all agog as to where your imagination has led you this time...'

This time? The audacity! He was speaking now with unnatural mildness and I wondered if the others found this as sinister as I did.

'But the fact is you're slandering me to my neighbours,' he continued, 'and that's a different matter entirely.'

My fury deepened at his use of 'we're all' and 'my neighbours', smoothly aligning himself with our colleagues in opposition to me. 'A spy camera was fitted in Pixie's shower,' I said, regaining Dee's and Noel's attention, 'and she and I called the police about it. As for where my "imagination" has led me, it's to a vulnerable young woman who clearly needs my protection.'

'Vulnerable my arse,' Alec said.

'A camera?' Noel said. 'Are you saying you've seen pictures, Gwen?'

'No, but I can only imagine how many people have.'

'There *are* no pictures,' Alec said.

'I only saw the camera,' I said. 'I've taken a photo of it. And the substance used to conceal it.'

'The officer told me about that,' Alec said. 'I explained I was plugging the gap with putty following an insect infestation. I said I'd have pest control come in and have a look.'

'That sounds wise. The last thing we want—' Dee began but I cut in.

'There's no infestation, that's nonsense. It was a camera. If they wanted to, they could trace it through your bank card,' I added.

'This is crazy talk.' He was chuckling now, by which I deduced he'd bought it with cash.

'If you were really innocent, you wouldn't be laughing, you'd be apoplectic,' I told him.

'Oh, believe me, I'm apoplectic. And I suggest you back off before I show it.'

'If I could ask you both to note the implicit threat,' I said to Dee and Noel, who were processing all of this with increasing alarm. Even the mildest of rows was unprecedented in our meetings.

'This is a very disturbing allegation, Gwen,' Dee said at last.

'Yes, it is. And I'm sure you can understand that as a woman I cannot consider it safe to work with this man on the other matters we're here to discuss. So if you'd prefer *me* to stand down ... ?'

One look at her face and I knew *as a woman* had swung it. What would the young feminist Stella say if she didn't automatically believe one of her sisters?

She turned to Alec, grimacing. 'I'm sorry, but Gwen's right, we can't just carry on with the meeting as normal after an accusation of sexual misconduct. I think it's prudent for us to err on the side of caution while we talk to Pixie and try to establish what's been going on.'

Alec held up his palms in mock surrender. 'Sure, Dee. Why break from the new normal, guilty till proven innocent? How about I accuse Gwen of, I don't know, stealing cash from me? Should we err on the side of caution on that as well? Maybe a bit of background on her business practices would be helpful? I'd be happy to supply it.'

I snorted. I should have known that was coming. 'Dee and Noel know all about that.'

'Well, *I* didn't. Are you even allowed to be a director?'

'I'm only not allowed to be a trustee of a charity,' I said. 'We are not a charity.'

'It's really not relevant to this discussion, Alec,' Dee said.

'Maybe it is,' I said, seeing a way to reframe this. 'I was the victim of male misconduct all those years ago and now it's poor Pixie who is.'

'Yeah, yeah.' Alec scrambled to his feet. 'You're right, we can't work together in these circumstances. Just let me know when you'd like to talk this through, Dee. I'm at your disposal.' He made infuriatingly dignified farewells and left, Dee on his tail. There was no slamming of the door in *her* face.

'Well,' she said, returning. Alec's beer remained untouched and she slid it to the centre of the table as if it were now up for grabs. 'I'm not sure what to say.'

'Can we see this picture of the camera?' Noel asked me, but his response to the image was not as positive as I might have hoped. 'It's hard to tell what it is.'

'Pixie will confirm it was a camera. She saw it as well. He's removed it of course. That's what I was looking for yesterday, Dee, when Karishma saw me.'

'Right.' A flicker of distaste crossed her face. She would never stoop to such unsanitary vigilantism, but if we left matters to people like her we'd never root out the criminals in our society.

Noel returned my phone to me. 'Even if we accept that there's a camera in this image, is there any evidence that Alec was the one to install it?'

'Well, I'm fairly sure it wasn't Pixie!'

'And if it *was* him, can we be certain it was installed without her knowledge?'

'Good point, Noel.' Dee rested her chin on her knuckles, thoughtful. 'I did hear a rumour that the two of them are romantically involved.'

'Really? Then it *is* possible it's a consensual thing between them,' Noel said. 'Each to his own and all that. You said yourself, Gwen, that you're sensitive to the idea of a woman being exploited.'

'Pixie was as horrified as I was,' I insisted. 'Why are we not being believed here?' My patience wearing thin, I made a decision then that I can now identify as instrumental in the disaster that was to follow. 'I wasn't going to tell you this, but I think you need to know that this camera business is part of a larger concern.'

'What larger concern?' Dee said.

'Alec hasn't been taking rent from Pixie, he's been asking for sexual favours instead.'

Her brow creased. 'I don't understand, if they're boyfriend and girlfriend ... ?'

'They're not, that's the point!'

'So she doesn't pay any rent at all?' Noel said. He and Dee shared an incredulous look.

'Not monetary. She pays with her body. It's an abhorrent practice and I hardly need remind you not what we intended when allowing the Rent a Room scheme in the building.' Again, I eyed Dee, transmitting severe sisterly disapproval.

'Of course not,' she agreed hastily. 'Leave this with me, Gwen. I'll talk to Pixie *and* Alec and report back to you both. Let's keep it between us for now.'

'Meanwhile, he's off the board?' I pressed.

'Yes.' At her suggestion we would make no announcement of any suspension on WhatsApp, but temporarily remove his name from our website and disable his email access.

'Where is Pixie now?' Noel asked. 'Did you say she's staying with you?'

'Yes, she's sleeping on the sofa until she finds a safe alternative. Daniel is with us, of course, but can I ask you both to keep an eye on her while I go in for my knee surgery later this week? I'll only be in the hospital for two nights if all goes well, but with emotions running high as they are, I'm worried about leaving her.'

'Of course,' Noel said.

'You focus on the op, Gwen,' Dee agreed, covering my hand with hers. 'You can count on us.'

25

As you're aware, I haven't said a great deal about my daughter Maya so far, the reason being that she was never directly involved in the crisis. But I think we've reached the juncture where an introduction might be helpful.

Before she appears in the present – at my hospital bedside, no less – I'd like to rewind a few years to the only occasion pre-Pixie that Columbia Mansions was embroiled in something resembling a scandal.

The problem on that occasion was perceived colonial links – perceived by Maya and a group of passionate young comrades with moral outrage in spades but rather less history education to support it. Not only was she the chief agitator, but also to my knowledge the only one to regularly cast her principles aside in order to eat a Sunday roast in the very cradle of evil she sought to expose.

The group's objection was this: Charles Reynolds, the gentleman architect who'd designed the building in the 1890s, had previously created a country house for a family descended from plantation owners. He'd subsequently married one of the daughters and proceeded to get fat off their old sugar money.

'Columbia Mansions was literally built on the bones of enslaved Africans,' Maya informed me, along with the news that a demonstration was planned.

'Not literally at all,' I said. 'Slavery was abolished in 1834. This building went up in 1896.'

'Fine,' she huffed, 'not literally. Sometimes I use literally metaphorically.'

'Okay. Good to know.' (You see what I was dealing with?) 'What you're talking about is inherited profits.'

'That doesn't make it right.'

'No, it makes it history. Different times, different cultures, different sensibilities. If Reynolds were alive today, we could alert him to the dangers. Or he might alert us, who knows. But there's nothing to be gained from comparing apples and pears.'

'Oh, I think apples and pears are similar enough,' she said, in her high-minded way.

I won't record the entire debate. Just picture me regarding this millennial firebrand with more weariness than severity when I said, finally, 'Just admit it, Maya.'

'Admit what?'

'That you're only doing this to annoy me. You could choose any of this man's buildings, so why the one *I* live in? Look, I'm really sorry you have parents who brought disgrace on the family, but that was your dad, not me. I don't deserve to be punished.'

This gave her pause for all of five seconds before she retorted, '*He* thinks it's great what we're doing.'

'Yes, I imagine he does.' Brian would love the idea that I was being harassed in my own home by my own daughter. 'It's easy to cheerlead when you're on the other side of the world. Let's see how he feels when you try to seize his home for the Māoris.'

Nothing wrong with sowing the seed, eh?

Anyway, to cut a long story short, she and her group assembled at our railings with placards saying things like 'STOLEN

PEOPLE, STOLEN DREAMS' and 'SAY YUH SORRY', and challenged anyone going in and out who failed to sink to their knees in apology. Liz got jostled in the melee and lost her balance, sustaining a cut to the temple which Jeanette treated from her first aid kit.

The stink made the papers, with the *Mail* taking the opportunity to quote the latest 'eye-watering' purchase price for one of the flats. Many of Maya's more utopian proposals were reprinted in all their glory and remain online to this day:

> *'If every resident of this shameful block paid a percentage of what their property is worth into a fund for the descendants of slaves, that would be a start. We propose ten per cent. It could be a decolonization tax, like the council tax.'*

Luckily WhatsApp had established itself by then as the go-to comms for neighbourhood groups and I was able to field objections with a level of efficiency that would have been tantamount to witchcraft in the eyes of our long-departed Mr Reynolds.

Hester
Does anyone understand this? Have they not heard of William Wilberforce?

Elliot
Just youngsters spouting ideology from across the pond. I blame Horrible Histories. *Watched it with the grandkids. Riddled with inaccuracies.*

Noel
I think that's unfair, Elliot. It's a really respected show.

Sadie
Agree with Noel. I've used it to teach the twins about structural inequality.

Elliot
Blimey, bet they love that!

Hester
tbh I don't think this is funny. What happened with Liz was out of order.

Gwen
I can only apologize for my daughter's activism. I'm confident it will blow over.

Dee
We're going to have to get used to this. This is quite an 'engaged' generation, especially the girls. Stella's the same.

'You don't think it will affect property prices?' I asked Dee privately.

'I very much doubt it. If anything, it establishes us as elite and upmarket.'

'We won't tell Maya that,' I said, laughing. (It saddens me now to think how swimmingly Dee and I got on in those early years.)

Not one to commit for long, Maya moved smoothly on to other causes: the climate crisis, Ukraine, and #MeToo, of course, which soon segued into a more militant feminism called The Patriarchy Must Die or some such.

The latter made her current incarnation all the more unfathomable.

*

I'd noticed a change of personal style since she'd turned thirty, left her job as a counsellor and moved in with her boyfriend Jason, a trader in the City who she'd met on a dating app; it had become more overtly feminine, sexier I suppose. Any placards and flyers that had moved with her to his house in Greenwich were systematically replaced by cookbooks and framed slogans like 'Happy Him, Happy Me!'

It was Daniel who'd tipped me off to her TikTok account, where she'd developed a following as a 'stay-at-home girlfriend' or 'trad wife' (her handle was @stayathomesiren). Evidently, this involved posting inane instalments in which she dressed as a maid or a hooker and extolled the virtues of serving her man.

'I don't want to be all things to all men. I want to be one thing to one man. *My* man,' she simpered in one video, exposing half of her bosom as she made some sort of virility-promoting smoothie in a big shiny mixer straight out of 1950s suburbia. Her hair, now Marilyn platinum, was intricately curled and she'd done something to her mouth to make it plumped and shiny, putting me in mind of a glazed strawberry tart.

Jason did not appear in the videos. He was a purely off-stage muse. 'He's the breadwinner,' Maya explained in another reel. 'I'm the muffin maker.'

I ask you!

Daniel called it cosplay (I had to look up what that was), while Dee said it was a reaction to feminism. 'It's hard being a young woman, at least according to Stella. She says they're pushed to extremes like no generation before.'

We both chortled at that, asking each other for the nth time what either of them knew about the challenges faced by their grandmothers and great-grandmothers. Did they know, for instance, that women hadn't been able to get a mortgage until as recently as the 1980s without a man's guarantee? Or that marital rape had only been illegal since 1992?

And before you point the finger, we acknowledged our part in this too. By protecting them from the bleaker of these realities we'd created young women who had no clue that what had been so hard won could be withdrawn with mind-blowing ease. Or, in the case of Maya and her ilk, returned with pleasure. Jason mustn't have been able to believe his luck.

'Let's talk about sex,' she suggested coquettishly in one clip. Even her voice had been modified, breathier and more intimate than it used to be. 'I make it my business to be available on command ...'

Of course, it was clear to me that all of this was a reaction of a more obvious sort. She'd tried being a strident activist, better at good causes than her disastrously flawed parents, but she'd found it exhausting and frustrating and ultimately thankless.

Whereas now, judging by all those likes on her social media, the thanks were pouring in.

*

She came to the hospital alone, her master being too busy wage-earning to accompany her, dressed in a silk dress with a slit up the thigh and a lilac fake-fur bolero. She bore a plate of home-baked cookies covered in cellophane so the perfectly imperfect treats could be admired by all, including her followers as she filmed her own arrival with the help of a selfie stick.

I asked her to put her equipment away as I had no wish to be in one of her videos. ('Leaving my brave boy to fend for himself while I care for Mommie Dearest ...')

'Well, this is nice,' she said, taking in the comforts of the private room. 'I didn't know you had medical insurance, Mum.'

'I don't,' I said.

'How can you afford this then?'

'I can't really, but I was in agony, so please don't give me a hard time about spending your inheritance.'

'I'm completely self-financing now,' she protested. 'Dan's the one who needs money. I can't believe he's applied for a job in a café. He's never made me a cup of tea in his life. Has he you?'

'No. Actually once, yes. The other day.' I suspected her objection was not to the downgrade in status on her brother's behalf but the fact that she believed all service roles should be filled by women. I said nothing more, just let her chat to the surgeon when he came by, brazenly flirtatious.

'Thank you so much for restoring her joie de vivre,' she cooed, even though I was drained of colour and faced a period of considerable pain once the morphine had left my system. When he'd gone, she updated me on her other news. The lucrative sponsored content she'd been offered; Jason's bonus; the luxury holiday in Thailand planned for Easter. 'I'm not being funny, but they still respect the patriarchy there,' she said.

'You mean without a social security safety net women have no choice but to take money from sad old sex tourists?'

'You always want to see the underbelly,' she complained.

'I don't *want* to see it at all. It keeps flipping up before I have a chance to avert my eyes.' Hard not to think of Alec then, his dressing gown falling open at the door. 'And may I remind you it's not so long ago that you had a few causes of your own.'

'All right, calm down,' Maya said. 'Aren't you supposed to be groggy from the anaesthetic? Let's try and get you a top-up.'

That made me laugh. Preposterous – and, yes, I admit shameful

– as I found her new persona, there was no denying we got on better now than at any time before.

I decided not to tell her about the crisis raging at Columbia Mansions and was relieved to deduce that Daniel had not yet passed on news of our temporary guest.

Cameras in bathrooms, sex for rent 'whenever he liked': there was too much of a risk she'd side with Alec.

26

I heard very little from my household while I was in hospital, just a cursory checking in by text from Daniel and responses of 'OMG' to pictures I sent Pixie of my strapped and swollen leg. Neither thought to help with arrangements for my discharge and so the hospital booked a taxi to return me home.

Then, an hour before I was due to leave the hospital, Dee phoned to suggest she pick me up.

'Goodness,' she said, clocking the paraphernalia I'd been supplied with for my recovery: surgical stockings, inflatable boots, walking frame and crutches. By contrast she was a light-footed sprite in tailored jeans, a beautiful mohair blazer and snug-fitting leather boots. A new blunt-fringed haircut enhanced her sexagenarian glamour. 'You must have a whole physio regime, do you?'

'They said about ten days recovery and six weeks before full mobility. I think I'm going to be out of action for a little while.'

'But worth it, I'm sure.' There was a faint air of 'I wouldn't know' about her manner. I could tell she assumed an alpha specimen like her would never have need of surgical renewal.

A wheelchair took me to the car park and a member of staff helped me into the passenger seat of Dee's Jeep, even securing my seatbelt for me, though I protested my arms still worked perfectly well. The kit for my recuperation was stacked in the boot, along with my overnight bag.

'Has Pixie been okay?' I asked as we departed.

'Yes. No harassment from you-know-who, I'm pleased to say.'

'Hopefully you'll be able to speak to them about this sex-for-rent business soon.'

'Oh, I already have.' Dee hit the accelerator, hurtling through the dying embers of an amber light as if being given chase, only to have to join the queue for a roundabout fifty metres on. 'I sat down with both of them yesterday.' She flicked me a wry glance. 'Separately, of course. I don't think we're at the mediation stage quite yet.'

I felt my blood surge. 'And?'

'On testimony alone, I'm inclined to find in her favour.' The phrasing suggested she'd taken to her role as judge and jury like a duck to water, but that was not the point. The point was she'd judged correctly.

'Good,' I said. 'I agree.'

'Lunatic!' She'd pulled onto the roundabout, somewhat cavalier in her assessment of the speed of an approaching vehicle. 'The thing is, Gwen – and Noel agrees with me – in a he said/she said situation like this, I'm not sure there's anything we can take to the police. Even if Pixie wanted us to, which she seems adamant she doesn't.'

'I know. She was reluctant enough about reporting the camera.'

'Which they didn't do anything about,' Dee reminded me.

I wasn't sure where this was going and could only pray it was not the appeasement of Alec and his reinstatement to the board. He'd buttered her up before and, with me out of the way, he had the advantage. 'So he just gets away with it?'

'In terms of police involvement, yes. But there are other sorts of investigations. That's partly why I wanted to speak to you before we see the others.' She moistened her lips with the tip of her tongue, eyes fixed on the road. 'I've suggested to Pixie we go to the media.'

'The media?' You could have knocked me down with a feather – until I remembered one crucial detail. 'You mean Stella?'

'Possibly, yes. She's been looking for an issue like this to pitch to TV. Something a bit harder-hitting than her column stuff, to extend her brand.'

Though Dee spoke casually, I knew there was no 'possibly' about it; she'd already discussed it with Stella. Not that she would have gone to her like some scurrilous informant, more likely she'd confided she was enquiring into particularly sensitive circumstances and Stella, sniffing a story, had drawn out the details.

Sex sells – even sex that someone's negotiated for free.

Sensing my scepticism, she added, 'When I say brand, I mean journalistic range. Shine a light on an issue that needs more attention than it's getting. I hadn't even heard of such a thing as sex for rent before, had you?'

'No, and I agree it would be wonderful if Stella could use her platform to warn other young women of the dangers. It puts the victim at risk of domestic violence and other types of controlling behaviour.'

Dee nodded. 'I could see this as a feature-length documentary, couldn't you? Or even a drama series. Look at what ITV did with the Post Office scandal. Toby Jones was outstanding. Brenda Blethyn could play you,' she added. 'I know you love *Vera*.'

'I do.' I suppressed my instinct to laugh out loud at the notion of *Columbia Mansions*, the TV series. Clearly imaginations (hers and Stella's, anyway) had run riot in my absence.

'I'm really not sure Pixie sees herself as a poster girl for the issue,' I said delicately. 'Either in news or dramatic form. She's such a private person and very upset and embarrassed by it all. You just said yourself she's not keen to escalate things.'

'With the police, no, but as I say …' Dee braked to allow a menace on an e-scooter to swerve in front of us and I took the opportunity to steer the subject back to Pixie's well-being.

'Well, I'm glad to hear Alec hasn't tried to confront her, but I don't think we can count on that continuing, especially if he feels he's been unfairly judged. How did he respond to your conclusions?'

'I haven't followed it up with him yet. I thought I'd phone him when we get back and ask him to resign from the board. Noel agrees, but we wanted to check with you first.'

'Fine by me. And if he refuses?'

'We'll discuss procedure to remove him. But you're right, Gwen, Pixie is embarrassed and needs to feel more empowered. What difference will it make to her if he's on the board or not? That's where a journalist can be of service to us.'

So much for moving the subject on.

I adjusted my throbbing leg. 'No disrespect to Stella, but journalists can do more harm than good.' I thought of the press coverage of our charity scandal and Brian's prosecution. Though relatively minimal, it had caused me enormous anguish, not only reading it at the time but also the fact that it stayed online afterwards, waiting to be discovered by one's enemies. Look how Alec had weaponized it when it suited him. I did not want that for Pixie. 'It needs to be mutually beneficial, otherwise it's just exploitation.'

'I completely agree. For goodness' sake, man, do you *have* to tailgate?' A white van was inches from our bumper, too close for me see the driver's face in any of the mirrors, but I guessed he'd clocked the sensible car, the older woman at the wheel and put his foot down. 'Perhaps we can reconnect them and see what happens? They got on very well at the bonfire party.'

I sighed. 'What does Pixie say about it?'

'She wanted to talk to you first.'

This, at least, was gratifying. 'I'm not sure, Dee. We don't want to drag Columbia Mansions through the mud. Remember that business with Maya.'

'Oh, I imagine it could be reported without letting on where it occurred.' Again, her casual confidence told me this had already been discussed. 'But you know her better than I do,' she added as we turned into Clayton Street.

'If Pixie wants to meet with Stella, that's up to her,' I said, though I already knew I would not be actively promoting the idea. It was all too easy to envisage Dee making the introduction and then strategically withdrawing, leaving me to manage any emotional fallout. 'What was the other reason?' I asked as she rolled down her window to touch her fob against the entrance pad to the car park.

'I beg your pardon?'

'You said that was partly why you wanted to speak to me before I came home. What was the other part?'

'Just that you're my friend, of course. I wanted to make sure you got back in one piece.' She reversed into her parking spot, careful to allow extra space on the passenger side. 'Right, let me get the walker in position for you and I'll buzz Daniel to come down for the rest of your stuff. They'll be waiting to welcome you home.'

But when I finally inched through the door, I was dismayed to find no special signs of welcome. Not that I'd been expecting balloons and bunting, but a bunch of tulips might have been nice.

Still, at least Pixie was home, albeit not yet dressed. She advanced for a hug. 'Gwen, you poor thing! How are you feeling?'

'Sore and tired, but the worst's over. Maya came to the hospital,' I said to Daniel, who was setting down my things in the middle of the room, no thought as to the tripping hazards they created.

'I thought you wanted me to stay and look after Pixie,' he said, instantly defensive.

'I did.' I eased myself into the most upright seat I owned. 'Dee says there's been no trouble from Alec?'

'None at all,' Pixie said. Remarkably, she'd managed to avoid him entirely during my absence. 'But Daniel's got an interview at Bageri Møller,' she added, as if that were the really important news. 'He's heading off in a minute.'

'Well done,' I told him, as if congratulating a teenager on his first Saturday job, not a man in his thirties who really ought to be applying for roles better suited to his experience and seniority.

He nodded. 'Not sure whether to mention the New Zealand trip, you know?'

'I would,' Dee advised. 'Honesty is always the best policy.' (She really did say this, I'm not making it up!) She bent to give me a squeeze goodbye. 'Are you okay for dinner? Would you like me to bring you a shepherd's pie from my freezer?'

'Thank you,' I said, 'but I'm sure Daniel and Pixie will have shopped.'

'Actually, I'm still a bit nervous about going out,' Pixie said, which was poppycock because she'd been to work at least once in my absence and could have picked groceries up on her way home.

As for Daniel, he could have shopped at any point during the sixteen hours a day Tesco Express was open. 'There's milk,' he said. 'But we drank the wine.'

'Honestly, guys,' Dee teased. 'Invalids need more than fluids. They need nourishing home-cooked food.' I began to protest the invalid label but she was focused on Pixie, smiling winningly at her. 'Could I have a quick word?'

'Sure,' Pixie said.

'Why don't you come up to my place for a drink. We'll leave Gwen to get herself settled in.'

'You could bring the shepherd's pie when you come back down, Pix?' Daniel suggested.

'Perfect,' Dee said, as if we had a logistics genius in our midst, the man who thought of everything.

From my chair, feeling hobbled in more than just the physical sense, I could see them in the hallway, Dee peering out onto the landing, Pixie backed up behind her.

'Coast's clear,' Dee said in a stage whisper, and Pixie trotted after her with nary a backward glance at the post-operative wretch who may have needed a little assistance 'settling in'. Daniel, meanwhile, just about found it in his heart to fetch me a glass of water before departing for his job interview.

I admit there was a moment there when I disliked all three of them.

27

By the time Pixie returned from Dee's, Daniel's interview had been and gone (as expected, he'd got the job) and the two of them immediately hooked headphones over their ears and began gaming. She was non-committal regarding Stella's bid to extend her brand – sorry, range – saying only there was 'no harm' in having a chat with her.

Evidently having turned her attention to Alec, Dee texted Noel and me not long after with unwelcome news:

Dee
He won't back down. He insists he's done nothing wrong.

Gwen
I'll resign from the board then.

Dee
Let's not be hasty. He's agreed he'll sit out the next meeting, which buys us time.

Noel
Yes. Let's see how things develop between now and then.

I could only assume Noel was not aware that the 'buying time' that Dee referred to had as much to do with her daughter's pitch for a broadcast news feature as any soul-searching on the part of the perpetrator.

'Things' certainly developed with hair-raising speed. No sooner was Pixie relaying the news that her chat with Stella had been 'interesting' and there was 'no harm in Stella making a few calls' than Dee was knocking on our door with posh biscuits and some 'exciting news'.

'Stella's pitched the idea to a contact at *News Radar* and they're interested.'

'*News Radar* is a big BBC show,' I told Pixie, guessing she would not have seen it.

'And their features go on the BBC website and get millions more views,' Dee said.

'Really?' Pixie said, and I caught the panic in her eyes. She hadn't thought Stella would succeed, I guessed, and certainly not so quickly.

In contrast, Dee was pleased to the point of holy radiance. 'It's early in the process, of course, but they've asked for a meeting.'

'Do *I* have to go?' Pixie asked.

'No, just Stella, I think. She'll ring you today, I'm sure.'

In fact, the call came as we were having coffee and, sure enough, Pixie concluded that there was 'no harm' in Stella having an 'exploratory' meeting with the producers.

'What do you really think?' I asked her, when Dee had gone. 'You can be honest with me. Assuming Stella gets this commissioned, do you want to talk publicly about your experience?'

She had an air of weary bewilderment about her as she struggled to answer. 'I mean, I want to raise awareness, like Stella says, but ... I don't know, I hate being the centre of attention. I hate it even when it's something good, you know?'

'I do know,' I said, for it was part of our bond that we were countercultural in this respect. Women like Stella and Dee and Maya yearned for the spotlight, for attention and acclaim and *relevance*, but Pixie and I, all we wanted was for life to be a little fairer.

Laugh if you will, but I genuinely believed that. I still do.

*

I know very well what turned the dial from doubt to agreement: her first meeting with Alec since she'd moved out of number 4.

If I remember rightly, it was the day after that call with Stella, when she was returning from work. Whether he'd been watching from the window and seen her walking through Winifred Gardens or it was by pure chance I do not know, but it was exactly as she was coming up the stairs that he chose to show his face. I'm very grateful I happened to be there to intervene: hearing voices, I manoeuvred out with my walker and propped myself at the balustrade, an excellent position from which to witness their exchange on the half landing, where he was barring her path. Dressed in drab grey, his face screwed-up and scowling almost to the point of parody, he put me in mind of the troll in *The Three Billy Goats Gruff*.

'I said can I get past, please?' Pixie said in a polite voice, a box from the bakery held in front of her as if in protection.

'I thought you'd be out of here by now,' he said, deftly shadowing her sidesteps to block her. 'On to your next victim.'

'Pixie *is* the victim, Alec,' I called down, 'as well you know.'

He shot me a hostile look. 'There she is, your very own battleaxe in shining armour.'

'I would ask that you do not insult me in this way,' I snapped.

He looked up at me with a sneer. 'Fuck off, you interfering sow.' Then, as Pixie took advantage of the distraction to dip past him, he muttered, 'Airhead slut.'

'I heard that!' I told him. 'I'm making a note of everything you say.'

'Likewise. Hey, I need my key back, yeah?' He was addressing the back of Pixie's legs now, as she scurried the half flight to safety.

'When I get my stuff back!' she shot back.

'Are you all right?' I struggled back into the flat after her and closed the door.

She nodded. 'He shouldn't speak to you like that.'

'Or you. He's a misogynist, plain and simple.'

'What are we going to do?'

'Well, for starters, we're not going to let him intimidate us. What's in the box?'

'Cinnamon slices from work. Do you fancy one?' She put the kettle on for tea and plated the pastries. Next thing, she was on the phone, the call on speaker.

'Stella?'

'Pixie? Lovely to hear from you. Have you—'

Pixie interrupted: 'I'm going to do it. One hundred per cent.'

There was a dramatic intake of breath before Stella exploded with joy.

'That's wonderful news! Oh my God, I'm so proud of you.'

'Like you said, he probably won't even watch it, but we can do that silhouette thing so no one knows it's me.'

'Precisely. We can protect your identity, no problem. And I've just had the most amazing talk with a girl in Leicester who's had a similar experience to you. I'm going up there tomorrow to meet her.' Stella chattered on, before adding, 'Can I just say it's a privilege to be your conduit.'

Pixie did not answer, likely not knowing what a conduit was.

'I'm so grateful to you for entrusting me with your story,' Stella went on, by way of clarification. 'I'll phone you as soon as I have a date for the interview, hopefully this week and then we can talk through the specifics of how we're going film it. In the meantime, you are somewhere safe, aren't you?'

'I'm still at Gwen's.'

There was a short silence. 'Of course. Good old Gwen.'

'Less of the old, Stella,' I said loudly, though Stella had probably thought the call private. 'The interview won't be here, will it?' I added, picturing crew lugging camera equipment up the stairs and into my flat. 'We don't want Alec getting wind of what you're up to.'

It felt important, that 'you'. What *you're* up to. Now Pixie appeared to be on board, I wanted to establish boundaries. This was Stella's project, hers and Dee's, not mine.

'Good point, Gwen,' she said. 'We'll do Pixie's in the studio.'

Pixie turned to me, her expression plaintive. 'Will you come with me, Gwen? You know, for moral support?'

'I think Dee should do that,' I said. 'She's the one who set this up.'

'We actually thought that might not be the best idea, Gwen,' Stella said, 'because we're related? It could look like it's not totally legit.'

'I'm not sure I understand,' I said. 'The fact that they live in the same building is how you've made the connection in the first place. Plus, I don't know if your mum told you, but I've just had knee surgery, so I'm not exactly mobile.'

'Broadcasting House is fully accessible,' she said. 'We can arrange for one of those taxis with a wheelchair ramp.'

'Even so,' I began, but Pixie interjected, her lovely eyes full of pleading.

'I'd prefer you, Gwen. You were the one I told first. I trust you.'

'Gwen,' Stella cooed, 'will you at least consider it?'

And in the end that was that. Pixie trusted me and I knew what a precious gift that was. I wasn't about to fail her as others had.

One young woman had been badly let down on my watch and I was damned if I was going to let it happen again.

28

Brian had denied harassment, of course, in just the same way as Alec did – and presumably men like them will till kingdom come. His tryst with Cyndi had been consensual, he maintained, if not exactly romantic. 'Tryst' was *his* word, by the way. The furthest he would concede was 'misunderstanding'.

As for any pain of sexual betrayal on the part of his wife, well, let's remember I was already standing in the ruins of my home, my business, my reputation. By then, when face to face with his bespectacled grey eyes, his homey features and oafish mannerisms, I did not see a man who attracted me. I did not see a man who had ever attracted me.

'Cyndi is the least of our worries, Gwen,' he said, when I took her accusations to him. Both kids were out and we were alone in the house I'd taken for granted for twenty years and would now be relinquishing to the first stranger who made an offer. 'Can't you just get rid of her.'

I glared at him. 'Get rid of her? I'm not the mafia.'

'No, but she listens to you. Tell her whatever you need to tell her.'

'I'll do no such thing. She needs an apology from you. Recompense of some sort.'

'There *is* no fucking recompense!' he cried. 'We've lost everything.'

'*You've* lost everything,' I corrected him.

'I know. I know. Don't make me feel worse than I already do.'

His self-pity sickened me. I had my phone in my hand and was turning it in agitation. Suddenly the screen lit up with the wallpaper photo of Daniel and Maya as young children, their little faces unbearably innocent. 'You should feel worse,' I said.

His tone hardened. 'It would be very easy for me to say you were in on it, you know.'

'You know I wasn't!'

'That's not what I said. I said it would be very easy for me to *say* you were.'

I couldn't, in the maelstrom of my rage, identify if this was blackmail or bribery or some other kind of marital deal. 'It would also be easy for me to back up Cyndi's story. Say she told me as soon as she got back from Edinburgh.'

'She didn't though, did she? She's only saying it now because her job's on the line.'

We stared at each other, entirely estranged and yet never more indivisible.

'I want a divorce,' I said finally. 'No arguments, no stalling. Anything left from the house sale is mine. The kids come with me.'

'You sure about that?' he said.

'What do you mean?'

'Come on, we all know you're not a natural in that department.'

It was true that Maya in particular was proving a challenge in her teenage years, but it was hardly surprising given the chaos at home, and I deeply resented his criticism. 'Well, they can hardly go with you,' I said. 'Not where you're going.'

I caught the animal scent of fear before he conceded. 'Fine. Shut Cyndi up and I'll make sure you're okay.'

*

With bank accounts inaccessible, I had to hunt for cash in pockets and drawers to take her out for a sandwich and cup of tea. We met near her shared house in a grubby part of southeast London that's now as chi-chi as Queen's Oak.

I looked at her across the café table and did my best to summon a rational, plausible tone. 'I've thought about what you told me and I want to say how sorry I am. It's terrible that you've had this experience while in our employment. Or in any circumstances.' I hesitated. 'Have you talked to anyone else about it?'

'Not yet.' She looked confused. 'You asked me to wait.'

'Yes, of course. I wanted to think what was best. To be honest, Cyndi, with this financial investigation going on, I think it will complicate things if you make a complaint.'

'For him, you mean?'

'For everyone. I worry it could be a distraction. It would be impossible to prove as well, so many weeks after the event. I know that sounds harsh but, unfortunately, it's the reality.' Though she nodded, I saw in her eyes her concerns about future young women, future victims. 'He's going to jail, so the result's the same. He won't be bothering anyone else any time soon.'

Doubt passed across her face – then vanished. She trusted my judgement. She trusted me. 'Okay,' she said. 'I get that.'

I'll come back to what happened to her later. Suffice to say that I was wrong about Brian's fate. He escaped jail time, then kept his powder dry for the duration of the suspended sentence. He met the partner who would become his second wife, a younger woman from New Zealand apparently gullible enough to swallow his tales of a miscarriage of justice, before leaving with her for her homeland with the swagger of a buccaneer.

Not only was he not sorry for what he'd subjected his young colleague to, he gave every impression of having erased her from memory.

As for me, I couldn't even get the poor girl that last month's salary.

29

I was disappointed not to see any famous faces in the reception of Broadcasting House. Adrian Dunbar, perhaps, or the lad who played young Morse. That would have been tremendous.

'Have you discussed this with your father?' I asked Pixie as we waited, security lanyards around our necks, for someone to come down and collect us. I'd heard her on the phone to him in recent days, but she'd been tight-lipped afterwards, seeming to be, if anything, more untethered than ever.

'No way,' she said. 'He doesn't know anything. He'd totally lose his shit.'

'He knows you've moved out though? He's happy about you staying with me?'

She nodded, running the pad of her thumb along the edge of her lanyard. 'I've told him all about you. He says you sound like a right champagne socialist.'

'Well, you can tell him I hardly ever drink champagne.' I pulled a face. 'It gives me gas. Why would he say that, anyway?'

'Because you used to run a charity. I told him you're not preachy, but he says charity is a hobby for rich people.'

'My goodness, what a bleak outlook.'

'I know.' And she smiled, a small uncertain smile, as if wanting to be polite to me while retaining loyalty to him.

'Maybe if I meet him, I can persuade him he's wrong about me,' I said.

Her gaze clouded, but I was saved from further character assassination by the arrival of an assistant, who escorted us in the lift to a waiting Stella. She hugged us both, telling Pixie how fantastic she looked, which was true. Even though her face would not be shown on screen, she'd spent hours applying make-up glamorous enough for a night out clubbing and styling her hair in a little beehive. Stella, meanwhile, was as pink and wholesome as a farmer's wife's, her baby bump prominent.

She explained arrangements to her interviewee with the studied patience of someone who'd already done so several times. It was to be a closed-set situation, with shadow used to obscure Pixie's face – 'but not in a theatrical way' – while her voice would be manipulated at the edits stage, her name switched for a pseudonym.

'Can I choose my name?' Pixie asked. 'I really like Christina.'

'What about the crew?' I asked Stella. 'Will *they* know her real name?'

'They're used to working with strict confidentiality. Nothing for you to worry about, Gwen.'

After that it was all business, starting with Pixie being introduced to the producer and crew. All were female, including an assistant who supplied us with hot drinks; Pixie's hands shook so badly I worried she might spill hers all over herself.

'Try to relax,' Stella said, taking the drink from her as if she were an infant and sandwiching her hand between hers. 'We've been through the questions. You know there's no right or wrong answers. It's just what happened and how it made you feel.'

If I'd imagined myself on the studio floor, mouthing assurances to Pixie from behind the cameraman's shoulder, I was mistaken for I was settled in some sort of ante-chamber and left to watch proceedings on a monitor.

Once set up and underway, Stella gained Pixie's trust with general questions about the challenges of finding affordable accommodation in the capital and by the time they reached the nitty-gritty her nerves had dissipated and she was speaking more freely.

Stella: What kind of sex were you expected to have?

Pixie: Any kind. Whatever he wanted. Yeah.

Stella: And you didn't feel able to refuse?

Pixie: It wasn't that I couldn't refuse, but I knew if I did, I wouldn't have a home. I could be kicked out at a moment's notice. It sounds horrible, but I ...

Stella: Go ahead. You can say anything you like.

Pixie: Just ... Sometimes I felt lucky to be honest. I had my own room. Even my own bathroom. I could close my door and be alone. And the other neighbours were really friendly.

Stella: They didn't ever suspect what was going on?

Pixie: No. Unless you were in the flat with us, you wouldn't know. Like I say, it was bad, but I got used to it.

Stella: It sounds as if you're saying it started to feel normal?

Pixie: Not normal, but … it could have been worse. It definitely could have been worse.

It was a shame her voice would be distorted for broadcast, I thought, because it was very moving how young and defenceless she sounded.

It had been agreed in advance that Stella would not bring up the issue of the spy camera in the shower, but stick to the sex-for-rent narrative, but even so, as I watched, I allowed myself a brief fantasy of that numbskull police officer watching the report and recognizing his negligence. Then I remembered that without her real face and voice and with only 'South London' given as her address, he would have no way of matching this story to the flat he visited or the people he'd spoken to there.

As they were wrapping up, I hauled myself through the corridors in search of a loo, approaching two young staff who were talking about how the story was going to 'blow up' on the socials and be part of a bigger conversation about the risks involved in renting as a single woman.

They obviously considered *this* woman to be either deaf or invisible because one of them asked the other, 'Who's the old girl on that frame thing?' just seconds before I reached them.

'A very good friend of the victim,' I said, sharply. '"Old girls" can be crucial in these situations. We've been around the block and know which pitfalls to avoid.'

The idea that I had any talent for avoiding pitfalls was laughable, but they didn't know that and pulled identically contrite expressions, no doubt fearing I'd complain about them to their boss.

'It's so brave what she's doing,' one gushed. 'Blowing the whistle like this.'

'A total queen,' the other agreed.

I waited politely till they were finished with their inanities before asking them to point me in the direction of the disabled toilets.

*

In the taxi home, Pixie was a volatile mix of emotions, one moment a child, delighting in the Christmas lights of Regent Street, the next older than her years, shoulders hunched, eyes downcast. I'd already praised her several times for her performance since we'd waved goodbye to Stella, but she roused from her reverie to ask me again.

'Did I do okay? Really?'

'Yes,' I said, 'I thought you were excellent. Very sympathetic.'

'I know you didn't think I should go ahead with it,' she said. We were crossing the river by then, always a cinematic experience after dark, the streetlamps and headlights blurred in the drizzle. I could see the driver eyeing Pixie in his rear view and I wondered if he was listening in.

'It doesn't matter what I think,' I said firmly. 'It's done now. The hard bit's over.'

Was I confident of that? I suspect now there must have been some element of wishful thinking because, in this life, isn't there always?

What I certainly didn't expect was for the opposite to be true.

For what we'd just taken part in to turn out to be the easy bit.

30

Her changeable moods continued, one day self-confident, even victorious, the next full of qualms, scarcely able to open the flat door for fear of running into Alec and his somehow divining her 'guilt'.

Since that skirmish on the stairs, he had not raised his ugly head, but, to be on the safe side, Daniel continued to accompany her to work, a service made all the easier now he'd requested the same shifts as hers on mental health grounds. Whose, I wasn't sure, but I encouraged him to take all the shifts he could get. Once he'd got a few weeks under his belt, I would ask him for a contribution to the household expenses.

Money was by now becoming a serious worry for me. I think I mentioned my £40,000? Well, it was running through my fingers like water, starting with the knee expenses: a follow-up appointment at the hospital was covered in the original fee, but the recommended physio home visits were extra. As for day-to-day costs, my pension income, perfectly comfortable for one, did not stretch to the startlingly increased utility and food bills run up by three and I now routinely plundered my savings to make up the shortfall.

On the morning of transmission – or TX as Dee insisted on referring to it – I overheard Pixie on the phone to Stella saying she'd changed her mind.

'Can't they just cancel the whole thing? Oh, did I? Okay. I just ... Yeah. No, I'll just watch it here. With Gwen.' Ending the call, she turned to me with an air of hopelessness. 'Did you hear that? There's no way of pulling out.'

'It's a bit late in the day for that, Pixie. An entire team will have worked on it and they'll have planned the running order.'

'I haven't slept a wink,' she said, groaning. 'I'm so worried.'

'Hold your nerve. Remember no one's going to know it's you. Only us and the TV people. And they've never been told *his* name. If he or anyone else treating women in this horrendous way happens to watch it, then it might jolt them into a conscience and make them stop.'

She nodded. 'Maybe something big will happen and they won't have time to show it? Like a terrorist attack or a new war or something.'

'Yes, let's hope for that,' I said wryly. 'Should I invite Dee down for the viewing?'

'I'd rather it was just us,' she said. 'I don't want to make a big deal of it.'

This suited me and also meant Dee would be free to celebrate more openly, doubtless in the company of an equally gratified Richard. Their daughter's first TV news feature, gateway to the next stage of her illustrious career: the champagne corks would be popping in the hallowed turrets of flat 32.

Stella, we'd learned, was out of town for another project, but would be watching from her hotel room. You certainly couldn't fault her work ethic.

News Radar aired at 10 p.m. and Pixie, Daniel and I gathered on the sofa as it began, Pixie in the middle, all of us with large fortifying glasses of wine. There was an update on Westminster politics to sit through, the new ways the UK was going to the dogs and all our own fault, according to the government, and Daniel and I grumbled along. Too nervous to speak, Pixie broke her silence only once and that was to comment that the presenter's blouse was a really horrible colour (and so it was, a kind of deathly sludge brown).

Next up was some new royal to-do indistinguishable from the last, which roused Daniel to make a brief plea for republicanism and made me wonder, idly, if that had ever been one of his sister's causes.

Then, finally, it was time.

> **Presenter:** Britain's housing crisis rolls on, with every week bringing plenty of new scandals but precious few practical solutions to the country's worst shortage since the Second World War. As renters grapple with ever-shrinking options, a shocking new trend has emerged. Stella Wilcox reports ...

'Oh fuck,' Pixie whispered. She was squeezing her wine glass so tightly I feared it might crack and slice her hand open.

'It'll be over in a couple of minutes,' I assured her.

It opened with the Leicester-based victim, who, like Pixie, was in her twenties but exhibited more of the worn-down desperation you'd associate with a victim of abuse. Stella handled her very ably, her tone gentle and compassionate, with a subtle awareness of the fact that she and her interviewee were of similar youthfulness. You could see Stella was in the advanced stages of pregnancy and there was a poignant disconnect between the happy evidence of her conventional male-female mating and the squalid corruption of it experienced by her subject.

In the next scene, she grilled a junior housing minister, whose heart went out to vulnerable renters and insisted legislation was on the cards to stop this and other 'harmful practices'. A housing charity spokesman was next.

'Have they cut you out or what?' Daniel said to Pixie.

'I hope. Might as well slay this,' she said with bravado, distributing the rest of the bottle of wine between our three glasses.

It was as she slid the empty bottle to the floor that she finally appeared on screen. In the promised silhouette, of course, the inference being that she'd be at grave risk if her identity was revealed and must therefore be the victim of a more dangerous landlord than that of the first girl. Her words, dubbed by an actor, were new to Daniel and I could see he was shocked.

'You'd never know it was you,' he said. 'That's not even your voice.'

'I know. Yeah. I did say all that though,' Pixie said, the release of tension tangible now she knew she'd been protected as agreed. She was swiftly replaced by a domestic abuse campaigner talking about blurred lines and desperate decisions.

This was followed by a surprise: Stella had secured an interview with a perpetrator, filming him from behind, his hood up, sitting across a table from her. Whether by accident or design, she was beautifully sunlit, an almost celestial inquisitor.

Stella: How do you respond to domestic abuse campaigners who say what you've been doing is a form of rape?

Landlord: I wouldn't call it rape, no. Definitely not. It's more like they're escorts or something.

Stella: But an escort is hired for a self-contained job before they return to their homes. Your tenant lives with you. This **is**

their home. Doesn't that make it more like a kind of domestic slavery?

Landlord: I don't think of it like that. It's just, I don't know, mutually convenient, you know what I'm saying? The way I see it, she's saving herself quite a bit of cash. I could've got market rate for that room.

'Incel bastard,' Daniel muttered.

'Brave to allow himself to be questioned, though,' I pointed out. And clever and resourceful of Stella because it was clear this final interview balanced the piece, elevated it. She'd done well to unearth him, when most of these monsters were probably like Alec, denying their violations and threatening anyone who dared suggest otherwise.

All in all, it was slickly produced, with an important feel. *Well done, Stella*, I thought. She'd done the two girls proud.

It was right at the end, as she was wrapping up, that the problem arose. Immediately after the first girl was seen turning into the gate of a terraced house in the Midlands, the shot switched to an indistinct female figure in a shapeless coat and woollen hat walking through what looked suspiciously like Winifred Gardens.

Stella: Remarkably, while one of the women we interviewed has now moved to another part of the city, safe from her abuser, the other still lives in the same building as the landlord she's accused of taking advantage of her ...

To my astonishment, the figure was now seen crossing Clayton Street and approaching the main doors of Columbia Mansions. Pixie wasn't recognizable, scrupulously shot from behind, the oversized coat masking her build, but, as she slipped inside, the camera closed in on the doors and clearly showed the date painted above: 1896.

> **Stella:** Which only underlines the point that when it comes to housing, even at the upper end of the market a safe haven is criminally hard to come by.

The feature ended, the studio presenter offering an earnest line of summary and a helpline number for others affected by the issue, before introducing the next item.

Concerned for my racing pulse, I took a succession of deep breaths before speaking. On Pixie's other side, Daniel's silence told me he too understood the cause for alarm.

'Say something, one of you,' she said, finally. 'Was I that terrible?'

'I thought you came across really well,' I began, 'but … Did you know they were filming you here? That last little bit,' I clarified, when she looked puzzled. 'I thought you only did the studio interview?'

'Oh, yes, I forgot all about it. It only took a couple of minutes.'

'I don't remember you mentioning it at the time.'

'I think you were back at the hospital that day, maybe? Your post-op thingy?' Tiny stitches appeared in her smooth forehead. 'What? Should they have got permission from the board? You couldn't tell it was me, could you? I was wearing the camera guy's coat.'

'No, it could have been anyone. It's not that, Pixie.'

'They showed the date above the door,' Daniel explained.

'Not the name though,' she countered.

'The building's very distinctive,' I said. 'Anyone could do one of those picture searches and find the address in seconds. Plus all the locals know it. *And* all the people who live in it.'

'But how would they know it's about *him*?' Pixie said. She still didn't get it.

'There are only thirty-two flats, Pixie, and how many have single male owners?'

'Loads, I would have thought.'

'Three.' I named them: Alec, Elliot, and an American expat called Reid at number 12. 'And only one of those has been renting out a room to a female tenant. A female tenant currently sleeping on her neighbour's sofa.'

There was a silence. Daniel coughed into his hand, then kept it there, covering his face.

'Is this bad?' Pixie asked at last.

'It could be. We need to pray Alec doesn't get wind of it.'

She brightened a fraction. 'I'd never heard of this show before; maybe he hasn't either? Or any of the other neighbours?'

It was the same tone she'd used when hoping for a terrorist attack. She was mind-bogglingly naive. But so was I in my own way, I thought, as my phone sprang to life with the first alerts from the residents' WhatsApp group.

So was I.

31

I didn't think to blame Dee at first. Yes, she'd initiated the connection between Pixie and Stella – you could go so far as to say brokered – but I believed it was purely Pixie's foolish agreement to be filmed here that brought the scandal to our door.

The door to a building that was architecturally flamboyant, with turrets and bays and cherubs, with beautiful gardens and private parking. The door to a building where affluent people lived – as Stella had put it, *the upper end of the market*.

I'd noticed recently that tall poppy syndrome had acquired itself a machete. A new generation of media wanted not so much to take the successful down a peg or two as hack them into strips (even when said journalists were, like Stella, among their number) and I didn't need to google it to know that the other property featured in Stella's report would escape all but minimal notice. Not only was it of the red-brick terraced variety common up and down the land, but Stella had explicitly stated that the victim had moved from the address where the abuse occurred.

Neither victim nor perpetrator still in residence to be doorstepped.

The first outlet to pick up on the story was the *Standard*:

Sex for Rent Scandal Rocks Historic Mansion Block

One of South London's most desirable buildings has featured in a BBC news story about the escalating rental crisis. Columbia Mansions in Queens Oak has been caught up in the growing trend for sex for rent, an arrangement whereby tenants – usually female – pay landlords for their accommodation in the form of sexual services. According to the BBC News Radar *report, both landlord and tenant remain in the building.*

The landlord is said to be a man in his late forties or early fifties who has lived in the block for several years.

'Is said to be,' I repeated aloud, though it was 7 a.m, and I was alone in my bedroom. 'Said by whom?'

A separate box detailed the market rate for a rental flat in the building and placed it in a league table of 'South London's Poshest Blocks'. Pictures of the building, as well as one of the gardens taken with a comically wide lens that made it look like Brideshead levels of parkland, accompanied the feature.

I'd long since preferred reader comments to actual articles and these ran the usual gamut:

What a sleazoid, omg.

Saw the News Radar doc. The girls are so much younger than them, super icky. Bet they wouldn't want some old perv doing that with THEIR daughter. Makes me want to vom.

I'd screw him for a flat in that building. Mind you, I'm a 20-stone bloke in my 60s so I might not be his type

Simple solution – DON'T LIVE IN LONDON! It's a cesspit!!!

Our WhatsApp group had been in overdrive since the previous night, Dee having been unable to make it to bed without committing to an emergency town hall at 9 a.m. A quick scroll first thing told me that Alec had neither left the group nor been removed from it; it was impossible to know if he had notifications on, but he hadn't contributed since his ejection from the board meeting. Was he even aware yet of the story breaking? And if he was, would he come to the meeting?

I was full of dread as I had coffee with Pixie. She wasn't in the WhatsApp group, but I shared the *Standard* piece with her and watched her face turn pale as she read it. 'This is why I was so worried last night. Has Stella got back to you?'

At my urging, she'd phoned Stella immediately after the programme had ended and left a voicemail expressing her concern about her address being traceable.

'Yeah, she just messaged. She said she had no idea they'd show that.'

I suppressed a snort of disbelief. There was not a cat's chance in hell Stella hadn't known about the filming. She was the creator of the piece, the narrator – and presumably writer – of that damning 'upper end' line. She'd known a shot of glamour, the inclusion of some obvious 'haves' in a story concerning 'have-nots' would attract attention and so it had.

'Can she at least get it edited out before it goes on the BBC website?' I suggested.

'I'll ask,' Pixie said, and began texting at once.

'Are you coming to the meeting?'

She looked up from her screen. 'Do I have to?'

'Of course not. It might be best if you don't, to be honest. It's possible he'll be there and names will be named. Let's keep you out of the fray.'

*

We met in Hester's flat directly below mine – Dee's suggestion, ostensibly to save me having to climb so many flights of stairs to hers, but I wonder now if she wasn't already putting space between her and the brewing scandal. I'd known that the *Standard* report would act as a clarion call, but it was still a shock to see a gathering of strangers in the street – media, presumably, or amateur gawker types. Most had their phones turned to the building and some tried to engage with those residents leaving their front doors and walking the short distance to enter ours.

Hester closed the shutters on them and turned on the overhead lights, which gave proceedings a stark, institutional air. All in all, there were about twenty of us, including retirees, homeworkers and one or two who'd been able to delay going into the office.

Alec was not there, thank God.

Whether by prior agreement with Dee I do not know, but Noel took it upon himself to lead the session. 'Just so we're clear,' he began, 'is everyone aware who this story concerns?'

Everyone was, confirming my instinct that this was one of the world's easier mysteries to solve; if those gathered outside did not yet know the identities of the two parties, they surely soon would. What was still news to some in attendance was the relationship of the reporter to the chair of our board. The longer-standing residents knew Stella from when she'd lived here with Dee as a student, and some of the rest had met her at Bonfire Night and other parties, but a minority needed bringing up to date.

'How did she get permission to film the building?' one demanded.

'Why did she *want* to, more to the point?' another asked.

'It's doxing, isn't it?' Sadie said, explaining for the benefit of

Liz and the other elders that this meant publicly identifying private information about an individual.

'Usually with malicious intent,' Elliot added.

Though she surely must have been expecting something like this, Dee looked mortally offended by this last remark. 'Oh, I can assure you there was nothing remotely malicious about Stella's intent. I think she was as surprised as we were that the shot was included.'

The same fudged line Stella had fed Pixie. I admit I was disappointed; I'd thought Dee might express at least mild disapproval, perhaps citing Stella's inexperience in the face of pressure from cynical BBC staff.

'Did she not see the finished video before it was broadcast?' I asked.

'She helped edit it, of course, but it was all very last minute as I understand. Let's face it,' Dee continued, gesturing towards the street, 'she wouldn't wish this sort of attention on her own mother, would she?'

'Or on the victim,' I said delicately.

'That goes without saying.' Dee turned crossly from me to address the group. 'For me, the important thing is we've put a stop to a horrible and exploitative situation. I wouldn't have known about it myself had not Gwen informed the board – for which we should all be very grateful.'

That was a skilful deflection, I thought, as everyone looked at me. Now they knew just who'd got this ball rolling.

'Many of us have been here before,' she added, 'we know the ropes when we're under siege like this. It will blow over and until then we stick together. Right, Gwen?'

Oh, cleverer still, reminding me – if not the others – of her support when it had been *my* daughter to stir up trouble. 'Dee's right,' I said. 'There was never any intention on Stella's part to bring Columbia Mansions and our residents into disrepute and it won't help us if we get distracted by infighting. Before we do anything else, I'd like to suggest that we remove Alec from the WhatsApp group so we can freely share information and suggestions between us.'

This was unanimously agreed and Dee removed him on the spot. Would he get a notification, I wondered? It was a moot point given that as we talked we could hear the clamour in the street getting louder, not to mention flat buzzers going up and down the stairwell. Unless Alec had overslept to the point of coma, he must know by now that something unusual was happening.

Dee then answered a few questions about the investigation she'd undertaken on behalf of the directors and how Alec had been told in no uncertain terms the practice of sex for rent was unacceptable.

'How are we only hearing about this now?' Hester asked.

'Because we hoped to protect Pixie,' she said, adding fervently, 'We still do.'

'We should mention that he denies the allegation,' Noel said. 'We're going to talk to him again as a matter of urgency and try to find a solution.'

Several residents wanted to know if Pixie had gone to the police with her accusations and I found myself echoing her phrase about the practice not being unlawful.

It was then that one brave soul asked what everyone wanted to know: 'But what did she actually have to do?'

'She answered that in her interview,' Hester said. '"Whatever he wanted, whenever he wanted" were her words, I believe.'

'Oh. How horrible. The poor girl.'

'Yes,' I said. 'Which is why whatever we decide to do, it needs to be in the interests of keeping her safe.'

'Absolutely right, Gwen,' Dee agreed. 'Now, we need to get these people to leave. Before Alec decides to come down and make things worse.'

Disputing Stella's story in the process, I thought.

It was agreed that she and I would go out and try to reason with the mob. And a mob it had become, we saw, as we surveyed the scene from the steps. Maya couldn't have orchestrated it any better in her heyday, there were even a few signs: 'WOMEN'S BODIES ARE NOT FOR RENT!' and 'NAME HIM NOW!' It was breathtaking how quickly they'd convened, but that was social media for you. Outrage was the typhoid of our time.

At the sight of our arrival, those who'd been trying other doors raced to ours, causing passing drivers to slow and check out the drama. Across the street in Winifred Gardens, several people gravitated to the railings. Everywhere you looked there was the small rectangular gleam of a phone screen.

Standing dead centre on the steps, with me to her left, Dee addressed the assembled in the steely style of the wife of an MP who'd been caught with his trousers down. 'I'm Dee Carmichael, chair of the directors of the building, and I'd like to make a short statement.'

She did not introduce me, either by name or role, and I could only look on mutely as she spoke. Already irked by her manipulations in the meeting, I resented the way she'd taken control of this too, not even conferring with me about the intended wording.

'We are aware of the BBC *News Radar* feature and the story in the *Standard* and we do not intend to speculate on either of these or on any further stories that appear. We politely request that you respect the privacy of our residents. There are no celebrities or public figures in this building, just ordinary people, the vast majority of whom had no prior knowledge of this matter.' Her resolve wavered slightly as she finished, perhaps recognizing that 'vast majority' had been a mistake.

'That's all, thank you,' she added, but sure enough, someone had picked up on the blunder.

'How many residents *did* know then? Why didn't they blow the whistle?'

'I'm really not in a position to say,' Dee said. 'We're conducting an internal investigation and—'

But hecklers drowned her out. 'Who's the landlord? Which flat's he in?'

'What nationality is he?'

'How long has he been taking sex for rent?'

'Did the rent include bills as well or were they extra?'

The last caused a shower of laughter and Dee lifted her chin in disgust.

'Who is he?' screeched the young woman holding the 'NAME HIM NOW!' placard, and Dee pulled back her shoulders.

'I will *not* be telling you that.'

'How old is the victim?' another woman demanded. 'Is she millennial or Gen Z?'

'Is she British?' someone asked at the same time.

'I believe the BBC feature answered those questions,' Dee said, back on safe ground. 'She is British and in her twenties. I have nothing more to add, so please move on and let's all get on with our day.'

As the racket intensified, she stepped back over the threshold, signalling for me to follow almost as you would summon a pet. As our eyes met, I was shocked to see satisfaction in hers, even relish, and all at once I understood that she had not only found it in her heart to forgive Stella for allowing our home to be besieged in this way, but was also ready to make a virtue of it. After all, further attention, if not a full-blown storm, would keep the video in the spotlight, enhance its currency; it would be amassing views by the second on the BBC website and social media.

'*Gwen?*'

A more sinister thought struck: was it beyond the realms of possibility that Stella – and indeed Dee – had intended throwing Pixie under the bus from the outset? Identified her as a chronic people pleaser with a doozy of a personal problem and used her entirely for their own ends? Intuition told me the answer was yes, bringing about an internal gear change that made me feel morally unassailable.

'I'll be with you shortly, Dee,' I said curtly, and stepped away from her to address the throng myself. 'Hello, everyone. My name is Gwen Healy and I'm a resident here. I'd just like to say that the most crucial thing in a situation like this is to protect the victim's anonymity and that is what we will continue to do.'

I swear I intended leaving it there; I'd only wanted to add my voice, to be heard as Dee had been heard, to demonstrate that I was not the puppet she took me for. And had the chant not started up, I'm sure I'd have turned on my heel, my need quenched.

'Who is she?' voices shouted, instantly joined by others in a ghastly refrain: 'Who is she? Who is she?'

Somehow this had turned from a demand for *his* name to a demand for *hers*.

'Stop! This is harassment,' I cried, my anger spiking. A carousel of faces began spinning through my mind – Dee, Pixie, Brian, Cyndi – before arriving at the correct one. 'If you're going to harass someone, harass *him*, the sex offender.

'His name is Alec Pedley.'

32

Adrenaline sustained my self-belief in the immediate aftermath of this unplanned denunciation, long enough to get me back inside the building and behind closed doors. Most of those who'd been at the meeting had gathered in the lobby to support us in our amateur press conference and their dominant reaction was shock – expressed by a collective hush.

'We're wondering,' Dee began, as flustered as I'd ever seen her, 'was that a good idea?'

'Oh, they'd have found out sooner or later,' I said, with feigned nonchalance. 'They can easily get a list of residents' names from the council or wherever. Freedom of information and all that.'

'I wonder if we need to get some security in place?' Noel said, his face pinched with stress.

'We don't need security,' I said crisply. 'It's not the Profumo scandal. Like Dee said, it will blow over.'

She didn't agree or meet my eye and I could tell what she was thinking: *That was before you veered so disastrously off script.*

Elliot gestured to the stairwell, drawing the group's attention to the resumption of the mass ringing of buzzers. 'I don't understand why he hasn't come down.'

'He must have headphones on,' Hester suggested.

'I think I'd better go and talk to him,' Dee said. 'I can break the news gently, urge him to lie low for a while for his own safety.'

'He's not the victim here,' I protested.

'No, but we need to contain this. Regain control of the narrative.'

I wondered if she'd already texted Stella word of my misstep. If not, then she soon would.

'I'll come with you,' Noel told her.

'Would one of you mind carrying my rollator?' I asked. As I began my agonizingly slow ascent, Dee hastened to take my arm while Noel brought the walker. Neither spoke, obviously wary of what I might do next, and I felt my bluster begin to ebb.

In the flat, Daniel was in his room, door closed, and Pixie in the living room, still in her pyjamas, headphones on. It appeared that neither was aware of the scene at the front of the building or had heard our buzzer going and for once I was grateful for their self-absorption.

I could hear Dee on the landing: 'Are you in there, Alec? Can you come to the door, it's important!'

'It's just us,' Noel added. 'Dee and me, no one else!'

Not Gwen, he meant. I was no longer in the circle of trust.

Our buzzer went again and I took a moment to disable it before ducking into my bedroom to check the window. There was still a sizeable horde below, many on the steps, presumably working the doorbells and hoping the mad old lady would come back out and make some more ill-judged disclosures.

Googling Alec's name, I quickly encountered the very problem my comrades had feared: since he was a director of a company, he was listed on the government Companies House website, one of the top results. There he was: *PEDLEY, Alec Robert*, along with his date of birth and full address, including flat number.

Oh dear.

Cracking open our front door, I saw that Dee and Noel had given up on Alec and left, though the faint drone of his buzzer could be heard. If he didn't want to lose his mind, he'd need to follow my lead and remove the batteries.

I could delay debriefing Pixie no longer.

'You're back! How did it go?' She lowered her headphones and looked at me nervously. 'Did they all see the show? Are they going to be okay about it?'

'I'm not sure. A few journalists have arrived, actually ...' I paused. 'They know Alec's identity now so I imagine their focus will be on him.'

Colour flooded her cheeks. 'Wait ... What? Does that mean they know mine as well?'

'No, and hopefully they won't. But let's keep on top of social media, just in case.' A thought occurred. 'Pix, is your dad on anything? Twitter? Facebook?'

'Don't think so, no.'

'He hasn't ever been here, has he?'

Again, no, which meant he would not know the building if he saw it online or in the papers.

'Well, let me know if you need any advice talking to him. And you might want to check in with Ash and any other friends who could recognize the place. They'll be worried about you.' I sounded like some sort of spin doctor, across all angles, but I knew I was just playing for time, obscuring my own blunder. As Pixie's fingers began working her phone, Dee called on mine and I moved out of earshot.

'He wouldn't come to the door so I've gone back up to my place. He knows what's going on, though, because I've just had a very unpleasant message from him. He seems to think I'm the one who gave his name to the media.'

I felt my face blaze with heat. 'Did you say it was me?'

'I haven't answered yet, but since a whole bunch of people videoed it, he's obviously going to find out the minute it's online. I'm going to text him back now and say he needs to stay in his flat. We'll tell the rabble out there he's on holiday or something.' She sighed heavily. 'In retrospect, that impromptu press call wasn't our best move.'

At least she said 'our' and not 'your', I thought.

I returned to the living room to find Pixie's horrified gaze already on me.

'Look at this, Gwen. Oh my God, they know everything.' She passed me her phone.

Columbia Mansions Sex Pest is 90s Pop Has-Been

In the last few minutes, a representative for the building caught up in the BBC News Radar *sex-for-rent controversy named the alleged offender as former 90s pop star Alec Pedley.*

Pedley was in grunge act Empty Cloud, scoring a hit with 'Take Me If You Want Me'. Though the band appeared on The Chart Show*, the song would prove to be a one-hit wonder and the group disbanded in 1998.*

Standard Online *has reached out to Mr Pedley for comment.*

'They don't know *everything*,' I reminded her brightly. 'They don't know who *you* are.'

'What representative?' she said as I handed her phone back. 'Was that Dee? Why would she do that? Does Stella know?'

I grimaced. 'It was me, actually.'

'You?' It took her less than thirty seconds to find the damning footage, newly dropped, my words broadcast to all who cared to listen and now filling the space between us: *If you're going to harass someone, harass him ...*

'I was trying to stop them from focussing on you,' I said, speaking over my own recorded indignation, 'before they find a list of names.' Only now did it occur to me that Pixie's name would not be on any formal registers for flat 4. She didn't pay council tax or utility bills.

She didn't pay *anything*.

'Right. Okay. Wow.' I could tell she felt she was in no position to criticize me given she had outed us in the first place and I reminded her that neither of us was to blame for what was happening, *Alec* was, and we went together to listen at the flat door. By now, reporters were in the building and on the landing, calling out to Alec that they were pushing notes under his door with their phone numbers. Given their resourcefulness, I figured they'd soon get his phone number and abandon these vintage methods.

'What's going on?' Daniel asked from the doorway, having finally emerged from his room, marks on his cheeks from his pillow.

'Pixie will update you.' Hearing voices out on the landing, I snatched up my crutches and dragged myself back out, where three people – all young activist types – turned as one. 'Leave now or I'll call the police!'

They responded with the usual cruel jibes and so I began prodding them with one of my crutches. Daniel came out and between us we shooed them from the building.

'Take the battery out of your buzzer,' I yelled through Alec's door.

'I can't stay here,' Pixie said, when we were back inside. 'I can't face him. He's going to come after me.'

'Has he contacted you?' Daniel said.

'No, but he will, won't he? What if he comes into the café later and has a go? What if he, I don't know, grabs me on the stairs? Just shuts me in his flat, tapes over my mouth and keeps me prisoner?'

'I don't think he's going to do that,' I said, noting how quickly her imagination grew wild. My phone was ringing: Dee again. I put the call on speaker this time in the hope of her being able to help calm Pixie.

'Elliot says there's been trouble on your stairwell. Was it Alec?'

'No, just the mob. We sent them packing. Alec's still holed up, so he's obviously following your advice.'

'Good. My guess is he won't confront you. He'll know any attempt at intimidation will come back to bite him.'

'What do you think we should do moving forward?' I asked.

'Let's wait it out. See if it calms down. I'll send a message to the group chat asking everyone to be vigilant.'

'What does she mean, "come back to bite him"?' Daniel asked me when the call ended, still not up to speed on the morning's mayhem.

'Just that it will look bad if he assaults an old woman like me.'

'It's not you I'm worried about,' he said, somewhat ungallantly.

He and Pixie had an afternoon shift together and we agreed they should go in as planned, both under strict instructions not to divulge anything to curious colleagues or customers.

'Say you've never met him, that you hardly know any of your neighbours. Have you mentioned him by name to anyone?' I asked Pixie.

'Not really.'

I found this hard to believe. She was sociable, even garrulous, and while I didn't think for an instant she'd have disclosed the sex-for-rent detail, she must have referred at some point to her live-in landlord.

'What about Instagram?'

'No. Never.' On this score, she was more certain and I had an inkling of what might be the psychology behind it. She hadn't wanted to validate Alec in the primary way her generation validated their actions, preferences, their very existence. In her curated social media world, he had no role.

'Try to look like a couple when you leave,' I advised them. 'If anyone asks, say you heard the girl's moved on. Beyond that, just keep schtum.'

33

I was fearful of being alone in the flat, but, in the event, the hours passed without interruption. If Alec knew to reassign blame from Dee to me, which he surely must by now, then he'd evidently decided against issuing any immediate reprisals.

Online, updates dropped constantly, attracting hundreds and then thousands of comments until there were too many for me to keep up with. On WhatsApp, Dee circulated her promised instruction to everyone to be on their guard:

> While we are subject to media interest, please go down to meet guests and collect deliveries in person. DO NOT buzz anyone in.

There followed multiple messages about Alec from those who had not been at the meeting and were now catching up.

> Reid
> This guy isn't still in the building, is he?

> Dee
> He's in his flat, yes

Sadie
You sure? I haven't heard a peep from above. How is Pixie? Is she on here?

Gwen
She's fine.

Karishma
Just looking at X right now. Holy smoke. Not sure why you said what you said, Gwen, tbh. This has really blown up.

Gwen
Maybe not the best tactic in retrospect. I apologize to everyone for the increased scrutiny.

Noel
It's done now. Let us know if any argy-bargy, Gwen.

The afternoon delivered a tabloid interview with the girl I'd met in Station Square who'd been offered Alec's room before Pixie:

Lucky Escape for South London Gen Z Renter

A Gen Z renter has spoken of her near miss with 'pop perv' Alec Pedley, alleged to be in the habit of waiving rent in exchange for sex. Cara Rowland was confident she'd bagged his spare room in swanky Columbia Mansions before it went instead to the unnamed lodger who has since appeared on BBC TV to expose the carnal demands of the Empty Cloud rocker.

'He showed us the room in a group of three,' says Cara. 'There was no suggestion of sex for rent, at least not to me, and I wasn't aware of him propositioning either of the other girls.

He said the rent was £1,500 minimum. He drove a hard bargain, actually.' Though initially offered the room, just days later she got a message from the landlord saying he'd had a change of heart.

He even tried to pass his preferred sex tenant off as a relative, Cara added. 'He told me she was his niece, which is super unsavoury. I really feel like I've had a lucky escape.'

Not daring to look outside, let alone step out onto the landing again, I put my phone aside and did my knee exercises, before spending a fretful stretch making a moussaka for dinner. Luckily, I'd stocked up on ingredients in an online order delivered the day before and so did not have to leave the premises and risk attracting – or causing – any more trouble. An old Wimsey dramatization on Radio Four eased my jitters somewhat.

Maya had left a voicemail earlier and while the moussaka was baking, I returned her call. As @stayathomesiren, she'd long surrendered her appetite for political engagement, but it was inevitable that column inches about Columbia Mansions would stir old outrage.

'I *knew* there was something weird about that building,' she tutted.

'It's nothing to do with the building,' I said. 'It's one rogue resident.'

'That's all it takes,' she said darkly. 'So is Pixie still staying with you? Shame our new garden room's behind schedule or she could have used that to hide out.'

'What?' I was taken aback that she knew Pixie – a woman she had never met – was the figure at the centre of this. Thank God for slow builders; I had visions of Pixie being roped into her trad wife routines, Alec's camera lens replaced by hers.

'Quite clever to keep her there,' she said, after running through the costly programme of renovations she and Jason planned once said garden room was finished. 'After that TV doxing, everyone'll assume she got the hell out of there. Yeah, that's clever, Mum.'

'Let's see,' I said modestly. Her assumption that our current state of chaos was the result of considered planning, not blunder and improvisation, was more comforting than I might have expected.

But the feeling was short-lived, for Pixie and Daniel returned from work with tales of grappling with TikTokers in conditions just short of hand-to-hand combat. I began to understood that the siege conditions I'd helped create might very well get worse before they got better.

'There's people with, like, a proper TV camera,' Pixie said as we ate dinner together, heads angled from our plates towards our news feeds. 'Not just phones.'

'Way more true-crimers than earlier as well,' Daniel said, and played us a video of some moron proposing all landlords be chemically castrated.

'They're vultures. They see others circling and they circle too. Maybe you shouldn't watch this stuff,' I said to Pixie. 'It could be triggering for you.'

'It's all right. I'd rather know what was being said. How much they know.' Including whether she'd been named, she meant, and the answer, mercifully, miraculously, continued to be no.

'Has Stella not offered you sanctuary at her place?' I asked, remembering Maya's remarks. 'She must be back home by now, is she?'

Pixie gulped from her water glass. 'She says it's almost as bad there. Her phone hasn't stopped ringing.'

'That's good for her, though, isn't it? I expect we'll see her on TV talking about it.' It seemed laughable now that we'd viewed the *News Radar* item as a self-contained piece of work and hadn't anticipated that even without the leaking of the address it would spark further interest. Hadn't Stella said all along it would be a conversation starter? And yet I'd never considered how that conversation might sound or how long it might last.

'I'm not being funny,' Daniel said, 'but do you think he's okay over there?'

I looked at him, surprised. 'Alec?'

'I mean, has anyone even heard from him today?'

'Haven't seen him since on the stairs that time,' Pixie said. 'When he called me a slut.'

'He communicated with Dee this morning,' I said. 'He was quite rude, apparently.' I continued to be amazed I hadn't received any abusive messages of my own – and to try to take the win at face value.

'He hasn't been out much at all, has he? Even before today, since Pix moved out?' Daniel looked from Pixie to me, uncertain. 'I mean, this is quite hardcore. He wouldn't self-harm, would he?'

Pixie looked terrified. 'What?'

'I'm sure he's fine,' I said, though I wasn't sure at all. I didn't know him *that* well and everyone had their vulnerabilities, their personal cut-off points in terms of stress. Maybe he hadn't confronted me today for a far simpler reason than I had believed ... My mouth felt dry as I recalled Sadie's text – *I haven't heard a peep from above* – and I put down my fork. 'Go and knock on his door, Daniel.'

'I haven't finished eating,' he protested.

'You're the one who's worried! It'll only take a second.'

I got the sense he would have refused had it not been for Pixie sitting fearful-eyed across from him. While hardly the Lancelot of this piece, he wanted to avoid giving our damsel the impression he was chicken.

She and I waited out of sight while he rapped on the door to number 4.

'Alec? Alec? Are you okay? We're a bit worried.' He asked a second time before adding, 'Do you, um, need any food or supplies?'

'Tell him he can have some moussaka if he likes,' I called. 'There's a portion left.'

Daniel repeated this through the door and we all jumped when Alec replied in the phlegmy tones of someone who had not spoken in a while: 'Stuff your moussaka up your arse, Gwen.'

'Charming,' I said, but I felt lighter of spirit both in knowing he was alive and that he shared my preference to avoid a face-to-face confrontation.

The sense of respite didn't last long, however. As the other two stacked the dishwasher and I rested on the sofa with my leg up, my phone pinged with a message from my nemesis:

You have made a big mistake

As if I hadn't had all day to come to the same conclusion myself.

*

Sleep was fitful for all of us. I could hear Pixie up in the small hours, turning on the kitchen tap, pottering about. Then Daniel's voice as he joined her. At some point after dropping off again, I was startled back to consciousness by the sound of an engine firing in the car park below. I found my glasses and struggled to the window just in time to see headlights sweep through the gates and down Clayton Street.

Wide awake now, I rolled my walker into the kitchen to make myself a hot drink.

'Did I wake you?' Pixie said, her head emerging from her nest of duvets and throws on the sofa.

'I can't sleep,' I said, turning on the kettle and rootling for my preferred peppermint teabags.

'Me neither. I keep thinking he's going to, like, break down the door. Come for us with, I don't know, that knife he uses to chop garlic.'

'A paring knife? That's quite specific.' What strange associations her mind made. 'He's not coming for us with anything, so don't worry. He's left.'

'Really?' She bounced upright. 'Left the building? How do you know?'

'I just saw his car. Makes sense that he'd wait till the dead of night to make his getaway.'

'I wonder where he's gone.'

'Who knows. Let's just hope he doesn't come back for a while.'

'Or ever,' she said, sinking into contemplation.

Waiting for the kettle to boil, I caught sight of her expression in the gloom and found myself thinking of those true-crime reconstructions on TV, the shot when the ordinary, decent person has her first thought of doing something wicked. A secret, revelatory moment not meant for others' eyes.

34

Pixie slept in late after the broken night, so I delayed going through for my morning coffee to avoid disturbing her. I wondered if it might be an idea to install a kettle in my bedroom for the remainder of her stay.

Opening the curtains, I checked for activity in the street below. A small group had already assembled, whether newshounds or nosy parkers I couldn't tell, but all appeared to be taking photos or video of our front door. One girl stepped into the road to get a better shot, causing an approaching car to brake and the driver to peer out the window to see what she was filming.

It didn't take long to discover what it was. In the residents' WhatsApp group, a photo had been shared of graffiti daubed overnight: *RAPIST*. This was met with a string of outraged comments and Dee's promise to ask Steve to remove it as a priority.

I shared my news:

> You'll be pleased to know the 'rapist' has left. I saw him drive off last night.

But this did little to pacify the residents. They'd reached for their pitchforks and were demanding Alec's permanent expulsion from the building.

Sadie
If he's gone, can we change his locks?

Dee
I think that's illegal.

Noel
Definitely illegal.

Hester
Can't we do anything via the terms of his lease?

As the thread lengthened, Dee rang me. 'Noel and I think we should have another meeting to answer all these questions. Are you free for a Zoom at ten?'

I said I was. 'Before you go, Dee, how's Stella holding up?'

'Oh, bless you for asking,' she said. 'She's good, I think. Absolutely inundated, obviously. Deciding who she should speak to and who she should keep at arm's length.' There was no attempt to smother her pride and if I'd had any remaining doubt that she considered the pros of our scandal to at least equal and possibly outweigh the cons, I didn't any longer. 'Don't worry, Gwen,' she added, and I pictured her rearranging her face. 'She's got Pixie's back. She would *never* name names.'

Unlike *you*.

Heading online, I saw that the story had gathered pace.

Breaking news: Pop Sex Pest Flees Home

Breaking news? For heaven's sake, this wasn't international conflict or the death of a monarch. And how did they know this anyway, had someone been staking us out all night? I pictured a buff young journalist, though it was more likely to have been some obsessed amateur with bad skin and nothing better to do than sit shivering in an unheated car, phone at the ready.

New images had been procured, I saw, including ones of the graffiti, as well as shots of our lobby, stairwell, and of Alec's door, presumably captured by yesterday's invaders. But one picture, from the bonfire party, could only have been supplied by a resident or one of our guests: in it, Alec stood with Steve, both wielding long-handled tools and looking vaguely demonic against the red flames. The headline read:

The Building Where Morals Went Up in Smoke

Very witty, I thought, rolling my eyes.

Also, true.

*

The Zoom picked up where WhatsApp had left off as everyone clamoured to 'get him out for good'.

'To answer Hester's comment about the lease, I could ask a contracts specialist to go through it and see if there's anything I've missed?' Noel suggested, adding that this might not be the year to incur unnecessary costs such as additional legal fees, what with roof repairs looming (thank God we'd not yet issued notice of the additional service charge).

'Don't we have some kind of morality clause we can invoke?' Elliot asked.

'We're not his employers,' Noel said. 'The fact is even criminals need to live somewhere – not that he's one officially, I hasten to add. We could make a request that he leave on a more informal basis?'

'Should we wait and see if he comes back?' Dee suggested. Playing for time, I suspected.

'Maybe he'll stay away?' Karishma said. 'Rent the place out?'

That raised a few eyebrows.

'Goes without saying he needs to resign from the board,' Elliot said.

'He's already been suspended,' Dee assured him.

Don't get me wrong, I was baying for blood with the rest of them – indeed I had set this witch-hunt in motion – but now, with the benefit of hindsight, it's striking that no one challenged the notion of Alec's guilt, just as they had not at the previous meeting. Even Noel's legal cautions failed to emphasize any presumption of innocence. Pixie was unanimously believed, Stella's TV report had ratified her truth, and the public rushed in to comment and cancel. It was trial by media, an expedited new form of law, which was hugely satisfying – unless you were the accused.

As I say, it suited me as far as Alec was concerned, but I can't tell you how grateful I am that Brian's and my downfall had taken place in more rational times.

*

Immediately after the meeting, a text from Dee alerted me to the fact that Stella had decided on her preferred media partner: she would be on Sky News within the hour.

She's in the green room right now!

I noticed the message hadn't been sent to the wider group and nor had she given any inkling on the Zoom. She was keen, no doubt, to protect her reputation as a firefighter not a fanner of flames.

I tuned in, of course. Under glossy studio lights, Stella was hale and shiny-haired, while her fellow panellist, a spokesman for the Met, needed a shave and was visibly sweating. The backdrop was corporate, the female presenter standing up behind some sort of counter, dressed in one of those tailored dresses that look about as comfortable as a girdle.

As I joined, she was demanding the Met guy justify why the police hadn't yet questioned Alec Pedley and he was struggling to explain that the police had no powers to act on 'so-called sex for rent'. Even I could see it was a rookie error for the police to have put a male spokesman in the firing line like this and not a woman.

'On what basis *might* you get involved then?' the presenter snapped. 'You have to admit there's considerable public interest in this story.'

'If there were an accusation of assault, rape or harassment, then we would want to make inquiries,' he said. 'Or if the matter involved a false allegation.'

Stella cut in then, her sultry voice indignant: 'There's no false allegation, I can assure you of that.' She turned from him to the presenter. 'It seems to me journalists are doing the job of the police these days. Which might help explain why confidence in the police is at a historic low.'

'I'm not sure that's fair,' the Met guy protested. 'As I say, if any individual feels able to report a sexual assault, they will be treated with absolute sensitivity and confidentiality.'

Not long after, Stella's latest *Sunday Times* column dropped online early. In it she discussed the strains of her *News Radar* story having gone viral, leading to her being pursued by her own colleagues in the media. *I would hate anyone to think I was poacher turned gamekeeper*, she suggested in her right-minded way.

Her photo had been updated, I noticed, her high cheekbones now strikingly lit, presumably by a professional. Googling, I saw she'd acquired an agent and the same headshot was on her page on their website. Such upgrades could not possibly have been arranged overnight.

I returned to her column, skimming to the end. *It's a circus*, she concluded (was there was no end to her passion for metaphor?):

> It's a circus and I've accepted that I'm powerless to stop the show. I can only do my damnedest to help keep the headline act as far from the spotlight as possible.

Powerless to stop the show? What a joke. She was the bloody ringmaster.

35

It was, if I remember, the next morning that I trundled down to the kitchen for my morning coffee and noticed that Pixie's duvet and pillow remained in a bundle by the side of the sofa. Either she'd got up earlier than this seventy-year-old lark or she hadn't slept on the sofa in the first place.

Murmurs could be heard from behind Daniel's door, followed by her unmistakable giggle, and I felt my heart rate pick up as if in detection of an emergency. How long had this been going on? Even in the context of the wider crisis, it worried me, given their manifest unsuitability for one another. Pixie was vulnerable and in need of support not seduction, while Daniel was adrift and would benefit from a clear route forward, not the drama an entanglement with Pixie offered.

I knocked gently. 'Are you in there, Pixie?'

The giggling stopped at once. She did not reply so I said no more, made my coffee and settled in my armchair by the living room window. Sadie's twins were in the garden, kicking a ball before school, and I enjoyed a harmless five minutes watching their game before their mum called them in to put their coats on and I succumbed to news of our more scandalous activities. *Mail Online* had the morning's big update:

'Kinky Alec' Spotted in Peak District

Sleazy Nineties rocker Alec Pedley, who has been accused by his lodger of demanding sex for rent, has been tracked down to the Peak District where his old Empty Cloud band mate Barney Cole is believed to live. The two has-beens were seen drinking in the village pub, the Black Hart, Pedley – who has been dubbed 'Kinky Alec' by social media users – wearing ripped jeans, sports jacket and baseball cap.

A photo of two shambolic middle-aged men at an outdoor table with pints, cigarettes and a retriever on a lead, suggested the stay might be more than that of a fugitive passing through. From what I could tell, the 'sports jacket' was Alec's boules team strip, which I doubted would please the rest of the club members.

The story had only recently been published and had so far attracted just two comments:

They look rough. All that 90s partying catching up with them, LOL.

Saw them at the Forum in 97, they were really crap, people were booing.

Five minutes later, Pixie and Daniel appeared – seconds apart, both dressed – and conversed in private tones as they made tea and toast. I felt as if I were in one of those theatres where the audience sits in the middle of the action, the performers moving deftly around you, not making eye contact.

'Is there a reason you're ignoring me?' I said finally.

'Mum! I thought you were in your room,' Daniel said.

'This *is* my room – or one of them.' I stopped short of reminding him that I owned the property and paid all the bills. 'What's going on, guys? Pixie, did you sleep in Daniel's room last—'

Daniel interrupted, addressing Pixie: 'You don't have to tell her, Pix.'

'I know,' she replied.

'Tell "her" what?' *What am I, chopped liver*?

'Nothing,' he said, palms bared in exasperation.

But if he could be obdurate, she was a more sensitive creature. 'We'll let you know if there's anything *to* know,' she promised, advancing with her plate.

'Okay,' I said, adjusting my legs. Too much use of the stairs and not enough sleep was playing havoc with my recovery and when the buzzer went, I let out a long groan. I'd reactivated it after Alec left, which may have been premature. 'Can one of you get the door?'

It turned out just to be the postman with some bits of Christmas shopping – I was spreading the cost this year – and a stack of mail. Among the bills there were a few Christmas cards, including one from Yasmin. *PS,* she'd scribbled, *I'm shocked by this stuff about Alec*, and I wondered if the media had tracked her down as they had Cara. It seemed unlikely; most of those opining on the story – including me – had volunteered themselves.

'I'd like to give you something for my board,' Pixie said, joining me as she munched her toast, and though my instinct was to refuse – 'board' spoke of a long-term arrangement and no one had agreed to that – the pile of bills on my lap was evidence enough that I needed any extra I could get.

'Perhaps a small contribution. Thank you. I keep meaning to ask, did you ever hear from the ombudsman about your appeal?'

'No.' Her forehead crinkled. 'I'm in a queue. I asked around online and everyone says it can take months.'

'It's a disgrace,' I tutted.

'I don't know why I'm so unlucky,' she said, suddenly self-pitying. She had a smear of jam on her chin that looked a little like blood.

'Try not to think like that,' I said. 'Did you see they've tracked Alec down? But they still haven't found you.' As each hour went by this seemed to me more remarkable. Was it possible Maya had been right and that hiding Pixie in plain sight had been a strategic triumph?

'They've tracked him down? Where?' She looked stricken, almost stunned, as if she'd genuinely believed he might simply have vanished without trace. As I found the *Mail Online* story for her, she looked for somewhere to put down her plate, eventually balancing it on the arm of her chair. 'Where even is the Peak District?' she asked, scrolling through the report.

'Derbyshire.'

'Is that far away?'

'Far enough.'

This seemed to console her. 'I should get the rest of my stuff back then. From my old room?'

'Good idea,' I said. In the furore of recent days, I'd forgotten all about that. 'I'll come with you.'

*

I'm not sure what we expected to have changed. For the flat to have been transformed into a werewolf's lair perhaps? For Pixie's clothes to have been torn to pieces in a savage fit of revenge? On the contrary, her room appeared to be untouched, the door closed on the same jumble she'd left in her wake.

One alteration we'd been forewarned of by the police officer: in the shower room where the camera had been fitted there was now fresh grouting. It felt like an age since that day of charged confrontations, when Pixie's affairs were a private concern not known even to our fellow residents, much less a public scandal.

This being our first moment alone that day, I was tempted to ask her about this new development with Daniel (shades of my early enquiries about Alec – what was it I'd said? *I'm not sure that's an advisable dynamic for a romance* ... You don't say!) but guessing any criticism would find its way back to him, I decided against. Besides, she'd promised she would keep me informed.

Leaving her to stuff clothes into bin liners, I went into the living room and explored Alec's work zone. The computers and other kit he used for his music had the power turned off, but opening an Apple laptop, I found the screen lit up with the usual prompt for a password. I tried a couple – 'emptycloud', 'winifredboules' – before closing up again. Even if I'd struck lucky, I knew there'd be nothing to find; he'd have cleared his devices of anything compromising long ago.

In the kitchen, the full and slightly whiffy bin suggested our concerns about his not having fed himself had been unfounded. He'd obviously forgotten to empty it and so I called Daniel and got him to take it to the main bins downstairs; the last thing we needed was mice in the building.

'I'm finished,' Pixie announced, flushed from her clearance exertions, and Daniel had to be called upon once more to help drag the bags into our flat.

There wasn't space for them all in 'their' room, so half had to be stored in the living room, but again I bit my tongue, making no comment about not liking the clutter.

'Did you leave your key?' I asked her, remembering.

'Nah. I'll say I've lost it.' She sent me a mischievous look, a flash of the playful Pixie of old. 'Let him pay for a new one.'

'The power of small wins,' I said wryly.

'Maybe he'll stay there forever,' she said, suddenly earnest. 'In the Lake District?'

'*Peak* District. Yes, he might. That would be good.'

It was pure wishful thinking, of course. As his public denouncer – and recipient of that threatening text, I knew it was not a question of *if* he'd return but *when*. That as soon as he was ready to defend himself, he'd be back.

I take no pleasure in having been right about that.

36

Febrile though the mood was in the building, the board could no longer delay sending out demands for the service charge, complete with the extra £3,000 per household for roof repairs, and letters were duly dropped in pigeon holes, emails circulated.

If Dee, Noel and I hoped the shock would be eclipsed by the ongoing Alec-related chatter then we were woefully naive, because the outrage was both immediate and unanimous:

Elliot

What fresh hell is this service charge demand? Three words to our overlords: No way José.

Noel

We are not 'overlords', Elliot. We represent you.

Elliot

Not in this case you don't.

Hester

It's a crazy amount, Noel. Can't we postpone the repairs for another year?

Karishma
Think I'm going to have to sell up at this rate

Elliot
Not sure I'd want to be on the market while it's common knowledge a sex pest lives here

Karishma
You're right – we're being held to ransom here!

And so on.

Dee tried to take the heat out of it by confirming the date for the Festive Fizz, our annual drinks held in her apartment on the final Sunday before Christmas, but everyone knew this was paid for from the sinking fund and when Elliot retorted that he'd rather put the money towards the roof repairs there was a flurry of agreement. Dee countered that she would personally cover the party expenses this year 'to promote togetherness at a challenging time for us all' and even the most disgruntled could find no fault with that.

I had my own reasons for feeling ambivalent about the Festive Fizz but that's by the by. Dee's Mother Teresa piety notwithstanding, she was right. Infighting would get us nowhere. We needed to stay united for when the true enemy returned.

*

An update to the Peak District sighting duly appeared, reporting that an 'elderly' woman had been seen at the window of Kinky Alec's London flat. If he was following his own press, which he surely was, then he'd know I'd entered his property. Had

I officially trespassed? Pixie too, since he was no longer receiving 'rent' from her.

I was cross about the 'elderly' but not surprised. Judging by the grammar, the originator of the item was barely out of short trousers.

This hold-the-front-page scoop notwithstanding, it seemed to me that the story was starting to lose heat. New outrages had caught the attention of the media: an MP denounced as racist; a footballer in court for a child-support prosecution; a pensioner on a mobility scooter paralyzed by a mum speeding in her Tesla to her son's rugby practice. And Christmas was coming, of course, which meant celebrities were flaunting their curves at parties and supermarkets had seasonal bargains for shoppers to snap up while being condemned for colluding in shrinkflation.

Rain was expected and travel chaos predicted.

Even Stella had been downgraded, from TV to radio. While Pixie and I decorated the tree Daniel had transported over his shoulder from the florist's on Station Square, we tuned into a Radio Four consumer rights programme on which she'd been booked to opine on the rental crisis. I made some mulled wine and Pixie described the Christmas trees of her childhood ('She couldn't get enough fairy lights, my mum') and asked what Daniel had been like as a boy. It was the nearest we'd come to feeling normal since she'd moved in.

Then, quite unexpectedly, she said, 'What happened to that girl you told me about?'

'Who? You mean Dan's wife, Nella?'

'No, the girl you hired as your assistant. Are you still friends?'

As I think I've illustrated, Pixie was an instinctive, solipsistic thinker, and I wondered if she was considering *our* friendship, whether it would survive this crisis we were navigating together.

'We lost touch,' I said. 'It's something I have a lot of regrets about.'

'Not too few to mention then,' she said, quoting Dee, and we exchanged a smile.

Stella came on the radio then, speaking passionately about the shortage of affordable rentals in the capital and extolling the virtues of one particular senior living complex in North London that would make ideal accommodation for young people in need of a leg up.

Just got to wait for us to die first, I thought.

37

Amateur though my writerly instincts are, even I can sense that a calm-before-the-storm opportunity presents itself here, so I'm minded to circle back to Cyndi, since she's on my mind following that exchange with Pixie.

After she lost her job with us, I tried placing her through my network of contacts in the charity sector, but perhaps understandably no one was inclined to do me a favour – or to want to hire someone tarnished by her bosses' malpractice.

Once it was clear we would not be able to honour salary payments, she rang to ask me for a private loan. I had to explain I was barely scraping by myself.

'Could you do shop work or waitressing while you hunt for something new? Where are you living? Still in the houseshare?'

'No, I'm in this hostel now,' she said vaguely.

'Hostel?'

'I've been here before. As soon as I get a new job, I'll look for a new share.'

'You could come and stay here,' I offered, 'if you're desperate?' But with Brian still in residence, awaiting his hearing with an increasingly bad grace, this was a non-starter and we both knew it. 'I'll be in touch as soon as this is all settled,' I assured her.

I didn't know till later what came next for her. What with the complications of keeping a roof over the heads of two teenagers while simultaneously trying to sell it, not to mention the lingering threat of being charged myself (irrespective of Brian's promises), I confess I allowed myself to presume the best.

When, years later, the #MeToo movement exploded, I scanned those thousands of Facebook posts for one from her. I never saw her name, but it didn't mean it wasn't there, swept downstream in the deluge.

38

I was alone in the living room, doing my knee exercises, when the dreaded news broke on WhatsApp:

Hester

Have you seen AP's back? Saw him in the car park just now. Acting like nothing's happened

Instantly the thread was ablaze again, a bonfire of fear and outrage:

Sadie

Wtf?

Karishma

I feel really anxious

Sadie

Is he still going to be working in the garden? Tbh, I really don't want my boys having any contact with him.

Dee

Remember what we said. He won't be looking for trouble.

This last proved to be correct, for it quickly transpired that while Alec was no longer prepared to hole up day and night – as Hester reported, he was now going about his business freely – he intended to behave impeccably, even when bearing the attentions of the last of the doorsteppers. Photos and video clips of him inevitably found their way onto social media, but there was not the traction of the earlier phase of the scandal, the rampant liking and sharing and rushing to judgement. The mainstream press had mostly lost interest, beyond one 'Disgraced Rocker Home for Christmas' update in the *Standard*.

Meanwhile, details of his encounters with neighbours circulated almost in real time.

'Is it true what they're saying?' Elliot asked him outright, when their paths crossed in the lobby. 'That you *forced* that young girl?'

Alec smiled at him, his tone respectful as he replied, 'Don't believe everything you read, mate.'

Liz, it was reported, muttered, 'Shame on you, Alec,' when they passed in the street, but in place of the expected 'Fuck you!' he said nothing at all, choosing to rise above it.

On a third occasion, when his ally Steve, who had continued with his gardening duties throughout this period, came to his defence in the face of another resident's vitriol, Alec told him to let it go. 'Let them believe what they want to believe,' he said, and within moments this was being shared on WhatsApp:

Karishma
Not sure I can trust Steve if he's defending Alec.

Hester
Typical. Could've told you they'd stick together.

Sadie
Should we look for a new gardener?

Noel
Steve is entitled to his opinion. We all support free speech, don't we? Plus decent gardeners are a nightmare to find and his rate is very competitive.

Ironically, given our proximity, our household was among the last to come face to face with him. Pixie was first, bursting into the flat in great agitation having met him on the landing and been wrongfooted by his politeness.

'He really didn't say anything at all?' I said.

'Just "Hi, all right?". That kind of thing.'

'Okay, well that sounds manageable.'

Only with the large glass of wine she was pouring herself, it seemed. She consumed half of it in the first swallow. 'It's creepy how calm he is. It's worse than having a big argument.'

'I can only imagine how awful it is for you,' I said. 'Maybe it's time to ask around again? See if any of your friends have got a spare room going, or a sofa?'

'They haven't.' She paused, regarded me over the top of her wineglass. 'Daniel said he would lend me the deposit for a new place.'

'Really?' I was taken aback by this. 'I don't think Daniel has anything to lend.'

'Doesn't he?' She looked amazed.

'You know how much he earns, Pixie; you have the same zero hours contract. Plus, he's in the middle of financial negotiations with Nella.'

'What about the flat in Stoke Newington? I thought they owned that.'

'They do, but the deposit was hers and they've got a big mortgage. She'll buy him out, I imagine, but it won't be much and there'll be solicitor's fees to pay out of anything he gets.'

'Oh.' Still clutching her glass, she began plucking at her hair with her free hand. It was terrible to see her so distraught again. What was Daniel thinking raising her hopes in this way? As I'd feared, their 'romance' amounted to little more than the blind leading the blind.

'Let's give it a few days, see what the general reaction is to Alec being back,' I suggested. 'I haven't even seen him yet.'

'Because you haven't left the flat,' she pointed out, and I realized this was true.

'I will tomorrow. I've got Scrabble Club at Hester's. If I see him, I'll find out if he plans on staying.'

*

In fact, it took a couple of encounters for me to register how things were going to be. That Alec's faultless conduct with the rest of the residents, Pixie included, did not extend to me.

The first time, as I was leaving for that promised excursion to Hester's, I assumed it was a coincidence when his door was thrust open a second or two after mine, his dark-clad, rough-haired figure easing into view. Instantly bottling that promise to interrogate him – there'd be better opportunities, I told myself – I simply headed towards the stairs as if I hadn't seen him. Stairs were still giving me serious gyp and since he didn't overtake me, I surmised he'd either changed his mind or was, for whatever reason, heading up the stairwell not down.

But as I turned on the half landing, I started at the sight of him watching me from the balustrade, a reversal of that scene when

I'd watched as he harassed Pixie. Our eyes met and I frowned in query, but he neither spoke not moved, just stared at me cold-eyed.

As I say, I thought it a coincidence, a little opportunistic intimidation on his part, but when the same thing happened on my next two outings, I had to conclude that this was some sort of campaign.

'What?' I challenged him the third time. 'What is it?'

Again, he just stared in that same silent, disquieting way.

'Say something, man!'

Nothing.

'Well, stop staring then!'

From then on, any time he heard our door open he would come straight to his, but if it were discovered to be Pixie or Daniel – or, more often than not, the two of them together – he simply went back inside. The strange unsettling staring was reserved for me.

I decided not to discuss it with Pixie, who would naturally fear that this malevolence might at any time be applied to her, the original complainant. Ditto Daniel, who would automatically share my confidences with her. It crossed my mind too that such hypervigilance on Alec's part might lead to his deducing the altered nature of their relationship (after all, basic nosy neighbour behaviour had alerted me to hers with him). If so, he might be able to argue – or at least delude himself – that she simply slept with whoever she happened to be living with. How could he be a sex-for-rent landlord when the woman in question was working her way through every available man in the building?

I decided instead to consult Dee.

It had not escaped my notice that ever since my fateful doorstep announcement, she had kept a low profile both in terms of our friendship and Pixie's welfare. During the early part of my knee recovery – which happened to coincide with Stella's seduction of Pixie – she had stopped by almost daily with treats and offers of help, but lately she had not been seen at our end of the building at all and I struggled to remember the last time I'd seen her IRL, as they say. She'd missed the Scrabble session I'd attended and Pilates was out of the question for me for at least another few weeks.

Since I was still avoiding the four flights of stairs up to her place, I phoned her.

'Alec's giving me the silent treatment.' I tried to describe our face-offs without becoming emotional. 'He refuses to utter a single word.'

'I'd call that a win, Gwen,' she said smoothly.

'I find it menacing, to be honest.'

'Menacing? It sounds plain childish to me.'

'Have you or Noel been able to find out anything about his plans?' I asked, remembering my offer to gather information before Pixie and I resumed discussions about her moving on.

'I'm afraid not. He keeps fobbing us off. Says he's getting advice and will come back to us.'

Getting advice from whom, I wondered. 'Has Stella heard from him?'

'No.' Dee sounded surprised. 'But his beef isn't with her. She was just the messenger.'

The conduit, I thought. 'Well, so was I,' I protested, 'and with a significantly smaller audience.'

There was a rather pointed silence. No need for her to state the obvious that I had been the one to issue his name publicly – Stella, like most of the press, covered her back with the liberal use of 'alleged'.

'You called the police about the camera that time, didn't you?' she reminded me at last. 'So as far as he's concerned, you've pointed the finger twice now.'

This was an excellent point and not one I'd considered.

Dee sighed. 'I'm not sure what else to say, Gwen. He'll let us know what he intends to do in his own time. Until then, we have no choice but to live with the new normal.'

Well, thanks for the support, I thought, hanging up. I felt, in that moment, entirely alone.

*

The next time I ran into him in our respective doorways, I gritted my teeth and tried a different tactic, adopting a more conciliatory tone.

'Alec, I wondered, do you have a minute?'

Silence.

'Just five minutes, to talk this through?'

Silence.

'Okay, then I'd like to say on the record that I'm finding your surveillance of my movements threatening.'

Silence. He might at least have queried that 'on the record' since there was no witness and no evident device filming or recording my declaration. This was the kind of nit-picking he used to thrill to and his refusal to indulge in it only deepened my unease.

I sighed. 'You can't go on refusing to engage with me.'

Silence; even his breathing was inaudible. He couldn't have been less like his wise-cracking ebullient old self, the neighbour I'd once shared a bottle of Madeira with and howled with laughter.

But I don't want to think about that.

No sooner had I gone inside and stepped out of my shoes than I received a text message from him:

Oh, we'll be engaging soon enough, don't you worry.

39

I don't recall exactly which day it was, but not long after I'd received that second single-line taunt from my mute antagonist, Pixie asked me at breakfast if I was doing anything that morning.

'I'm going to look at a flat,' she said. 'Do you want to come?'

Obviously, I had questions, not least ones to do with funding and this loan Daniel had offered her, but instinct told me to let her lead. 'If there aren't too many stairs, yes. I'd love to.'

Knowing Alec would come to his door moments after I opened mine, I sent her down ahead, but it turned out something more important occupied him for once. Work, perhaps, or the call of nature. No one could make themselves available for glaring 24/7, could they?

In the street, Pixie consulted Citymapper and we took the bus towards Battersea. I was confused to be heading into town and not out, but she was tight-lipped about details, saying it was to be a surprise and remarking instead on my free bus pass.

'It must be great to be old. Free travel. Your amazing flat. You're so lucky.'

'I'd far rather have working legs,' I said. I worried about her mental health to be thinking this way. It was becoming clearer by the day that she had not fully processed her ordeal, and would not be able to while remaining neighbours with the man who had subjected her to such torment. And she was right to think that a passive Alec was at least as dangerous as an animated one, his indifference to her almost certainly a ploy. I crossed my fingers that the room we were about to look at might supply the solution.

We got off the bus near Battersea Park and she led the way to a mansion block near the main gates. 'Here we are.'

'Here?' I was flabbergasted. The building was far grander in scale than Columbia Mansions and even more ornate in style. There was no way Daniel would be able to stump up for this on her behalf. Was her 'surprise' news of her fraud repayment, or even of secret savings? She'd been working long hours, but even so, it would have to be a boxroom in the basement to be even halfway affordable in this pricy postcode. 'Where did you hear about it? On one of the spare room sites?'

She beamed at me. 'It's not a room. It's the whole flat.'

Before I could voice my trepidation, a young man approached from a nearby Mini Cooper branded with upmarket estate agent's livery and introduced himself as a 'negotiator'. 'Christina Boulter?'

'That's me.' Pixie spoke with a blithe confidence as obviously fake as the name she'd given, but he didn't seem to notice, ushering us through the main doors and into an immaculately conserved lobby dominated by a magnificent curved staircase that wouldn't have looked out of place in Kensington Palace.

However, it was only once inside the flat itself – all 1,800 square feet of it, with two huge bedrooms, plus a smaller one that was once the maid's room and that Pixie declared 'incredibly useful' (for self-guided meditation or gift-wrapping, perhaps?) – that I understood. This was one of her fantasy viewings. What had she said the very first time we met? *I'm just a time waster.* And now, by extension, so was I.

I'd seen this sort of prank in TV dramas, of course, usually women attending open house events and doing something childishly transgressive like stealing an ornament or sneaking into areas they'd been expressly asked not to enter, but this felt different. As she stood by the high windows overlooking Battersea Park, the trees a spindly mesh over the winter sky, well-heeled denizens arriving with dogs in quilted coats, Pixie radiated a happiness that was all too real. This was a precious interlude when she could believe she deserved the best, when she became the woman who the agent took her for, moneyed and privileged and entirely accustomed to the good life.

'Can I ask what you do?' he asked her.

'I'm an actor,' she said. 'In theatre.'

'Would I have seen you in anything?'

'Oh, I use a different name.'

This did not answer the question but had the desired effect of discouraging his line of questioning. He turned his attention to me, the picture of trained respect. 'And you're mum, are you?'

'No, I'm just a friend.'

'A very good friend,' Pixie said, reaching to take my hand. She really was the most affectionate creature. 'I love it,' she told him. 'I'm just waiting to hear about a play in New York, then I'll know where I'll be based.'

'Broadway?'

'Off Broadway,' she said, as if that were even better.

He still gave no impression of suspecting that she was delusional. Even if he was unaware that stage actors earned little more than minimum wage, he probably thought she was independently wealthy, some nepo baby with a trust fund.

According to Dee, the entertainment industry was full of them – and she should know.

'I assume that was just for fun,' I said as we walked back to the bus stop. A slicing wind attacked my face as I fought to keep up with her pace. 'There's no way you can afford that place.'

Noticing I was struggling, she slowed, lending me an arm. 'Don't freak out, Gwen, but there's something I haven't told you. I've been offered money by a journalist.'

'What?' I felt my heart pound under my ribcage. Though I'd known it was inevitable she'd be identified, it was still shocking to hear of the breach having finally been made. 'One of the vultures outside Columbia Mansions, you mean?'

'No. I've never met them.'

'How did they find you?'

'On Instagram. A few days ago?' She paused to help steer me around a broken paving stone. 'It was in hidden requests.'

Just like Alec's original proposal. 'What did they say?'

'They just asked if I was the girl in the story and if I would do an interview. I deleted it, but they keep getting back in touch and, like I say, offering a fee.'

'How much?' I asked. We'd reached the bus stop by now and, facing her, I saw a flare of excitement in her eyes that worried me.

'Five thousand pounds.'

This sounded modest given the media storm but as I say, interest was on the wane and, in any case, I was not about to propose she enter into negotiations.

'It wouldn't be anything I didn't tell Stella on the TV thing,' she added. 'But I couldn't stay anonymous this time. They'd want photos.'

Behind her, the lights were red, traffic completely stationary, as if the whole street and not just Pixie awaited my verdict. 'I'm not sure,' I said carefully. 'The fact that you've been able to keep your identity hidden is the one advantage you have coming out of this. Right now, you can get on with your life like any other person.'

She sighed, and it was hard to tell if she was disappointed or relieved. 'That's what Daniel says as well.'

Which explained his offer, at least. He was prepared to get into debt so that she could preserve her dignity. He didn't want to see her to sell her soul – as well as her body – any more than I did.

'But if I *did* do the interview,' she said, rallying, 'if I could get them to up the money, then I could live somewhere like that flat we just saw.'

This was magical thinking even by her standards. 'The rent was what? Three and a half thousand a month? But they probably want a year's contract, which is over forty thousand pounds. Then there's the council tax, all the utilities, that's another five thousand. They'd want evidence that you have the funds to cover all of that. Could you up the interview money that far?'

'Oh. No. Not *that* far.' As ever with Pixie, the high was chased by the low and no sooner had the bus arrived and we'd settled in the disabled seats than she'd begun sobbing. 'I just want to be free,' she wailed, attracting attention from nearby passengers.

'You *are* free,' I soothed.

'I mean free of *them*. Men. All of them. No offence to Daniel, he's great, but I need to be on my own, you know?'

'Oh, I do know. Believe me.'

The bus was heavy with passengers and their Christmas shopping, the heating oppressive, progress slow. I watched as she drew a face on the steamed-up window, knowing before she added the features that it would be a sad mouth, not a smiley one.

'Where do you see yourself?' I asked. 'I mean, realistically. Not that place we just saw.'

She scrubbed out the face. 'Anywhere. Just on my own. Somewhere like that studio in New Cross? I just want to go back to the beginning.'

The downgrading of her dream in the space of five minutes stirred fresh tenderness in me and I heard myself voice what I now think I'd been subconsciously planning ever since she told me about her awful plight with Alec: 'Then let's see if there are any other units available. I'll lend you what you need.'

Her chin snapped up, eyes sparking. 'Really? No. I can't ask you to do that.'

'I didn't hear you ask. But if it helps you forget this interview and keep your privacy, I'd be happy to.'

'Really?'

'Yes. Just promise me you'll tell this journalist they've got the wrong girl and block them from contacting you again.'

'I promise. I'll pay you back,' she added. 'As soon as this om-whatsit makes the bank pay.'

'Ombudsman.' I must have reminded her of the word a dozen times. A thought struck. 'Won't you need that money to pay back your dad?'

'It was a gift,' she said. 'That's why it was so awful. He gave me his savings and I lost them.' Before I could reply her mind had raced on and she was asking me if I thought dogs would be allowed in her new rental. 'I'd settle for a cat. A rescue, maybe? One of those ones with a chunk out of their ear, they are *so* cute.'

'They are,' I agreed.

Some might say I should have predicted what happened next, that I was throwing good money after bad, but as far as I was concerned the matter was simple. She needed to be relocated somewhere safe and there didn't seem to be anyone else who could help her.

Not without demanding something in return.

40

Her escape was arranged at speed. I transferred £5,000 to her account and helped her contact letting agents in the New Cross area. Multiple units in a new building were coming on the market in the New Year and it was agreed that if she got ahead of the game with her paperwork she stood a very good chance of securing one. Until then, she would stay with Ash, whose parents were going on a cruise over Christmas, and contribute by helping with Draco's walks.

Her job at Bageri Møller could not be held open and so she resigned with the aim of reapplying as and when she was back in range.

'If I even need to,' she told me. 'I just had a message about a freelance content job that sounds completely amazing.'

It was truly a joy to see her so buoyant after all she'd been through. 'Feel free to come and visit any time over the holidays,' I said. 'I'll be on my own. Daniel will be in New Zealand of course.'

I wasn't sure how she'd framed her departure to him in terms of their relationship, whether as a break, a break-up or neither (complicated new categories seemed to exist in the dating landscape of the 2020s), but he seemed sanguine enough as he helped load her possessions into Dee's Jeep that Saturday morning. It wasn't ideal that Dee should be the one to spirit

Pixie away, to muscle in on the moment of freedom funded by me, but my main priority was that she should leave without any interference from Alec.

'Look how beautiful the building is,' Dee said, taking pictures for her social media as we stood at the car waiting for the youngsters to bring down the final load. Columbia Mansions was always at its most picturesque at this time of year, the brickwork a rich copper red in the creamy winter light, Christmas trees glittering at the windows.

Only one window was open – Alec gazing down from it.

'Bugger. Look, Dee,' I murmured. 'This is what I was telling you about. This staring.'

'I can't tell what he's looking at,' she said doubtfully, and I wondered if she might need to switch her reading glasses for bifocals (even glamourpusses suffered the effects of ageing). 'Maybe it's good that he sees she's leaving,' she added in an undertone. 'He might be more inclined to negotiate next steps.'

'Maybe.' He had still not come back to Dee regarding the 'advice' he'd been seeking and now Noel had left for a two-week skiing trip, which created a further delay.

'We'll insist on a proper powwow as soon as everyone's back after the break,' she promised, which made me think briefly of Maya. 'Powwow' was offensive cultural appropriation, or at least it had been when she'd liked to lecture me on such things. 'And don't worry, he's not invited tomorrow night.'

I looked blankly at her before remembering the Festive Fizz.

'You and Daniel *are* coming, aren't you? And you haven't forgotten you always do your cinnamon stars? The Konditor recipe with all the lovely spices? They were such a hit last year.'

'Um, sure.' I found myself floundering. Dee might have the capacity to juggle climactic dramatic moments and trivial details but it was beyond me to talk about biscuits while Pixie prepared to leave and Alec hovered at his window casting hexes my way.

Daniel and Pixie arrived then with the last of her things. It seemed to me she was leaving with less than she'd arrived with, but that may have been psychological, my being so painfully aware of all she'd lost during her time here. In a trice, Dee was in the driver's seat, engine firing, and Daniel and I were hugging Pixie goodbye. It felt absurdly casual after everything we'd been through these last weeks, as if she were going away for the night and not marking the end of an extraordinary personal crisis, but what would I have preferred? A formal debriefing in an interrogation chamber? A scene of weeping and wailing for Alec to enjoy?

'Off she goes,' I said to Daniel, as the Jeep sped off down the street, braking violently at the junction. 'Hopefully she'll get to Ash's in one piece.' I lowered my voice in case Alec was still in earshot. 'I don't know if she told you, it was me who lent her the money for her flat deposit?'

Daniel glanced at the icy sky and turned his collar up. He was wearing his green peacoat, which still sported a few dog hairs from Pixie's outing with Draco all those weeks ago. 'Yeah, she said. Cool. Thanks, Mum.'

I was grateful that any notion of my having wished to separate them did not seem to have occurred to him. 'She said *you* offered her a loan as well. Did you?'

'Yeah, but not for that. She wanted to pay back her dad the money she lost in the fraud.'

This threw me; hadn't she said her father had gifted her the lost deposit? And that Daniel's offer *had* been for the flat? I suspected no subterfuge on her part, however, only a mind too tangled to grasp financial detail, decisions made on the hoof. I felt a rush of sureness that my own loan had been the right course of action, even if my savings balance was now running alarmingly low. 'I don't understand where you'd have got the money if she'd said yes? I thought you were broke?'

He toed a clump of leaves into the gutter. 'Nella's lawyer just told us she'll cover legal fees if we go for the clean break.'

'That's great news!'

'Plus I did an extra job. A side hustle.'

'What side hustle?'

'Just a quick thing for a friend.' He checked the time on his phone. 'I ought to head off to work. You should go back in, Mum, it's really cold. Do you need help with the stairs?'

'I'm fine.' I watched as he crossed Winifred Gardens, a real purpose to his stride, and marvelled at his transformation from glass-half-full hermit to a really rather agreeable member of our community.

I had Pixie to thank for that, I realized.

*

As if that recent lapse in our friendship had never happened, Dee dropped by after delivering Pixie, a bottle of Crémant in hand, which struck me as a prematurely celebratory choice.

As ever, Alec's door opened within moments of mine, but seeing Dee, he simply raised a hand to her and withdrew. I took the opportunity to explain once more his attempts to mess with my mind. 'It's only when I'm on my own, so when I complain about it, it looks like I'm imagining it, *doesn't it*?' I added, loudly enough for him to hear through the door and for Dee to startle. 'I know your game, Alec! I've been keeping a record of your attempts at intimidation!'

Dee looked perplexed. 'Let's just go in and have a drink, Gwen.'

‘Of course.’ But her scepticism only illustrated my point and I kept to myself the new fear that had lodged in my gut these last few hours. With Pixie now gone and Daniel and most of the rest of the residents set to decamp soon after the drinks party, Christmas would be a perfect opportunity for Alec to escalate his campaign against me. To stage his own interpretation of *Gaslight*.

‘Was Pixie all right?’ I asked as she followed me to the kitchen. You could hear the swish of luxury fabric as she removed her coat and scarf.

‘She was fine. A very alternative young man helped at the other end. I was careful not to use any pronouns just in case.’

‘Ash? I think he’s just a regular he.’ I collected a couple of champagne flutes and set about uncorking the wine.

‘I saw your message to the group,’ Dee said as I poured the pale frothy liquid. I’d already updated the residents on Pixie’s departure and accepted a flurry of big-hearted wishes on her behalf. She cast a glance towards my oven. ‘Oh. I thought you might have started baking.’

‘Why would I be baking?’

‘The cinnamon stars, Gwen!’

‘Of course. I’m sorry, I’ve had so much on my mind.’

‘Haven’t we all? What with dealing with everyone’s hysteria about Alec and the service charge, and organizing the Festive Fizz, I haven’t had a second to myself.’

‘I thought we hadn’t seen much of you lately.’ I objected to that ‘hysteria’, the implication that the fallout from a sex-for-rent scheme and an increased service charge demand were on a par, but did not say.

We settled on the sofa. In the fading light, Dee’s profile was elegant, her cheekbones attractively shadowed. Perhaps it was being alone together for the first time in a while, but I understood in that moment that her charisma wasn't simply a case of looking good *for her age*, it was the accrued confidence of having looked good all her life. The rosy filter of admiration through which she'd navigated her life.

No doubt Stella would one day evoke similar thoughts in some lesser friend of hers.

Dee sipped her Crémant, which I now realized must be from her Festive Fizz stocks. 'I didn't like to say in front of Pixie, but it's probably for the best she won't be at the party. With neither of them there we can all just be ourselves. Try and forget this drama for a couple of hours.'

Neither of them: again, that false parity, as if Pixie and Alec were equally qualified to spoil our fun. I countered my annoyance with the reminder that she'd just given up hours of her day, the day before her own party, to ferry Pixie to safety. As we used to say at the charity, you couldn't do better than direct action.

'I keep meaning to ask you,' Dee continued, 'would you like to come for Christmas lunch? With me and the kids? I know you'll be alone.'

'I'd love to,' I said. 'Assuming Alec doesn't make me a better offer.'

She guffawed at that.

'Thank you, Dee, that's very kind. I'll make the stars first thing in the morning.'

She crossed her legs, took another sip. 'If you think there'll be time for the icing to dry.'

*

It was only after she'd left, when I went into my bedroom for the first time since seeing Pixie off, that I noticed a card propped against the lamp on the bedside table. It had my name on it in blue ink, with the distinctive tail of her capital 'G'. The thickness of the envelope promised more than a thank you card and when I opened it, I found a small tissue-wrapped gift of some sort. I read the message first.

To Gwen,
Thank you so much, you've been awesome. This is in case you have suspicions about the next girl!
Love Px
PS I told him I lost it and I think he believed me.

The package contained a key. I didn't at first understand – she'd already returned the spare key she'd been using while she stayed here – but quickly deduced it must be her old key to Alec's flat. How and when she'd convinced him she'd mislaid it I did not know.

I read the message a second time and suppressed a shudder at the idea of my letting myself into number 4 and sweeping a second time for cameras, of the mere possibility that the violation that had led to one girl's flight might be repeated.

Over my dead body, I thought, and you'll remember, perhaps, that I've uttered the pledge before in this account.

Well, this time I meant it.

41

It took me almost ten minutes to get to Dee's top-floor flat the following evening, by far the most stairs I'd attempted since my surgery and a feat possible only with Daniel's aid. But once there I used my remaining energy to take my hat off to our hostess – for this Fizz was without question the most Festive of them all.

The table in the turret had been removed to accommodate a glossy ten-foot fir strung with hundreds of silver baubles, and everywhere you turned there was an artfully artless floral arrangement – blood-red roses, holly berries, winter foliage, pussy willow. Even the finger buffet was a feast for the eyes: antipasti arranged on boards in Christmas wreaths, with sprigs of rosemary in place of pines, and mountains of pigs in blankets and devils on horseback. Orange fire crackled in not one but two fireplaces; otherwise, light was limited to hundreds of candles and fairy lights.

The background carols were familiar from previous years (Dee favoured the choir of King's College) and Daniel and I arrived to 'We Three Kings of Orient Are', though we were now a two.

'Have you heard from Pixie today?' I asked him, as we scooped up glasses of fizz and joined Hester, Liz and the rest of the gang. I detected unease: it *had* been a break-up then, or at least a significant downgrade. 'I'm sorry. I know you don't like me interfering.'

'No, it's all right,' he said. 'I'm sure she's just fine.'

If he didn't want to discuss Pixie, then he was, alas, alone in that aim. In spite of ongoing competition from the service charge heist, there was still plenty of disapproval of Alec to share and a good hour was devoted to what the community needed to do to prevent our resident sex predator from thinking he'd got away with it. Few, if any, knew of Pixie's relationship with Daniel, but everyone knew she'd been living with us and so we were the focus of a bombardment of questions about her departure. Had there been any showdowns since he'd been back? Where had she gone and were we quite certain Alec did not have the address to track her down? How would she ever get over something so degrading and was she getting counselling?

Daniel said then what I, what with my town crier infamy, could not. 'I think the worst thing for her is knowing people are having these conversations about her. I mean, she wanted to put the issue out there, that's why she did the TV interview in the first place, but she did it anonymously. She never wanted her personal life to be dissected like this.'

'Agreed,' I said. No need to mention how close she'd come to being tempted to tell all to a journalist who'd hunted her down on Instagram. The earnest simplicity of Daniel's words shamed the group and conversation settled on the safer ground of everyone's plans for Christmas Day itself and how their various hosts' talents could not possibly surpass Dee's.

As if in illustration, her toast included the famous quote from Napoleon – 'In victory you deserve champagne, in defeat you need it' – and I suppose you *could* accuse her of co-opting our humble drinks for her own coronation. But that would be unfair. By the time her helpers supplemented the savoury nibbles with mince pies, miniature cranberry tarts and, of course, my spiced biscuits (the icing had dried in good time, as I'd been confident it would)

I felt as thankful to her as everyone else in the room. Maybe she'd been right about Pixie's absence being a positive thing. Living at the level of crisis we had been was not sustainable.

It was as 'Joy to the World' gave way to 'In the Bleak Midwinter' and Liz was telling us of her daredevil grandson's plans for a 'budgie jump' from a bridge in South Africa that we became aware of some sort of to-do at the door. Conversation sank to a murmur and Dee could be heard talking in unusually vexed tones: 'Hang on a minute, I really don't think it's a good idea—'

'Calm down,' a male voice interrupted, and I felt the hairs on my arms stand up before my conscious brain could catch up and identify the caller as Alec. 'Don't worry, I'm sure they all know you wouldn't dream of inviting the social pariah in.'

'He's like the wicked fairy,' Hester murmured. 'Who's he come to curse?'

'All of us,' Sadie said.

'Just give her this, will you?' he could be heard insisting, and Dee's apparent agreement brought an end of their exchange, the door clunking shut. He'd delivered something of Pixie's, I guessed. Having watched her removal in Dee's car, he took Dee to be her new principal contact, and likely had not been aware the residents' Festive Fizz was taking place until he'd got to the door. Hard to believe it was only six weeks or so since he'd hosted his Bonfire Night after-party. Been one of the lads, Pixie's 'romantic' partner.

As conversation swelled once more, Dee advanced through the gathering, dismissing her guests' curiosity with shrugs and platitudes. 'Nothing to worry about. I've sent him on his way.' To my surprise, she made for our group and handed me a letter. 'I said I'd give it to you, so here you are.'

'What is it?' I asked, thinking of those cryptic texts he'd sent, of my unerring conviction that he'd been biding his time. The envelope was creamy white, with my name and address typed and centred, giving a yesteryear feel to it that could only portend bad news.

'If it's something we can use to help get rid of him, keep hold of it,' Karishma said with a touch of melodrama, and now I thought of the poison pen letters of Agatha Christie novels, words cut from newspapers and rearranged in messages of hate and menace.

I limped to a quiet corner and perched on the side of an armchair before sliding my thumb under the flap and removing two stapled sheets of premium-quality A4.

'Why didn't he just put it in our pigeonhole or shove it under the door?' Daniel said, joining me.

'Because it's something he wanted me to read in front of our neighbours,' I said, knowing now that he'd been all too aware of our gathering. I tried to absorb the contents – not a poison pen letter, but a missive from a City lawyer:

Dear Ms Healy,

Re: Your defamatory statements on news and social media

We are acting for Mr Alec Pedley in connection with the identification and pursuit of instances of libellous statements across national broadcast, published and social media. We have been made aware of statements you have recently made that were covered by several social media channels and national and local news outlets that make reference to our client.

We have evidence to prove that the statements made by yourself contain serious, untrue and highly defamatory comments towards our client, which have been communicated to millions of people throughout the United Kingdom, posing a serious threat to the reputation of our client.

Under the law of England and Wales, a defamatory statement is one which is false and causes damage to a person's reputation or otherwise does them harm.

Legal proceedings

In order to protect our client's interests, we are considering proceedings against you in the High Court. These proceedings would seek remedies including but not limited to the following:

- *Substantial damages*
- *An injunction to restrain you from publishing the same or similar statements in the future*
- *Costs*

The letter went on, but I couldn't read beyond the words 'damages' and 'costs', the agonies of past losses colliding with fear of those to come. I had a finite amount of money in my account and no way of coming by more; how would I conjure up whatever it was these lawyers demanded?

'What is it, Mum?' Daniel took the letter from me and scanned it, frowning. 'He's taking legal action?'

Together, we cut past the other guests to reach Dee at the buffet, where she was explaining to Reid, our resident American, and his girlfriend how long they needed to soak cranberries in Grand Marnier to achieve the culinary orgasm they were experiencing by eating hers. Seeing my face, she excused herself and read the letter at once.

'What's he playing at?'

'I think it's quite clear,' I said, my voice trembling. 'He wants to bankrupt me.'

'This is what he must have meant about getting advice. Noel and I assumed any pushback would be against us as a group.'

'Just me,' I said weakly.

Those bright hazel eyes darkened. 'You need to respond with a legal letter of your own. Let's ask Noel to recommend a specialist in this sort of thing.'

'He's on holiday, isn't he?'

'He won't mind us messaging. This is an emergency.' Putting down her glass, she texted him on the spot and minutes later a recommendation arrived for a lawyer who Noel happened to know would be in the office until Christmas Eve.

'Phone her first thing in the morning,' Dee urged. 'You can't have this hanging over you over the break.'

Unable to continue socializing, I left the party, Daniel linking his arm through mine to help me safely down the stairs. The night air was sharp as we walked the short stretch along the pavement, our breath visible in front of us. The envelope felt spiky in my pocket, dangerous as a switchblade.

For the first time, as we reached our landing, I willed Alec to emerge, but of course he did not, this particular act of his drama now complete, and so I thumped on his door with my fist.

'Alec? This letter is nonsense and you know it!'

Daniel tried to wrestle me aside. 'Don't, Mum. It's not going to help.'

I ignored him, screaming at the door: 'You won't get a penny from me, you scheming bastard!'

'I'm sure it will be all be sorted by the lawyer,' Daniel said, finally getting me into the flat.

I could not agree. In the living room, the tree Pixie and I had decorated together looked pedestrian and diminished, and not only in contrast with the grandeur of Dee's. I knew it would be impossible for me to take pleasure in Christmas now and that this was precisely what Alec had intended. I'd been right to fear his exploitation of the festive exodus; he knew I'd be alone in the flat, just me and my fears for my future.

He'd punish me for his crime if it was the last thing he did.

42

Frances Voss was nothing like any of the lawyers involved in the furore surrounding Brian's and my removal from the charity and its subsequent disbanding; those had been male, thin-haired and self-important, dry as a bone. Nor did she resemble the legal eagles in the American TV shows Daniel and I watched, who wore tailored dresses and heels and spoke conspiratorially to clients from under immaculate fringes. This woman was more how I pictured a senior civil servant: grey-suited, impassive, desk-bound, the edge of said desk not quite cutting into a thickened midriff that spoke of junk snacking, the window behind in dire need of a clean.

Since she'd been booked up well into the New Year, I had the fact that some poor soul had come down with a gastric infection to thank for the surrendered slot that meant I could buy advice mere hours before the holiday shutdown. A Zoom had been offered, but I'd insisted on meeting in person, keen to escape the space where the man threatening to destroy me sat glorying in his revenge on the other side of the wall.

'You're familiar with what libel is?' she began, her gaze no-nonsense and searching.

'Yes,' I said, 'though I would have thought this fell under slander.'

'Because there is film recording involved, it meets the criteria of libel.' Her voice was accentless, authoritative, and I was nervous of her air of settling me into a complex discussion. Far from dismissing Alec's move as game-playing theatrics, as I'd expected her to, she was quoting the Defamation Act – citing the line 'has caused or is likely to cause serious harm to the reputation of the claimant' with particular weight – and explaining that I was not being accused of a crime but a 'civil wrong'. She then proceeded to run through the passage in the letter that urged me to produce an apology and pay damages, actions I had no intention of undertaking.

'No way,' I said when she'd finished, and she bit into her lower lip causing the colour to drain from it, a tic I soon learned meant my response was unsatisfactory.

'Yes, you said on the phone your position is to refute the claim. Talk me through your thoughts on the public statement you made on Tuesday December the tenth.'

I'd done very little else but think about it these last hours and so was well prepared. 'Well, it can't be slander – sorry, libel – because that involves a false statement and my statement was true. His name *is* Alec Pedley and he *is* a sex-for-rent landlord. The victim had just been on national TV to describe her experience with him, which is how I came to be commenting on it – and can I just say that it was other people, not me, who filmed it and posted on social media.' Outrage rose, my voice growing shrill. 'This whole thing is crazy! He's just looking for someone to blame because he got found out and now no one wants to know him. When it comes down to it, all I did was give his name to a bunch of reporters who would have found it on their own a few hours later.'

She heard me out without a hint of agreement or disagreement. 'Okay. I've familiarized myself with the BBC *News Radar* item and the *Standard* article that followed and in both cases the parties involved were treated with strict anonymity, were they not?'

'Yes, other than the fact that their address was identified. That's how we came to be besieged by this mob in the first place. I was the one who named and shamed him, I can't deny that, but the point is it's true. He *did* take sex for rent.'

A faint nod and a discreet pursing of the lips seemed to signal a level of support. 'We'll accept that as stated fact for now, though he denies it. But I'm convinced it was a honestly held judgment on your part.'

'It's honestly held because it's true!'

She eyed me with curiosity, as if genuinely intrigued that I should not understand what I'd done wrong or what trouble I was in (perhaps both). 'I've studied the YouTube clip of the recording of you and your neighbour speaking to the media and I'm afraid it's not a matter simply of naming and shaming, as you put it.'

'What do you mean?'

'You describe him as a sex offender.'

I swallowed. 'Yes. That's my interpretation of what a sex-for-rent landlord is.'

'Your "interpretation". I'm glad you see the distinction.' Indeed, she looked as if an important obstacle had been overcome: I was not a simpleton after all. 'Because he's not actually a registered sex offender, is he?'

I paused. 'I don't think so, no.'

'So that's *not* stated fact. Do you see the difficulty?'

'I suppose so, but I wasn't saying he was a *registered* sex offender, was I? I was saying he's a sex offender because of what he did as a sex-for-rent landlord.'

'Except sex for rent is not technically a crime, hence his not being subject to police investigation.'

'Well, it should be,' I said. 'It probably will be in the future.'

'We'll come back to the police in a minute,' she said, 'but for now let's look at the issue of reputational damage. I noticed you used the phrase "No one wants to know him" just now and that's very much the problem, not least in terms of his ability to earn a living. According to his solicitor, at least two offers of work have been withdrawn since you made your statement and a third client is on record as saying she was influenced by the media coverage to withhold a commission she'd been intending to give. Of course, this is still playing out so there may be more lost revenue to be cited, though it's easier to prove reputational harm when an offer has been made and withdrawn.'

I said nothing. I had not considered Alec's work situation other than to assume exile had been an opportunity to throw himself into it.

Frances chewed her lip again; something else bad was coming. 'I explained that this is a civil matter, but I'm concerned it could escalate into a criminal investigation.'

'You just said ... Oh.' She meant me, I realized, not him. 'In what way?'

'If your actions were to be construed as a campaign of harassment, for instance.'

My mouth dropped open.

She referred to her notes. 'Is it correct that you phoned the police on November the sixteenth to report a surveillance device and accuse Mr Pedley of intent to publish pornographic material?'

'I don't know about publishing pornographic material, but I saw the camera with my own eyes. It was in her shower. The victim's shower.'

'But the call was made by you, yes? The victim herself has never made any complaint against him or used his name in any report or interview?'

'She was right there with me! I phoned on her behalf.' I was starting to get agitated again: whose side was this woman on?

She must have sensed this because her manner grew fractionally warmer. 'I know it may be frustrating and can feel as if words are being twisted against you, but I can only advise you according to the law and it can sometimes be a blunt instrument, I'm afraid. And there are other grievances that don't do us any favours either.'

I looked up, indignant. 'Like what?'

Again, she checked her notes. 'Mr Pedley says the press knew things only a neighbour could have told them and his assertion is that you were an informant.'

'Nonsense,' I said. 'What things?'

'His car registration. Details of his travel plans, which led to the media hunting him down at a friend's home and generating further negative publicity.'

'I don't know anything about that. I saw him leave, but any of us could have worked that out in the morning when his car was gone from the car park. We were relieved. We were scared of him!'

She allowed a sympathetic tutting at this. 'You were also seen in his flat without his having consented to your being there. Is that correct?'

'I was just helping his victim move her stuff out! Honestly, if we're talking about "incidental grievances", I can give you a list of dozens by him against me. He's been harassing me on a daily basis, can we countersue with that?'

She brightened. 'Give me some examples.'

I outlined his various intimidation tactics, trying not to exaggerate. 'He's been lying in wait. Coming to his door whenever he hears me at mine, but refusing to reply if I speak to him, just glaring at me. He's created a constant sense of menace.'

'Has anyone else witnessed this?'

'Not really. The whole point is it's only for me to notice. But I've told lots of people, including my son, who lives with me.'

'Any stated threats?'

'In texts, yes.' I pulled up the thread on my phone to show her and she read them aloud.

'You have made a big mistake. Oh, we'll be engaging soon enough, don't you worry.' Perhaps it was her matter-of-fact tone but they didn't sound nearly as sinister as they had when I'd received them.

'Thank you. If you can send me a screenshot of these.'

'He's called me names as well,' I said, remembering.

'What names?'

'Battleaxe. Gargoyle. Interfering sow. And I witnessed him calling the victim a slut. It's all contributed to a feeling of hostility and threat.'

'Have you complained to the police about it?'

'Of course not. I don't trust the police as far as I can throw them.'

'Okay, I've made a note of that. Be sure to log any incidents from now on.'

But I already knew there would be no more stalking, no more staring. He'd bullied me into a state of profound disquiet and then, when I was at my least stable, served me with my papers. It had come naturally to him, all of this. He had an instinct for cruelty, for revenge.

Frances made a steeple with her fingers, bowing her head a touch. 'Now, in terms of my advice, I think you should consider settling this before they can pull together more evidence. Nip it in the bud.'

'Nip it in the bud? This is bonkers!' I cried, unable to think of anything more intelligent to say.

'Allegations of sexual offences are considered very serious and damaging. I'm going to send you links to some defamation cases where damages were awarded and I want you to read them carefully over the break before deciding on next steps.' She fixed me with an unsmiling gaze. 'Gwen, you need to understand that if this went to court and you lost, you could be liable for costs as well as any damages he wins. That could run into hundreds of thousands, which is a crippling amount for most people.'

'It is for me as well. Yes, very much so.' I had a strong suspicion settling might not be so great either. 'What sort of sum are we talking about to make this go away?'

'Mr Pedley has indicated that he will settle for £75,000.'

'Seventy-five thousand?' I was stunned. 'For one sex offender slur?'

'Which they can prove was repeated and shared until it reached a national audience, and subsequently lost him earnings.'

'But he knows I can't afford that,' I protested. 'I'm barely surviving on my pension. He's much better off than me, even without these few jobs he claims he's missed out on.'

'That's not the point, I'm afraid.'

I was beginning to wish I had a pound for every time she said 'I'm afraid'; it would go some way to helping with her fees. Then a darker thought occurred. 'Would they ... Would they be allowed to mention my history? If we went to court?'

Her eyebrows shot up halfway to her hairline. 'Your history?'

'I was involved in a financial investigation years ago.' I gave a brief outline of the charity debacle, of Brian's prosecution and sentencing. 'I was never prosecuted but I was disqualified from being a trustee.'

'All right.' She scribbled a note. 'Well, I certainly think it's worth bearing in mind that Mr Pedley has never been involved in anything criminal.'

Just my luck he was the first rock musician in history not to have had a drugs conviction!

'Can I think about it?' I asked.

'Of course. Read the cases I send you. Meanwhile, I advise you not to have any contact with him. Keep well out of his way.'

I had an image of my thumping on his door after the Festive Fizz, Daniel manhandling me away. 'That's not going to be easy. Our doors are a few feet apart.'

'Even so. If you see him, say nothing. You don't want to give him any reason to increase his demand. I won't sugar-coat this, Gwen,' she said, bringing an end to a session that could not have been more disheartening, 'he's in the stronger position. And he knows it.'

43

I returned home to find Daniel in utter chaos with his packing. He, Maya and Jason were flying to New Zealand that evening and yet he'd barely begun to get organized. Damp laundered clothes were jumbled up with worn dry ones on his unmade bed, toiletries and yet-to-be-wrapped Christmas gifts strewn on the pillows. Quite the contrast with the sponsored social media post Maya had shared earlier that morning in which she was pictured in an off-the-shoulder floral frock sitting demurely atop a trio of vintage trunks that wouldn't have looked out of place on the *Titanic*.

Amid the scent of wet cotton was a note of rose from a diffuser Pixie had installed and not taken with her and all at once I was rocked with the grief of her having once been here, central to our household. As close a family member as Daniel himself.

'How did it go?' he asked, pausing to look at me. He badly needed a haircut.

'Not great.' My expression hardened as I recalled the one phrase from the meeting that had looped through my mind on my bus ride home: *He says they knew things only a neighbour could have told them* … 'You gave reporters information about Alec, didn't you?'

His face went slack and I knew I was right.

'That's where you got the money you offered Pixie, wasn't it?'

There were the beginnings of a shrug in his shoulders before he thought better of it. 'It was just a few bits.'

'Like his car reg? What else?'

He'd supplied the photos from the bonfire party, it emerged, and 'mentioned' Alec's friend in the Peak District. 'I didn't know the address, but he told me they go to this pub called the Black Hart.'

Hence the photo of 'Kinky Alec' and his pal leaving that same establishment. 'That was a huge story, Daniel! Without that, the media might have lost interest a lot sooner.'

'What does it matter?' he said. 'The guy's literally his old bandmate. They'd have caught up with him sooner or later.'

Exactly my ill-conceived justification for releasing Alec's name in the first place. 'It could matter more than you imagined. The lawyer said I need to pay him damages and I'm now thinking I'd better do that pretty damn quickly before he finds out you've been running this little sideline. It looks coordinated, Dan. Does Pixie know what you did?' It would be more damning still if it transpired that the original accuser had profited from his actions.

'No,' he said with a hint of his old sullenness. 'She's got no idea. Look, why don't you use the money I got to pay these damages. Then we'll be quits.'

'Is it seventy-five thousand pounds?'

He looked astonished. 'No, nothing like that. That's crazy money!'

'You think? If anything, I got the feeling the lawyer thinks I'm getting off lightly. They can probably run that up in legal fees alone if it goes to court.'

Daniel groaned. 'I'm sorry if I've made things worse, Mum.' He gestured to his packing. 'One thing I *can* do is get out of your hair before I do anything else to screw things up.'

Leave me to deal with this on my own while you go on holiday, you mean, I thought. Only now was I seeing that I'd grown to value his support these last weeks, his arm in mine when I needed it – and not only physically.

'I'll move out as soon as I'm back,' he added, but before I could address this my phone began ringing. Dee, asking how I'd got on with Frances.

I gave her the headlines and she reacted similarly to Daniel, bar the offer of a monetary contribution.

'It's a mess, Dee.' I felt my throat tighten. My voice was reedy as I continued. 'I don't see how I can do anything but apologize and pay, but if I do then *he'll* be the innocent party. We can forget trying to get him out of the building. He'll be petitioning to get *me* out.'

'Oh, Gwen, we would never allow that. Try not to panic, I'm sure there'll be a compromise to be had. How did you leave it? I'm assuming nothing can be done now till the New Year?'

'She's going to send me her advice in writing. I've got some cases to look at before I decide.'

'Good. Okay. At least you have her in your corner. I'm so glad we were able to arrange that.' A subtle reminder that she'd been instrumental in this. 'While I've got you ... about Christmas Day.'

'Would you rather I didn't come?' I guessed.

'No, not at all, we're really looking forward to having you. But would it be all right if we didn't discuss this latest development? Stella's only two weeks away from having the baby and I don't want to cause any unnecessary strain.'

I almost laughed out loud at this. Stella was the last person I would entrust with news of my latest humiliation; she'd be sure to shoehorn it into her column or next interview. Her social media continued to feature regular posts about sex for rent with clips from the *News Radar* feature, the Sky News interview and the other media appearances she'd made, and for all I knew she was cooking up a follow-up report.

Hanging up, I saw a text message had arrived while I'd been on the call – from the man himself:

Had any interesting seasons' greetings, Gwen dearest?

And even though Frances Voss's sober no-contact warning still rang in my ears, I fired off the only response he deserved:

Go to hell, pervert.

*

His possessions crammed into a rucksack the size of a conjoined twin, Daniel finally left for Heathrow. I didn't envy him the journey by public transport but equally would have been furious if he'd booked a taxi – at £100-plus an extravagance at the best of times, let alone now I faced being taken to the cleaners.

Once alone, I settled down to study the defamation cases Frances had emailed me. The first involved a distinguished academic who had faced a campaign against him by two associates that included online allegations of rape potentially seen by hundreds of thousands of people, including his students. He'd been awarded £70,000. The next was a teacher incorrectly reported as guilty of assaulting a primary school child. Given it was seen in the national press and online, it was judged to have seriously damaged his professional reputation and he was awarded £50,000.

In the last one, a local branch of a political party had published a photograph of the claimant alleging that he was being investigated for the sexual assault of a neighbour. In fact, the police had discounted any criminal inquiry, but the defendant refused to withdraw the allegation, resulting in an award of £40,000 being made.

Sobering reading indeed. All claimants had been successful and the implication was that Alec would be too.

Next, I made a forensic study of my recent and foreseeable spending. The surgery had been £14,000, plus physio; I'd lent Pixie £5,000; I would soon owe the unwelcome £3,000 surcharge on the coming year's service charge. Increased expenses during Daniel's and Pixie's occupation took care of another couple of thousand. And in spite of the unadorned style of my legal representative, her fees were going to be in the thousands even if I chose the 'nip it in the bud' route, which I was by no means inclined to do.

That left me with £10,000-15,000, disastrously short of the amount Alec was demanding. Where was I going to find the rest? Extending my mortgage was out of the question at my age and in any case how would I meet the increased monthly repayments when every penny of my pension was budgeted for? I had no other assets, not even a car.

When Frances's written advice arrived, I tried – and failed – to find some new clue as to a solution. She'd been right about Alec having the stronger hand: while my complaints amounted to little more than unwanted staring and a few text messages, he had meticulously logged every actionable infraction of my own. *You described him as a sex offender ... You were seen trespassing in his flat ... You reported him for intent to publish pornographic material ... You were an informant to the press ...*

On it went, everything she'd quoted in our meeting and more, the reframing of every last encounter, every line of communication, to give the impression that I had nothing better to do than make his blameless life a misery. No doubt that text I'd just sent calling him a pervert was already in the evidence file too.

About to give up for the day, I felt my mind snag on one of those damning lines – *You were seen trespassing in his flat* – and gently release a reminder. The key Pixie had left and that she'd told Alec she'd lost. I went to check the bookshelf where I'd put her thank you card and there it was, nestled behind out of sight.

My head told me to return it to him, or better still dispose of it, but gut instinct compelled me to keep it. It compelled me to take it from its packaging and slip it behind the sofa cushions, the same sofa on which Pixie had slept during her time here. It also compelled me to take down the card and read again that scribbled message – *In case you have suspicions about the next girl!* – before tearing it to pieces and dropping it in the bin.

44

Christmas Day dawned with the gift of an unexpectedly glorious winter sun – and the scarcely less sublime bonus that Alec's car was gone from the car park. Like most residents, he'd chosen to spend his Christmas elsewhere. The Peak District, perhaps. Roast turkey with all the trimmings at the Black Hart.

Mercifully there'd been no reply from him to my 'pervert' text, but I'd received lovely 'Merry Christmas' messages from Pixie in Kent, sent in the early hours – evidently, she and Ash been up late partying – and from Daniel and Maya in Wellington, safely landed after a day in the air. Maya included a link to her TikTok message to her followers, which involved her turning sausages on the barbecue while wearing an itsy-bitsy bikini; it seemed unlikely she'd had time to create this content in New Zealand, so she must have filmed it in near-zero conditions in the garden of her cottage in Greenwich.

Either way, it no doubt added an erotic frisson to her male followers' family Christmases.

After an idle morning, I took my time getting ready and then braved a little gentle exercise in Winifred Gardens before heading to Dee's for lunch. There was an air of holiday amnesty about my fellow *flâneurs*, even the most arrogant males willing just this once to acknowledge the old bird in their midst. I seemed to have made progress with my knee, too, taking barely half the time to climb up to Dee's than I had for the Festive Fizz and arriving with a genuine smile on my face.

'Merry Christmas!' I offered her the bottle of champagne I'd bought before learning I could no longer afford it.

'Here she is!' she cried. In contrast to my own rather formal woollen dress, she was wearing leather jeans, a type of cowboy boot suitable for a woman half her age, and a shimmery silver blouse with sleeves that fell to her knuckles and were surely quite impracticable for stirring gravy and other catering tasks.

Andy Williams crooned 'It's the Most Wonderful Time of the Year', which may have been overstating it, but as I say my mood was buoyant, improved further by the tableau that greeted me of Stella, Cam and Rafferty gathered by the fire. A silver wine cooler – containing Dom Perignon no less – sat on the coffee table among half a dozen expensive French candles, each with silver carousels of birds turning in the heat of their flames, and the surviving flowers from the residents' party had been upstaged by an enormous bouquet of roses, their crimson heads cradled in lush foliage.

'Oh, Dee. This all looks so beautiful. The roses!'

'From Richard.' Dee handed me the flute of champagne already poured and waiting. 'He sends them every year, more for Stella and Raf than for me.'

Both adored offspring, plus Cam, stood to greet me. The men wore jeans and cashmere sweaters and smelled of the upscale urban male: expensive Italian leather and smoked cedarwood (I thought briefly of Alec in front of the bonfire, cooling his forehead with his beer, and dismissed the image). Stella, now hugely pregnant, wore a berry-pink jersey dress and incongruously dainty ballet pumps.

She kissed me and gripped my hands tightly in lieu of a hug. 'I haven't had a chance to say how sorry I am that things escalated the way they did. I can't believe how insensitive some people have been. Those TikTokers, oh my God they really ran with it, didn't they? I know Pixie was really shocked.'

She spoke in 'all's well that ends well' tones, as if our problems were in the past, not knowing of course that I had the sword of Damocles hanging over me.

'We can't blame them. It was a good story,' I said with the faintest hint of accusation, but she was no fool and picked up on it at once.

'I feel *so* bad that she was driven out.'

'It wasn't feasible for her to stay. She's much better off out of his orbit.'

She nodded very solemnly, as if respecting a wisdom superior to her own. 'Same for the other girl. The one in Leicester? She's just sorted out a new job and things are really looking up. I'm so proud of them both. I need to update them, actually. I just heard yesterday that the domestic abuse charities have had an amazing response to the feature since it's been on the BBC website.'

'Really?' So the BBC classed it as domestic abuse but I wasn't allowed to call Alec a sex offender? Might I really lose my home over a linguistic discrepancy? I felt my mood dip, but only momentarily because Cam was now handing Stella a posh gift bag adorned with gold ribbon and she was passing it to me.

'*Un petit cadeau* for you ...' she said, beaming.

'Oh,' I said. 'Dee and I agreed no gifts.'

'I know. I totally broke the rules. You've been such a superstar, Gwen, I can't not give you something.'

It was a costly set of Penhaligon's bodywash, hand cream and scented candle, far more expensive than the gifts my own children had given me: Daniel's, not wrapped, a bottle of Hotel Chocolat liqueur, which admittedly I would enjoy; Maya's, a framed piece of hessian with the words 'We Are All Born Beautiful' embroidered on it. Utterly moronic.

'I don't know what to say,' I said.

'That's a first,' Dee said, circling with the champagne, and I was surprised to see I'd already drained my first glass.

At lunch, a salad of some sort with ricotta and roasted peach, then turkey with an incredible chestnut and pumpkin stuffing, I was seated between the two men and quickly guessed that Rafferty had been tasked with entertaining me. I'd met him before, of course, and had always found his careless, jocular manner disconcerting in light of his profession – I preferred to think of pilots as poised and serious-minded types, not fools guffawing in the cockpit – but thankfully we were not on a plane now. Talk was mostly of their family, the new baby in particular, but far from excluding me it was as if I were, just for one day, a clan member myself.

Everyone but Stella drank freely from a succession of costly wines and digestifs.

After lunch, in place of charades, there was social media, but I was in no position to protest. Even Dee was at it. 'I'm up to sixty-three likes on Instagram for my Christmas tree,' she told us with girlish glee.

'I'm surprised it's not thousands, Dee,' Cam said. 'It's easily the best I've seen this year.'

'The one in Claridge's was pretty nice,' Stella reminded him. 'Did we tell you we had a babymoon dinner there, Mum?'

'How much did *that* cost?' Rafferty asked, and I started to think, *More than Pixie and the Leicester girl could afford*, but then I remembered the Penhaligon's present and was able to find it in my heart to forgive her.

'One more!' Dee exclaimed, still counting her likes, and

catching up on messages. 'Oh, that's nice! Pixie wishes us all a merry Christmas.'

'Festivities went on late last night, I gather,' I said, secretly pleased that I'd been remembered ahead of Dee, even before Pixie had gone to bed. 'She messaged me at three a.m. I can't imagine staying up that late, even on Christmas Eve!'

'Well, with the time difference,' Dee began, then stopped, flushing.

I glanced at her, curious. 'What time difference? She's only in Tunbridge Wells.'

'Where the time difference can be measured in decades, not hours,' Rafferty quipped. 'Remember that club we went to that time, Stells? It was like it was still the Noughties.'

She cackled. 'Oh my God, remember how they all went wild to "Rhythm of the Night"?'

'What? It's a classic banger,' Cam said.

Ignoring this joshing, I repeated my question to Dee – 'What time difference?' – which caused her to pout at her phone as if dismayed by its role in this sudden unpleasantness.

'I said I wouldn't say, but I'm not telling you anything you can't see for yourself on Instagram.'

'I'm not on Instagram. Show me.'

She swapped seats with Rafferty to share her phone with me, switching from her own grid to Pixie's and demonstrating how to pull up posts and scroll through comments.

What I saw staggered me. The last few posts made it quite clear that Pixie was about as far away from Tunbridge Wells as she could get – Wellington, New Zealand, having travelled with Daniel, Maya and Jason on what looked to be a very boozy flight. The most recent post was a selfie with their hosts on the deck of Brian's back yard, beers and beams all round.

I doubted she had thought to check with Daniel about the likelihood of my stumbling on this treasure trove of memory-making, but if she had he'd probably – correctly – have said it was fine because boomers were only on Facebook. He didn't bother with social media himself, so there'd been nothing to give the game away on that score, and, as I've said, Maya was only concerned with self-promotion.

The point was, none of their text messages had made mention of the fact that Pixie was with them. They'd colluded to keep it from me, even involving Dee – *I said I wouldn't say anything* – who'd let slip when inebriated.

I felt nauseous, disorientated. My vision dimmed at the edges.

'Gwen?' Dee said, her face puckered with concern. 'Try not to fret. I know she might not be your first choice for Daniel, but he does look very happy. They both do. That's all that matters, isn't it? Think of how they both used to mope around.'

'With good reason in her case,' Stella pointed out. I couldn't tell if she'd been in on this, but that was by the by; I already knew she was the most guileful of operators. 'How brilliant that she's gone on holiday, Gwen? A change of scene is the best possible cure for the trauma she's experienced. So healing. I've always wanted to go to New Zealand.'

'We'll go when Boo-boo can manage the flight,' Cam promised and was instantly mocked by Rafferty.

'Remind me not to be working the day you take "Boo-boo" intercontinental for the first time. It's sure to be a screamer like you were, Stells.'

'I can't believe they didn't tell me,' I said.

'I'm sure they will,' Dee said. 'They've only just got there and I got the impression she was quite a last-minute participant. You mustn't think it's some big conspiracy,' she soothed, even though she'd already admitted it was. 'You could have joined Instagram and followed her at any time, couldn't you?'

'Is her account private though?' Rafferty asked. 'She could have refused Gwen's request to follow her.'

'A situation you're all too familiar with,' Stella teased, but Dee sent them a stern look.

'Why would she want to do that? She and Gwen are great friends. I'm sure she plans to tell her all about it the minute she's settled in.'

'I'll text her later and ask,' I said, not caring for the surreptitious looks they were exchanging. All at once, I was an outsider again.

I managed a further subdued half hour before saying, 'Do you mind if I head down? I'm feeling a bit bloated after the champagne.'

'Don't forget your pressie!' Stella said and Dee collected it before tailing me to the door.

'I feel terrible if I've upset you.'

'You haven't done anything, Dee,' I said, then, remembering my manners, 'other than be a wonderful host. Thank you for inviting me, it's been very special. The food was magnificent. And the kids are great fun, a credit to you.'

She met this string of compliments with a doubtful expression that remained even as she closed the door.

*

It was between the third and second floors that I stumbled – spectacularly so, literally launched into the air, my stick flying from my hand and my glasses from my face. But even with blurred vision, my understanding of what was happening was acute: *I was going to die. This was it.*

And I wasn't scared at all

Then I landed face-down on the carpeted stairs and self-preservation prevailed: I snatched at a strut and gripped, my body weight continuing its fall until I felt an agonizing wrench in my shoulder. I feared for a second that it had dislocated, but after a few uncertain seconds I found I was able to heave myself up. I was badly winded and had twisted my wrist, but I knew instinctively there were no broken bones. My knee felt no worse off than before and I hadn't hurt my head beyond a light bump on the carpeted stair edge.

I located my glasses and stick and went gingerly on. Whether or not I glimpsed then what I would later face down with valour I can't say for sure, but given the intense strain I was under, the bullying I'd endured, not to mention the fresh callousness heaped upon me by my own family, well, it's a viable theory that the fall might not have been wholly accidental.

That I'd divined in some last flash of anguish or self-loathing that death might be the simplest solution to my heartache.

A blessed end to it all.

45

Only after treating my wrist with ice and swallowing a prescription painkiller with a glass of Daniel's chocolate liqueur did I allow myself to examine my feelings of betrayal, which were complex and multi-layered.

Quite apart from the humiliation – both as mother to Daniel and friend to Pixie – of being the last to know about her having joined him on the trip, there was also the question of how she had paid for it. Daniel had pledged his ill-gotten cash to my legal fees, and it seemed unlikely her long-awaited ruling by the financial ombudsman had borne fruit over the holiday season.

Which left … No, she couldn't have, could she?

She couldn't have taken the money I'd lent her for a longed-for flat, for the safe harbour she deserved, and spent it on a jaunt Down Under?

As for any previous subterranean desire on my part to keep Daniel and her apart – which Dee had taken as read and I deduced to be the reason for her secrecy – well, that had seriously backfired because it looked very much as if I'd made it possible for them to spend time together in paradise … with the man who had done his level best to impoverish me in the first place.

I messaged the three of them in turn:

To Daniel: Am I right in thinking Pixie is with you?

To Maya: I didn't realize Daniel had company on the trip?

To Pixie: I hear you're in New Zealand?

I tapped out a follow-up message to her – *That money was supposed to be for your rental*! – then had second thoughts and deleted it.

It was the early morning where they were, so I couldn't expect any replies for hours, but one thing I could do while I waited was open an Instagram account. What with the effects of alcohol and painkillers, this involved a few false starts, but eventually I managed to post a picture of my Christmas tree with a few bland words before locating @pixiegray321, the account I'd scrolled through on Dee's phone. As Rafferty had speculated, it *was* private and I would have to wait for my follow request to be approved before I could view the posts again and study the comments – or add any of my own.

*

I woke bruised in both mind and body. The memory of falling, of finding myself spreadeagled on the stairs, occupied me for several dark minutes before my spirits revived at the sight of new messages on my phone:

Dee

I hope you're OK, Gwen. Thank you for being such great company yesterday, we loved having you with us for Christmas. How's your head this morning?

Not great, Dee.

Daniel
Yes, she decided to join us last minute.

Last minute? I'd been there when he'd left for the airport and she was on the same flight! He *must* have known by then and had cravenly kept it from me.

Maya
I said he should have told you. Catch me (if you can!) on TikTok @stayathomesiren

Pixie had not replied, and nor had she accepted my Instagram request, so I checked my email in the hopes that she'd opted to express herself in more detail; she'd surely understand I was owed an explanation, given such a radical change of plans since we'd last spoken. There were no recent mails in my inbox, but hope flared at the sight of the new mail icon in my spam folder; she must have set up a new address, something I'd repeatedly urged her to do when the scandal was at its height.

But clicking on it, I found something far less welcome, indeed deeply objectionable: a message from the police, dated December 23:

We are writing to invite you to attend a voluntary interview at Queen's Oak Police Station regarding an allegation of harassment. Please contact us to arrange a convenient time to come in.

Alec's name wasn't given, but he was undoubtedly behind this – more of the 'seasons' greetings' to which he'd alluded in his vile little text.

Though it was a bank holiday, I forwarded the email to Frances Voss and left a succession of increasingly frantic messages on her office phone number. Truly, I do not know how I managed my mind during the wait for her return call. Certainly, the rest of the bottle of chocolate liqueur was consumed – or 'slayed' as Pixie would have put it – as was the rest of the alcohol stored on the premises.

At least Alec stayed away, so I could not be tempted to confront him.

Frances finally rang back on the afternoon of the twenty-seventh.

'I'm sorry to bother you over the break,' I said, regretful by then of the sheer volume of messages I'd subjected her to.

'It's fine, Gwen. I know it can be distressing to receive these sorts of emails out of the blue.'

'It really is.' The sound of an ally – even one I was paying – brought a choke to my voice. 'I thought you said this would only be a civil matter?'

'The libel is, yes, but a complaint of harassment is something the police can choose to investigate. I did warn you things might escalate.'

'Can I refuse to be interviewed?'

'You can, but that might prompt them to arrest you, so I would advise cooperating. I'll attend with you so try not to worry.' She paused; an awkward question was coming, I could tell. 'Gwen, there's no history between you and Mr Pedley that we didn't cover in our meeting, is there?'

I felt my pulse stutter. 'What do you mean?'

'These current hostilities, they don't follow any previous bad feeling, do they? With harassment, pattern of behaviour is a key factor.'

'It's not "bad feeling",' I said, insulted, 'it's my reaction to his mistreatment of a friend, a young woman who would otherwise have been defenceless.' I felt a spike of self-pity at the thought of Pixie with Daniel in New Zealand, perfectly placed to forget the whole saga. At the present moment, *I* was the defenceless one, not her. 'He'll be doing this to put more pressure on me for the damages claim, to scare me into agreeing.'

'It does have the feel of a pincer movement,' Frances said in enviably level tones. 'But the police can't be used in the way you're suggesting, as part of someone's private vendetta. They wouldn't want to speak to you unless they judged they had solid evidence. Let me come back to you on timings. It might not be today, okay? Most people aren't back in the office till next week.'

'Of course. Thank you, Frances. I'm really grateful.'

While I waited for further intelligence, I must have started and abandoned twenty episodes of my favourite TV shows, but not even *Morse* could hold my attention. The continuing soreness from my fall was a diversion of sorts and I spent long hours in the bath and in front of the mirror looking at my body, repelled by the colour of my bruises, no longer the rainbow displays of youth, but shades of blue and grey. It was a long time since I'd examined myself in this way, morbidly fascinated by the view from both front – the slack ropes of fat over my ribs – and rear, the artless oblong from shoulders to hips. I remembered again that serene acceptance of death I'd felt mid fall.

I checked Instagram incessantly, but Pixie had still not yet accepted my request. Maya's feed supplied a regular diet of holiday vignettes: some sort of mountain trail; an outdoor bar, beers borne aloft to a pink sky; a market stall selling jewellery and sunhats – with Pixie occasionally visible at the periphery. I also searched for Jason, Brian, even Brian's wife, who I had never met, hoping for other scraps.

For a woman who'd never set foot on the app before, I was a fanatic. I'd already attracted a hidden message, a string of gobbledegook, the only legible phrase being 'Live sex clips & hot camera'.

These people were fixated on sex. No wonder Instagram was such a honeypot to Alec and his depraved ilk.

46

Thanks to the inconvenience of the weekend, during which rain pounded the windows and violent winds blasted the gardens, it was three days before Frances came back to me.

'It *is* Alec Pedley,' she said, a superfluous verification for I had no other opponents in my ring. 'We'll get disclosures before the interview—'

'Voluntary chat,' I cut in, correcting her.

'Yes, all right, but don't make the mistake of thinking it's only casual, Gwen. It will be under caution and recorded. We'll meet ahead of time and have a look at what they've got, so you'll know what to expect.'

'What's the strategy? Should I just answer each question honestly?'

'Actually, I recommend you give no comment.' She explained why at length, the upshot being she thought that if I was not reined in then I might indulge my unhelpful habit of flinging my own allegations about and in the process provide more evidence of malicious communication.

In other words, I was my own worst enemy.

'So you know where you're going?' she asked before we hung up.

There was a larger question in this, to which I could have offered myriad answers, but I gathered she meant the address of my local police station, a mile or so north of Columbia Mansions. I'd passed it on the bus a hundred times, idly curious about who might languish in its bowels, confirming or denying, confessing or concealing, and maybe – it presumably still happened in these godless times – praying for dear life. Sometimes on those bus rides I'd shudder as I recalled my formal interviews in a Surrey station years ago, as police tried to judge if I was Brian's accomplice or dupe. Perversely, his protection had been all that separated me from his crimes.

You know, friends asked me sometimes if I thought our marriage would have been long and happy – or at least longer and happier – had it not been for the fraud, but the truth was the marriage *was* the fraud.

Most of them are, aren't they, one way or another?

*

Frances and I were greeted at the station with a 'Happy New Year' that sounded sincere enough, but how on earth could it be? If someone had a meeting with a detective then plainly something unhappy had befallen them. I, for one, had spent New Year's Eve alone, guzzling cheap wine and googling women's prisons, wondering if I might soon be joining what one described as its 'diverse and complex' population.

The interview room was dismal, as if the apprehension of those who'd lost their way in life ranked too low even for a once-a-decade paint job, and I had to hope the detectives themselves were in better nick. In fact, just one was present for our interview, female and perhaps a little *too* well-groomed, with that weirdly vaudeville make-up you saw on social media and sharp polished nails a cheetah would have been proud of. Her voice was sultry and well-modulated, not unlike Maya's, a disconcerting detail I could have lived without.

Frances's presence went some way to easing my anxiety, as had her reaction to the disclosures file beforehand. 'It's pretty thin. They might have kept something back to surprise us, but if this is it then I can't see it having legs.'

Formalities over, Cheetah lady began: 'On Sunday the 16th of November last year, did you make a 101 call to the police regarding a complaint about Mr Pedley that was judged to be false?'

'It wasn't false—' I began, before sensing Frances stiffen and curtailing my reply: 'No comment.'

'Did you want to elaborate, Gwen?'

'Ms Healy. No.'

'On the same day, did you tail Mr Pedley from his home to Tesco Metro on Winifred Gardens Parade, Queens Oak?'

'No comment,' I said firmly.

'Did you search a public bin directly after he'd used it?'

'No comment.'

'Well, you might be interested to know a witness described you doing exactly that.' Here she quoted from an encouragingly slight file on the desk in front of her: 'They said you were "acting in a feral and eccentric manner".'

I shot her a defiant look. 'I'm not interested to know, no.'

She raised an impossibly flawless eyebrow before continuing. 'The next day, Monday the 17th of November, did you, in the presence of Dee Carmichael and Noel Rudd, your neighbours and co-directors of the management board at Columbia Mansions, accuse Mr Pedley of publishing obscene images?'

'No comment.'

'Did you use false allegations both publicly and privately

regarding his relationship with his lodger with the intention of having him removed from his role of director?'

'No comment.'

'On Tuesday the 10th of December, did you make a public statement in the street outside Columbia Mansions in which you described Mr Pedley as a sex offender?'

'No comment.'

She made her first use of props then, sliding a print-out towards me and saying, for the benefit of the recording, 'I'm showing Ms Healy a print-out of a screenshot showing a WhatsApp message dated Wednesday the 11th of December. The highlighted text reads: "You'll be pleased to know the 'rapist' has left. I saw him head off last night." Do you recognize that text, Ms Healy?'

'No comment.'

'Does "the rapist" refer to Mr Pedley?'

'No comment.'

'On Saturday the 14th of December, did you enter his property without his permission?'

'Whose property?'

Another raised eyebrow. 'Mr Pedley's property. Flat four, Columbia Mansions, Clayton—'

'No comment,' I cut in.

'Did you, on the same occasion, remove bins from his property with the intention of searching their contents?'

I couldn't help bark with laughter at that. 'No comment.'

There was a change of medium then. An iPad was fired up, a video clip played. 'This video was taken from Mr Pedley' door camera on Sunday the 22nd of December. Ms Healy, do you recognize the person in it?'

It was laughable to ask because it was clearly me, coat unbuttoned over the pleated navy dress I'd worn to the Festive Fizz.

Judging by the fish-eye lens, the camera had been fitted behind Alec's peephole, the perfect height from which to capture my anger as I struck the door with one my crutches. There was no audio, but doubtless a competent lip reader would be able to supply my words if they had not already: '*You won't get a penny from me, you scheming bastard!*'

I made a mental note to ask Noel if permission was needed to install a security device like this one – not that Alec was in the habit of asking permission to fit his surveillance equipment. At least now I knew how he'd been able to arrive at his door so promptly whenever I was at mine: he'd been watching a live feed, like a security guard.

'No comment,' I said.

Next came another print-out. 'Did you send this text message to Mr Pedley on Monday the 23rd of December calling him a "pervert", specifically "Go to hell, pervert"?'

'No comment.'

The detective took a moment to straighten her print-outs before placing the iPad on top. 'Ms Healy, you do understand that this is your opportunity to give your side of the story in what is being investigated as a campaign of harassment against your neighbour?'

'No comment.'

She treated me to the infantilizing gaze of a weary parent before saying, 'If that's the case, then we'll finish there.'

I felt like sticking my tongue out at her, but resisted.

My debrief with Frances in the Costa across the street barely lasted the time it took us to drink a cup of tea.

'I can't believe they think it's worth spending resources on pettiness like this,' I said.

'Not petty to them. We've talked before about interpretation,' she reminded me, but I could tell she was relieved. 'It's good that they didn't have anything too explosive up their sleeve.' Given her question on the phone, I assumed this meant any historic unpleasantness that might have strengthened the investigators' suspicions of my character.

I was glad I hadn't told Dee or anyone else that I'd be speaking to the police – or, rather, that they'd demanded to speak to me. Of course, I might have confided in Pixie had she still been staying with me, not least because the police might at some point want to interview her as a witness to my various episodes of 'harassment', but as she continued to ignore my efforts to contact her it was a moot point. I told myself I didn't want to spoil her trip by worrying her, which wasn't to say I'd forgotten about her suspected misuse of my loan, simply that I recognized that it was now of secondary concern and best addressed in person.

Frances finished her tea, saying, 'I think there's a very good chance of their No Further Actioning this.' She checked her phone and gathered up her effects. 'Right, I have to scoot. And Gwen? Contact with Mr Pedley … No more texts, okay?'

47

As it happened, there *was* some historic unpleasantness, something Frances and the cheetah detective would have been very interested to hear and that no one in Columbia Mansions knew about, least of all Alec.

Brian, yes.

I might as well just come out and say it: I physically attacked him.

It was the conclusion to that argument about Cyndi, when he'd swept aside her accusations and threatened to implicate me in his embezzlement if I chose to side with her and not him.

'You are a hateful man,' I told him.

'You are an ugly woman,' he replied.

Which sounds childish when I write it like that, but at the time felt profoundly, diabolically adult. It certainly caused me to lose control: I picked up my phone and hurled it at his head, causing both a serious wound near his right eye that would need stitches and a concussion that rendered him briefly, thrillingly, incoherent.

In A & E, having recovered his speech, he told staff he'd been whacked by the low-hanging bough of a tree in our garden, which was barely a degree more convincing than saying he'd walked into a door, but for once I benefited from being a woman. Had it been me with the head injury, we might both have been questioned a lot more seriously.

Still, I think you'll agree he only got what he deserved.

It remains to be seen if you'll think the same about me.

48

The first week of January was a strange period of limbo – purgatory, if you like. One by the one the residents came back from their breaks, none of which, I could only assume, had been quite as godforsaken as mine. Noel and his husband returned from the Alps, Sadie and family from her in-laws in Guernsey, Hester from friends in Norfolk, and Liz from her daughter's home in Bath. As for Dee, following her Christmas hosting marathon, she'd taken a spa break in the Cotswolds, 'Refresh, Recharge, Reward' or some such. I couldn't spare the energy to judge its success.

She and Noel were prompt in checking in on my 'legal wrangle' and I was prudent with my updates, limiting them to the civil suit. I was taking my time over a decision, I said, reassessing my financial position before entering into negotiations. Noel reiterated his confidence in Frances and I thanked him again for the recommendation, praying that confidentiality protocols prevented her from telling him about the police investigation now running in parallel.

I pictured myself in that dilapidated interview room, how I must have looked to the young detective. A bitter old woman guilty of criminal malice.

Alec arrived home, too, and in a markedly less performative manner than last time – so discreet was his reappearance, in fact, that we only realized when his car was found to be parked in its spot. And even then, no one felt the need to debate it ad nauseam on WhatsApp; for the majority, a little perspective had re-entered the building.

It was different for me, of course. Sitting alone in my living room, I imagined him on the other side of the wall on the phone to his lawyer, discussing their strategy, discussing *me*.

I encountered him just twice during this period, both times on the landing. On the first occasion, I couldn't control my reflexes, flinching with a loud gasp in what I believe is known as a jump scare. By the second time, I gained control of myself sufficiently to recoil only faintly. As for his reaction to me, the menace of his previous incarnation had been replaced with what I can only describe as a state of emptiness, even serenity.

I don't think I would ever have the capacity to do what he did, to look through a human being as though through glass. To convince himself – and maybe, for a moment, her too – that she wasn't even there.

*

Daniel was the last to return, ten days into the New Year, looking the opposite of how I felt: sun-burnished, brimming with health, at ease with himself – all of this after a day on a plane – and of course I was pleased to see him looking so Refreshed, Recharged and Rewarded.

After his enquiries about my knee and mine about his jetlag, I made us a cup of tea and got straight to the point: 'Was Pixie on your flight back?'

Whether owing to guilt or disorganization, she still had not replied to my messages or approved my request to follow her on

Instagram. Having guessed she'd travelled home with Daniel I'd left a voicemail to suggest we meet for a coffee.

'No, she flew back a couple of days ago.' There was a casual note to his reply that I found both irritating and a little ominous.

'How did she pay for the trip, did she say?'

'What?' He looked genuinely surprised by the question.

'Come on, the flight alone would have been a couple of thousand. Did she use the money I lent her?'

'I don't know. We didn't discuss it.'

'I don't believe that,' I said. 'But, to clarify, *you* didn't pay for her?'

He raised his eyebrows. 'To *clarify*, I did not.'

'Why didn't you tell me you'd invited her? I know she was on your flight out. I saw Maya's pictures.'

'Yeah, but it was totally spur of the moment and you were all het up about the lawyer, so I didn't say anything.' He slurped his tea, eyes watering at the temperature. 'We *knew* you'd overreact. It was a holiday, that's all. With Dad, the person you hate most in the world, so it's not like we thought you were gonna suffer any FOMO.'

I tried to process this litany of insults: *I* was overreacting, *I* was full of hate, *I* had been too 'het up' to be entrusted with news of a good friend's plans. Why was he treating me like this? He'd been so supportive before he left – I remembered his helping me down the stairs after the Festive Fizz, patient and devoted. 'Do you *really* not see why I might be upset?'

'Uh, you lent her money and you think she wasted it on a holiday? But even if that *is* what she did, it's not a crime, is it? Might be the best decision she made for her mental health, after everything she's been through.' He spoke as if I were not the very person who'd identified and rescued her from 'everything'.

'It's more that I have financial issues of my own,' I reminded him. 'My situation with Alec hasn't gone away, in case you're interested. If anything, it's got a lot worse.' I had about as much desire to relate my recent humiliations to him as I had Dee or Noel, but still, a part of me died when he didn't even ask what I meant by this, only yawned and rubbed his eyes.

'So she's back at Ash's, is she?' I said, breaking the silence.

'Yeah, down in Tunbridge Wells.'

And if I was right and she had spent her deposit, she'd be there for as long as Ash and his parents would have her. 'Wasn't she supposed to be looking after their dog?'

His mouth twisted with impatience. 'You make it sound like it was some kind of animal welfare issue. Ash was home the whole time. He totally agreed she needed a proper break.'

Again, it was if he'd completely forgotten my part in caring for her. 'Okay. Well, if you're speaking to her, will you ask her to phone me? I've been messaging her since Christmas and she hasn't replied. It's been over two weeks now.'

Daniel placed his mug on the coffee table. 'I don't know.'

I stared at him, confused. 'You don't know if you'll be speaking to her or you don't know if you'll ask her to phone me?'

'I mean, I don't know if I want to get involved in this.' He stretched his neck, yawned again. 'I'm really knackered, Mum. Can we do this later?'

'Do what? What's going on?'

'Just ...' He raised his palms in surrender. 'Okay. Fine. We talked a lot when we were away about everything that went down here.'

My pulse began to speed. 'And?'

'And we all agreed none of it *would* have gone down if you hadn't broken her trust when she told you about Alec. The whole thing could have been handled in a completely different way.'

Though I could not deny this – Lord knew I'd come to the same conclusion myself, punished myself relentlessly by imagining what those better ways might have been – that 'we all agreed' stung. It was all too easy to imagine Brian putting his oar in (the man who'd been accused of assaulting a young woman himself!), thrilling at the opportunity to damn me. 'Dee was the one who got her involved with Stella and the BBC,' I pointed out.

'But *you* told Dee. She asked you not to tell anyone but you did. You say you're her friend, but that's not what friends do.'

'Nor is selling information to journalists,' I snapped. 'Does she know about that yet?'

'She does actually. I told her when we were away. She understands I was desperate. Financially.'

I felt my colour rise. *Desperate financially?* What a selfish pair they were!

'Anyway,' he said, struggling to his feet, 'I need to go and get some shut-eye.'

'Your bed's all made up and I cleaned your en suite,' I told him. 'And I've made a beef casserole if you're hungry later.' This was his favourite meal and he thanked me with a faint air of defiance, no doubt thinking I should have told him about these niceties before letting him say such hurtful things about me.

Straight out of the Old Daniel playbook and without a shadow of a doubt the result of Brian's malign influence.

*

Jetlagged, he slept on and off for the rest of the day, then rose early the next. By the time I got up at 7.30 a.m., the washing machine was already groaning, with further loads waiting to go in. From what I could gather, he was laundering every stitch he owned. The rest of his things he was packing.

'This is a hive of activity.'

He glanced up from his boxes. 'You did ask me to leave, Mum.'

'When?'

'Before the trip?'

'I didn't ask, you said you wanted to.'

He shrugged as if I were splitting hairs.

'Where will you go?' I asked.

'Maya's. For a while anyway.'

'Won't having a roommate interfere with her TikTok filming?'

'Don't see why. I'll be in their new garden room. It's got its own bathroom.'

Of course, the quarters she'd considered offering Pixie in her hour of need. Perhaps the plan was for Pixie to join him there. 'What about work? You've only just started at Bageri Møller.'

'I'm switching to the branch in Greenwich. Just need to go in and meet the manager.'

I didn't have the energy to interrogate him on his career plans beyond this. For all I knew he'd resolved to follow Pixie's footsteps in moving from place to place, casual job to casual job. Digital nomads who'd dispensed with the digital.

'What's this?' He'd stumbled on the box I'd brought back from Nella's.

'Looks like stuff from your old flat.'

'Oh. Can I leave it here?'

'You don't want to keep any … ?'

'What, souvenirs?' He scoffed at the notion. 'Why, do you keep any from *your* marriage?'

'That was different,' I snapped. 'Your father was a convicted criminal, which doesn't tend to promote sentimentality. But as far as I'm aware, Nella remains a law-abiding citizen.' I took comfort, not for the first time, in the fact that they did not have children to complicate their parting – or to suffer from it.

Daniel scowled. 'Look, I'm not getting back with her if that's what you're hoping. I'm not splitting with Pix.'

So they were still romantically involved then. All at once, I was struck by the way these last months had been defined by a series of rivalries, a vying for Pixie's affections. Between Alec and me, between Dee and me, and now, apparently, between Daniel and me. 'Perhaps I'll ask your sister if I can move in as well,' I said, growing tearful.

His expression clouded. 'Why would you do that?'

'Because I'm going to have to sell this place, aren't I? To pay Alec's damages. That's if I'm not in jail.'

'What are you talking about, why would you be going to jail?'

'I told you yesterday, things have gone from bad to worse. The police are investigating me for harassment. I've been in for questioning and now I have to wait to see if they'll charge me.'

That jolted him out of his heartlessness. 'Harassment? Are you serious? Why didn't you tell us?'

I blotted my nose with a tissue. 'Because I didn't want to spoil your trip. And look how you repay me? By saying these horrible things.' Tears dripped down my face and I dashed them away. I could see he regretted his comments.

'Have you been over there to have it out with him?'

'He's been away until recently. Anyway, I'm not allowed to speak to him. Everything I say gets noted and used against me. He's even got a camera watching to see if I approach his door.'

Daniel looked so appalled I had a fresh insight into the trouble I was in. 'This is awful, Mum. Is there any way I help?'

'Yes. You can get Pixie to answer my messages. Tell her it's imperative that we meet.'

He'd walked right into *that*. 'I will. Of course.'

And that was that with Daniel. Nine months of his company and in the blink of an eye, he was gone. Not spirited away by Dee, at least, hers the last word, the final smile of sympathy, as had been the case with Pixie, but in an Uber, its backseat crammed with his things.

Only the box from his old life was left behind. Consoling myself with a large gin, I revisited his vacant room, perched on his stripped mattress and pictured myself making my home among those unwanted Valentine's cards. Miniaturized, like the Incredible Shrinking Woman or one of The Borrowers.

*

Almost three weeks since I'd last heard from her, Pixie finally texted. Daniel had evidently made good on his promise and the column of thirty-odd messages from me was now countered with a line from her:

sorry gwen but I don't plan 2 come 2 london any time soon

I replied at once:

Then I'll come to you. Just say when and where?

She did not answer at once, so I added:

Please Pixie. One coffee. You owe me that much.

The dots came and went for several minutes as she composed her reply and I'd almost given up by the time it landed:

tmrw @11? cake stand cafe, high st, tunbridge wells

The elation I felt was disproportionate to the smallness of the bone I was being thrown, but I couldn't help it.

I'll be there!

But there were no ticks or 'read' or even 'sent' for this one and when I googled why, it transpired she must have sent that last message and then immediately blocked me.

49

I took inordinate, almost ritualistic care in getting ready. In choosing what to wear (comfortable trousers and a fuchsia sweater that once drew a compliment from Pixie) and how to style my hair (a rare blow-dry); even in deliberating which body wash to use in the shower (the Penhaligon's was easily my fanciest but would its scent make me think of Stella when I needed to concentrate on Pixie?).

Ridiculous, I know, behaving in such a lovelorn manner.

The trains being less reliable than at any time in living memory, I allowed an extra hour to get to Tunbridge Wells and spent twenty minutes of it waiting to depart Charing Cross while a signal failure got fixed down the line.

The train had just started moving when my phone rang. Dreading a last-minute cancellation, I was relieved to see Frances's name flash on screen.

'I've just come off the phone with the police. There's an informal caution on the table.'

'What does that mean?' I asked.

'It means they caution you verbally and there's no admission of guilt.' When I failed to respond, she added in galvanizing tones, 'It's an excellent outcome, Gwen.'

'An excellent outcome would be if *he* was cautioned,' I said.

There was a silence. You could almost taste her amazement. 'That was never going to happen,' she said at last.

'Can I have the rest of the day to think about it?' I was fretting about Pixie, of course. Now just minutes from seeing her again, I worried that to accept the caution was to let her down, to become a deserter where once I'd led the charge. I needed to get a sense of where she was at before I made my decision.

Frances turned brisk, even cold. 'Of course. But I strongly recommend you take it, Gwen. Take it, pay the damages, extricate yourself from all of this before the costs get too ruinous.'

She meant financial costs, of course, but there were emotional ones too, and I wonder now if I hadn't already passed the point of no return in that respect.

*

If Royal Tunbridge Wells, with its historic societies and passion for gardens, seemed an unlikely home for Pixie, then the Cake Stand café only emphasized that incongruity. It was all faux Tudor fittings and antique crockery, Victoria sponges under tall glass domes, absurdly genteel, defiantly out of date. The last place I'd have expected her to choose.

But then she'd chosen it with me in mind, hadn't she?

She arrived with Ash in tow (I supposed I ought to be thankful it was not Daniel) and after stiffly succumbing to a hug settled opposite me, he to her left. If I'd been in any doubt before that our friendship had been subject to revision, I wasn't any longer for her body language confirmed that she'd turned against me. Was she going to answer all my questions with 'no comment'?

'You look well,' I said cheerfully, and so she did. Her face was tanned and freckled from the Antipodean sun, her punkish bob grown out, the ends fanning softly over her collarbone. Whether her choice of top – a Māori print – had been consciously worn to remind me of the holiday, I couldn't say. The same went for the many leather and silver bracelets she wore on both wrists.

A teenage waitress with false eyelashes that would have put Twiggy's in the shade (literally) came to take our orders – luxury hot chocolates for the two of them, an ascetic single espresso for me – and then I made my opening gambit.

'You've probably heard from Daniel about my misgivings about your trip?' I'd given careful consideration to the word I wanted to use before settling on 'misgiving'. It communicated disappointment without accusation.

A scowl passed over Pixie's face. 'So I'm not allowed a holiday, am I?'

Instant confrontation was not in her personality and I suspected she'd been coached by Daniel or even Brian. *Make sure you get in there first or she'll walk all over you ...*

'Of course you are,' I said. 'It was just what you needed and I'm really happy about that. Everyone agrees,' I added, to show I was by no means out in the cold, that *she* might have blanked me, but no one else had. 'My misgivings are only that the money I lent you was supposed to be for you to get yourself a new rental. One of those studios in New Cross, remember?'

'You can't dictate my spending,' she said, not quite snapping and, again, it was not her phrasing. Her voice would come through eventually, I trusted. Her natural sweetness could not be erased. She could be determined, but she was not spiteful.

'Not normally, no, but this was a loan with a specific purpose, so it *was* conditional. I know you know that, because otherwise you'd have just told me where you were going. Instead, I had to find out from Dee. On Christmas Day.'

She shrugged. 'I thought you were on Instagram.'

'I am now but I wasn't then. Remember you had to explain to me what hidden requests were? And anyway, you haven't accepted my request to follow you so you know I haven't had access to your posts.' I paused to allow the delivery of our drinks and for Ash and her to scoop their whipped cream and marshmallows into their mouths like infants. 'And even if I *had* been able to see them, would that really have been the most appropriate way to let me know you were visiting my ex-husband? A man you know treated me very badly?'

She said nothing, eyes down, ostensibly concentrating on needless stirring. I had a sudden vision of her asking Brian about the scar by his eye, how he'd got it. Her aghast reaction when he explained.

'Look,' I said, 'I'm not stupid. I know there was some sort of conspiracy of silence because Daniel and Maya didn't say anything either. They're my children, Pixie, and I don't appreciate you turning them against me.'

She dropped her spoon to her saucer as if in protest. 'I haven't turned them against you.'

'Maybe it's the other way around then? Why did you block my phone number?'

''Cos I couldn't handle all the voicemails,' she said peevishly. 'I was trying to forget Columbia Mansions, not have these constant reminders.'

Already a sense of stalemate was thickening between us. My assumption that her natural kindness would surface was looking shakier.

'Did you spend it all? All five thousand?'

She said nothing, which I took to be a yes.

'And has Daniel told you about Alec's claim against me?'

Again, she said nothing. Then, inspired: 'See, there's stuff you haven't told me either.'

'Because I was protecting you, I didn't want you to feel guilty. But now I see you're more robust, I'll share my situation. I'm going to have nothing left, Pixie. I'll be completely wiped out.' There was a tremor in my voice, like that of an elderly person. 'It's one thing to put myself at risk knowing a friend has a roof over her head, but it's another to know it just funded an expensive holiday.'

As she again resorted to silence, I lost my cool, crying out, 'Do you not realize I could lose my home?'

'At least you've got one to lose,' Ash piped up, speaking for the first time and with a knifing resentment.

I treated him to my most baleful gaze. 'I'm in my seventies. It's not easy to bounce back at this age.'

'Not even with your new leg?'

'What? Are you trying to be funny or are you just thick in the head?'

Pixie turned to him with a gentler admonishment. 'Ash, don't. Maybe I should do this alone.'

'Yeah. All right. I'll wait outside.' He got to his feet, dragging his jacket from the back of the seat, and took his chocolate to the counter to have it transferred to a takeaway cup.

'Do what alone?' I said to Pixie, sounding like a lover on the verge of a spurning. A rapprochement between us felt out of reach now, our lovely old closeness unrecoverable.

'Reassure you that I'm going to pay you back.' Her brow furrowed. 'It's really insulting that you act like I won't. I'm working again.'

'The project you mentioned when you moved out? Who's the client?'

She pressed her lips together. 'I'd rather not say.'

'Why not? This is ridiculous, I'm not some kind of stalker!' My vehemence was drawing glances and I lowered my voice, relying instead on an injured gaze. 'Are *you* going to accuse me of harassment as well?'

'What d'you mean "as well"?'

'Nothing. Forget it.' Clearly Daniel had kept news of the criminal investigation to himself. He was capable of *some* discretion then. 'And however you get your next injection of cash, you'll need to use it for rent, so there won't *be* any left to repay me – or whoever else you owe. Money burns a hole in your pocket, Pixie.'

There was of course a more sympathetic point of view and one my enduring affection for her led me to prefer: she didn't know the value of money because people like me kept bailing her out. She'd evolved to expect it, the moment one benefactor was exhausted the next must be sought.

I glanced out the window to the street, where Ash was loitering, cup in one hand, vape in the other, oblivious to an attempt by a trio of middle-aged women to manoeuvre past him. Looking back, I found that Pixie was gazing at me with a franker, more receptive expression than previously and I felt a twinge of hope.

'Daniel told me you've done a lot of reassessing since you left Columbia Mansions and if you've come to see my motives in a new light then I have no choice but to accept that. All I ask is that you keep in mind who was really to blame for your unhappiness there.'

It was then that it happened – and I might so easily have missed it, if I'd teared up, for instance, or checked again on Ash, but instead I caught its full glare. Dilemma, no, puzzlement, as she processed my comment about blame.

She didn't immediately think of Alec.

I felt myself go cold, my lungs tightening, even as my brain herded excuses for her. She'd not automatically thought of him because she'd done such a good job of healing herself, of 'reassessing'. Or she'd learned to use CBT to replace thoughts of him with ones of … who knew, her future menagerie of fur babies, perhaps?

But there was also a third possibility.

'You do know who I'm talking about?' I said.

''Course I do.' Her countenance had refreshed, all doubt banished as she pushed back her seat and began gathering up her coat and bag. 'I need to go. Ash'll be freezing by now.'

'Wait.' I reached for her arm to stop her, careful to keep my grip gentle. 'Please, just tell me one thing.'

She paused: *Go on.*

'It *was* true, wasn't it? What you said happened with Alec?'

Her gaze toughened with that new defiance. 'I did that TV interview, didn't I? I put myself through all that shit.'

'That's not what I asked. I asked if it was true.' Bile rose in my throat – liquid dread – and I swallowed it, feeling my face contort. My hand was still on her arm.

'He told me, you know,' she said.

'Told you what?'

'You know.' There was a giddiness in her eyes, a sense of disbelief in her own temerity. 'He told me after that thing with Draco. He'd said stuff before, like you were jealous, but I had no idea what he was on about. It explains a lot, I reckon.'

I drew a deep breath, staving off panic. If this was an attempt at a diversion, she couldn't have picked one more likely to throw me off balance. 'I don't want to talk about it.'

'No, you only want to talk about me. To question me.' She extricated her arm, rubbing it with her hand as I'd hurt her. 'Maybe everyone's right, you *are* obsessed.'

Everyone? *Obsessed*? We stared at each other, our individual griefs failing to connect. 'It wasn't, was it?' I whispered at last. 'It wasn't true.'

She gave a sad little sigh as she finally stood, thrusting her arms into the sleeves of her coat, hooking her bag over her arm. 'You decide, Gwen. You obviously know best. You always do.'

50

It was all I could do not to vomit on the train back to Charing Cross, for it rocked me, that exchange, it rocked me to the point of nausea. As if Pixie's rejection of our friendship weren't painful enough, as if the revelation that she knew secrets concerning Alec that predated her own didn't undermine, *overturn*, what that friendship had meant ... Well, the suspicion that she'd misled me about her original allegation was worse. It was harrowing, sickening.

Because everything I'd said and done, all the dilemmas I'd wrestled with, was predicated on the truth of that allegation.

Instinct told me deliberate lying was too cunning an act for her, that it must have been a question of embellishment. What verb had Alec used that time? *Reimagine*, that was it. Had she *reimagined* herself as the victim? Had she *reimagined* relations between the two of them and then encouraged her saviours' assumptions so that they might more readily extract her?

If so, the odds had certainly been in her favour, and not only because I, the self-elected leader of those saviours, had old axes to grind. Another victim's memory to honour. There was also the fact that in this new light of shifting allegiances, in this age of young women changing their personas as regularly as underwear, a TV interview – *all that shit* as she'd so inelegantly put it – the truth was malleable as putty.

Pixie's generation regarded news as a means for self-promotion as much as for the reporting of real events. Look at Stella: she'd certainly done her share of old-school fact-finding, but had she fact-*checked*? Had she been so scrupulous about not offending her female subjects – *I believe you* – that she'd failed to subject them to the correct degree of scrutiny?

Sitting on the train, the world through my window as dreary and indistinct as I'd ever known it, I thought it likely that the answer was yes.

Which meant the real victim might still be at the scene of the crime – or should we say non-crime.

Flat 4, Columbia Mansions.

51

My knee having stiffened with the travel, I made heavy weather of the single flight of stairs to our landing and, in contravention of Frances's orders, rapped loudly on Alec's door. Though highly agitated, I had the presence of mind to keep out of range of his peephole, from which his covert camera presumably still transmitted images to his phone or laptop. The tactic worked, and as he opened up, I eased a foot across the threshold before he could catch sight of me.

When he did, his face soured. 'Contact me through my lawyer, please.'

'Alec, we need to talk face to face. It's about Pixie. I've just seen her.'

'Bully for you.' He began to close the door. 'And move your foot if you don't want your toes broken.'

Knowing he was a man to make good on his threats, I withdrew my foot and the door clicked shut in my face.

'Listen to me, please!' My mouth was so close to the timber my breath misted the paintwork. 'There are things I'm not so sure about any more. I think I might … I think I might owe you an apology.'

There was a moment's silence and then the door reopened a fraction. 'I know *that*,' he growled through the gap. 'My lawyer's been waiting on it since before Christmas.'

I thought about Frances's call, the police caution I'd been offered that suddenly looked pretty damn generous. 'Please, there are things we need to discuss. Just give me five minutes?'

'It had better be worth it,' he said, still barring the door.

'Will you come over to mine and I'll make us a cup of tea?'

He stepped aside, ushering me in. 'Something stronger might be better. Lead the way, you know your way around.' As I hobbled down the hall, his taunts followed in my wake. 'Enjoy yourself, did you, poking about when I was away? Making off with the rubbish? What is it with you and bins? Bit of a fetish, is it?'

I flushed. 'We emptied it for you, that's all. It was starting to smell. To be honest, I was surprised you hadn't changed the locks.'

'I was going to after that, but then she texted to say she'd lost her key, which figures. We all know what a dozy bird she is.'

I knew he was challenging me to protest the sexist slur, but I said nothing. In the brighter light of the kitchen, I was better able to assess his appearance. He looked sallow but well rested, a creature who'd been hibernating for winter – as opposed to having braved hellfire as I guessed *I* must look, with my burning face and wild-eyed desperation.

He collected two glasses from a cupboard. 'Whisky or gin?'

'Gin, please.'

He poured the drinks neat and handed me mine, signalling for me to join him in the armchairs overlooking the gardens. He sat with his legs open, forming a diamond shape, and started on his whisky. 'So, the penny's dropped, has it?'

'I think it has, yes.'

'Well, eureka, Gwen.' His face broke into a smile, albeit a mean-spirited one. 'What took you so long?'

I took a tentative sip of the gin; it was sinus-clearing potent. 'I maybe shouldn't have waded in the way I did.'

‘What, without a scrap of evidence, you mean?’

I sipped again before braving a proper gulp. ‘If it was just a normal rental arrangement then you’ll have her regular deposits on your bank statement, won’t you? Would you show me?’ Had Dee demanded such evidence from him, I wondered? In the whirlwind of the *News Radar* business, I’d neglected to get a detailed account of her ‘investigation’.

‘Why would I do that?’ he said.

‘So I know you’re telling the truth.’

‘Can’t help you there. The first three months were paid by her dad and after what happened with the flat before, he wanted to pay me direct. Cut out the middle woman, if you know what I mean.’

I did. I could hardly contradict the notion that Pixie was not to be trusted with large sums of money. ‘What about after that?’

‘She was going to pay cash. And don’t start on about tax evasion, I don’t want to hear it. Anyway, turned out she had the room for less than three months so I didn’t need to get anything more from her.’

‘Fine. Show me his payment.’

He regarded me with mild impatience before tapping at his phone, thumb scrolling. ‘It came through a firm owned by a mate of his, what was it called … ? Ah, here it is.’ He showed me a deposit from September for £4,200 from Sweeney Ltd. ‘The first three months.’

‘I thought the rent was £1,500 a month?’ I queried. ‘That’s £4,500, not £4,200.’

‘Get you with your mental maths. This was what we agreed. I came down a bit. Call me a soft touch.’ He chuckled. ‘No good deed goes unpunished, huh?’

‘It doesn’t,’ I agreed sadly, knowing I might have arrived at this juncture long ago had I been thinking logically and not been swept up by my own hero complex. I frowned at the name of the remitter. 'Sweeney Limited? His name's Gray. Anyway, I thought he sold his business?'

'This is where the rent came from, Gwen, okay?' Alec said, getting impatient. He took the phone back, laid it on his thigh. 'Some mate of his in Bromley, I think she said.'

'Mate?'

'Well, it wouldn't be *his* account, would it? There're banking restrictions when you're banged up.'

'Banged up? What do you mean?'

He looked at me in amazement. 'Tell me you're not serious? You don't know her dad's in the nick?'

A bolt of shame sped through me. 'I didn't know, no.'

'Well, that says it all, doesn't it? She's obviously been highly selective with her personal information.'

I blinked, discombobulated. 'How do *you* know?'

'Came out one night when she'd had a bit of a session. Don't think she was happy she'd let slip, mind, when I reminded her the next day.'

This, presumably, was when confidences in the other direction had also been shared. I swallowed. 'What did he do?'

'Some sort of burglary charge. Look him up, his name's Colin Gray. And I strongly recommend you don't go confronting him with a whole load of questions. People like him don't take kindly to interference in their finances, even from fellow cons like yourself.'

Given this new intelligence, his unjust dig at me hardly registered. I drained my gin, scouring my mind for any last holes. 'What about the camera in the shower? I don't care what nonsense you told the police, I saw it with my own eyes.'

He nodded. 'I've been thinking about that. I think that must have been fitted by Yasmin.'

'Yasmin? Why would she do that?'

'Why do you think?'

I looked dumbly at him as he rubbed his nose with his knuckles, smirking. 'How do you think someone on an NHS nurse's salary got the money together to buy a flat?'

'I assumed she and Casper saved up. Or they had help from their parents.'

'Not the case. She was on OnlyFans. You do know what that is?'

'Yes.' I'd looked it up when overhearing Daniel tell Pixie he predicted Maya would migrate to the platform. Perhaps by now she had. 'I don't believe it. Yasmin's not like that.'

'Of course that's what *you* would think. You think chicks like her and Pixie are nice little Pollyannas. But unlike you, when I make an accusation, I have evidence to back it up.' He fiddled with his phone again and flashed a video at me, a woman visible from the neck downwards, soaping herself in the shower.

I turned away, shocked to think it could be the kind, care-giving Yasmin. Thoughtful enough to send a Christmas card to her old neighbour. An educated girl with choices.

'This is where the money is,' Alec said, reading my mind. 'Bet she does stuff in her nurse's get-up, as well. She'll be raking it in.' He acted as if this were entirely normal, which it clearly was to him since he'd had the app at the ready.

'What about your original message to Pixie. You said, *We can come to an arrangement*. What did that mean? Just a discount?'

His gaze narrowed. 'There was no message.'

'She told me all about it. It was a hidden request on Instagram.'

'I'm not on Instagram, Gwen. I have no idea what a hidden request is.'

'Your username was @queensoaklandlord, something like that.'

'Come on, even if that exists, which I very much doubt, how

many landlords are there in Queen's Oak? Could've been anyone.' He regarded me with honest sympathy. 'Sorry, not me.'

'Why make it up? It makes no sense.'

'I assume it was to explain why she was sleeping with an old goat like me.'

It was a horrible image and I suppressed a grimace. 'Explain to who?'

'To you. And then whoever you blabbed to. We agreed we'd keep it to ourselves, but then you found out. I'm still not sure how, to be honest with you.'

Outside, down in the garden, there was the sudden yowl of a cat. As Alec got to his feet and went to fetch us more drinks, I felt my throat constrict. Could it really be as simple as he said – and as Daniel had implied? That if I hadn't peeked and pried, a consensual relationship might have run its course and we'd all have returned to our original positions?

'Plus she was skint,' he continued, returning with the drinks. 'Think about it: she wasn't getting any more money from her dad after those first few months. He'd already thrown good money after bad and it wasn't like he was around to slip her a bit of cash when she was short. She was earning peanuts at that café. Creating this sob story and getting you all riled up about it meant she could walk straight across the hall to a rent-free scenario.'

It was excruciating the way his account filled the gaps I'd been so determined to overlook.

'And I know she started shagging Daniel once she was in there. More fool him. You've been played and so has he.' He looked thoughtful. 'The media stuff wouldn't have been in her game plan, mind you. I'm amazed she did that fake interview. Didn't think she had the bottle.'

I swallowed another mouthful of gin. 'She wanted to pull out, but Dee and Stella persuaded her. We all really thought she was being abused.'

'I know you did.' He tipped back his whisky, rolled the empty glass between his fingers. 'But the only person being abused here is me, which is why I instructed my solicitor to sue for damages. Not just you, by the way, but every media outlet that's printed my name and repeated your original slur. I have no choice but to recoup lost earnings.' As I fell silent, he leant forward to twist the knife. 'Come on, Gwen, you must know there's no way you can fight this defamation claim. You've just admitted you've got fuck all.'

He meant evidence, but it applied just as easily to my financial position. I began to cry. 'I lent her money. With that and my knee and the extra service charge … This lawsuit … I'm going to have to sell the flat.'

Through my tears I saw his expression soften a fraction. 'Can't you just remortgage?'

'I've looked into it but I'm too old.' I drew a tissue from my pocket and blew my nose. 'I'll have to downsize.'

'That's rough.' He sounded properly sympathetic now. 'You've lived here how long?'

'Just over ten years.'

'You've got yourself in a right mess. I'm sorry. I really am.'

I felt hope spark, all pride gone. 'You said you're suing other people as well, so maybe you could—'

He cut me off. 'No can do. You were the one who said it first. You're the apex offender. I have to clear my name, Gwen. It's not just the lost earnings, to be honest. I don't need Pixie's dad getting out of the slammer and coming after me. And Dee and Noel have made it clear that unless I can prove I'm innocent, I'll no longer be welcome here.'

‘The board doesn’t have the power to remove a leaseholder,’ I said.

‘I didn’t say I’d be removed. I said I wouldn’t be welcome. Which means more of what I’ve already been subjected to. Keep clear of the sex pest and all that. Not even allowed to rake up the leaves in case some kid gets exposed to my deviant influence. I need it formally established that I’m the victim. Damages show that. Because I’ve been damaged, Gwen, and I think you’re starting to appreciate that.’

I nodded. ‘I am. I’m really very sorry, Alec.’

He exhaled, his puffed cheeks deflating very slowly. ‘I knew you would be, eventually.’

52

Back in my own flat, in a state of near collapse following these back-to-back confrontations, I drained a glass of water to mitigate the gin and then googled Pixie's father's conviction:

Herne Bay Man Jailed for Burglary and Affray

A Herne Bay resident who was arrested by police after carrying out a burglary in Whitstable has been jailed.

On 3 February 2023, Colin Gray broke into a property on Preston Parade and made threats to the victim before stealing cash, designer clothing and jewellery. He pleaded guilty to burglary and affray and was sentenced at Canterbury County Court to a year and ten months in prison. PC John Billings of East Kent CID said, 'The victim was subject to a frightening ordeal but thanks to the swift actions of officers the offender was stopped in his tracks.'

I am no psychologist, but I do believe now that this helps explain Pixie's erratic behaviour during the period covered by this account. Her reframing of the facts, her exaggerations and fantasies. The human mind is an instrument prone to playing out of tune, after all, and to have your only parent convicted of a crime and removed from society must have been destabilizing.

The situation was doubly affecting for my knowing that some variation of her mortification – *It's shaming ... I don't want anyone new to know* – must once have been felt by Daniel and Maya. Had I paid enough attention to this when *their* father fell from grace? Not to mention his subsequent relocation to the other side of the world.

Was it possible Daniel and Pixie's bond was less a by-product of convenience than of a profound shared sorrow?

I turned my mind to the new complications I'd unleashed by reversing my position on Alec – in his presence, no less. Had I made a strategic mistake? If he were to pass on the contents of our conversation to his lawyer and, in turn, Frances, both the civil and police cases would be strengthened at a stroke. I needed to get back to her without delay.

Before doing so, I checked my bank account a final time for evidence of miscalculations on my part or miraculous skin-saving deposits from others, but found neither. There was no repayment from Pixie, of course, and for the first time, I wondered if her story of the New Cross fraud were even true. I, for one, had never seen any emails or correspondence from her bank or the ombudsman. Alec had talked of her father throwing good money after bad, but wasn't it possible, given her other falsehoods, that the bad had never existed?

But it hardly mattered. Alec's damages would take me well past the point of no return, with or without her £5,000. With only time left to lose, I rang Frances and told her I would accept both the police caution and Alec's demand for damages.

'You've made the right call,' she said. 'We'll start drafting the documents.'

Next, I emailed Dee and Noel to signal my intent to sell my flat. I couldn't dally in putting it on market; the board had a complex list of requirements that I remembered from having been the purchaser and knew to expect a drawn-out affair.

*

Just as I guessed she would, Dee dropped round the following morning. She must have been on her way to a meeting or a nice lunch for her get-up was box-fresh – cashmere tie-neck sweater, wide-legged trousers with a sporty side stripe, spotless white trainers – her hair and make-up beautifully done. She could have passed for half my age.

'Any news on the baby?' I asked. 'Stella's how many days overdue now?'

Dee looked a little thrown by the question. 'Four, I think. What on earth's going on? You're not serious about selling the flat?'

'I've agreed damages with Alec,' I said. 'This is the only way I can pay them.'

'Oh, Gwen. I must admit I'm sorry to hear that. We thought you'd fight our corner to the bitter end.'

Fight our corner? Was there no limit to her disingenuousness? 'Some new information has surfaced,' I said coolly. 'You may not want to hear this, but it's possible Pixie misrepresented her situation to us.'

The delicate lines in Dee's forehead deepened. 'In what way?'

'In that there was never any sex for rent. I'm not saying she and Alec didn't have a sexual relationship, or that there wasn't a cause for concern, just that I've seen evidence that during the months she lived with him her rent *was* paid. Monetary rent. Which means she can't have been paying in kind.'

Dee's lipsticked mouth opened in shock. 'I can't believe that. Really?'

'Yes. Did you not ask him for evidence of rent when you looked into it? When I was in hospital?'

She looked flustered by the question. 'I'm trying to remember.

That's right, I asked *her* and she showed me the payments on her banking app. It was all just coffees and bus tickets and bits and pieces. Nothing anywhere near the amount rent would have been.'

'Because her father paid it for her. It didn't come from her own account.' I sighed. 'It's good news, in a way, though, isn't it? It means she didn't suffer as we thought.'

'True, yes. Wow. Okay.' Her conflicting emotions were not hard to fathom: relief, yes, that a young woman she'd been fond of might not have experienced the living hell she'd believed, but also irritation for the inconvenience of this volte-face when she'd worked so hard to contain residents' ire regarding a different narrative entirely. And, perhaps the one that overrode all others, horror that her daughter's break-out journalism had been based on shaky if not false grounds – and that this might so easily become publicly known. 'What on earth was she thinking?' she cried in a rare loss of self-control. 'Misleading us all like that!'

'We mustn't blame her.' Still processing the collapse in my own faith, I had limited energy for schadenfreude. 'She's been dealing with a lot in her life and I think maybe she convinced us because she'd convinced herself. I don't think we can ever know what happened between them, but what is abundantly clear is that Alec's case against me is even stronger than I thought.'

'Yes, yes, I see that.' Dee had recovered from her outburst, her poise restored. 'Maybe we can crowdfund to help with the damages?'

I pulled a face. It was a game suggestion but we both knew it would only draw attention to the original scandal, the last thing the residents would want now we'd entered a period of relative tranquillity. Certainly, the WhatsApp group chat suggested appetites were returning for more trivial matters: a spate of local car break-ins, a group of addicts smoking drugs in Winifred Gardens (*Too much to expect the boys in blue to put two and two together here?* Elliot commented).

'I'm selling up,' I said. 'It's the simplest solution.'

*

There was one silver lining to my defeat, albeit gossamer thin. Selling meant I could gift Daniel a small sum to get him back on his feet and also set aside funds for Maya for when she grew tired of being a TikTok caricature of female subjugation.

I phoned them jointly to break the news, careful to couch the turn of events in purely pragmatic terms – 'I have to accept that his case is stronger than mine', 'I'm quitting while I'm behind' and so on. It's fair to say I was not expecting the pushback I got.

'But you still believe her side of the story?' Maya demanded, with a note of her old zeal.

'I think it's not cut and dried and I made a mistake presenting it that way.'

'We knew this would happen,' Daniel said. 'She told me you'd started to doubt her.'

Though it was entirely predictable Pixie had given him an unflattering account of our meeting in Tunbridge Wells – and that he would slavishly back her up – I took offence nonetheless. 'To be fair, Daniel, I think you of all people know *she* doubted *me* first. It's clear you've decided between you I'm as much a culprit in all of this as Alec.'

'No one said that,' he protested.

'Well, it doesn't matter any more. This is between Alec and me. I have to end this while I still have a chance to sell up and start over.'

'Where will you live?' Maya asked.

'I'll find somewhere.' A one-bedroomed flat in one of those co-living complexes for seniors Stella had waxed lyrical about, perhaps? It wouldn't be Columbia Mansions. It wouldn't be my home. But it would be *a* home, which I think we've established was more than many citizens of this city have to their name.

Not long after the call ended, I phoned Maya again and asked her not to put the call on speaker this time.

'It's fine. Dan's just left for work anyway.'

I sucked in my breath, gathered my nerve. 'I just need to ask, Maya, the reason you've adopted this new domestic goddess …' I was going to say 'guise', but stopped myself in time. '… this new identity. Was there anything in particular that set you on that path?'

There was a silence. I pictured her puzzlement. 'What are you talking about?'

'I mean, I know what happened with the charity must have been traumatic, and it was obvious that led to your own activism, but this … This is so different. I wondered if there was something else. Something I did.'

Or didn't do. The answer to my question arrived as I asked it. I'd modelled marriage badly. I'd given the impression it was an unholy place to build a life, not the sanctuary she now sought to create with Jason.

To my surprise, she burst out laughing. 'You are funny, Mum. You act like you're, I don't know, our pole star or something.'

'Pole star?'

'Yes. Directing us from above. Making it all align.'

I didn't know what to say to this and it was left to her to supply the sign off.

'Not everything is to do with you, you know.'

53

If memory serves, it was just a day or two after that session with the whisky and gin that Alec asked to meet again. I suggested coffee at my place and, since it was a Saturday morning, I broke my strict economy drive and bought cinnamon buns from Gail's. I thought of all those Saturday mornings with Daniel and pictured him in Maya's new garden room, working his way through a plate of blueberry muffins fresh from her oven.

'It's so much lighter in here than in my place,' Alec remarked. He'd come straight from the barbers and though the shearing had exposed spikes of grey at the temples, he looked ten years younger.

'It's the extra windows. It makes such a difference having them on three sides.'

'This is really tasty,' he said, tearing at the bun. 'Pixie used to bring those slices from the Danish place, but these are better.'

This innocuous domestic detail caused a flutter of regret, self-disgust. 'Did your lawyer tell you I've agreed to pay the seventy-five thousand?'

'Yup. Called me yesterday.'

'I've also started the process of putting the flat on the market,' I said, brushing pastry flakes from the corners of my mouth. 'I was hoping you might be flexible in terms of a payment schedule? A bridging loan will come with a horrendous interest rate, if I can even get one in the first place, which I probably can't. The apology and police caution will be much sooner, of course.'

'Actually, I wanted to talk to you about that,' he said.

'Oh yes?' I felt a clutch of panic and yet his expression was affable, even chummy. He had suggested this meeting, I remembered. I was only hosting it.

He finished chewing and looked me square in the eye. 'Here's the deal. If you write to the board, retracting all accusations and copying in all the residents, I'll withdraw the claim for damages.'

My mouth fell open. 'Are you serious? You mean I wouldn't have to pay after all?'

I couldn't believe what I was hearing, not least because a full retraction of comments had been agreed through our lawyers in addition to the damages.

'*And* I'll withdraw my complaint to the police about the harassment,' he added.

'But I'm due to go in next week to accept a caution.'

'They might decide not to bother once they hear what I've got to say.'

I almost burst into spontaneous weeping. 'Do you mean it? Do you really mean it?'

'Yeah. Totally.' He was being exactly as he'd been at his neighbourly best, as if none of the ugliness between us had happened.

'That's so incredibly decent of you, Alec. I ... I can't believe it.' I felt my whole body sink with relief and gratitude. Yes, there was still the service charge supplement and Frances's legal fees, but without any damages to pay I'd be able to keep the flat. 'Why have you changed your mind like this?'

Even as I posed the question, the explanation landed: either of her own accord following our meeting or, more likely, prompted by the news of my capitulation passed on by Daniel, Pixie must have contacted Alec and pleaded my case. The bonds of friendship had not dissolved completely.

Alec was smiling, evidently enjoying my response. 'Let's just say I've had some good news from my solicitor regarding another party I brought a claim against.'

Not Pixie then. The bonds *had* dissolved. 'One of the papers or social media sites?' Thank the Lord for corporate riches! The amount won must have knocked my £75,000 into a cocked hat for him to relinquish it so easily. 'Maybe Dee and Noel would welcome you back on the board?'

He looked surprised that this was my first thought. 'Oh, I don't want that. Let's leave all this admin crap to them and elect some new directors.'

'Agreed.' It was all I could do not to whoop.

'I'm glad you're happy.' He licked his finger and used it to mop up the last of the sugar, not a habit I cared for, but I was not about to say. He could clean the plate with his tongue if he wanted, given his extraordinary generosity. 'One condition,' he added.

'What?' I said, happily. 'Name it.'

'You sell your flat to me.'

'What?' *That* wiped the smile off my face.

'Don't get me wrong, I'll give you market rate. But without that, there's no deal.'

I gaped at him in fresh disbelief, before realizing he must have misunderstood my position. 'But the damages are the reason I have to sell in the first place. If your claim goes away, I won't need to put it on the market.'

He nodded, all understanding, but a glitter had appeared in his eyes that I struggled to read. 'I get it, sure. But that's still my condition.'

A silence spilled between us, broken only by children's squawks from the garden, a furious yell of 'You pushed me!', followed by the wearied tones of parental intervention.

'This sounds a lot like blackmail,' I said at last.

'Does it?' He drew a hand over his cropped hair, smoothing it where it had sprung on end. 'I'd be careful not to go bandying another accusation against me if I were you. I can be quite litigious when I need to be.'

Now I understood the glitter: spite. Relish in turning the screw. I felt my face grow hot. 'Well, it's something, isn't it? Something underhand. Unseemly.'

'*Unseemly*? Oh, Gwen, you're like something out of the Edwardian era.' As I began to breathe heavily, he added, 'Hey, before you get upset, I haven't finished. Hear me out, you might like this next bit.'

'I won't,' I said, my voice thick with emotion.

Something of his earlier reasonableness returned and he sounded almost sporting when he said, 'You can stay on. In this flat, I mean. As my tenant. I'll be wanting to rent it out for a while so why not to you?'

'Are you insane?' This was so preposterous it had to be a joke. I waited for him to break into laughter and say he was having me on, that his original offer of conciliation stood, but his expression was quite unchanged. He actually meant this. I tried to recover my composure and calculate the basics of what such a rental would entail. I thought of the £3,000 a month the building's renters paid for their flats. That was a colossal £36,000 a year, even before council tax and utilities. Not much less than the sums I'd cautioned Pixie against paying in the Battersea block.

'It's an interesting proposal,' I said, my tone flat, 'but I wouldn't be able to afford the rent.'

'Why not? You'd have a whole wad of cash from the sale.'

'I have a big mortgage to pay off. There's no way I'd have enough left for eighteen years of rent.'

His eyebrows met. 'Eighteen? I don't follow.'

'My life expectancy is eighty-eight.'

He gave a heave of laughter. 'How the hell do you know that?'

'The government has a calculator.' Again, this made me think of Pixie, not understanding, not *wanting* to understand. *I think it's better not to know.*

Advice I could have used a long time ago.

'I see,' he said. 'Well, assuming the government is right, I wouldn't want to let it for quite that long. But long enough for you to take your time making your plans. Five years, maybe? And in terms of the rent, I'm happy to – what was the phrase I'm meant to have used? – "come to an arrangement".' He chuckled at my appalled expression. 'Too soon to joke? Look, I'm serious. You can do some admin for me. Maybe some cooking. No reason why everything shouldn't feel exactly the same.'

Admin? Cooking? What on earth was he talking about. 'Couldn't you just buy another flat?'

Another wry smile. 'Yours is the only one that would work.'

'Work in what way?'

'To knock through. If the board approves the work, of course, which I imagine they will. Considering the way I've been mistreated, I'm guessing they'll want to play nice.'

Knock through? I tried to picture such a super-flat. It would be an enormous 'U', the living room a run of six windows, including two sets of French doors and twin balconies, across a full quarter of the building. It would be beautiful, probably the most valuable apartment in Queens Oak.

'You could afford to do all this? How much are you getting in these other settlements?'

His eyebrows twitched. 'That's for me to worry about. But like I say, not for five years or so. When I'm ready to retire. Plenty of room for me and my team of sexy nurses. What? Too soon, again?'

I was starting to feel weak. His blend of casual blackmail and lascivious humour was too much to process. 'I need to think about it,' I said, my voice little more than a scrape in my throat.

But he heard it well enough, springing up, revitalized by sugar and avarice. 'Sure thing. Don't take too long.'

*

It was surprisingly less tortuous a dilemma than you might think.

In the pros corner: both the criminal and civil cases against me would vanish, no minor consideration given the anguish they'd caused – and continued to cause – me. And since I'd already made my peace with selling the flat, then why not to Alec? No other buyer was going to offer a concession for me to remain in it indefinitely, protected by a tenancy agreement.

In the cons: to capitulate in this way, to be downgraded overnight from owner to tenant, felt humiliating, not to mention downright peculiar. The thought of explaining it to Hester and Sadie and the rest of my neighbours was beyond the pale.

But all things considered, my degradation wasn't anything for the history books, was it? It wasn't biblical, a case of how the mighty have fallen.

Plenty of others had suffered greater losses.

54

I believe I neglected to tell you what became of Cyndi.

As you already know, without the pay she was owed or any immediate prospects, she'd lost her room in her houseshare and found a temporary spot in a hostel – it was one she'd lived in before, when she left the care system. There, attacked by a fellow resident, a young woman with addiction issues, she sustained injuries from which she later found she'd contracted hepatitis C.

She died last year. I didn't need to personally investigate her final years to know they must have been medically complicated and full of sorrow. It's possible, even likely, that the support of a mentor – or loyal friend – could have made a difference to the outcome.

I discovered the news by chance, from one of those 'sad news' posts you see on Facebook, in this case by the colleague of an acquaintance in another charity. It was just before a board meeting at Dee's and, as usual, I walked the length of Columbia Mansions with Alec towards the main doors.

'Not your usual self, Gwen,' he said. 'Something wrong?'

I told him I'd seen news of a friend of a friend who'd died far too young and he asked how it had happened. To my surprise, he said he was aware of such dangers. 'Yeah, Yasmin said they had a warning about that at the hospital. Never get in a scuffle with an addict, that's what they're told. You definitely don't want to let them draw blood.'

We'd reached the main doors and he entered the code, held the door open for me. 'One scratch is all it takes.'

55

I'm not a skilled storyteller, as you will have gathered. I have little control of the pace of this thing. Like all journeys, it is subject to stalls and diversions. So you'll forgive me if I motor through the next six months at full throttle, my justification being that life during this period was if not *uneventful* then at least relatively predictable.

Picture me, if you will, in late July at my open French doors, breathing in pure green. The gardens had just that day emerged resplendent from a month under cloud and the scaffolding for our roof repairs was not due to go up for another week, so there was that splendid sense of reprieve. Where once it had been uncommon, the sound of children playing was constant now for a previously dank and shady zone on the bottom right-hand side of the gardens had been reconfigured as a play area. It was basic stuff, just swings, a slide and a climbing frame, but the building's youngsters and their friends made daily use of it. Sometimes I'd see Dee down there with her baby granddaughter in her arms, safely delivered back in January with the help of the vaunted male doula.

Alec donated the funds for the playground. He did the work himself, with the help of his old mucker Steve, which had gone a long way to helping rehabilitate his reputation in the community.

He and I had resigned from the board and new elections saw

Hester and Karishma selected in our place. My formal retraction of my accusations towards him had been accepted and reaction among the residents to the news that I'd Got It Wrong, as I believe modern parlance has it, had been skilfully moderated by Dee. The consensus was that it was very decent of Alec to accept my mea culpa (and my flat, I itched to comment) and many wanted it known that they regretted accepting rumour as fact. They'd allowed the evil tech giants to lure them onto the rocks of misinformation, where they'd indulged in lazy groupthink.

Elliot asked if Pixie had also withdrawn her accusations and apologized to Alec, but Sadie pointed out that you would have to be very troubled to go to such lengths to besmirch someone the way Pixie had him and we should all wish her well in addressing her mental health issues. Dee quoted a line about walking forwards not backwards that she said was from Abraham Lincoln but sounded very much to me like one of Maya's embroidered inanities.

Then came the playground and before long, if Alec's name came up on the WhatsApp group (to which he had been reinstated), it was only to be asked if he might have a look at a post or a chain or some such, or what he thought about adding a sandpit in phase two, or maybe one of those walking barrels we'd had when *we* were young, before the elf and safety madness took grip.

His purchase of my flat had gone through quickly, there having been no chain involved, and to all intents and purposes you'd never have known anything had changed. The space was the same, my furniture arranged no differently. If anything, it was *more* homely because I'd been able to reintroduce the touches that had been sacrificed when I'd had to subsidise Daniel and, briefly, Pixie. Better wine, fresh flowers, candles, a well-stocked fruit bowl. A Gail's bag on the kitchen counter whenever the fancy took me.

Alec had proved to be uncharacteristically sensitive on the

matter of my fall from grace, not once rubbing my nose in it – or complaining about the service charge, which he now paid on both properties. At the board's request, the camera in his peephole had been removed. Yes, I felt twinges of anger and self-pity, but time healed, memories were short, and for many hours a day I simply forgot that I was no longer the owner of flat 3 Columbia Mansions, my pride in being a resident there as strong as ever, my friendships less damaged than they might have been.

True, Dee and I were no longer as close as we'd once been and I tried not to be triggered by news of Stella's commissions by the BBC and other broadcasters. Her *Sunday Times* column had continued uninterrupted and, as Hester had predicted at that dinner party in prelapsarian times, she used it to espouse the many luxury beliefs of an affluent young woman who treated her baby as the world's first (she'd even named her Eve!).

I still did Older Bodies Pilates and, since my new knee was by now fully functioning, had joined an urban ramblers' group.

What else? Daniel and Maya had put their modest inheritances to good use. Maya entrusted hers to Jason to invest (not as hard to swallow as you might think since he was, as she referred to him in her content, a 'finance bro'), while Daniel, his divorce from Nella finalized, used some for a short-term rental and saved the rest for the deposit on his next flat. As for his relationship with Pixie, he'd been cagey on the few occasions I'd enquired and eventually I'd stopped asking, tired of being made to feel as if I were some sort of stalker, not to be trusted with even the sketchiest update.

Romantically attached to my son or not, Pixie was keeping her head down and protecting that precious anonymity she'd almost given away, evidently trusting in Stella and others with careers to defend to keep a lid on any controversy that threatened to ignite. New scandals seduced those who'd once swarmed to our doors.

She never had accepted me on Instagram.

And that could have been that. This could have been my wrapping up, a little status report on the players in this story, the winners and the losers. But I'm afraid to say it was not. Not by a long chalk. And had it been, I really don't think I would have felt the need to record any of it in the first place. All those scenes, the confessions and the showdowns, the parties and the drinks, would have been buried with us, and the meek – or in our case those infants now swinging and sliding in the playground below – would have inherited the earth.

Instead, several things happened. I like to think it would have been out of the question, even immoral, for me to rein in my suspicions, turn the other cheek. But I know that's not true.

I made a choice.

Actually, I made a series of choices.

56

First, right when I'd thought she'd consigned me to the past, Pixie unblocked my phone number and messaged me:

> Fraud people found in my favour. Just transferred your money + 10% interest. TY for the loan and sorry it took so long to pay back, Pixie

I opened my banking app and checked my balance; a deposit of £5,500 had just landed. I texted her back:

> Safely received, thank you. How are you? I've been thinking of you.

Expecting to find myself reblocked, I was startled when she replied straightaway:

> Would rather you didn't think of me tbh. I heard you said I lied about Alec.

I texted back:

> Pixie, I understand it was complicated emotionally, but I saw your dad's rent deposit with my own eyes.

Again, her response was instant:

> There was no rent. Believe what you like but you can't change the truth.

I scrambled to reply, only to find that this time I *was* blocked. What on earth was going on? How could she *still* be insisting one thing when evidence had proved the opposite? Accusing me of 'changing' the truth when in fact I'd acknowledged it at considerable personal expense? Feeling my old friend indignation rise in my chest, I left the flat, hurried along the block, and made my way up to Dee's.

Opening the door in a flared raspberry-pink dress, she was a split second late in concealing her dismay at the sight of me.

'Do you and Pixie still follow each other on Instagram?' I asked, breathless.

'Hello to you too, Gwen.'

I ignored her sarcasm. 'Do you?'

She looked warily at me. 'I think so, yes, though I haven't used social media in a while. I find it toxic.'

She found it toxic?

'Could I possibly look at her feed on your phone? She won't accept my request.'

She made a reproachful little moue at me. 'I can't help thinking if someone doesn't want you to follow them on Instagram then it's not good practice to persist via a third party.'

My outrage ignited. 'And *I* can't help thinking that while I've been scapegoated and humiliated, other parties have come out of this whole saga smelling of roses – and *you're* one of them!'

Shocked by this, my first explicit challenge of her personally, she stepped aside to let me in; she wouldn't want Karishma or other neighbours overhearing such inelegant talk. 'Fine. But I'm in the middle of my emails, so I won't be able to help you.'

'I don't need help,' I snapped. 'I'm not educationally subnormal.'

'I don't think that's an acceptable term any more, Gwen.'

'So report me to the language police, *Dee*.'

She raised a palm. 'For goodness' sake, let's not bicker. I'll get my phone for you.'

She brought up Pixie's feed and passed the phone to me before retreating to her laptop in the turret.

Having not been offered a seat, I hovered in the hallway as I scrolled through Pixie's recent posts. The last was from two days earlier, a selfie of Daniel and her in what were recognizably Maya's yesteryear patio chairs, vintage teacups in hand, and looking incongruous in their modern clothing, like time travellers. It answered one question, anyway: he *was* still seeing her.

Unable to resist, I scrolled back to the date of our last meeting, back in January. A post from the next day was a clip of a TV actress with tears rolling down her face. Music began playing – 'Cry Me A River' by Julie London – and caused Dee to glance over, so I muted it. The caption said:

> When you discover a great friend doesn't believe your trauma is real. Doesn't even know you.

I scanned the top comments:

> *Not a friend then. Better off without.*

> *People can be soooo disappointing.*

Here for you, hun.

And so on. I scrolled back towards the present, my attention snagging on a graphic with white letters on a pink background: *Sign petition to Stop Sex for Rent!* It came with an unusually lengthy caption:

> Please support this issue as it's very close to my heart. I got caught up in sex for rent myself last year and I know how easy it is to find yourself trapped. To blame yourself, even convince yourself you're OK with the arrangement. I don't want to hide any more, I don't want to lie to myself. I can't name the man who used me in this way because of legal shit, he's already sued someone else who called him out, but names don't matter anyway imo. All that matters is we ban this horrible dehumanizing practice – pay it forward to the next girls. I support Women Against Sex for Rent, link in bio #WASFR

Inside my rib cage my heart knocked painfully. I caught my breath, read it a second time to be sure I'd understood. Located the link that led to the website for Women Against Sex for Rent, a formal campaign to outlaw the practice. My instincts lurched from horror to denial. Was this another fabrication, an extension of the original lie? Even part of a strategy by Stella to put protections in place should the news of Alec's exoneration leak from Columbia Mansions?

It seemed awfully elaborate – and sincere – if it was.

If it *wasn't*, then did that mean Pixie had been telling the truth about Alec after all?

I returned to the post and read the comments. They were

all supportive, bar one critical one that had attracted multiple castigations and an apology from the poster. Stella had been one of the first to comment:

> *So proud of you, Pix. It's always hard to put your head above the parapet but future generations of women will thank you for it.*

Back atcha, Pixie had replied, adding a string of flexed biceps emojis.

There was no comment from Dee and if she'd known about this twist in our tale, she hadn't cared to tell me. Since I'd apologized to Alec and cast doubt on Pixie's account, I was the last person they'd recruit to the cause.

Why, then, had Dee given me access now? My hunch was she didn't think it would make any difference what I believed because no one trusted my beliefs any more. I could stand on our doorstep and make the most outlandish pronouncements and no one would listen. I wasn't a director; I wasn't even a leaseholder any more. I was just a pensioner who'd lost touch with reality.

I was irrelevant.

I became aware of her bearing down on me. 'All done here?' After our tiff at the door, her voice had returned to its customary charm-offensive purr.

'Yes, thank you.' I closed the app and returned her phone to her.

'Look, Gwen, I don't know what you meant just now about smelling of roses, but I think you've possibly misunderstood the situation. This last year has been incredibly challenging for all of us.'

'Some more than others,' I said with grim politeness.

She conceded this with a jerk of her right eyebrow. 'I think we're old enough and ugly enough to be able to live with the occasional difference of opinion, aren't we?'

It was my turn to concede. 'We are.'

'Will I see you at Pilates tomorrow? Mind you,' she added, without waiting for me to answer, 'I might have to sit it out myself. My hip's been giving me gyp.'

'Nothing serious, I hope,' I said. 'You're a bit young for a transplant.'

She looked at me, baffled. 'Transplant?'

I admit I was surprised by my own playfulness, given my inner turmoil. 'Just something Pixie once said.'

'I see.' She saw me to the door with a game smile. 'Bye then. Glad all good.'

57

Believe it or not, I'd learned *some* lessons from my past mistakes and one of these was never again to rush headlong into a confrontation, especially not with someone as fleet of foot as Alec. Time and again he'd proved himself capable of outsmarting me.

What I needed was ammunition, not emotion.

My first investigation was that rent Pixie's father had paid via a 'mate in Bromley'. The name had been memorable for being the same as one of my favourite old shows and after some googling, I found a likely candidate in Sweeney Events, Beckenham. It was a trendy agency, describing itself as an 'alchemy of action, incubation and invention', whatever that meant, though if the owner *was* a friend of Pixie's father, this might very well have been the source of some of her 'content' work in the past.

Somewhat against the communications zeitgeist, my call was picked up by a living human.

'This is a bit of a long shot,' I said, 'but do you have any dealings with a man called Colin Gray? He's an associate of yours, I believe, and you handled a payment on his behalf last September?'

'I can check for him on the staff list?' she suggested. This was futile, but she was only trying to be helpful and so I kept my impatience in check. 'No, there's no one with that name working here.'

'Perhaps I could speak to someone in your accounts department?'

'Accounts are outsourced to an external firm. I can give you a number?'

I noted it and thanked her. Before ringing, I prepared my lines with greater care, hoping that whoever handled my enquiry would be junior and not fully au fait with confidentiality protocols.

'This is HMRC,' I said, friendly but professional. 'We're investigating the accounts of an individual called Alec Pedley and I'm trying to verify that Sweeney Events made a payment to him in September last year. I believe it was on behalf of a third party.'

'I'm not sure I'm with you. What third party?' The tone of brisk authority suggested I'd not been fortunate in where my call had landed.

'The amount was for £4,200. I don't have a reference, but if you wouldn't mind looking up the name?'

'I'm afraid I'll need your request in writing. Details of freelancers' fees are confidential.'

My pulse leapt. 'You mean Alec Pedley is a freelancer? Commissioned by Sweeney Events?'

'I didn't catch a name, you're with Client Investigations, did you say?'

'That's right. Christina Boulter,' I offered, remembering Pixie's alter ego.

'As I say, Christina, I'll need you to write to us so we can give your questions due consideration. Would you like to take this email address down?'

I pretended to do so, then hung up and returned to the agency's website, finding my way with increasing foreboding to the 'Our projects' page. Among the newsworthy commissions of the last year, one stood out: a 'hypnotic soundscape' for a children's museum. It didn't require the investigator credentials I'd just faked to surmise that professional composer Alec might have contributed to this soundscape.

Sure enough, a few minutes' digging brought up an official credit. The payment he'd shown me had been nothing to do with Pixie's rent and had not been arranged on behalf of her father, a thief who would likely pour scorn on the 'alchemy' offered by this agency. Alec had simply scrolled through his deposits, calm as you like, and found a figure in the right ballpark. He'd hoped – no, assumed – I wouldn't follow it up and he'd been right.

I *had* questioned the amount, if I remembered, because it was less than the £1,500 a month that he'd told me he charged, but he'd explained that away with some fib about giving her a discount.

It hadn't added up, but I'd swallowed it anyway.

*

No subterfuge was needed to find Yasmin's number; I still had it in my contacts from when we'd been neighbours. I messaged to ask if she might be free to meet for five minutes and she suggested a time the next day at her place of work.

It was one of those London hospital complexes where the original building had been dwarfed by dozens of wings and additions, with mobile MRI units parked in the street. Off-duty staff gathered at a departmental entrance to smoke and vape and make calls on loudspeaker, as if neither their patients' nor their own privacy was of the slightest concern.

Inside the main building, the air was humid, no doubt swimming with viruses, and I was grateful to be led by Yasmin to an outdoor seating area out of view of the main drag. Our messages had talked of a coffee but there was no way I was paying £5 a go at the mediocre chain franchise; in any case, Yasmin had a water bottle with her.

'You look well,' I lied. Though a very pretty girl, she looked washed out, careworn, and the blue of her nurse's tunic only accentuated her pallor. 'How's the new flat?'

'Great. The commute's a killer, though. Takes me over an hour to get down here. I was spoiled before though.'

'I suppose nursing isn't one of those jobs you can do from home,' I said wryly.

She pulled a face. 'Maybe when there's an AI version of me. We can split the pay.'

I remembered Liz mixing AI up with the A1 and Pixie giggling next to me, that feeling of optimism I'd had that we were entering a golden era as neighbours. It felt like decades ago, before the revolution.

'That scandal with Alec last year,' I began, and she jumped in.

'Is that what you wanted to talk about? God, that was completely mad! I had journalists trying to get quotes from me, but there was no way I was saying anything.'

'Was there anything *to* say? Nothing like that happened to you, did it?'

'No. I mean, he tried it on once or twice when he was hammered, but as soon as he met Casper he backed off. I wasn't scared.'

'Good. I'm glad to hear that. And if you had been, I hope you know I'd have been there for you.' I said this without thinking, only recognizing my hypocrisy a beat too late. Look where my 'being there' for Pixie had got her! To support someone and then withdraw your support was arguably worse than not supporting them in the first place. 'I'm sorry to have to ask you something so intrusive, Yasmin, but a camera was found in the new lodger's shower and Alec gave me the idea that you had it fitted. Is that true? It was in the grouting on the wall opposite the showerhead, about shoulder height.'

Yasmin flushed, clearly shocked. 'What? Why would I do that? Come on, Gwen, you might as well tell me.'

She was right; this was not the time for me to be coy. 'He said you used it to film material for a porn website. That's how you funded your flat deposit.'

'*What?*' She shook her head as if to free it of the very idea. 'No. Absolutely not. This is ... Oh my God. Did he show you any of this "material"? If so, I'll need to go to the police.'

'He showed me a couple of seconds of a video, but ...' I hadn't seen the woman's face, I remembered. Again, I'd simply accepted Alec's 'evidence', done none of the due diligence I'd been so quick to suspect Stella of bypassing. What a fool I'd been. 'The way the camera was positioned, it could have been anyone. He just said it was you.'

'Wow. Okay.' She shook her head, quietly furious. 'At least it's not some deepfake shit. Well, I'm one hundred per cent sure there was no camera.'

'He was probably just winding me up,' I reassured her.

'I'd prefer it if he didn't lie about me in his wind-ups. I'll phone him after my shift and—'

'No need,' I said firmly. 'I'll make that clear to him for you. He must have fitted it after you moved out.'

'You know what?' she said, still aghast. 'He *was* doing some DIY in the en suite before the next tenant came. What a sleazebag.' Her shoulders quivered. 'Makes my skin crawl.'

'The camera's been removed now,' I said. 'I don't think he'd try it again. He wouldn't want a furore like the last one.'

'Hmm. Well, it's good that you're still there to keep an eye on him.'

Shame pooled in my stomach. What would she say if she knew

I'd withdrawn my allegation and apologized? That the Columbia Mansions community had had no choice but to welcome him back into the fold?

'Was he ever charged with anything?' she asked as we prepared to part.

'Unfortunately not. That kind of rent arrangement isn't technically illegal and it was always a case of his word against ours.'

Ours. Mine and Pixie's. I felt physical pain then, deep in my centre. Any sliver of doubt that I'd been royally deceived by Alec was now gone. I'd aligned myself with him and in doing so rubbished Pixie's side of the story. I was estranged from her, a woman who'd made me feel good about myself, to be in league with him, a man who made me cringe.

A man to whom I now paid rent to live in my own flat.

58

Alec answered the door in grubby overalls, having come from the garden, I surmised. His face was ruddy with exertion and sweat had beaded above his upper lip. He was wolfing a Snickers and the aroma of peanuts wafted towards me.

'Is this a good time?' I said coolly.

'Gwen, hello.' His gaze lowered automatically to my hands, clasped together in front of me, my fingers interlaced, and disappointment crossed his face. He was accustomed to my bearing a casserole dish or Tupperware with a home-cooked meal, which I did two or three times a week as part of my rental deal. 'Come in. I was taking a break anyway.'

Inside, it was clear from the obstacle course of hoover, mop and dustpan and brush, and from the smell of lemon and eucalyptus, that the chore occupying him was in fact a deep clean of the flat. The carpets were pristine, the windows shining and there was not a speck of dust on the woodwork. I couldn't help thinking of those crime scene cleaners you see on TV, hired to sanitize and disinfect, to erase signs of trauma.

In the living room, he offered me a coffee, but I declined. In the anxious, furious minutes before my arrival, I'd resolved that I would never accept anything from this man again as long as I lived.

He poured himself a glass of water and downed half of it with his back to me. 'Have a seat,' he said, surprised to find me still hovering.

'I'll stand, thank you.'

He frowned. 'What is it? You're being very peculiar, even for you. Come on, at least take a load off.'

He flopped into the centre of the Chesterfield and I lowered myself at the far end of the smaller sofa, sitting rigidly upright. My jaw had tightened, my eyelids felt stiff with each blink; every part of me was clenched and unyielding.

'She wasn't lying, was she?'

'Who?' he said.

'You know who.' I felt like a bereaved parent facing her child's killer. I didn't want to sully Pixie's memory by saying her name in his presence. 'Just be straight with me, Alec. It can't make any difference now. You've got what you wanted.'

He tilted his head as if in consideration. 'I don't think I ever said she was *lying*.'

'No, but you denied everything she said.'

'I think you'll find I denied everything *you* said.'

'We were saying the same thing!' I snapped. 'It was you who lied and you know it. You said you took rent from her, but that payment you showed me wasn't from her father like you said. It was for a music job you did for a client.'

He raised his eyebrows, mock-impressed. 'Quite the Poirot. Look, if you really want to rake over this again, I'll tell you exactly how it rolled. I made a suggestion and she agreed to it. End of. No one forced her.'

'Circumstances forced her.' My tone was prim, my posture still rigid. 'She didn't *want* to have sex with you.'

'With the best will in the world, Gwen, you weren't in the room.'

He grimaced as if there could be no more repellent a notion and I felt fresh fury burn in my chest.

'I didn't need to be. She told me exactly how it worked.'

'And yet not so long ago you decided none of it was true,' he pointed out. 'Forgive me if I'm finding this is all getting a bit Groundhog Day.'

'I was wrong,' I said.

'You were wrong,' he repeated with satisfaction, as if I'd applied this disavowal to a different statement altogether. 'And tomorrow, will you think you were right again?'

'No. I won't be changing my mind again.'

He regarded me with mild annoyance. 'Really, does it matter, anyway? You just said it made no difference. It's all in the past now.'

'Yes, a pretty disastrous past from my point of view. You stole my flat!'

'I didn't steal it. You were paid market rate. You still live in it.'

'Not only that, you destroyed one of the best friendships I've ever had.' As my heart registered the depth of this truth, my eyes brimmed tears. Friendship hadn't always come easy, but it had with Pixie.

Alec sniggered. 'Come off it. You knew each other for five minutes. You're better off without her. I know I am.'

'Because she called you out!'

'Again, it was *you* who did the calling out. You dragged her into a situation she would never have got into on her own. She'd have got herself sorted eventually, moved on. Put the whole thing down to experience.'

I gulped, all too aware of uncomfortable echoes of sentiments expressed by Pixie herself. What had she said? *This is just a bump in the road*, that was it.

'There's something else.' I'd almost forgotten. 'I spoke to Yasmin and I know the camera wasn't there when she had the room. That video you showed me, it wasn't her, was it?'

He straightened – this was something that actually interested him – and there was a beat or two when I sensed he was conjuring a denial. But just as swiftly he abandoned the charade. 'If you must know, it wasn't her, no.'

'It wasn't … ?' I had to ask, I couldn't not. 'It wasn't Pixie, was it?'

He shrugged. 'Don't know who it was. Could've been any of the ten million trollops on that site. You lose track after a while, know what I'm saying?' He gave another snigger. 'No, I don't suppose you do.'

'So you used the camera in the shower just to watch? It was your dirty little secret, was it?'

'*Our* secret, Gwen.' He gestured in exasperation. 'Do you *really* not get it? The camera was part of the deal. Pixie knew all about it. So long as I didn't share, she was cool.'

'I don't believe you.' But as I processed this latest nugget, I had to admit it fitted with my having had to persuade her to let me search for the camera. She'd looked sick when I found it, been distressed when I'd called the police; she must have been terrified of the humiliation that awaited her were the truth to surface. Even after agreeing to Stella's interview, she'd insisted that detail be left out.

'She wasn't cool,' I said. 'She was never cool. She was coerced and exploited and downright disrespected.'

He shrugged. 'You say potayto, I say potahto. Now, much as I like a catch-up with my valued tenant, I do need to finish cleaning. I've got viewings for the room first thing in the morning.'

I couldn't believe what I was hearing. 'The board have allowed another Room for Rent?'

'How could they not? My name's been cleared, everyone's falling over themselves to show how much they trust me. And we do have a housing crisis in this city.' He pulled a ghastly mock-virtuous expression. 'Hey, I'm just doing my bit to alleviate hardship. Maybe you should do the same – provided you get your landlord's permission, of course.' He actually winked then, adding, 'Plenty of middle-aged toy boys out there. My sort of age, you know what I'm saying?'

I got to my feet, glaring at him. 'You're despicable.'

I expected him to jump up, get in my face, but he did the opposite, lounging back as if I were his court jester, my skit passably entertaining. 'What, coz I don't want to shag some old girl? Pixie found it so funny, you know. "How could you?" she goes. She kept saying it, "I know you were off your face, Alec, but how could you?"'

My chest was about to explode with the heat of my temper. 'I hate you,' I hissed.

'Yeah, I'm sure you do. Whatever turns you on, Gwen.'

I could still hear him laughing as I let myself out.

59

This is a difficult scene to write – and, to be frank, if I'm writing it then I know for sure I won't be sharing this document with anyone else.

Dear reader, it's official: *you don't exist.*

Maybe you never did. Maybe you were always the imaginary friend of a friendless old woman. Empowering me, consoling me, keeping me company. My very own Harvey. My Stig of the Dump.

I should point out (dear Harvey, dear Stig) that the following dialogue is of course only as accurate as any recollection of a drunken episode can be, just the gist really. The slurring and giggling and other tomfoolery should be taken as read.

It happened after the Festive Fizz the year Alec moved in. Stella, then a recent graduate, had been recruited with a couple of friends to circulate with magnums of Prosecco and this they did with such dedication that every last guest to tumble back out of the door was three sheets to the wind.

Alec and I staggered back to our landing and he accepted my invitation to join me in a glass of the Madeira Liz had given me for Christmas. She'd just been on holiday to the island, as I remember. On my sofa, we touched chunky crystal glasses with a dangerous crack, laughing at our own clumsiness, and downed it like water.

I lived alone then, of course.

'Come on,' he said, when we were on our third glass. 'Tell me what you're hiding.'

'What d'you mean?'

'You know, this headmistress act. You must be hiding something. And I don't mean a cane.' As I rocked with laughter, he went on, 'I can't tell yet, do you do it with everyone. Or is it just me? Because I'm such a bad boy?'

Our faces were close to each other's, the Madeira in our glasses close to spilling, and then to my amazement we were kissing, *I* was kissing for the first time since Brian, which was years, many years, but the rhythm of it, the moves, were still there. I might not remember our words with full clarity, but I remember the taste of burnt sugar and orange peel on his mouth, I remember the solidity of his bones under a friendly padding of flesh. I remember his large hands roving.

I remember enough.

Waking up in bed the next morning after the dreamless sleep of the dipsomaniac, I surrendered to the process familiar to anyone who has caroused a little too hard the night before. First, the sense that something wasn't right, followed, seconds later, by drilling head pain and spangles behind the eyes. Then the selective release of memories – in this case, the residents' Christmas do, the chatter and the laughter and the dancing – swiftly pursued by self-doubt: had I said anything I would regret? Been rude or judgmental or too ... too *headmistress-y*?

That was when I became aware of breathing.

I prised open dehydrated eyelids and saw him. My new neighbour Alec, the twice-married one-hit-wonder musician. Jocular, extrovert, a little off-colour in his humour. Twenty years younger than me.

Shocked, I covered my face with the edge of the sheet, leaving a sliver through which to view him, and tried to piece together what had led to this unanticipated, electrifying turn of events. Prosecco and Madeira, essentially. My pulse quickened as I recollected that I had been the initiator of the kiss on the sofa that had led to the groping that had led to the migration to my bedroom – a reckless, if not self-destructive, urge for I surely must have expected him to reject me. I whimpered in shame to recall the deluge of lust when he had made the opposite choice.

Some minutes into consciousness by now, I began to register a small, simple happiness. I liked this new friend of mine. Did he … did he like me?

Beside me, he was waking. I watched through almost-closed eyes as he blinked and frowned, not recognizing the room he found himself in, not knowing he was being watched. Then he turned towards me.

The expression on his face was one I will never forget and that I know now went on, at least partly, to inform the events of this account. Incomprehension, disgust, alarm. There was a moment of paralysis as if to shut down physically would render him invisible, a held breath as he tried to assess from my breathing how deeply I was sleeping. Then, last and worst of all, *panic*.

There followed a cartoon-like sequence as he slid from under the covers, his back to me, before creeping out of range. I had to strain to hear him dressing and leaving the room. There were no sounds of the bathroom being used or the front door opening, so I guessed he must be stealing down the hall towards the living room, perhaps to locate a forgotten item. A minute later, his prowler's footsteps returned and I heard the flat door brush open, then click shut.

When I got up, face and chest aflame, I trudged into the kitchen and found a note from him on the counter:

Gwen,
Cheers for the drink,
Alec

No kiss, no promise to be in touch, not the smallest trace of intimacy.

Just a regret too huge and horrifying to mention.

60

There is kicking a woman when she's down and then there is grinding her face into wet tarmac and flattening her with a steam roller. The latter was closer to how I felt when, just hours after leaving Alec's flat in a state of bleakest torment, I read the email that popped into my inbox:

Hi Mum,

I'm emailing because it's the only way to say what I want to say without being interrupted and criticized.

Since I moved out, Pixie and I have got a lot closer and we plan to get married now my divorce is through. It will only be a register office thing and I hope you'll understand that it's not appropriate to invite you, not after everything that's gone on between you and her. Also, Dad is flying over for it and we don't want our day marred by bad feeling. (Pixie's dad might be able to come as well and I'm sure you can appreciate that could be awkward.)

But I thought you had a right to know and I'll give you a call at some point after,

Love, Daniel

If it weren't for that 'love' I swear I might have climbed onto the roof and thrown myself off. Instead, I opened a bottle of Cab Sav and set about drinking the whole thing in the space of an hour. *Married?* So soon after splitting from Nella and mere moments since meeting Pixie? The man was a lunatic!

And where was Maya in all of this? In favour, presumably, and hoping to recruit Pixie to the ranks of the stay-at-home sirens or whatever the fools called themselves. Did she know about Pixie's commitment to the Women Against Sex for Rent campaign? Even if they'd squared their sexual politics somehow, they were unlikely sisters-in-law by most people's standards.

As the alcohol released wilder imaginings, my future unfurled in fully formed vignettes. A wedding celebrated without me but with Brian and his second wife in proud attendance (not to mention the ex-con father – even he was deemed less offensive than me!). Grandchildren who I wouldn't be allowed to spend time with but could only glimpse from the sidelines, pitied by Dee, who enjoyed unfettered access to her own – and perhaps to mine, too, if Pixie and Stella remained on 'back atcha' terms. Life alone at Columbia Mansions until such a time that Alec decided to issue me with a no-fault eviction order and fill his mega-flat with hot young attendants, like some latter-day Benny Hill.

Gwen the outcast, the rejected, the wretch. The *old girl*.

I turned the TV on, knowing I had to stop this churning paranoia, and found an old episode of *Vera* I hadn't seen for a few years. But unable to concentrate for more than ten minutes, I turned it off again and scrolled through the news on my phone, wallowing in story after story of the moral decline of our once-great Britain.

My radar picked up one particular story:

Users Slam Year-long FOS Delays

Most of us have grumbles about our bank, mortgage lender or other high street businesses, but customers who choose to take their case to the Financial Ombudsman Service are facing the added stress of the longest delays in its history. In the last year, fewer than half of cases were tackled within six months and in some areas of London, staff shortages have meant not a single case has been resolved.

And it's not only the delays that are causing the public's frustration to mount. Once resolved, the number of upheld complaints has also fallen.

'In the past five years, fewer than a quarter of cases were upheld,' said Matt Ringwood of Which *magazine.*

'This is completely unacceptable,' a spokesman for the Treasury said. 'British customers deserve better.'

Addled though my brain was with the wine, the calculations were not hard to manage. Pixie had filed her complaint last September, or more likely October given how she'd procrastinated, which was well under a year ago, meaning the money she'd used to repay me was unlikely to have come from any reimbursement to do with the fraud. It must have been supplied by new fiancé Daniel, in all likelihood taken from the early inheritance I'd gifted him.

I'd paid myself back, which felt bitterly defining.

Just as I was about to turn off my phone, a notification popped up for an email from Alec and I scanned its contents with horror:

I write to give you notice of an increase in rent for Flat 3, Columbia Mansions, Queen's Oak … From September 1 the new rent will be £3,200 per calendar month … This represents market rate for the property …

Over three thousand pounds? He was proposing a fifty per cent increase! Not proposing, demanding. There could be no doubt he'd been enraged by our row, by my insults, my insubordination, and had lost no time in setting about a plan to oust me. Flinging down my phone in fury, I succeeded in spilling wine over myself and the sofa, and went in search of kitchen roll. I removed the seat cushion to mop up the dark stains, too drunk to do a decent job, but what did it matter? It was a battered old thing and would soon be tossed in a skip.

Just like its owner.

As I eased the cushion back into place, a glint of silver caught my eye and I fished for what I initially assumed was a coin but discovered was in fact an item I'd secreted there myself and forgotten all about.

Pixie's key to Alec's flat.

61

Extraordinary as it may sound, none of what happened next was premeditated. I simply acted as if under the auspices of a puppetmaster, my marionette limbs knowing precisely what to do and when.

It was 2 a.m. when I left the flat, too dark to see properly, but I hadn't brought my phone or a torch and didn't want to turn on the communal light for fear of attracting attention. Having not in the end undressed for bed, I wore the clothes I'd been in all day – now wine-stained – along with a battered pair of sheepskin slippers Maya and Daniel had gifted me from New Zealand years ago.

I waited for my vision to adjust before crossing to Alec's door. I did not feel as drunk as you might think – the counteraction of adrenaline perhaps – and turned the key in the lock without mishap. The weight of his door as I pushed it open was exactly like mine, as was the gentle click as it closed behind me. I pocketed the key and stood for a moment in his hallway, absorbing the silence. There was a note of expectancy in it, I thought, the residual energy of his housework earlier, possibly. I could see surprisingly well thanks to milky moonlight filtering through the open door of the living room, where the windows had not had their curtains drawn. All other internal doors were ajar and I noticed now the sound of snoring coming from the master bedroom.

Needing to be certain no one else was here, I tiptoed towards the living room, which looked much as it had when I'd been here earlier. Alec's water glass was still on the coffee table, the cushions flattened where he'd made himself comfortable, the better to mock me. In the kitchen, his dinner things had been abandoned, ready-meal packaging on the worktop, plate and fork in the sink. There was an empty wine bottle and wineglass, too – I was not the only one who'd been drinking heavily.

I looked at the wall that separated this room from mine and thought of the ballroom-sized space that would be created were it to come down. Were one resident's life to gobble up another's.

On my way back up the corridor, I slipped into the spare room. The closed curtains were pale and flimsy and the glow from the lightwell revealed the room to be as neat as a pin, with a new mattress cover on the bed and a duvet zipped into transparent packaging, two pillows stacked on top. That aura of expectancy was heightened in here. Would anything be expected of her, his next girl? Not formally, perhaps, not as an agreed condition as had been the case with Pixie, but if he were to gain confidence, secure in the knowledge that his enemies had been neutered ... what then?

I peeked into the en suite, curbing the reflex to pull the cord and start up that noisy fan. It too was pristine and smelled of a deep clean. In the walk-in shower, I ran a finger over the grouting where the camera had been fitted: still smooth. Oddly, I felt less of an intruder now than I had when searching the same space with Pixie in daylight, less nervous of discovery. It was as if I felt I had a right to be here. I had a mission.

I left the room and approached the main bedroom. The gap wasn't wide enough for me to ease through, so I pushed the door very gently. There was resistance this time, the brushing of timber against carpet pile sounding like a roar, and I waited at the threshold a moment or two to be on the safe side. Only when satisfied that Alec's snoring continued uninterrupted did I venture in.

The curtains on the left-hand window did not quite meet and a crack of light allowed me a decent assessment of his sleeping position. He was lying on his front, his head twisted to the left and mouth slightly open, hair flat to his skull as if combed before bedtime. The duvet was high, almost up to his neck, and beneath it his upper body rose and fell, rose and fell. To the other side of him – where Pixie had once lain, submitting to his attentions – were two redundant pillows.

I moved silently around the bed, tucking the duvet under the mattress as I went. It was a summer weight and easy to handle. On a second rotation, I tightened it an extra inch or two until it was as taut as a hospital sheet; he probably hadn't been swaddled like this since he was a baby in his mother's arms.

I lingered a moment on the side where his face was visible, imagining his confusion – and mine! – if his eyes suddenly opened and spied me standing over him, but he was a contented, peaceful sleeper, evidently not at all tormented by his waking actions.

I slid out one of the spare pillows. It was dense, weighty. Using both hands and all my upper-body strength, I placed it over his head and pressed. I knew from my crime dramas that it took a good five minutes to do the deed, a very long time to have to apply solid pressure. It was surprisingly a good minute before he began struggling, at which point I introduced a bent knee to pin him in place. I'd like to take credit for my surgically corrected muscle power, but the truth is the tucked duvet did the work, restraining him like a straitjacket, preventing him from kicking or punching.

Just in case he'd somehow developed the lung capacity of a pearl diver, I added an extra ninety seconds or so before finally stepping away, exhausted but satisfied.

I did not move the pillow aside; I was not at all curious to see what he looked like dead.

62

The same higher power that had brought me here now led me back across the landing to my own flat, where I slept, a heavy sleep at first, all physical strength obliterated, but then more restless. By 7 a.m., I was aware of a terrible mounting nausea and, when I could bear it no longer, dashed to the bathroom and regurgitated red wine into the toilet bowl. Then I emptied my bladder, undressed, and took a shower.

This might be my last in my own bathroom, I thought, and treated myself to a generous dollop of the Penhaligon's bodywash Stella had given me for Christmas and that I'd been using only on special occasions. Afterwards, I wiped the steam from the mirror and examined my face. I looked fatigued, still sick from the wine binge. There was something else too, a blankness to my eyes, a sense of evacuation.

As if I knew there was nothing left of interest for me to see.

Once dressed, I made myself a coffee and headed back to number 4, mug in hand. This was not one of those situations you read about when the bad guy wakes up under the misapprehension that he's committed his crime only in a nightmare. I knew full well that what I'd done was real and if I had any fear at all it was that I'd failed to kill Alec, that I'd go back in there and find his bed empty – like in that old French movie when the drowned man vanishes from the bath tub, somehow having survived and fled.

But he was just where I'd left him, his leaden outline beneath the duvet, and I slid away the pillow to find his head still twisted to the left. His deoxygenated skin had the gleam of putty, with small purple patches. His expression was one of outrage, outrage at having been robbed of life by stealth, of not having been offered a fair fight, though I could have been projecting that, knowing as I did what a keen combatant he'd been in life.

I leant closer and sniffed for evidence of rot, but could detect none, only my own bodywash. Perhaps my sense of smell had been, like my gaze in the bathroom mirror, compromised. Stripped of its power.

It was by now well past 7.30 a.m. and the building was stirring. Time to text Dee:

Could you come to Alec's flat. It's urgent.

She was an early riser and the two ticks appeared straightaway. Not even ten minutes later, I heard the main door open and shut and the weight of her footsteps on the stairs. I went to meet her at the flat door. She'd evidently dressed hastily, the buttons of her blouse one out, creating a single tail over the waistband of her trousers, and I felt pleasure in witnessing this rare slovenliness.

(Did I detect, too, signs of a slight discomfort in her hip?)

'What is it?' she said, a little out of puff. You didn't often see her without make-up and her skin was soft and squishy, enquiring eyes containing all the life that Alec now lacked. That I now lacked too. 'Is he not well?'

'He's not, no.' I waited till she was safely inside before telling her, in a bald tone, 'He's dead.'

Her face turned pink with shock. 'Gwen, that's awful. Was it in his sleep, d'you think?'

'Yes. I don't think he felt much.'

'Well, that's something.' She followed me into his bedroom and to his bedside, intoning gravely. 'Poor man. He's barely fifty, is he? I wonder if he had a—'

'No.' I interrupted her before she could waste her energy speculating on heart conditions and other silent killers. 'I did it. I suffocated him with that pillow.'

'Oh!' Her hand flew to her mouth. 'You don't mean that.'

'I do.'

'Then …' She took a step back from me, repelled. 'This is not good, Gwen.'

She made an attempt to tug the duvet over his face, presumably in a gesture of respect, but she was hindered by the tightly tucked edges. I saw her eye the pillow and decide against using that to conceal him – it would feel too much like she had administered the lethal smothering herself. Her demeanour was understandably very troubled.

'Well, we can't just leave him like this,' she said. 'We need to call 999.'

'Yes. Will you do it?' I drifted to the window and looked out onto the street and across to Winifred Gardens. Through the lime trees, beyond the boules pit, I could just make out a sliver of the bench where Pixie and I had sat when she'd told me about the sex for rent.

Behind me, Dee was talking on the phone. 'Police, please … Columbia Mansions … Queens Oak … It's my neighbour … He's been murdered by his tenant … What? Oh. I didn't witness it myself but that's what she's just told me. She's here with me now … Weapons? She says she suffocated him with a pillow. I wouldn't call it a weapon, not as such.'

I chuckled at that.

'A name?' She faltered then and I watched her more closely, trying to gauge the reason for her hesitation. Was she feeling the need to protect my identity till the final embers of freedom had been extinguished? To gift me a last period of grace? Because I'd be sleeping in a cell tonight, that much was certain.

'Oh, yes. Dee Carmichael,' she said finally, and I realized they'd asked for her name, not mine. 'No, it's too late for medics. He's definitely not alive and I don't think he has been for a few hours. Okay. Yes, we'll wait here in the flat.'

She hung up. Below us, there was the sound of a loud clunk, the door downstairs closing, followed by footsteps on the path. Hester leaving on some errand or other. 'They'll be a few minutes,' she told me.

I adjusted my vantage point at the window, almost as if expecting the police to be shimmying up the walls of the building, poised to enter through this very window.

'I'm not sorry,' I said very clearly, as if already speaking in court, addressing the judge. 'In case you were wondering.'

'I'm sure you will be,' Dee said, 'when you think it through.'

'I won't.'

'Well, don't say that to the police, will you?' she said, which made me remember talking to them before, 'no comment' after 'no comment'. Would I get the same detective as on that occasion, the woman with the talons? This was quite a leap from harassment and yet the two matters were clearly linked; she'd at least be consulted.

There'd be press interest too. This would be a scandal that made the last one look like child's play. I wondered how long it would be before Dee tipped off Stella. Within moments of handing me over, I predicted.

'We might as well go and sit in the living room,' she said.

Still clutching my mug of coffee, I followed her to the rear of the flat, where I sat in an armchair overlooking the garden. Sadie was releasing her kids from the terrace doors, shooing them off to the new playground with a warning not to get mud on their uniforms, presumably while she cleared up breakfast or gathered what they needed for school. They always left at 8.20 a.m. sharp. I wondered how she would break the news to them that a murder had taken place above their heads. That the harmless old woman they'd known all their lives was in fact a monster.

I noticed Dee had remained on her feet and was eyeing the dinner things in the kitchen. She was looking for something practical to do so she wouldn't have to sit with me. I'd forgotten the detail of Alec's last meal: M&S Tuscan Sausage Penne for two.

Thinking better of tinkering, she came to sit in the adjacent chair, keeping to the edge of her seat, the better to flee should I turn my violence on her. 'Why, Gwen? I don't understand. Was it all that business with Pixie? I thought you'd made your peace with that?'

I said nothing, just swallowed the last of my now-tepid coffee.

'You must have had a reason to do something so …' She couldn't find a suitable adjective for murder and I was damned if I was going to supply her with one.

Appropriate, I might have chosen. No, *honourable*.

I wondered what Pixie would think when she heard the news. Daniel and Maya, too, of course. I supposed they would support each other – with their criminal fathers' help.

A wedding would raise their spirits.

It didn't take the police long to arrive. I heard Dee talking to them at the door. 'She's in shock,' she told them. 'She's not herself.'

They took me downstairs. I was aware of other residents at their windows, some leaning right out as Alec had done when we'd spirited Pixie away and just as I would have myself had it been a neighbour of mine being arrested. A group of young women had gathered by the gates as I was being ushered to the police car and I couldn't at first think how they'd known to come, ahead of the pack and yet not filming on their phones or asking questions like the gannets who'd circled before. Then I heard Dee explain to them that the viewings had been cancelled and I thought, *Of course*. Alec's new round of prospective roommates.

A group of four, just as he preferred.

Three of them nodded and stepped away, but the fourth strode forwards, undeterred. It was only when she reached the police tape and pleaded her case to the officer guarding the door that she was finally convinced to give up on the rarely available room in iconic Columbia Mansions. As she marched back into the street, tutting to herself, our eyes met and she spoke to me as if we knew each other or had at least established something in common on sight:

'I knew it was too good to be true.'

And I nodded, answering with a sympathy that was genuinely heartfelt, 'Yes. It usually is.'

Gwen's note

I end this account by acknowledging how touched I am by the many messages of support I've received while on bail. Some dear friends have even offered me a roof over my head should I need one at a later stage. I hope to leave with their lovely faces in my mind.

And it's not who you might expect either. Not Dee, for instance – I've served my usefulness to her. Yes, she visits me, but only so she can be at the centre of relevance, only so she and Stella can continue to find ways to bleed us all dry. I wouldn't be surprised if she buys my flat. Completes her takeover.

She's got more up her sleeve, that vixen, you watch.

Greenwich, London

DEE

Six months later

She is no natural-born rebel (let's face it, she was head girl at both junior and senior schools), but she does feel that when you reach a certain age you've earned the right to take rules with a pinch of salt – even those ordered by the court. Until yesterday and ever since Gwen's arrest, she's been strictly forbidden from visiting her friend, what with being a prosecution witness at the forthcoming trial, but it's not as if there's ever been a police guard to stop her. It can't be considered *that* risky to the future of the British constitution.

Anyway, to all intents and purposes the person she's been visiting is Gwen's daughter.

Maya must have been filming one of her videos because when she comes to the door of her Greenwich cottage she's trussed up like Jessica Rabbit, her kohled eyes and cherry lips a 1950s ad man's wet dream. And, presumably, plenty of 2020s men too.

'Dee,' she says in her breathy, inviting way. 'I'm so happy to see you!'

'You too. Isn't it the most beautiful morning?'

'It really is. I've just been filming in the garden. Come on in.'

Dee knows from her previous visits that the property is undergoing renovations, a mustard-yellow vintage kitchen going in at the rear, complete with floral-print drapes, scallop-edged velvet bar stools and all manner of feminine flounces that must be costing a bomb. She doesn't ask Maya if she's using the money Gwen gave her after the sale of her Columbia Mansions flat or whether income from her influencer activities covers it. Maybe the banker boyfriend pays for everything? It's part of her brand to be provided for old-style, after all.

After the schlep from Queen's Oak, she's dying for a coffee and would love one from Maya's engine-sized machine, but Maya says Gwen will want to make her a Nespresso in the garden room. Images move constantly on the phone screen in her hand and she divides her attention equally between it and Dee. 'Before I forget, thank you so much for connecting me with Stella.'

'Oh, my pleasure. Do you think you might work together on something?'

'I hope so. She's going to do a bit of soft pitching.'

A prickle of guilt prompts Dee to say, 'The main thing is *you* get something out of it, Maya. I learned that with the Pixie situation. It needs to be mutually beneficial, otherwise it's just exploitation.'

She has an excellent memory and is aware she's repeating verbatim what Gwen said in her car on their way back from her knee surgery. She made a good point – she frequently did, to be fair, and Dee still finds it hard to believe that such a thoughtful and caring woman turned into a remorseless killer. It just shows how little you really know about friends and neighbours. There've been clues since the crime: according to Pixie, Daniel has hinted that his parents' marriage was stormy, for instance. And Noel is convinced there must have been more to Alec and Gwen than met the eye.

'Yeah, no.' Maya's eyes widen, no mean feat given the set of false eyelashes that wouldn't look out of place on a drag queen. 'It would be amazing for me. It would really extend my reach.'

'I have to say I think your reach is pretty impressive already,'

Dee says. Gwen has always been so ashamed of her daughter's anti-feminist schtick and yet it's as plain as the nose on Dee's face that Maya has made a splendid career out of not having a career – not one that's recognizable to boomers like them, at any rate. She's never understood this business of influencers, but can see from the numbers that Maya's value grows by the hour. Money for nothing, as Dire Straits said back in the day.

It strikes her now that she's probably getting the new kitchen for free.

'So how's your mum been this week?'

'Same.' Maya shrugs. 'Just writing and writing. Comes out every day, does her steps. Up and down. She's like that old guy in lockdown.'

'Captain Tom. Yes.' Except he was raising money for charity whereas Gwen has been bailed for murder. She addresses what's brought her here. 'What do you think of her change of plea?'

Maya's cheeks fill with air, which she swallows before exclaiming, 'Really pleased, oh my God! Bit frustrated we've all had to go through this pre-trial stress, though. I mean, why couldn't she have pleaded guilty from the start? It's not as if she didn't confess at the time, is it?'

'Only to me.' Since that terrible morning in July, Gwen has never admitted formally to Alec's murder. Her police interviews progressed from 'no comment' to outright denial; there was even a spell of crazy talk when she claimed to have been framed by the 'real' murderer, Pixie's father of all people! Even without the copious forensic evidence collected at the scene, timing was her undoing: Colin Grey wasn't released from prison until two weeks after Alec's death.

'I'm relieved as well,' she tells Maya, which is quite the understatement. It would have been excruciating – and possibly damaging to her reputation – to have had the events of last year picked over. It would be all too easy for the defence lawyers to accuse her of manipulation, of putting Stella's journalistic instincts above her friends' desire for privacy, turn her into the villain.

And they mustn't forget that, for all his faults, Alec was a real person with family and friends, all of whom must have been distraught at the prospect of a trial and the media's coverage of it.

A guilty plea is the best outcome for them all.

'It will be a shorter sentence now, won't it? Still, I hope the new hearing won't be too distressing for you, Maya.'

'I'll be okay,' Maya says. 'I've got Jason. He's my rock.'

Dee doesn't ask about Daniel. Pixie is a brave and wonderful girl, but she can't be expected to be anyone's rock in this situation. Their wedding plans were postponed following the murder, that much she knows, and thinks a very sensible decision.

The two of them pass through the building works – minus any builders – and into the garden. To the left, under the kitchen window, is a little patio area with cane chairs and a circular flowerbed crammed with oversized fake hydrangeas. Dee leaves Maya there and crosses to Gwen's garden room, a *Little House on the Prairie* wooden annexe furnished by someone (presumably Maya) with unlimited access to the Laura Ashley archive.

'Oh. Hello, Dee.' Gwen is at her desk, dressed colourfully in red trousers, a royal blue top and violet neck scarf. She's always dressed quite drably, but since her relocation here she favours vivid colours. There's an element of costume to it, with the scarf and the glasses on a chain, as if donning the plumage of a Golden Age authoress.

She gets to her feet and Dee moves to give her a hug. While Gwen doesn't exactly recoil, she doesn't yield either, sliding wordlessly away to tend to her Nespresso machine.

They sit side by side on her blue floral-print sofa, coffees in hand.

'How's the writing going?' Dee asks.

'Good. Yes. Thank you. I've actually just finished.'

'For the day?'

'No, the whole thing.'

Ah, now the news of her change of plea makes sense. She's been delaying the inevitable to buy herself time to write. She couldn't have worked like this in a cell, held on remand, at least it's Dee's assumption that you don't get handed a laptop as you step through the door, while pens and other writing implements could presumably be crafted into deadly weapons.

'That was fast. You're quite the William Faulkner.'

Gwen gives her a querying look.

'He wrote *As I Lay Dying* in six weeks.' They've just read it in the newly founded Columbia Mansions book group, but she doesn't say that because she doesn't want Gwen to feel sad that she's missing out on gatherings she might once have taken part in and now never will.

'I've never read it,' Gwen says. 'What's he dying of? The one who lay dying?'

'She. Just old age. She's worn down.'

Gwen nods. 'Understandable.'

'Anyway,' Dee says cheerfully, 'well done. They say writing about traumatic experiences is the best therapy there is.'

She knows Maya agrees, but Gwen dismisses the idea with a flick of her hand. 'I just wanted to get it all down before I leave.'

'Who's it for, I don't think you've said?'

'Just me. It's a diary really. My …' She hesitates.

'Truth?' Dee suggests.

'Coming to terms, you could say. I needed to figure out where I went wrong.'

'And what did you decide?' Dee asks, curious.

'It was long before, you know, the end.' Gwen sighs. 'I think it was when I stopped trusting her.'

'Pixie?'

She turns, affronted. 'Of course Pixie!'

Dee feels a prickle of irritation. Even in these circumstances, Gwen can be rather high-handed. 'To be fair, you didn't know her very well. None of us did.'

'I wish people would stop saying that,' Gwen says crossly. 'We had a real connection.'

Dee isn't sure she agrees, but she moves on because there's no sense in angering the poor woman. 'So have you printed it out? To store a copy somewhere safe?'

'No. I told you, it's not for anyone else to read. In fact ...' With sudden energy Gwen pushes herself up and reaches for the laptop, swinging it onto her lap. 'I'm deleting it right now.'

'What?' Dee is shocked. 'Don't do that, think of all that work!'

But Gwen has made her mind up. 'It's served its purpose. Like you say, it's just therapy. You wouldn't record it if it were a conversation with a therapist.'

Well, you *might*, Dee thinks, if it was a conversation with a murderer. There's the distinctive crunching sound of an item being dragged into the bin, then Gwen returns the open laptop to her desk and asks Dee if I'd like a second coffee. Dee remembers the cinnamon buns she's brought and Gwen is thrilled. As they eat them, she doesn't ask after Dee's health – her hip, for instance, which continues to trouble her – but that's fair enough. When you're about to be sentenced for murder, you have limited bandwidth for other people's well-being.

'Delicious,' Gwen murmurs. Now she's disposed of her magnum opus, she's noticeably calmer, rather as she was when Dee found her with Alec's body and called the police. *I'm not sorry* ... Dee shudders to think how she'll be when the reality of her situation sinks in. When will that be? When she's in the police van on her way to prison? When the cell door closes and she turns to find some meth-smoking whack job is her new roommate?

Gwen drains her coffee and says she needs the loo. There's a little bathroom next to the kitchen area. Dee's never been in it but she imagines more Maya touches, rose-pink towels and dried flowers. One of those silly ruffled covers for the loo seat. She hears the door bolting – it's stiff and grinds unpleasantly – and wonders why on earth Gwen thinks she'd want to come in after her.

Then, quite unexpectedly, she thinks, *Actually, it could be a useful warning for when she comes back out* ... After that, her body seems to act without her brain needing to be involved. She grabs the laptop, celebrating the discovery that the screen hasn't yet locked, and clicks on the bin icon. There it is, a lone Word document, titled rather tastelessly 'A Neighbour's Guide to Murder'.

She checks the garden and the house beyond. Two builders have appeared in the kitchen window, but they're absorbed in their work and don't spare a glance in her direction. Maya is nowhere to be seen.

She drags the document back onto the desktop and opens it. Gwen *has* been busy: it's over three hundred pages, thirty-plus chapters! Some are long, some no more than a passage or two, all rather chaotic and amateurish, but then Gwen *is* an amateur. (Dee would have liked to have written a book herself but has had far too busy and rewarding a life to have found the time.)

She scrolls to the end, to the last paragraph, thinking it might offer her a sense of where Gwen's mind was right before finishing. It's dated today: she really did type the last words just as Dee arrived.

I end this account by acknowledging how touched I am by the many messages of support I've received while on bail. Some dear friends have even offered me a roof over my head should I need one at a later stage. I hope to leave with their lovely faces in my mind.

And it's not who you might expect either. Not Dee, for instance – I've served my usefulness to her. Yes, she visits me, but only so she can be at the centre of relevance, only so she and Stella can continue to find ways to bleed us all dry. I wouldn't be surprised if she buys my flat. Completes her takeover.

She's got more up her sleeve, that vixen, you watch.

There's a knifing sensation in Dee's heart, followed by a flood of pain: how cruel and mean-spirited! (Fine, so it *has* crossed her mind about the flats – Rafferty is house-hunting at the moment and it would be lovely to have him in the building.) She glances again at the bathroom door – she hasn't heard the loo flushing, but there's the sound of a tap running, the faint whine of water pipes. Her attention returns to the document. There isn't time to search her name and discover any other slurs, she must simply be grateful no one else will read this vitriol.

She closes it and is about to drag it back to the bin when her mind snags on a phrase and she reopens it, reads that author's note a second time.

I hope to leave with their lovely faces in my mind ...

Her heart pumping so violently she feels its beat in every cell of her, she gets up and tries the bathroom door. As expected, it's locked. She pushes her good hip against it, but the bolt holds.

‘Gwen?’ she calls out. ‘Gwen? Are you all right in there?’

Nothing, just the sound of running water, the constant flow of it, the steady whine of the pipes. And she knows then that Gwen isn’t coming out of the bathroom – at least not in the same shape she went in.

Two years later

She and Pixie travel to the screening together. Owing to their roles as executive producers (EPs, it has a nice ring), they need to arrive earlier than the rest of the guests: they're needed for photos and, in Pixie's case, a briefing for the Q & A on stage with Stella. They don't talk much in the car, other than a quick update on the flat renovations.

'Gwen would be so happy to know you're living there,' Dee says for the umpteenth time and Pixie replies, as she usually does, 'I hope so.'

Probate on Alec's estate took over a year – 'That's Broken Britain for you,' Elliot said and Dee's inclined to agree – and his beneficiary, a cousin who lives overseas, put the two flats on the market long before it was granted, which meant an extended period of viewings, genuine buyers outnumbered by ghouls. But eventually the paperwork was finalized and sales were agreed on both properties.

Pixie and Daniel bought Gwen's old flat, helped with their deposit by Maya, whose income has rocketed. (Best not to question how, Daniel says, which Dee takes to be an opaque reference to pornography, God forbid.) Rafferty took a look at Alec's flat, but he was always going to opt for somewhere with easier access to his hub at Stansted and it was bought in the end by an empty-nester couple called Paul and Carol. They knew the recent history of the place – news of the murder had been in the press, of course – but said they were too old to believe in 'vibes'.

Carol has joined Older Bodies Pilates and the book group and proves to be an asset to both.

The premiere is at a private screening room in a Piccadilly hotel. It's an all-female team, a striking sight in the photos, with Stella – in white – at their centre. Dee couldn't be prouder of her clever, courageous girl. Watching her confidence and ambition develop alongside little Eve has been a beautiful thing. She said it herself in her brilliant column back when she was pregnant, you *can* grow both at once – if you accept you must suspend your social life. And yet those sacrificed friends are arriving this evening in force, which is lovely to see.

Some of Stella's other subjects are here too: Maya and her boyfriend Jason, who has an old-school masculinity that suits formal dress beautifully, the perfect accompaniment to his partner's choice of gown, so startlingly low-cut Jayne Mansfield might have thought twice about giving it an airing. Maya's not the only one to go all out, mind; their producer, Catriona, is close to a handful of celebrities, who arrive swathed in sequins and diamonds, each with their own unique light pattern.

Pixie stands out for the demureness of her look: a black jumpsuit with a high neck and wide legs, simple ponytail and minimal make-up. She carries herself with the same strength evident in the film, every inch the defiant survivor, fire in her eyes.

'This is so cool,' Daniel says, finding Dee in the swelling crowd. 'I mean, I knew there'd be a red-carpet vibe, but they've spent money on this, you can tell.'

Maya, meanwhile, is directing Jason in the taking of a video in front of an urn of flowers, with roses and foxgloves and masses of tumbling foliage. 'Got to get my content,' she tells Dee when she sees her looking.

'Of course. I'll be posting on Instagram myself.'

'You know how to invite a collaborator?'

'Sounds rather Second World War, I'm not sure I dare.'

'I'll show you,' Maya promises. 'Now get me in front of the banner,' she orders Jason, and Dee studies it properly for the first time. It features Gwen's and Pixie's faces, larger than life and turned to each other with an air of suspicion. The strapline reads:

One woman's secret is another's motive

*

In the screening room, Stella and Pixie take the stage for their Q & A before the film is shown, a well-known journalist asking the questions.

'The film tackles a very dark and traumatic experience for you, Pixie,' the interviewer begins. 'Does it make a difference to have been personally involved in the process? To help turn that challenging time in your life into a creative endeavour?'

Pixie nods. 'In a way, yes. Like I've worked through it and come out the other side? But it actually feels more like the beginning than the end.' And she speaks briefly but eloquently about Women Against Sex for Rent, the welcome boost the film is bringing to the campaign.

Stella gets the tricker questions, the ones about the morals of repurposing true crime as entertainment, but she's used to these. She's been doing press for weeks now.

'Our focus has always been on the events that led to Alec Pedley's death,' she explains, 'because that was the focus of Gwen's book. This is a close adaptation of a literary work, not a "loosely based on" situation, so it's true we are in Gwen's head and hers only. But there was never any intention to glorify a killer.'

'You sound as if you have sympathy for her?' the interviewer says.

'Not for the decision to take a life, no, but for the way she was confused and deceived by Alec, yes. She had complicated feelings for him.' Stella pulls a wry face. 'It might sound like an odd thing to say about a murderer, but Pixie and I both knew Gwen pretty well and I think we agree that most of the time her heart was in the right place.'

'Most of the time, yes,' Pixie echoes.

'She had all these young women in her life,' Stella continues. 'She seemed to connect with them more than any other group and anyone who's read the book will know their names. Her daughter, Maya. Her former daughter-in-law, Nella. An old colleague she was close to called Cyndi, who she felt such guilt about. Pixie here, of course. Even me, in a way. Like I say, she had room in her heart for all of us at one time or another.'

The interviewer nods. 'Maybe what's so fascinating about murder in a domestic setting is that it can involve surprisingly relatable people. A bad thing done by a good person, if you like?'

'I think so,' Stella agrees. 'It's not that cartoon kind of evil we know how to react to. It's uncomfortable. It's the last resort you wish had never been reached.'

Dee is flattered to be referred to in the next question.

'You mentioned knowing Gwen personally, Stella, and I think many people here will be aware that your mother, Dee Carmichael, was close friends with her and acted as editor and consultant on the publishing side. She's had creative input in the film too, hasn't she?'

'She has. She's our exec producer and is also on screen as herself.' Stella laughs. 'I know it probably looks a bit nepo, but as you say it was her great friendship with Gwen that was the basis of this whole project. Mum was the last person she saw, the only person she trusted with her truth, and without that we wouldn't be here now, sharing this incredibly compelling story.'

The interviewer remarks on how it might seem to an outsider to have fallen into Stella's lap, but there's no denying the sheer all-consuming graft of getting a film made.

'It was much, much harder than giving birth,' Stella agrees, with a lovely tinkle of laughter. She adds that it is two years since the events depicted in the film, the blink of an eye in TV terms, and only exceptional momentum has got this story over the line so quickly. She hopes it will the first of many meaningful feminist works by the team.

And without further ado, they dim the lights.

*

Straight away, even before the titles, Dee appears on screen. She's in the window seat of her flat in Columbia Mansions, laptop glowing in front of her. Even though she was expecting it, she feels her blood heat at the sight of herself, so much older than she pictures herself.

Stella's voiceover fills the auditorium:

Stella: It is a cold night in January when Dee Carmichael checks her email and finds a message from beyond the grave.

Typed words now appear across the screen:

Dear Dee,

You are the only person I trust to read this. Please do with it as you see fit.
Goodbye and thank you for your unwavering friendship,

Gwen x

Screen Dee is startled, instantly emotional. The scene is, by its nature, acted, one of the film's many reconstructed sequences, but Dee alone knows it didn't happen like this at all. Still, it wasn't hard for her to imagine how unsettling it would feel, how profound, to hear from Gwen this way. Her old friend, taken from them in such a heartbreaking way.

Stella's narration continues:

Stella: The message is from Dee's friend and neighbour Gwen Healy, who only a day earlier died by suicide. This is the last email she sent before taking her own life and Dee knows immediately what it is Gwen wants her to do ...

Now more text appears, this in a clean, modern font:

This film reconstructs events described in Gwen Healy's own confession. It uses AI to bring her voice back to life, allowing unprecedented access into the mind of an unlikely murderer ...

In the next seat, Pixie leans towards Dee and whispers, 'I'm getting shivers, are you?'

'Yes,' she whispers back, as screen Dee closes her laptop and turns to the window. There's an exterior shot of the turret next, her figure in silhouette, growing smaller as the camera retreats and retreats until fixing at last on an overhead view of Columbia Mansions and its grounds.

Only now does the title announce itself:

A Neighbour's Guide to Murder
A film by Stella Wilcox

As she watches, it's almost as if it's her first time. As if she wasn't the one who took meetings to decide who would be the best publisher for Gwen's story, wasn't the one who proposed that proceeds be split between Daniel, Maya and the Women Against Sex for Rent campaign. Who worked with Stella and Pixie and their wonderful production partners to create a film they can all be proud of. True to Gwen *and* true to them.

Oh, and who gave her manuscript a thorough edit before sharing it with any of the above – Stella included.

Naturally, she removed all those spiteful digs about her daughter, how she intended throwing Pixie under the bus and bleeding her dry and the rest of it. No one needed to read those awful fallacious sentiments. Cuts about Dee herself were rather more extensive for it transpired that Gwen had developed a warped and frankly paranoid private view of her friend. In the madness of it all, she had become fixated on the idea that Dee was some sort of terrorist stage mother with an agenda to exploit Pixie and scapegoat Gwen. It had been quite disquieting to read.

All of that had to go. Yes, it shortened the book by a few pages, but it created a more balanced sense of justice – and it isn't as if she *added* anything.

She didn't tell anyone about the cuts, of course, simply presented the edited manuscript as the original. Not that it succeeded in removing the pain completely. You can delete hurtful lines from a document but you can't erase them from your memory and they'll always be there, taunting her in moments of weakness.

She's only human, after all, just like everyone else in this affair, and God knows she has her regrets.

But then again, too few to mention.

Two years earlier

Gwen must have pills or razors in the bathroom with her, she realizes. She must have turned on the taps to hide any involuntary cries or other noises. It was Gwen herself who told Dee that leaving a tap running for five minutes uses fifteen gallons of water and she knows her friend well enough to know she'd have had serious misgivings about this wastage.

Before she can second-guess herself, she returns to Gwen's laptop and opens her email app. She clicks on 'new message' and auto-fills the recipient line with her own name. She titles it 'Goodbye' and types a short message:

Dear Dee,

You are the only person I trust to read this. This is the only copy. Please do with it as you see fit.
Goodbye and thank you for your unwavering friendship,

Gwen x

She attaches the document and hits 'send', before dragging the manuscript back to the bin and emptying it.

She waits precisely twenty minutes before leaving the garden room and hurrying across to the house. In the kitchen, the builders look up from their work.

'Have you seen Maya?' she asks them and one of them gestures to the hallway. They're like non-speaking actors, contributing to the sense that none of this is quite real.

She hastens down the corridor, calling Maya's name. The girl appears at the top of the stairs, her arms full of beautifully folded laundry.

'Is everything all right? I'm in the middle of—'

Dee interrupts: 'I'm worried about your mum. She's locked herself in the bathroom. I've been calling her name, but she's not answering.'

Maya frowns, not yet understanding. 'How long has she been in there?'

'About fifteen minutes? She was being very odd. Even after I arrived, she was at her laptop, said she had to send an email, acting as if I wasn't there.'

'She does that,' Maya says. 'I told you she's been obsessed with her book. She goes into a kind of trance when she's working on it.'

Dee nods, biting her lip in concern. 'She said she'd finished it, so maybe she's just exhausted. Could she have fallen asleep in there? Will you come over and see if you can help?'

They go back to the garden room together. The little espresso cups and plates sit next to the laptop. Should she have wiped the keyboard, Dee wonders? In the unlikely event that it will be checked for fingerprints, she'll say Gwen asked her to put it back on the desk for her after she'd finished her emails. 'That was when she went to the loo,' she imagines telling the police. 'She seemed absolutely fine, at peace with herself.'

'Mum? Mum?' Maya hammers on the bathroom door, but there's no response and she's getting alarmed now. 'Fifteen minutes?' she says to Dee. 'Did you check if the window's open?'

'I didn't know there was one.'

They go out to look. The window is a small square of frosted glass, open an inch or two but not enough to be able to see in, and certainly too small to escape through. The sound of running water is torture now.

'Should we call for help?' Maya asks.

'I think we should.' Dee digs in her handbag for her phone. 'To be on the safe side. We can always phone them back if she comes out, explain it's a false alarm.'

Maya begins to weep, black tears rolling down her face, and takes a tissue from her pocket. She blows her nose, taking the foundation off in the process and exposing pink nostrils. 'They might be ages. I'll go and see if the builders can break down the door.'

'Good idea,' Dee says, and as Maya scurries off, she dials 999. It's the second time in the last six months she's had to do this and both times have been on account of Gwen and her terrible, unaccountable recklessness.

Her hands are pleasingly steady as she makes the call.

Acknowledgements

A huge heartfelt thank you to the HQ dream team of Kate Mills, Lisa Milton, Claire Brett, Philly Cotton, Georgina Green, Emily Scorer, Grace Marshall, Abigail Soddy, Felicia Hu, Sarah Renwick, Angie Dobbs, Stephanie Heathcote and Ellen Rockell. Thank you too to Cari Rosen and Donna Hillyer for freelance copyediting and proofreading (without which my words would be infinitely worse off!).

On the agency side, my thanks to the Curtis Brown team led by superstar Sheila Crowley and including Helena Maybery, Tanja Goossens, Georgia Williams and Krys Kujawinska. At UTA I have exceptional champions in Veronica Goldstein and Christy Fletcher and at SLTM the brilliant Luke Speed makes all my screen projects happen. I am eternally grateful to you all.

Thank you to Into the Breach for research and also website stuff.

Librarians and library users: as many of you know, my local library was my second home when I was young and my 2024 CWA Dagger in the Library nomination was a career highlight – thank you so much for supporting my work!

Readers, booksellers, book reviewers, book bloggers, book buyers, book borrowers – book people generally: I thank each and every one of you for your part in making it possible for me to share another story.

ONE PLACE. MANY STORIES

Bold, innovative and
empowering publishing.

FOLLOW US ON:

@HQStories